Readers love the True Mates series by J.R. LOVELESS

Chasing Seth

"Chasing Seth was a VERY good story… I highly recommend this book to all who love to read."

--Night Owl Reviews

"I loved *Chasing Seth* by J.R. Loveless. Right from the start I was drawn in by the characters."

—Top2Bottom Reviews

"Another touching angst filled book by J.R. Loveless."

—MM Good Book Reviews

Forgiving Thayne

"I enjoyed the story… If you enjoyed *Chasing Seth* then you'll definitely enjoy this one!"

—The Blogger Girls

"J.R. Loveless has created an outstanding saga that I enjoyed immensely… *Forgiving Thayne* is beyond doubt a compassionate romance."

—Literary Nymphs Reviews

By J.R. LOVELESS

Love and Snowball Fights
Touch Me Gently
You Belong With Me

THE ADA CHRONICLES
His Salvation

TRUE MATES
Chasing Seth
Forgiving Thayne
Protecting Kai

Published by DREAMSPINNER PRESS
www.dreamspinnerpress.com

J.R. LOVELESS

PROTECTING KAI

Published by
DREAMSPINNER PRESS

5032 Capital Circle SW, Suite 2, PMB# 279, Tallahassee, FL 32305-7886 USA
www.dreamspinnerpress.com

Protecting Kai
© 2020 J.R. Loveless

Cover Art
© 2020 Tiferet Design
http://www.tiferetdesign.com/
Cover content is for illustrative purposes only and any person depicted on the cover is a model.

Trade Paperback ISBN: 978-1-64405-739-1
Digital ISBN: 978-1-64405-252-5
Library of Congress Control Number: 2019952831
Trade Paperback published February 2020
v. 1.0

Printed in the United States of America
∞
This paper meets the requirements of
ANSI/NISO Z39.48-1992 (Permanence of Paper).

CHAPTER ONE

"HAVE YOU found him yet?"

"No," Cole Ferris snarled into his cell phone, his fingers curling tight around the plastic. "It's as though he disappeared into fucking thin air!"

During a trip to deliver his latest order in Redwood City, the closest neighboring city to his home in Emerald Lake Hills, California, Cole had bumped into a young blond man and nearly shifted on the spot. His wolf perked up and tried to take control. Keeping a tight hold on his beast took every bit of his concentration, and Cole knew with certainty the young man was his mate. He'd tried to follow, but somehow lost him in an empty alley not far from the Whole Foods Market he'd been delivering to. He still didn't know how the man had outrun him or vanished without a trace.

"Do you need help?" his soon-to-be Beta, Nick Cartwright, offered.

Cole ran a hand through his hair in aggravation. "No. I think it's better if I find him on my own. Besides, right now isn't a good time for you to be separated from your mate. It hasn't been long since the bond between the two of you was completed. Being away from each other right now wouldn't be good for either of you."

"You shouldn't be out there on your own, Cole. Sara is worried about you."

Sighing, Cole stared broodingly out of the window of the hotel room he'd rented for the night. The trail had run cold in Phoenix, Arizona. The name David Freeman, discovered from the registry for the bus company that had brought his mate to Redwood City, had been, as Cole thought, an alias. He hadn't expected anything else, but it still frustrated him. "I'm fine, Nick. Tell my mother not to worry. I can't return home until I find him."

"The summit is in less than two weeks, Cole. Elijah expects you to be there for it."

He'd forgotten about the summit, actually. Sneering, he resisted the urge to punch the nearest wall, not wanting to have to explain the damage to hotel staff. When Nick's best friend and former Rho of the Emerald Lake Hills pack Seth Davies had mated with the soon-to-be Alpha of the

Senaka, Wyoming, pack, there'd been an agreement made between both of the Alphas to meet once every six months to give the unmated wolves in the Senaka pack a higher chance of finding their intended mates. Elijah's hidden intention behind the idea of the summit was to slowly introduce the other group to the idea of nontribal wolves as, until Seth's arrival in Senaka, they had believed only Native Americans were born and true wolves. The Emerald Lake Hills pack knew there were others out there, having established a treaty with three different packs close to their territory in an effort to form alliances and keep the peace between them. The treaties also opened the door to others in neighboring states and even farther out from there. Over time they'd come to discover there were, in fact, at least twelve more packs scattered across the US alone, and they knew of another two in Canada and three in South America.

Cole had anticipated the summit originally in the hopes of locating his intended half, but now he had no desire to attend. He hungered to track down and claim the one destined to be his. Only he couldn't ignore his duty to his father and their people. He would succeed Elijah Ferris as Alpha of the Emerald Lake Hills pack when his father stepped down, and the duties and responsibilities of the position would become his. His father, though still young by wolf standards, wanted to retire to enjoy his remaining years and have the chance to guide Cole through the trials of being an Alpha. Cole had argued with his father, telling him he wasn't ready, but Elijah wouldn't listen to him and announced his intentions to pass on the reins of the pack to Cole not long after the summit.

"I'll be there," Cole snapped.

"Keep me posted, Cole. Remember I'm here if you need me."

Cole slumped down on the bed. "Thanks, Nick," he murmured before disconnecting the call.

Where the hell had David disappeared to? It seemed as if he were a ghost and Cole had only imagined him. He'd managed to get a lead on David's whereabouts from a private detective he'd hired and followed the breadcrumbs to Phoenix, but now he didn't even begin to know where to look. Cole remembered the scent of fear clinging to David as if he'd bathed in it. What could cause his mate such terror? It brought out Cole's protective instincts, and he wanted nothing more than to find whoever had frightened David and rip them apart.

For the first time in his life, Cole felt helpless. He couldn't protect David if he couldn't find him. There had to be someone here who'd seen the young blond man in the grainy photo from the bus station security cameras. Cole's wolf prowled restlessly beneath the surface, demanding to be set free. He knew his wolf could find David by smell if he allowed it to take over, but he couldn't risk it in a big city, and it seemed as though David had learned to stick to big cities to hide in. While proud of his mate for being smart, it frustrated him to no end to not be able to call on the instincts of his wolf.

In the last few weeks, Cole hardly ate or rested as he tried to remain right on David's tail. He hadn't even had the chance to shift, and his skin itched with the need to run. But what really concerned him was where David slept and if David had food to eat. Cole figured David wouldn't be on the run if he had a lot of money in the first place. Was his mate sleeping on the streets where anyone could hurt him? What if David were starving? These thoughts haunted him anytime Cole stopped moving. His stomach churned more and more as the days rolled by.

Cole stood and snatched up his wallet and cell before leaving the hotel room. He needed to get out and walk around, work off the energy burning through his veins. With the approach of summer, the air outside was muggy and warm, causing his white T-shirt to cling to his upper chest, clearly outlining the large muscles he'd gained from the daily work in his greenhouses. Cole had never been a vain person despite his good looks or destiny to be Alpha. He had inherited his father's height, six foot six, but instead of his father's dark countenance, he'd been blessed with his mother's auburn hair, green eyes, and fiery temper. The moment he'd hit puberty, he'd begun to fill out, even with little to no exercise, his wolf maturing and growing in size. His heritage added to his stature, and by the time he turned eighteen, he looked more like he was in his late twenties, early thirties.

As early as the age of sixteen, he'd captured both men's and women's interest, but Cole hadn't been attracted to the idea of casual encounters as many other men were. He'd only had two relationships through high school and his early twenties: one girl and one man. Much to his parents' dismay, he found himself more attracted to men than women, and he didn't hide his preference from his parents. Now, at the age of thirty, he understood why, after having discovered his mate was male and younger by a good few years from what he could tell. He prayed David was over eighteen because he wanted to claim his mate more than anything he'd wanted in his life.

Cars rushed by as Cole walked. Phoenix seemed congested and dirty compared to Emerald Lake Hills. He hated feeling penned in by large buildings and crowds of people. His wolf didn't like the different smells and sounds, causing him to become skittish. Cole kept a tight rein on his inner beast and continued his aimless wandering. Maybe he could sleep for a few hours tonight, at least if he tired himself out enough.

"Hey, gorgeous," a female voice interrupted his thoughts.

Cole focused on the source and saw a woman in a tight miniskirt, high heels, and tank top—an obvious sex worker. Even if he hadn't already found his mate, he wouldn't pay for sex. "Not interested."

She smirked and approached him, trailing one finger along his bicep. "Won't cost you much. In fact, since you're so sexy, I'll throw in a blow job for free."

Gritting his teeth, Cole stepped away from her. "I said not interested, lady."

She glared at him. "Fuck you, mister."

Cole rolled his eyes. He opened his mouth to retort when he heard a loud cry of pain from an alleyway nearby. The woman glanced toward the alley, a scared expression on her face, and started walking in the opposite direction, ignoring the sounds of someone who needed help. Cole shook his head. No one cared enough to help each other when they needed it in this world.

He strode to the end of the alley and saw three men surrounding another who crouched close to the wall, shielding his head with his arms. There were tears in the man's clothing, and it was obvious the men intended to rape him or worse. He opened his mouth to shout at them to leave the poor bastard alone when his mate's scent hit him. His cock hardened immediately, and his canines lengthened in response. Cole growled, his eyesight shifting between human and lupine. They dared to touch his mate? He picked up the smell of blood and knew it belonged to David. His growl deepened, becoming more ferocious, and the humans finally noticed his presence.

One of them, a tall man with dark hair tied in a ponytail, turned to face him. "Well, well. We have a good Samaritan coming to the defense of a whore."

Rage burned even higher at that word being used to describe his mate. Cole snarled, lip curling upward at the corner. "Get your dirty fucking hands off of him."

A glimmer of fear slithered through the bastard's eyes, but it faded quickly when the other two thugs came to his side as reinforcements. "What you gonna do about it, asshole?" challenged the bulkier of the three.

Cole smiled, but the expression held no humor, merely deadly intent. "I don't think you want to challenge me."

"And if we do?" the third human taunted, pulling out a knife and flashing it at him.

When Cole didn't do more than deepen his sneer, the first man turned abruptly and kicked David in the ribs, hard. Cole heard bones break, and David howled in agony, hugging his chest to try to protect himself from the next blow. The man didn't get a chance to land another one. Cole roared in fury and charged, easily snapping the neck of the bulkier attacker. He felt the bite of the knife slicing through his bicep and backhanded the third human, sending him flying into the side of the building with a sickening crack. Warm blood dripped down his arm, but Cole didn't even falter as he gripped the one who'd dared to injure his mate by the throat. Cole snarled in the bastard's face, his teeth, sharp points, glinting in the moonlight overhead. "Never, ever touch *my* mate," he said ferociously and promptly twisted the man's neck.

Cole allowed the body to crumple to the ground as he struggled to regain control. Shit. Shit. Shit. This wasn't good. He'd just killed two of them and he could barely make out the heartbeat of the one he'd tossed into the wall, but he needed to focus on the man still cowering near the end of the alley. Cole carefully approached David and crouched close to his side. It broke his heart when David whimpered at his touch on his shoulder.

"It's okay," Cole soothed. "They can't hurt you again."

Cole sucked in a deep breath when shimmering hazel eyes peered out from under slim arms. He felt as if he'd been punched in the stomach at finally seeing his mate up close. Blood trickled from David's nose, and a bruise had already begun to form on his porcelain cheek, but the thing that struck him the hardest was how gaunt he appeared to be. His clothing hung on his thin frame, and Cole could just make out a black leather choker around the young man's throat. David slowly lowered his arms, crying out when his ribs protested his movements. Cole winced and attempted to help him. David scurried deeper into the corner, eyes wild with terror.

"I'm not going to hurt you," Cole murmured. "I promise. I want to help you."

"Ju-just leave me alone," David begged.

"I can't do that, David," Cole said in a quiet voice.

David's eyes widened in shock and horror. Cole could smell David's fear grow stronger still. "Wh-who are you?" David demanded, a bit of fire showing through.

Cole hid a smile. His mate had spirit, even if it was shrouded at the moment by his distrust. "My name is Cole Ferris."

"Did-did *he* send you?" David spat out, attempting to crunch himself farther into the corner while holding his side.

Frowning, Cole tilted his head to the side. "He?"

David studied him for a moment. "He really didn't send you?"

"I don't know who *he* is," Cole replied simply.

"How did you know my-my name?"

Cole lowered himself from a squat to his knees, resting his palms on his thighs. "I've been looking for you. I got the name from the roster of the bus you took from San Francisco to Redwood City."

The scent of David's panic increased once more, and Cole held up his hands. "I'm honestly not here to hurt you."

"Then what do you want? Why did you follow me?" David asked suspiciously.

How the hell did he tell the young man before him they were mates? It wasn't exactly something a human could understand, which made blurting it out not an option. Cole hesitated, and David shook his head, attempting to climb to his feet. "Wait," Cole said, desperation in the one word.

David grabbed at the wall to steady himself, and Cole could see David's face growing paler by the second. "Leave me alone."

Cole searched in vain for words to keep David by his side—nothing sounded right in his head. David took several steps but didn't make it far, his face becoming white as a sheet. Cole moved with lightning speed to stop David from injuring himself further as he passed out. Sighing, Cole slid an arm beneath David's knees and picked him up, cradling him close to his chest. He needed to get David to a doctor. The problem was there would be questions about his injuries. And what would Cole do with the men lying in the alley? His own arm still bled from the deep cut by the man's knife. Shit. This wasn't exactly how he'd expected to find his mate.

Looking around him at the bodies of the three men, Cole hoped no one discovered them before he could return to clean up the mess. The last one's heart still beat, but it wasn't likely the man would wake up anytime soon, if at all. Cole needed to tend to David first.

Despite the late hour, the streets were still crowded with cars driving by. Cole managed to flag down a taxi. He took note of the street and buildings around them before instructing the driver to head to the hospital.

"Mind if I ask what happened?" the driver inquired as he put the cab into drive.

What the hell could he tell the cabbie? Cole searched for an answer, but when the driver saw his hesitation the man said, "None of my business. I didn't see anything, mister."

"It's not what you think," Cole protested. "He was attacked."

The driver frowned. "Should I call the police?"

"No! Uh… no. We'll figure it out at the hospital."

The cabbie gave him a skeptical look but headed to the nearest hospital. The ten-minute ride felt like an eternity as he listened to the breath wheezing in and out of David's lungs. "Please hurry," he murmured to the driver, holding David closer.

"Almost there."

Cole let out a sigh of relief when he saw the lights of the hospital and the ambulance just pulling out of the parking lot. He managed to dig his wallet out of his pocket to throw forty dollars at the driver and climbed out of the vehicle to rush into the hospital. As soon as they took David to be seen to, Cole would call his father. There might be a local pack who could help with the disposal and maybe even keep the police off him for David's condition. "He needs help," he shouted as he strode into the ER with David in his arms.

A nurse and two orderlies immediately rushed out to take David and put him on a stretcher. Every instinct in Cole screamed to not let them take his mate, but he knew they needed to tend to David's injuries. Cole soothed his inner wolf and tried to hold on to his beast.

"Sir, I'm going to have to ask you some questions," a woman behind the reception desk called out.

Cole gave a jerky nod and walked to the counter.

"What's his name?"

"Ah… David Freeman."

"Date of birth?"

He had no idea when David had been born. "I don't know."

She frowned, but continued. "How old is he?"

"I don't know."

The same answer kept coming as she asked him a couple more questions. "Can you tell me what happened?"

Cole hesitated and then said, "Some guys attacked him. I managed to scare them off and brought him here."

A suspicious light entered the woman's eyes, and Cole knew his uncertainty had caused her doubt about "some guys" being the ones to hurt David. "I see. If you'll take a seat in the waiting area, someone will be with you shortly."

Yeah, sure, he thought to himself, you mean the cops. He gave her another nod and went over to the room they had set up for family members and loved ones of whatever poor bastard had been brought into the emergency room. Cole pulled his cell phone out of his pocket and called his father. He quietly outlined everything that had occurred, ensuring the humans in the room couldn't hear him relaying the information about David's attackers. "Stay put, son. I know a few people in the area."

"Thanks, Pop."

"Just come home as soon as you can," Elijah Ferris groused over the phone and then cut the connection.

Cole grinned, knowing he frustrated his father to no end sometimes. Except his father couldn't fault him for this. David was his true mate, and Cole couldn't begin to imagine not finding him. Seconds after he'd hung up, a couple of uniformed police stepped into the room. "Sir, we have some questions we'd like to ask you."

Cole's wolf snarled within him, knowing they believed him to have hurt his mate, but Cole knew they were only doing their job.

"Can you tell us what happened?" The officer, name tag giving the last name of Hawkins, eyed him critically, noting the blood on his clothing and the scrapes on his fists. The cut on his arm had already healed. Cole knew the shrewd man's gaze couldn't have missed the slice in the sleeve of his shirt but there being no wound.

He briefly outlined everything, leaving out the details of having killed two of them and critically injuring the other one. "They ran off, and I brought the man here," Cole finished.

"And you don't remember where this happened?"

Cole shook his head. "No, I'm just in town for the night and happened to be walking to my hotel when I heard the young man cry out."

"Can you give us a description of the men?"

Of course he could. Would he? Hell no. They wouldn't find them even if he did, and his father would make sure there were no bodies or evidence remaining. "I couldn't see them very well. We were in a dark alley."

Before they could ask him anything else, the second officer's radio squawked, and he walked off to answer it only to return with a sour expression. "Time to go, Hawkins."

"What? We're in the middle of a report here!" Hawkins protested.

"Captain said return to the station now."

Hawkins looked at Cole, furious, his mouth in a tight line. "Got some friends in high places, buddy?"

Cole gave him an innocent look, although he knew it didn't fool the cop. Hawkins glared at him and said, "We'll be back to check on the kid in the morning, so don't go gettin' any ideas about disappearin'."

The "kid" wouldn't be there tomorrow morning if Cole had anything to do with it. "Sure thing, Officer Hawkins."

Satisfaction dripped through him as the two cops left the hospital, Hawkins glancing over his shoulder more than once. Cole spent the next hour pacing the waiting room until he heard David's last name and spun on his heel near the far wall. A nurse stood in the doorway holding a clipboard and called out David's name. Cole rushed forward. "Is David okay?"

"Come with me, sir. Dr. Vernon needs to speak to you." She didn't wait to see if he would follow, merely turning and heading toward the doors leading into the ER.

Cole strode after her, his long strides making it easy to follow. He glanced around at the various curtained sections. He'd never been overly fond of hospitals, but then wasn't that something everyone said? As a shifter he'd never had the need to be in one. The scent of antiseptic and death stung his sensitive nostrils. His wolf sneezed and whined. Cole soothed him as best he could. *Not much longer.*

The smell of primal earth hit Cole, and he stiffened, knowing full well another shifter was in the hospital. He had to resist the urge to snarl and rush to David's side. The idea of another shifter close to his mate before he'd claimed him brought his wolf's fighting instincts even closer to the surface. He held on to the scruff of his wolf's neck by sheer force of will. The nurse stopped outside a curtained-off cubicle near the wolf Cole had scented. Lean muscles and dark brown hair were the first things Cole noted of the tall shifter with a lab coat encasing his upper body. He could sense the doctor didn't have much power. Most likely either a lesser wolf or Omega of his pack. Chocolate-brown eyes darted to him, and Cole could see reverence and fear in the depths of them. The doctor must have sensed Cole's true nature. Cole drew himself to his full height and waited, dying to rip open the curtain and see David for himself.

"Sir, I'm Dr. Vernon." The other shifter approached him and held out his hand tentatively.

Cole clasped the proffered hand and squeezed gently, immediately releasing him to reassure the doctor he wasn't a threat. "Is David all right?"

"I'm afraid he's had severe trauma to his rib cage. Three are broken. He's malnourished and dehydrated as well. We had to sedate him as he was hysterical when he woke up in the hospital." Dr. Vernon glanced at the nurse. "Mrs. Truman, could you give us a moment, please?"

The nurse nodded and left, walking toward the front of the ER, leather soles squeaking with each step. Cole knew whatever Dr. Vernon said next would make it even harder to hold his wolf in check. As soon as the nurse disappeared through the swinging doors, Dr. Vernon turned toward him and murmured, "There's evidence of longtime abuse. Scars, bones previously broken and set improperly. I know I don't have to tell you this has already been reported to the police, but I know you weren't the one to inflict the abuse on him." He looked around furtively and lowered his voice even further, knowing Cole would hear the mere whisper. "My Alpha has been in touch with yours and has told me the situation."

Cole's pulse roared through his veins, rage boiling inside him, muffling the doctor's voice behind a wall of pure, unadulterated fury. His hands balled into fists. Someone had been abusing his mate? Hurting him? He'd find the son of a bitch and rip the motherfucker's throat out. "Is he able to be moved?"

Dr. Vernon frowned. "We've wrapped his chest to stabilize the ribs, and we put him on an IV drip. I'm not sure it's a good idea to remove him from the hospital."

"Is it unsafe to move him?"

"Not exactly."

"Good. I want him home where he's protected."

Dr. Vernon put his finely trembling hand on Cole's forearm when Cole went to open the curtain. "There's something you should know, sir."

Cole stopped, his fingers curled over the edge of the ugly peach-colored cloth.

"When he woke up, he yelled something about needing to get away because someone would find him. He wasn't entirely lucid at the time, but he seemed terrified."

Cole tightened his grip for a split second around the fabric. "They won't get near him. Not if I have anything to say about it."

Dr. Vernon gave a satisfied nod and removed his hand from Cole's arm. "When you're ready to check him out, come find me. I would recommend you put him in a hospital as soon as you get him home. At least until he's recovered from the dehydration and is no longer starving."

"I'll try, but I'm not sure he's going to cooperate." Cole gave a wry twist of his lips at how stubborn his mate had seemed to be during those scant moments in the alleyway. "Thanks, doc."

He watched the doctor walk away before slipping behind the curtain. His breath caught in his throat at the sight of his mate. David's face appeared pale against the white sheets. A butterfly bandage had been applied to the bridge of his nose and Cole could see the edges of a dressing peeking out of the collar of the hospital gown. Deep, steady breathing calmed Cole. He approached the side of the bed and immediately picked up David's hand. A woodsy scent struck Cole, one he hadn't noticed before in his panic and fear for David's life. He frowned. It wasn't human or wolf. "What are you?" he asked unexpectedly, knowing he wouldn't be getting an answer, at least not right away.

Cole brushed the fingers of his other hand along the bruise on David's cheek. He sucked in a sharp intake of breath at the sight of deeply scarred flesh around David's throat. It explained the strange leather strap he'd seen David wearing earlier. The marks clearly indicated some kind of collar or chain had kept David shackled for gods knew how long. Who would do such a thing to another being? He gently touched the puckered skin near the beating tick of David's pulse, his jaw clenching as David whimpered in his drug-induced sleep. Whoever had done this would fucking pay.

Cole tended to prefer peaceful settlings of disputes, but when it came to someone hurting one of his own, he never surrendered or gave up. "I will protect you, my mate," he murmured in a soft voice. "No one will ever hurt you again."

Determined to return home before David woke up, Cole set about making plans. He fully intended on never letting David out of his sight ever again.

CHAPTER TWO

THE SOOTHING vibration of muffled engine sounds wormed their way into Kai Renard's consciousness. He struggled to remain in the dark depths of sleep. He felt comfortable and warm, safe even. Something he hadn't felt in years. His body seemed to have other ideas, though, and Kai slowly gave in to awareness, his eyes fluttering open. He lay in a bed in a small cabin of sorts. It took him a few moments to realize the engines belonged to a plane, and panic overtook him. He sat up, horrified at the small sound of distress he let out, but he couldn't stop it. Pain exploded in his chest at the abrupt movement, and he gave another cry, this one sharper and higher, and wrapped his arms around his rib cage.

The door swung open and someone rushed in. Kai struggled to gather himself enough to fight if he needed to. Sweat beaded on his forehead from the fire eating through his body. A deep voice issued a small oath, and the bed sank slightly to his right. Kai tried to move farther away, only to freeze up as the action caused more pain to shoot through him.

"Shh, it's okay," the voice murmured. "Here, open your mouth."

Fingers shoved a small pill through his lips, and he tried to reject it, turning his head and clamping his jaw. A sigh came from the unseen man, tears of agony still blurring Kai's vision. "I'm not going to hurt you. The pill is for the pain I know you are in. Please, take it."

Blinking to clear his eyes, Kai slowly looked toward the owner of the voice only to suck in a breath of surprise, one he instantly regretted. He groaned and moved his palm to his chest. Bandages were wrapped around him and secured over one shoulder. "What-What happened?" he asked.

The man who'd rescued him from the men in the alley sat beside him, holding a small white pill on the ends of his long tanned fingers. "You don't remember?"

"I remember the men—" Kai cut his words off, his face paling. They'd intended to rape him, maybe even kill him. Then out of nowhere the stranger had appeared. "Where are we?"

"On a private jet heading to my home."

13

Kai grew fearful again. Why would this man be taking him to his home? "Who are you?" he demanded, panic setting in again and causing his hands to shake.

The stranger grinned. "I guess you don't remember me introducing myself. I'm Cole. Cole Ferris."

"I remember your name," Kai snapped, and if he could have he would have shifted away from the man. He didn't trust anyone. They could all be working for the bastard or willing to turn him over to him for money. "I meant who are you? What do you want from me?"

Cole frowned and tipped his head a bit to the side. "I wish I knew how to tell you," he murmured, "without freaking you out."

Kai's eyes widened, and his heart started pounding in abject terror. "*He* sent you, didn't he? I won't go back! You can't make me!"

He struggled to get off the bed, shoving at the sheets only to squeak in horror when he saw he wore nothing but a pair of boxers. He hissed in anguish and grabbed at the sheet, trying to cover himself again, but Cole sat on top of the blanket, and Kai couldn't get him to budge. He eventually gave up and swung one leg off the side of the mattress.

"Hey, hey!" Cole reached out to try to stop him. "You're going to hurt yourself."

Kai glared at him and batted at his hands. "Don't touch me!" he shouted and managed to stand, huddling into the corner between the bed and the wall.

Cole held up his hands. "I'm not sure who *he* is, but I promise you I'm not taking you to him. Please take the pill, and we can talk, okay?"

"No," Kai replied stubbornly, at which the larger man heaved a sigh.

Reaching toward the little table near the bed, Cole picked up a small bottle. "Look," he said, indicating the label. "It's a pain medication from the hospital, issued by the doctor who patched you up."

Kai clenched his hand at his side, his other arm wrapped around his waist in a useless effort to stem the pain. "Liar," he accused. The throbbing made it harder to breathe, and he could barely remain standing. "How do I know you didn't just change whatever is in the bottle?"

"Jesus," Cole grunted. "You really are a mistrusting little thing, aren't you?"

"Little!" Kai squawked.

Cole ran a hand through his hair in a frustrated motion. "I'm not here to hurt you. If I wanted to, wouldn't it have made more sense for me to do it when you were asleep? Here, I'll prove it's not meant to do anything to you."

Kai watched as Cole tossed one of the pills into his mouth and swallowed, opening up after to show the white oval was gone. He still didn't trust the man's word. The pain grew increasingly worse the longer he stood there, but he would rather chew glass than believe Cole.

"Please, sit down before you fall down and hurt yourself even further," Cole pleaded.

Fiercely, Kai shook his head. "Not until you get off the bed."

"Then will you please sit?" Cole demanded.

Kai gave a jerky nod, knowing if he didn't get off his feet soon, he'd pass out. He watched in suspicion as Cole stood and crossed the room, deliberately leaving the bottle of pills on the bed. He waited until Cole stood near the door again before perching on the edge of the bed, intently studying Cole in case he tried anything. Cole smiled in relief, an expression that tugged at the muscles in Kai's stomach in a most uncomfortable manner. He didn't analyze the emotion fluttering in his belly, choosing to ignore it instead.

"Please take the pill. I promise it is only for pain. The ER doctor prescribed it for you."

Picking up the bottle, Kai glanced at the label, noting the doctor's name, the name of the medication, and the name he'd adopted to avoid using his real one. Not that he had a clue about anything to do with medical terms, but the instructions did say one pill every four to six hours for pain. He shook a tablet into his palm, tossed it into his mouth, and swallowed it dry.

"There's water on the nightstand," Cole offered.

Kai narrowed his eyes at him. "I took the pill. Now tell me who you are and why the hell we're on a plane! How did you even get me out of the hospital without my permission?"

Cole started pacing, which caused Kai to flinch and earned a disappointed look from the other man. For some unknown reason, the expression made Kai feel guilty. Why should he feel guilty when he was the one who'd been kidnapped? Kai shoved the remorse down deep, refusing to allow it to affect him.

"I already told you my name is Cole Ferris. I'm… shit, I'm not even sure how to say this, so it's probably best I just come out with it. I'm a shifter, a wolf shifter."

Kai's jaw dropped. "You're a what?"

"A wolf shifter."

A snort of laughter escaped Kai before he could stop it, causing him to groan in misery as his ribs protested the effort it took. "You expect me to believe you're some kind of werewolf? Like in the movies?"

Affront crowded Cole's features. "I am not a werewolf," he said stiffly. "We shift into wolves, not monsters."

Was this a new tactic by his uncle? Find someone to pretend to be the same as him and get him to trust them? Kai didn't know whether to keep laughing or break down and cry. He hadn't cried since the first time his uncle beat him. He'd refused to give Jerrod the satisfaction of seeing him broken. "Werewolves don't exist," Kai insisted.

Cole stopped in his tracks and gave Kai a saddened glance. "I truly wish I knew of a gentler way to do this, but there's no alternative."

Kai's fear deepened at Cole's words, and he pulled the sheet up over his naked form in an effort to shield himself. Cole closed his eyes a split second before a flash of bright light momentarily blinded Kai. Blinking, he tried to clear his vision. A mix of a gasp and a scream lodged itself in Kai's throat as he stared at the dark red wolf standing where Cole had been mere seconds ago. Horrified, Kai couldn't do anything except stare. "Holy shit," Kai whispered.

The wolf trotted toward the bed, and Kai crowded close to the headboard, gritting his teeth against the pain exploding inside his chest at the abrupt motion. "Stay away!" he yelled.

The animal stopped and sat down, tilting its head to the side. Kai wondered if the creature was separate from the human, or if Cole had control even in beast form. The wolf laid its muzzle down on the edge of the mattress and stared at him, giving a whine. Before Kai realized it, his hand was halfway to touching the animal. He froze and dropped his hand to the bed, shaking his head. "No, you aren't real. This isn't happening."

Kai turned away when a flash of light came once more and Cole appeared there again, kneeling beside the bed. "I didn't mean to frighten you further," Cole murmured.

It was all too much. Kai raised his hands to his head, digging his fingers into his scalp. "Please let me go," he keened. "I promise I won't tell anyone about you being a-a werewolf."

A soft grunt came from Cole's direction, and the mattress dipped beneath Cole's weight. Too exhausted to move, Kai waited for whatever Cole intended to do to him.

"I would never hurt you," Cole said softly. "I swear it on my very soul. I would give my life to protect you."

Cole's words struck deep, and Kai raised his head enough to look at the auburn-haired man who'd come barging into his world out of nowhere. "Why?" he asked hoarsely. "What do you want from me?"

Cole leaned against the headboard. "I don't want anything from you. The reason why, I can't explain right now. Just please… trust me."

The lost little boy inside of Kai wanted to believe Cole. He wanted to give in and let someone else take care of him for the first time in a long time, but the part of himself that had suffered through every beating, every barrage of foul words, screamed for him to run, to never give in. How could he possibly allow himself to trust a complete stranger, even if they offered him the very thing he'd been searching for over the last ten years?

Kai weakly shook his head. "I can't," he murmured.

"Will you please do me one favor, then?"

Kai tensed at whatever Cole was about to say.

"Give me one month to prove you can trust me? Please? After, if you still want to leave, I'll give you the money you need to start a new life somewhere else. I'll help you hide from whoever *he* is."

Kai lifted his head, his heart swelling, a tiny flicker of hope beginning to stir within him. He stamped it out immediately. "Why should I?" he demanded.

Cole shrugged one broad shoulder. "Because I saved your life."

Kai scowled then. Bastard! "I didn't ask you to!"

Cole grinned. "No, but I did. Come on, one month. That's not very long in the grand scheme of things. What have you got to lose?"

A lot, Kai thought sourly. He truly didn't understand why this guy wanted to help him when they didn't know each other. He'd begun to believe that he wasn't working for Jerrod. But had he somehow found out about Kai's ability? Cole hadn't given any indication he knew Kai's true nature, but he could be hiding the fact that he knew. Kai continued to argue with himself for several minutes. Cole didn't say a word, merely sat next to him and waited for him to answer.

"On one condition," Kai said finally.

"Anything."

"Tell me why you want to help me."

Silence met his request, the only sound coming from the engines reverberating throughout the jet, and Kai wondered if Cole would answer him. The response Cole eventually gave did nothing to alleviate Kai's reservations. "I can't give you the answer you want."

Kai scowled. "Then my answer is no."

Cole moved until he turned and faced Kai. The solemn expression on Cole's face stalled any further protestations Kai might have made. An odd sensation wrenched Kai's heart in his chest, and he had to keep himself from blurting out he'd changed his mind. His inner half chirped, shocking Kai at how much he wanted to reach out and smooth away the lines of sadness on Cole's face. *Why?* Kai wondered. A sharp, high-pitched bark, audible only to Kai, sent a shiver down his spine. He'd never had such an intense reaction before, to anyone or anything.

"Would you prefer to be on the run, hungry and sleeping on the street, than in the warm, comfortable bed I can offer you? Or spending every moment looking over your shoulder instead of knowing you're safe and protected by my pack?" Cole challenged softly.

Twitching at Cole's words, Kai tried not to let them sway him, but the tone of Cole's voice spoke to the part inside of him that wanted to give in. "No," he whispered.

"If you will give me the month I ask, I will prove to you I'm not going to hurt you and only want to help you." Cole reached out, his hand steady yet gentle, and picked up Kai's from where it rested on the mattress. He ran his fingers over the scar around Kai's wrist, where the shackles Jerrod kept him in night and day had dug in relentlessly.

The delicate touch sent tendrils of emotion trickling through him. Emotions Kai couldn't identify. He tugged at his hand, needing to think clearly and not be distracted by what he felt. Cole let him go immediately. Kai wanted to believe in the comfort the man beside him offered, but he wasn't sure he could forget the years of abuse he'd endured enough to let Cole in as he asked. Finally, after a long internal battle of wills, Kai capitulated and whispered, "Okay."

"Okay?" Cole asked, eagerness evident in his voice.

"I said okay," Kai huffed, not wanting to repeat it or dig deeper into his subconscious as to why he'd even agreed in the first place. He already regretted it. Didn't he? Another sharp internal chirp admonished him, and Kai grunted.

Cole offered a brilliant smile, and Kai swallowed hard. That smile made him appear even more gorgeous. "One month. No more," Kai repeated sternly.

"One month," Cole agreed and stood with a small bounce, much to Kai's dismay.

Had he made a mistake in agreeing? But if Cole stood by his word, Kai wouldn't need to scrounge for food anymore or sleep on the street. He could have a normal life. Well, as normal a life as he could have, he supposed. If Cole had lied and only a cage waited for him on the other end of the flight, he could run again, right?

"Will you do me one more favor?" Cole asked, still standing beside the bed.

Kai gave him a skeptical look, and Cole laughed. "It's not a lot. I promise."

"Okay," Kai agreed reluctantly.

"Tell me your real name. I know it isn't David."

"How do you know it isn't?" Kai challenged.

"Because you don't look like a David, and someone who is on the run isn't going to use their real name."

Should he tell Cole his name? What harm would it do to give him only his first name? He missed hearing it. His mother had named him Kai after his grandfather. "It's Kai."

"Kai.... I like it." Cole smiled again, a dimple in his right cheek deepening.

Kai scoffed and looked away, attempting to play off his embarrassment and the way his body warmed at the grin.

"We should be landing in another twenty minutes or thereabouts. We'll have to drive for a little bit to reach my home, though. There are no airstrips in Emerald Lake Hills." Cole walked over to a door near the one he'd entered the small cabin through. He opened it and removed some clothing, which he brought to the bed and placed at the end. "Do you need me to help you get dressed?"

Kai shook his head, unable to bear the idea of the virile man before him seeing more than he probably already had. His ribs stuck out against his skin, and his legs appeared thin and gangly from the lack of sufficient nourishment over the past several years. He'd been lucky if he'd eaten once every other day more often than not. His meals consisted of whatever he could find while on a job or whatever he could ferret away under Jerrod's cruel eye.

"I'll be fine," he muttered.

Cole nodded. "If you need me, shout. I'll be just outside the door."

Kai remained on the bed until Cole had left. He gingerly stood and made his way to the clothing. The jeans and T-shirt reminded him of his possessions. He panicked and hurried over to the closet. The bag wasn't inside. Tears burned behind his eyes, threatening to spill over. The only things he owned in the entire world were gone, including his mother and father's picture. Swallowing hard and forcing his emotions away, Kai returned to the bed and carefully pulled on the jeans. They hung low on his waist, held in place only by the sharp jut of his hips, and emphasized the slenderness of his legs. The jeans were easy to put on by himself, but when he went to put the shirt on, a hiss flickered from his lips as his ribs protested the upward motion of his arms.

It took some maneuvering, a lot of sweat, and five minutes before he had the shirt on. Kai would rather chew nails than call Cole in to help him. He found his sneakers in the closet and managed to shove his feet into them sans socks. Since he couldn't bend well, he figured tying them wouldn't happen and left them untied, tucking the laces inside the shoes. Taking a small breath, he exited the room to find Cole sitting in a plush leather chair and talking into a phone. Kai had only ever been on a plane once in his life, and this one looked completely different. There were only six seats, all of which were light tanned leather and apparently swiveled from the way Cole swished back and forth without thought. A television was mounted on the wall to his left, and a woman stood at the front of the plane in a flight attendant's outfit, waiting to be summoned forth. Jeez, how much money did this guy have? Did he own the plane?

Cole looked up and smiled at him, green eyes twinkling. "Hey, Nick, gotta run," he said into the phone. "We'll see you soon."

Kai carefully lowered himself into a chair across the aisle from Cole while Cole completed his call. Cole moved from his seat abruptly, surprising Kai, and he started, biting his bottom lip to stifle the groan of pain he almost let out. A sigh whispered from Cole as he knelt beside Kai and started tying his shoes. Guilt stabbed him once more. "Where did you get the clothes?" he blurted out in an attempt to ignore the emotion.

"Phoenix is home to another pack. They're just outside the city limits, actually. They were aware of my presence in the area, and they aided me and you. The Alpha's youngest son is about your size, and they gave you some clothing since some of yours ended up ruined in the… scuffle." Cole explained all of this and then stood and returned to his seat.

A shudder ran down Kai's spine at the reminder of what had almost happened. If anything, he at least owed the man for saving his life. "What-what happened to them?" he murmured.

Cole glanced away. "They won't be able to hurt anyone ever again." Kai's breath caught. "You killed them?" he whispered.

"It was an accident. I lost control." Cole ran a hand through his thick dark red hair.

The knowledge Cole had taken the lives of the three men who'd attacked him sent a new sliver of fear running through him. If Cole could lose control enough to kill someone, what would happen if Kai ever made him angry? Kai opened his mouth to ask another question when a voice came over the loudspeaker. "We'll be descending to San Carlos in ten minutes, Mr. Ferris."

"Can you secure your seat belt, or do you need help?" Cole asked, reaching for the straps of his own.

"I can manage," Kai grunted. It didn't take much effort to belt himself in. The plane bounced a little, and he let out an embarrassing squeak. A blush flooded his cheeks when he glanced at Cole and saw him hiding a smile.

"Never flown before?" Cole inquired.

"Once. A long time ago." Kai looked away, staring out the window at the clouds streaming past the wing. He didn't volunteer any further information and sat in silence as they went through the landing process.

Cole stood the moment the plane came to a halt. He took a black bag from under the seat in front of him and another from the seat beside his. Kai's eyes widened when he saw his backpack, and he undid his seat belt eagerly. He got up and snatched the bag from Cole, uncaring of how desperate it made him appear. He hugged it to his chest. Cole didn't say anything, leading the way down the aisle to the door to exit the jet. The flight attendant bid them goodbye as they disembarked. Kai gave her a weak smile before stepping out onto the top step. He blinked against the bright light and allowed his eyes to adjust for a moment.

Cole waited patiently at the bottom of the steps, turning to look up at him. "Coming?"

Kai took the stairs at a slow pace, trying not to jar his ribs. He remained mute as he followed Cole to a nearby black car. An attractive man with golden-blond hair leaned against the fender, hands deep in his pockets. Kai swallowed as alarm settled in his chest, and he eyed the man warily. A grin spread over the blond's face at the sight of them, and he shoved away from the car. Cole strode straight up to the man and clasped him in a backbreaking hug. A surprising jolt of jealousy ripped through Kai, and he almost gasped, managing to stifle the sound to avoid alerting Cole to his distress. "Welcome home, Cole!"

"Good to be home, Nick."

So this was Nick, the person Cole had been talking to on the plane. Kai studied Nick, noting the warm sparkle in a pair of deep emerald-green eyes, golden hair, and sun-kissed skin. "You must be Kai," Nick greeted and started toward him, only to stop when Kai retreated.

Cole gripped Nick's shoulder and shook his head, silently telling the man something. Kai could only wonder about the look between them. "Sorry," Nick said.

"Kai, this is Nick Cartwright. My best friend and soon-to-be Beta."

Kai merely nodded in acknowledgment of Nick's welcome. He wondered about Cole calling Nick his Beta but didn't feel comfortable enough in Nick's presence to ask.

"Let's get going. I want to get home and check on my greenhouses." Cole glanced at his watch.

"Everything is fine," Nick soothed. "Sara has been there every day to make sure your staff has everything under control. The place hasn't burned down yet. Relax."

Cole grumbled and opened the door, motioning for Kai to get in. Kai skirted around Cole and managed to climb in without causing any further pain from his rib cage, still clutching his bag. Cole closed the door behind him, leaving him alone for a few brief, blessed seconds of silence. He searched through his bag, cataloging all of his belongings with a sigh of relief. He spotted the leather choker he kept around his neck to hide his scars and yanked it out, then put it on quickly. The scars were ugly, even more than the ones on his wrists. He had learned to hide them after his escape, noting the way people's eyes were immediately drawn to the marks on his throat. Some were sympathetic, others disgusted. He didn't want to be memorable. If people remembered him, it would lead his uncle to him even faster.

The two men stowed the only bag Cole had with him in the trunk before Nick got into the driver's side and Cole went around the front to the passenger seat. If Cole noticed the choker, he didn't show it. They were on the highway shortly thereafter. Somehow, Kai could sense the anxiety to be home running through Cole.

Cole and Nick spoke about things Kai allowed to go over his head for the duration of the trip, instead staring out the window. After about twenty minutes, he saw signs for Redwood City and tensed when he remembered the encounter after he'd gotten off the bus. His eyes widened and his breathing grew shallow. Cole had been the one Kai had bumped into. Kai had been too upset to realize it before, but seeing the name on the road sign stirred his memories.

Kai wanted out of the car. Now. Why would the man he'd accidentally collided with want to take care of him? Why would Cole have followed him all the way to Phoenix? His blood pounded in his ears and his heart raced with pure terror. Had Jerrod followed him here and paid Cole to return him to Jerrod? Had Cole lied to him?

"Kai?"

A cry lodged itself in Kai's throat. He choked and reached for the door handle to open the door. Swear words exploded in the front seat as Nick swerved to the side of the road, tires desperately seeking traction as they skidded through dirt and grass.

"Kai!"

The door wouldn't open. Kai wrenched at the handle frantically, trying to get out of the car, hysterical. "Let me out," he screamed. "Let me out! I won't go back to him! I'd rather die!"

"Shit," Cole grunted and somehow managed to wedge his impossibly large form over the front seat to sit next to Kai. "Kai, stop! I told you I don't know who he is. I promise I'm not bringing you to him."

"I re-remember you," Kai stuttered still tugging weakly at the door handle.

"What?" Cole asked frowning.

"You chased me! I bu-bumped into you, and you chased me."

Cole reached out and gently pried Kai's hand from the latch. "I told you I had a reason I wanted to help you, right?"

Kai nodded and yanked his hand from Cole's warm grasp, tangling his fingers in the folds of the beat-up nylon backpack on his lap. His gaze darted between Nick, who was watching them in the rearview mirror, and Cole. "You refuse to tell me," he accused.

Kai saw Nick's eyebrow go up, but Nick didn't say anything, merely playing voyeur to their conversation. Kai wondered at the telling action. Why would Nick be surprised Cole hadn't told him the reason?

"I don't want to scare you any more than you already are," Cole murmured.

Tensing again, Kai crowded closer to the door, tightening his grip on his bag. Cole sighed and turned as much as he could, placing his leg onto the seat. He looked at Kai with a serious expression. "I told you I'm a shifter. The thing is... well... shit."

Nick turned off the car and got out, leaving the two of them alone. He leaned against the front of the vehicle, facing away from Kai and Cole.

"I didn't want to tell you this way." Cole sighed.

"Tell me what?" Kai demanded.

"When a shifter is born, their soul is shared with another," Cole began hesitantly. "We call them our true mates. When we meet them, we know instantly who they are. By smell and sometimes even just by sight." Cole paused and took a breath before he said, "You... you're my true mate."

CHAPTER THREE

COLE WAITED with bated breath as he dropped the bombshell, knowing Kai wouldn't accept it easily. He wasn't disappointed.

"You're crazy." Kai scowled, reaching for the handle once more. The door opened this time without issue.

Stopping Kai from exiting the car by snagging hold of the backpack Kai held on to for dear life, Cole searched desperately for something to say. "This is why I didn't want to tell you. I knew you would have a hard time believing me. Especially with everything you've obviously been through."

"I don't want to be your m-mate," Kai stuttered, his whole body trembling.

Cole ignored the hurt Kai's words caused and his wolf's immediate desire to kidnap and hold Kai captive until he accepted him. "I can't change what is the truth. I meant what I said on the plane. Give me one month. If you don't at least come to trust me, I will help you secure a new identity and start a new life anywhere you want."

Kai turned his head away from Cole and tightened his grip on his bag, fingers turning white. Cole would never admit the terror racing through him that Kai would reject him again. As the son of the Emerald Lake Hills pack Alpha and the successor to the position, Cole couldn't ever remember a time in his life when he'd been afraid of anything. Was this burning ball of acid in his stomach how Nick had felt when his own mate denied his claim? No wonder Nick had spent six months in hell!

"All right" came the whispered response.

Cole couldn't stop the whoosh of breath he let out. He hadn't expected Kai to give in so easily. The object lodged in his throat began to disintegrate, and he swallowed, hard. "Thank you," he murmured.

"I still don't trust you," Kai grunted, peering at Cole out of the corner of his eye.

"I know, but you will."

Skepticism shone in the hazel depths of Kai's eyes, but Kai didn't say anything in response to Cole's confidence. Cole slowly released his hold on the backpack and moved away, waiting for Kai to close the door again. The soft thud of it latching sent a swish of satisfaction to Cole's inner beast, and Cole smiled as he settled against the seat beside Kai.

Nick glanced over his shoulder toward them at the sound of the door shutting, and Cole gave a brief nod. Relief flickered across Nick's handsome features before he turned to climb into the driver's seat once more. "Are we heading to the hospital?" Nick asked after he'd started the engine and pulled out onto the highway again.

Kai started and glared at Cole. "I'm not going to a hospital."

Cole had already figured Kai would be resistant to returning to one with how his mate had reacted to the idea of being in one in Phoenix. "The doctor in the ER said you're malnourished, dehydrated, and need medical attention. I think we should at least—"

"No," Kai interrupted. "Let me out right now if you think I'm staying in a hospital for even a minute."

Sighing, Cole swallowed a frustrated sound and compromised. "On one condition, then."

Suspicion entered Kai's hazel eyes. "What?"

"For at least a week, you'll do nothing except rest and recuperate." Kai opened his mouth to argue, but Cole gave him a hard look. "It's the only way I will agree to not taking you straight to the hospital in Redwood City. I will not have my mate collapsing again."

Kai snapped his jaw shut with an audible sound and groused, "I'm not your mate."

Cole ignored the sharp twist of pain in his heart and instead chose to concentrate on having a solid month to win Kai over. "That's the deal. Your choice."

"Fine," Kai huffed.

"Nick"—Cole never took his gaze off Kai—"take us home."

"Sure thing, Cole."

The remainder of the ride, Kai stared stubbornly out of the window while Cole alternated between watching Kai and talking to Nick in the front seat about his greenhouses and other pack business. Several times he noticed Kai's ears perk up, and Cole noted it usually happened when they spoke of the pack. Kai being curious gave Cole an advantage, and he stockpiled it for later.

Cole's wolf grew restless the closer they got to his home, and Cole could feel his skin prickling, itching. It had been at least a week since he'd shifted for longer than the brief moment on the plane with Kai. He needed to run, to expel the energy built up inside of him. His wolf needed freedom. Tonight, after Kai went to sleep, he would head into the woods behind the greenhouses and set him loose.

"Cole?" Nick's voice interrupted his thoughts.

Cole blinked away the fog to realize they'd pulled up in front of his house. Kai sat staring out of the windshield, his eyes widened slightly and his lips parted in surprise. Pride exploded in Cole's chest at his mate's wonderment over his home. He'd built his business from the ground up over the last eight years from one small building to three massive greenhouses, which sat in the far distance. His home, a custom one-story, had floor-to-ceiling windows to allow as much light in as possible. The house was almost entirely made of glass along the outside perimeter. He'd done it deliberately, not wanting his wolf to feel penned in or confined. No curtains or blinds adorned the windows since he never had to worry about neighbors looking in—his nearest neighbors were over five miles away in either direction.

Cole opened his door, climbed out, and rushed around to open Kai's. He offered his hand. "Welcome to my home," Cole said.

Kai ignored Cole's proffered limb and stepped out on his own. Cole stifled a sigh and smiled. "Come on. I'll give you a brief tour before I show you where you'll be staying."

"I'll leave your bags inside, Cole. Thayne is waiting for me at the house," Nick called after them.

"Thanks, Nick!" Cole replied, never taking his eyes off Kai's face.

Cole unlocked the front door and guided Kai in with a hand on the middle of his lower back. Kai immediately sidestepped his touch, clutching his pack tighter, sweat beading on his forehead at the abrupt movement. "If-If I'm going to stay here, then I don't want you to-touching me," Kai stuttered.

Cole wondered if this would be harder than he thought. Kai seemed pricklier than expected, and a hands-off policy would be extremely difficult to follow the longer Cole was around his mate. "I'm not going to hurt you," Cole stated softly.

"I-I don't like to be touched," Kai growled. "Just... don't touch me."

"Okay. I won't touch you," Cole promised against his wolf's inner demand he dominate his mate and force him to do as he said and not the other way around. "Can we please call a truce? I don't want to spend the next thirty days trying to show you I don't mean you any harm only to have you constantly biting my head off."

Kai eyed him for several long breaths and finally gave a jerky nod. Cole hid his fleeting satisfaction and gestured for Kai to follow him. "This is the living room. I don't have cable since I don't watch TV much, but if you want me to, I can have it installed."

"No! Uh… no, I uh… I don't really watch TV," Kai mumbled.

Most of the house had wood flooring, with area rugs and runners here and there. The living room, however, had light beige carpeting and was furnished with a dark brown sofa and two dark brown leather chairs. A matching coffee table sat in front of a large fireplace embedded in a freestanding brick wall painted to match the carpeting. A flat-panel television was installed above it. Cole had picked out most of the furniture and color scheme with his mother's assistance. She'd been most insistent he wouldn't know quality if it bit him in the ass. Of course, she'd been right. If he'd done it on his own, he probably would have already had to replace several of the items since he'd accidentally shifted in the house on more than one occasion.

The dining area and kitchen were one large room, separated from the living room by a single half wall lined with photos of his family, pack, and a few key moments in his life courtesy of his mother. She loved pictures. The walls in his parents' home were littered with picture frames. Even the first time he'd shifted as a thirteen-year-old had been memorialized by her camera. Everyone in the pack knew to expect her to be taking photos at every event—it didn't matter how big or small an occasion.

Cole had purposely separated a small breakfast nook off from the larger dining table, knowing it wasn't necessary for him alone on a daily basis. The table seated eight, and he only ever had guests for employee events or small get-togethers with packmates. Full-moon runs were held at the pack manor. The only part of his kitchen for which he'd insisted on sparing no expense had been the refrigerator: huge, industrial, and stainless steel, with double doors and two pull-out drawers at the bottom for storing fresh vegetables. The cabinets and countertops were a lighter brown granite to offset the darker furniture.

"You can help yourself to anything you want to eat. There are plenty of fresh vegetables kept stocked, along with sandwich fixings, bread, and a number of meats. I'll be working in the greenhouses most of the day with the others, which means you'll have the house to yourself, but if you need anything heavy lifted, you're to call me, got it?" Cole instructed.

Kai rolled his eyes but nodded.

"There are intercom speakers near the front and back doors and in my bedroom in case you need to get ahold of me for anything during the day. They are connected directly to each of the greenhouse speakers. All you have to do is turn the dial to the number of the greenhouse, hold the button, and speak." Cole pointed toward a small white object in the wall beside the front door. "My employees will let me know you're trying to get ahold of me, and I'll come to the house."

"I'll be fine," Kai muttered.

Cole turned to look at Kai. "You aren't to do anything except rest. You have multiple broken ribs, you're dehydrated, and you're malnourished. Not only did you collapse yesterday, but you very well could have died. If you don't keep your promise of resting for the next week, I will take you to the hospital and tie you to the bed myself, Kai."

Kai squeaked when Cole mentioned tying him to the bed and stumbled away a few paces. His face grew pale, and Cole lifted his hand toward Kai only to stop and let it fall to his side. He'd obviously said the wrong thing. Cole mentally swore and ran his fingers through his hair in frustration. "I'm sorry. I'm not trying to frighten you, and I would never truly harm you. I just need you to understand how serious your condition is. If you have to lift anything heavier than a fork, I want you to call me, understand?"

Fear and mistrust clearly showed on Kai's face. Cole waited, hiding his uncertainty behind a façade of indifference, even though he wanted to grab Kai by the shoulders and demand he listen to him. When Kai gave a minute nod, Cole almost missed it in his distraction. The tension in Cole eased, and he smiled. "Good. Now, let me show you where the bathroom is and where you'll be sleeping."

Cole led the way down the hallway, indicating the restroom Kai would be using on the way, and then opened a door across from the bathroom. "This is your room. Mine is right next to yours. If you need anything in the night, all you have to do is call out. The door at the very end leads out toward the greenhouses."

The room had been decorated in similar tones to the living area: soft beige paint, sand-colored carpeting, and dark furniture. The bed, a queen-sized four poster with a nightstand on either side, dominated one wall.

"There are additional sheets in the hall closets if you need any, and you can put your things in the dresser," Cole explained.

Cole noticed Kai staring around him almost in awe, and his throat tightened. He clenched his fists at his sides. If he ever got his hands on whoever had hurt his mate, he'd do unspeakable things to the bastard. "I'll leave you to get settled here while I go check on some stuff in the greenhouses. Maybe you'd like to lie down and take a nap?"

Kai didn't look at him, merely fingered the ratty backpack he held and gingerly perched on the edge of the bed as though he would have to jump up at a moment's notice. Cole knew there wasn't much in the bag. He'd shamelessly dug through it in the hospital, eagerly searching for clues about his mate's identity. The only belongings inside were a couple of shirts, another pair of pants, socks, a change of underwear, a picture of a smiling couple who resembled Kai—which Cole figured were Kai's parents—the collar Kai wore around his neck, and a small notebook Cole found contained drawings of animals: birds, dogs, and foxes mostly. He'd been fascinated by Kai's talent, but it didn't actually reveal much about Kai.

"Well… I'll leave you to it, then," Cole said and left the room, half hoping Kai would stop him, only to be disappointed when there wasn't a single sound. He returned to the living room and found his own bag by the front door where Nick had said it would be. He picked it up and took it down to his room, where he put the bag inside the door before heading out to check on his greenhouses.

The greenhouses were set about a thousand feet away from the main house. He employed nine others to help maintain them, three in each, while he did the deliveries. They'd assist with any foot traffic they received from pickups or the occasional one-offs. Most of the pack bought from him as well, which kept his employees pretty busy and his business thriving. Each greenhouse contained different types of vegetation based on what they required for the growing process—the level of sunshine, soil, water, etc. He'd carefully cultivated degrees of temperature, fertilizer, and water level dependent on what he'd planted. Soy beans were a highly coveted item in California and were his number one selling crop. There wasn't much competition in the immediate area except for a local farmer in the next town.

Cole had run into the man more than once trying to get the Whole Foods Market in Redwood City to buy from him, but he couldn't beat Cole's prices or quality.

"Cole!" a cry went up when Cole stepped into the first greenhouse.

Cole grinned and waved at Julie Parker, a pack member and his right-hand woman when he went out on deliveries or, in the case of the last two weeks, longer. She ran up to him and threw her arms around him, hugging him tightly. "It's about damn time you came home!"

She grinned up at him. A brunet with bright green eyes, Julie had worked for him almost since the beginning when he'd opened the business eight years ago. He'd scraped by in order to pay her, but she'd stuck by him anyway. Since then she'd been promoted to manager and had the salary increase to boot.

"Where is he?" She peered around him, trying to get a glimpse of Kai.

"He's in the house, resting. He's been through a lot. Don't go pestering him, Julie," Cole warned, eyes narrowing at the corners.

Julie held her hands up. "What? Me? I'm just curious to meet the one who's managed to snag the next Alpha and had the unflappable Cole all tied up in knots lately," she said.

Cole knew she didn't mean anything by her teasing. She was right. It took a lot to get under his skin, but knowing his mate had been right there within his grasp and then gone again had left him agitated and frustrated. Something Julie had only ever seen when one of the orders for his clients went wrong.

"I didn't mean to snap, Jules. He's just... damaged. I almost didn't even manage to get him to come home with me. I don't want to take the chance of anyone scaring him off."

Julie dropped her hands and tilted her head to the side, questions immediately popping up in her gaze. "What do you mean damaged?"

Starting to pace, Cole swung his arms at his sides, trying to dispel the helplessness eating at him. "Someone abused him. Badly. I'm not sure which is deeper, the physical scars or the emotional ones. I've never seen someone so afraid, Jules. I've spent the last two weeks thinking of every possible scenario that might happen when I found him. None of them even came close to the reality. I have no idea how to talk to him. Everything I say makes him suspicious. Everything I do makes him flinch or want to run! How am I supposed to claim him if I can't even touch him?

31

"I actually made a deal with him! I promised him if he gave me a month and he still didn't trust me, I'd let him go! Willingly! What the hell was I thinking?" Cole found himself shouting by the time he'd finished, the last words bouncing off the walls of the greenhouse. He halted his movements and stared at Julie, needing an answer to his rhetorical question.

Julie came closer and touched his arm, sympathy on her face. "Desperation makes us do things we wouldn't normally do, Cole. Have faith. A month is a long time. You are a wonderful man with a very big heart, and he will come to see it, given the chance."

The idea of Kai leaving at the end of the month caused Cole's heart to clench. Cole gnashed his teeth together and closed his eyes. "What if he doesn't?"

"He will, Cole," Julie replied gently.

Gods, he prayed Julie was right, because he didn't think he could survive losing him again. Opening his eyes, Cole lifted his head and attempted a half-assed smile at her. He knew the best thing to do right now would be to stop thinking and dig his fingers into his beloved soil. Getting his hands dirty and working with the earth the gods had placed beneath his feet would help get his mind off the deadline before him. "Thanks, Jules."

"Anytime, boss."

"How about giving me the rundown of business since I've been gone while we plant some new tomatoes at the far end?"

Julie nodded, and she started in on the latest orders, crops, and news as they walked to the end of the greenhouse. Fresh beds of tilled soil lined either side of the aisle, and Cole breathed the scent in deep, a sense of tranquility trickling through him. The clean, earthy smell had always soothed his soul in times of trouble or distress. For the next several hours, the two of them worked side by side, planting, watering, and discussing the general business needs.

"I think we finally have a chance to land the Bryson's Market account," Julie said after about an hour.

Cole sat on his heels, swiping at his forehead with the back of his palm. "You're only telling me this now?" he demanded. "You know I've been trying to land that account for two years!"

She rolled her eyes at him. "Don't get your panties in a bunch, Cole. It's not for certain. George's brother Thomas happens to know the owners. They were just waiting for you to return to arrange a meeting."

Bryson's Market was a popular organic grocery chain that not only serviced Redwood City, but also had several other locations throughout California. Cole had been sending them samples of his vegetables and herbs for the last two years in hopes of luring them away from one of the bigger suppliers. "What finally brought them around?"

"Thomas said the owner's wife loved the peppermint bath salts. She said she's never found anything that left her skin feeling as soft or looking as vibrant. She demanded her husband give you the meeting. Personally, I think it's because she wants the recipe for the bath salts." Julie grinned teasingly.

About a year and a half ago, Cole had come up with a mixture of all-natural peppermint oil extract from the leaves of the plants he grew in one of the greenhouses, Epsom salt, and a few other all-organic ingredients to make a soothing bath salt for his mom for her birthday. She'd fallen in love with it and suggested he market it. He'd laughed it off at first but contemplated the idea long enough to see if any of his clients were interested. Before he knew it, he had more orders than he could keep up with. He'd placed Julie in charge of the process and imparted his ingredients list to her.

"Tell Thomas I'll meet with them anytime they like," Cole replied. "I can be available whenever they are."

Julie chuckled. "I figured you would say that. As soon as I knew you were on your way home, I made the appointment for Friday."

"You really are the best, Julie!"

"I know," she replied, cockiness in her tone.

COLE'S UNEASINESS over the situation with Kai had completely vanished by the time he looked up at the clock and realized it was almost dinnertime. "I'm going to wash up, Jules, and head back to the house."

"Sure thing, boss. Just going to finish up this last section, and then I'm going to head out for the day."

"Have a good night, and thanks again for watching over everything for the last couple of weeks." He stood and pulled her up into a brief hug again. "I'll see you tomorrow."

"Night, Cole."

Cole washed his hands, arms, and face and left the greenhouse, waving at several of the others as they were getting into their vehicles for the day.

The house still remained dark when he entered, meaning Kai hadn't left his room. He took a moment to listen for Kai's heartbeat to reassure himself Kai hadn't bolted the moment Cole had left the house earlier. The slow steady thud sent relief curling through him. A light shone around the edges of Kai's door, indicating Kai had at least turned one on inside his room. Sighing, Cole continued to his own bedroom to grab a quick shower and change of clothes. He could faintly pick up the same musky scent from the hospital throughout the house. It disappeared when he entered his room. Apparently, Kai had come out long enough to explore the house. If Kai remained locked behind closed doors whenever Cole was around for the next month, how in the hell would Cole be able to gain Kai's trust? He needed to come up with a way to get Kai to come out.

He didn't linger in the shower, rinsing off and towel-drying quickly. He chose a faded pair of jeans and a white T-shirt to wear, leaving his feet bare. The cool wood floor beneath him reminded him just how much he'd missed being in his own surroundings, and the peace from the work in the greenhouse deepened further at finally being home.

Cole stopped outside of Kai's door and knocked lightly. "Kai?"

No answer.

Knocking again, Cole called a little louder, "Kai?"

A muffled "Yeah?" came through the door.

"I'm going to make something to eat for dinner. Is there anything you don't like to eat?"

"Not hungry."

Cole scowled and swallowed a frustrated grunt. He closed his eyes and breathed in deep. "You have to eat, Kai. You promised. If you don't, then I have to take you to the hospital."

Several moments of silence met his words and then a muttered, "Broccoli."

He blinked. "Broccoli?"

"I hate broccoli."

Cole choked down a laugh and cleared his throat. "Okay. No broccoli. Anything else?"

Silence again. Then, "Peas."

"So... no broccoli or peas. I'll remember. How about some spaghetti? Think you can eat some?" A sound of what Cole took for consent came from the other side of the door. "I'll let you know when it's done, then."

Cole knew what Kai had revealed about himself wasn't all that personal, but he still held it close to his heart. It gave him hope maybe the month would be enough to convince Kai to remain with him. He began whistling as he made his way to the kitchen and started prepping everything for dinner. He set a pot of water on to boil, got out the package of organic pasta, and then grabbed a jar of his homemade tomato sauce from the small walk-in pantry. The sauces available in the supermarkets were atrocious. How anyone could call those pasta sauce was beyond him. He jarred his own sauce a couple of times a year and then added seasonings when he used it. Pack members were constantly asking him to sell it, but he had enough work on his hands with the greenhouses and the peppermint bath salts. There wasn't time to produce something else right now.

He set another smaller pot on the stove and emptied the contents of the jar into it before taking several jars of dried spices from the nearby cupboard. It wasn't even necessary for him to measure the different seasonings anymore as he knew it by heart. He stirred the sauce as he added the flavorings. The smells immediately started filtering through the house. While the water began to boil, Cole picked up a remote sitting on the bar between the kitchen and the living area. He hit the power button, and soft sounds of a saxophone filtered through the air.

Next he broke up the spaghetti into the water, lowered the heat, and then put out a couple of plates, silverware, and napkins at the small breakfast table. It didn't take long for the noodles to cook and the sauce to heat thoroughly. He drained the water and then dumped the noodles into a bowl to place on the table. The sauce followed shortly after.

Finished, Cole went to get Kai. The door hadn't opened, something he anticipated being a regularity. He knocked and called, "Dinner's ready, Kai."

Kai didn't answer, and Cole frowned, sighing internally. Would he have to fight every step of the way? "Kai?" he repeated, knocking again.

The door cracked open and hazel eyes peered out at him. "Come eat," Cole said softly.

CHAPTER FOUR

KAI HAD heard Cole enter the house long before he knocked on the door. His heart tripped a beat when the footsteps stopped in front of his room momentarily before carrying on. For what reason he couldn't really be sure. Fear maybe? Anxiousness? His inner self chirped at him, reminding him of Cole's ability. Was Cole working for Kai's uncle? Maybe he wanted to lull Kai into a false sense of security to keep him from running until his bastard of an uncle could arrive. The chirp came again, a denial in the tone. Somehow, his other half seemed convinced Cole wouldn't betray him, but Kai still didn't trust him.

The war within him frustrated him. He'd never disagreed with his other half. What the hell had he been thinking to agree to stay here for a month? He needed to leave as soon as he healed. A few days and he'd be well enough to take off. Just until his strength returned. He'd start by stockpiling whatever food he could take with him. The man surely wouldn't notice it missing with everything he had. While Cole had been gone, he'd walked through the house, looking into each room and learning where the windows and doors were in case he needed to make a fast escape. He'd found the loaded pantry and even snooped vaguely through the cabinets and refrigerator. He snagged a couple of packs of crackers to start with, stashing them in the back of the closet in his room. The one room he'd avoided going into smelled like Cole. Somehow, the idea of stepping over the threshold scared him. He didn't quite understand the feeling. After all it was only a room, but somehow it seemed extremely... intimate.

When Cole knocked a little while later, Kai jumped, wincing at the jarring movement. He begrudgingly answered the man's questions and then went quiet, listening as Cole moved away and the muffled sound of whistling reached his ears. His stomach began growling as soon as the smell of something delicious cooking reached his nostrils. Kai breathed the scent in deep, closing his eyes. He hadn't had a hot, home-cooked meal in years. His mouth watered, and he gripped his belly, trying to stifle the intense hunger gnawing at his innards.

He couldn't be sure how much time passed before Cole came to his door again. "Kai?"

At first, he debated about not replying. Giving in meant showing weakness, except his stomach let out another louder, longer snarl. Kai sighed with capitulation, slowly stood, and made his way to the door. He opened it a crack and peered up at Cole. "Come eat," Cole said.

If he weren't starving, Kai would have told him no and shut the door in his face, but he knew being stubborn and not eating wouldn't help him get out of there any faster. Kai waited for Cole to move and then opened the door farther, noticing the way Cole's eyes darted down his form, as if checking for something. He gave Cole a defiant stare and waited.

Cole walked toward the front of the house, clearly expecting him to follow. Kai hesitated for a split second and then started after Cole. Soft music played from the stereo in the conjoined living room, and he found the small table near the windows covered with a heaping bowl of spaghetti and a smaller gravy boat full of sauce, waiting for them. His throat tightened at the scene. Years of loneliness swamped him, and Kai curled his fingers into his palms, fisting his hands at his sides. He'd missed out on so many things: the comfort of his parents' embrace and love, the way his mother used to cook dinner for them, the sounds of their laughter and voices as they talked and joked around over dinner. He'd lost sight of their faces in his mind a long time ago. The picture he carried with him was the only way he could remember what they looked like.

"Is everything okay, Kai?"

Kai shook himself and glanced at Cole. He tried to keep the misery he felt inside from his expression, but something must have shown through. Cole frowned and took a step toward him, stopping when Kai moved away. "What's wrong? Are you in pain? Did you take another pill yet?"

"I'm fine," Kai replied in a stoic manner.

"You're not fine," Cole insisted. "I can see it on your face."

Kai glared at him. "I said I'm fine. You wanted me to eat, so let's eat."

Cole started to say something else and then seemed to think better of it. He gestured Kai to one side of the table and sat down across from him. Kai gingerly lowered himself into one of the chairs and waited for the okay to serve himself. Cole reached out and picked up the serving silverware. He started dishing the pasta onto Kai's plate. "I can do it myself," Kai protested.

"I know you can, but I want to do it," Cole said.

Cole continued to pile noodles onto his plate, filling it almost to overflowing. "I can't eat all of this!" Kai exclaimed, eyeing the heaping mound.

"Eat whatever you can," Cole replied while picking up the gravy boat and starting to pour sauce all over the spaghetti. He emptied about half the bowl onto Kai's pasta before setting the dish onto the table to scoop noodles onto his own plate. "Will you allow our pack healer to take a look at your injuries?"

"No."

"He may be able to expedite the healing process," Cole explained calmly. "If Seth were here, he'd be able to heal you completely, but we'll have to settle for Jack. He's an empath and has the ability to seek out and coax the cells of the body to repair the damage. It's slower, but it works. He's actually Nick's second cousin by marriage."

Dazed, Kai stared at Cole. Healers? Empaths? What the hell were these people? "I don't want anyone touching me," Kai finally snapped.

Cole sighed, dropping his fork onto his plate. "Is this how the next month is going to play out? Constantly fighting everything I try to do for you? I already told you I could no more hurt you than I could myself. You are a part of me, the other half of my soul is yours. You can't see it yet because you aren't wolf, but eventually you will. Even now you must at least feel something is different between us."

"I don't feel anything," Kai lied, stuffing a forkful of spaghetti into his mouth to keep from having to say more.

Cole must have realized Kai wasn't planning on admitting anything and let the subject of them being mates drop. "At least let Jack take a look at you, see if he can help. Please."

Kai furiously shook his head. "No."

"Damn, you are stubborn!" Cole exclaimed. "Do you like being in pain? Is that it? You have lived in pain for years and don't know how to function any other way?"

Kai stared at Cole, his fork halfway to his mouth. His hand shook, the pasta shivering on the tines. He slowly set the utensil on his plate and stood. "You don't know anything," he whispered.

"Then talk to me! Help me understand!"

Kai felt penned in, cornered. Panic and alarm pounded through his veins. He lifted his hands to grip at the sides of his head. "Just leave me alone."

Cole's chair scraped against the floor, and Kai flinched, stumbling backward into his seat. He'd smart-mouthed someone stronger than him. When would he learn to stop opening his mouth? Kai cowered into the corner between the table and the chair, ignoring the pain in his ribs, as he sensed Cole coming closer. The heat from Cole's body enveloped him first. The surprisingly gentle touch on his bicep brought out a small sound of abject terror, a weak sound he couldn't stop, but the punishing blows he expected never came. Cole started to lightly stroke Kai's upper arm and shoulder. Small unintelligible sounds came from Cole, and Kai's inner self responded to him. The desire to fling himself against Cole's broad chest scared him even more than the fear of being physically injured.

The gentle caresses moved to the nape of his neck, and Kai shuddered, his nails digging into the flesh of his scalp. He needed to pull himself together, to run, to get away from the man beside him. Why did he want to lean into the touch rather than escape?

"Calm down, shh. I'm sorry I pushed you."

Kai clenched his eyes shut tighter in response to Cole's words. The callused fingers massaging his neck sent alarming shivers of awareness down to Kai's groin. A sharp, high-pitched bark echoed in his head, urging him to accept the touch and the comfort offered by the stranger who'd blazed into his life, running over him as thoroughly as a high-speed train. Kai fought against the feelings surging inside, a violent storm of emotion he'd never felt before rushing over and through him. The invisible cord spiraling straight through his core stretched thin and snapped, sending Kai crashing into Cole's chest. He found himself sliding his arms around Cole's back and burying his face alongside Cole's neck. A sob caught in his throat, unissued out of trained instinct to never cry in front of anyone.

A sense of peace he hadn't experienced since before his parents' death spread over him. Suddenly an image of a young boy, eight or nine years old, laughing and running through a field while holding the string of a kite burst into his mind. Auburn hair shone brighter than a copper penny in the sun overhead, the wind causing strands to flutter unchecked along the boy's smooth, baby-soft cheeks. Eyes green as emeralds sparkled in the tanned, freckle-spattered face. The image changed to another of the same boy, now a few years older. He stood in the pale glow of a full moon's light, excitement evident in his posture. Kai could feel the power surging through the teenager, and with a blinding flash of light, the boy disappeared and a beautiful red wolf stood in his place.

Kai sucked in a deep breath, eyes flying open wide to stare unseeingly at the wall as he realized the boy in his vision was Cole. Were these memories? How could he see what only Cole could know? What if Cole could see into his memories too? Kai panicked, shoving away from Cole to go running through the house. At first, he headed for the outside door at the end of the hallway, but Cole cried out his name, and Kai backtracked and rushed into the bedroom he'd been granted for his stay. He slammed the door and locked it, allowing the hard wood to hold up his weak limbs, and panted for breath. Oh gods, what if Cole could see the horrors he'd lived?

When no knock at the door came, Kai carefully lowered himself to the ground, bringing one knee up to his chest. His ribs ached from all the abrupt movements, but it didn't even come close to what he'd experienced in the past. Cole's words from before echoed in his ears. *"Do you like being in pain? Is that it? You have lived in pain for years and don't know how to function any other way?"*

Each word had struck him in the gut harder than a fist. Of course he didn't enjoy living in pain, even if he'd known nothing else for the last ten years. Cole had no idea what hell his life had been. The days had begun to blend together. The only time Kai had ever really come alive had been whenever his uncle allowed him the freedom to carry out whatever scheme the man had concocted. Kai tilted his head to rest on the door and closed his eyes, fingers gripping tightly to the loose fabric of his jeans. The fear and anxiety of the constant beatings had disappeared for the brief moments he'd been allowed off his leash. Each day he'd wondered how long it would be before he was killed, either by the barrage of blows from his uncle or a bullet from the gun of whichever unfortunate victim his uncle had targeted. There had been many close calls, but Kai always managed to flee before someone ended his life. On several occasions, he'd considered standing there, letting a stranger shoot him, but his other half wouldn't allow it.

Distracted by his memories, Kai didn't hear Cole approach the door. The soft sound of his name being called through the wood caused him to jerk in alarm. "Kai?"

Kai refused to answer.

"Please open the door, Kai."

Silence.

Cole sighed—a slither of breath, but Kai still heard it. Kai's inner self chirped, urging him to let Cole in. "I can't," Kai murmured.

A whine trickled through his mind. Kai covered his ears, but he knew it wouldn't keep out the next keening cry. After all, they were only in his head.

"I'm sorry," Cole whispered. Kai heard Cole's hand touch the wood of the door softly before fading footsteps signaled Cole's departure.

Kai opened his eyes, dropping his hands to the floor beside him. A few more days, and he could leave. He wouldn't need to stay for long. Another mournful howl issued from Kai's other half. "Stop it," Kai demanded. "Just stop! We can't stay here."

A shrill cry caused Kai to wince. He'd never fought against his other half as much as he had in the last couple of days. He'd always trusted the instincts of his animal self and relied on them to save his life on more than one occasion, but on this they would never agree. They needed to leave. No one could be trusted. Cole had a hidden agenda. Kai just hadn't figured it out yet. Cole's claims of Kai being his mate were outrageous and ridiculous. Besides, they were nothing alike. Cole was a werewolf for cripes' sake!

It took some time for Kai to gather up enough energy to move from his seat by the door. He headed to the bed and curled up on top of the comforter, his head pillowed on his arms, eyes closing immediately. He just needed a few more days.

THE NEXT day, Kai jerked awake, eyes opening wide. It took him several breaths to remember where he was. Some of his tension eased, but he waited for any sounds outside his room. He didn't hear any movement in the house. Cole must have already gone to the greenhouses. Kai unfurled from the bed and stepped off of it, his bare feet padding softly on the carpet. His ribs still protested, but he could already feel a difference. It wouldn't be long before the pain dissipated completely and he could carry through with his plan to leave.

He cracked open the door and stopped to listen again, to ensure Cole had already left the house. No noises met his attentive eardrums, and he let out the last of his tension on a deep exhale while making his way to the bathroom to relieve himself. With his bladder empty, Kai's stomach growled, loudly. He hadn't eaten much of the pasta from the night before, and he had run out of funds for food a few days prior to Cole finding him. He wondered if there were any leftovers from the night before and if Cole would mind if he had some of it. Cole's words from the previous day echoed in his head, and Kai let go of his reticence to take food from the fridge without permission. Cole had said he wanted Kai to eat, so why shouldn't he?

Kai wandered down the hallway to the kitchen and found the bowls of pasta and sauce Cole had placed in the refrigerator. Once he'd put some spaghetti and sauce in a bowl, covered it with a paper towel, and placed it in the microwave to heat, Kai turned and noticed a sheet of paper on the countertop. Curious, he moved closer and found a note addressed to him in strong, scrolling writing.

> *Kai,*
>
> *Please accept my apologies. Once again. I promised you you'd be safe here, and I haven't been keeping my word by pushing you to relive something you don't want to. I will not ask you again. If you ever want to talk, I'm here to listen. Last night's dinner is in the fridge. Please make sure you eat something.*
> *Cole*

Kai traced over the elegant curve of the letter *C* in Cole's name with the tip of his index finger. His mind wandered to the remembered sensation of Cole's touch on his arm. The only people to touch him without anger and hatred had been his parents and now Cole. Even the occasional women his uncle brought home were nasty, vile human beings. They either ignored him or laughed when his uncle beat him. Kai remembered one of the women suggesting his uncle "pimp him out" to other men when he turned sixteen, suggesting they would pay top dollar for a chance at such a slender young boy. He'd been horrified at the time, believing his uncle would say yes, but his uncle's immediate scoffing and use of the word "fags" alleviated any fear of being raped for money. Kai hated the woman afterward and couldn't have been more relieved when his uncle dropped her a few weeks later.

The ding of the microwave echoed across the kitchen, disturbing Kai from his thoughts, and he dropped the paper as if scalded. He shook his head and moved to take his food out. Steam rose from the plate, and the smell caused his stomach to growl once more as he set the dish on the table. He grabbed a fork from the drawer he'd found while exploring Cole's home the day before and plunked down in a chair. The hunger pains urged him to eat the first several forkfuls in heaping quantities before he slowed to a more reasonable amount and speed. His belly clenched at the sudden nourishment, and Kai forced himself to go even slower.

Once he'd cleaned the plate, he stood and placed the dish and silverware in the sink and then wandered down the hallway. Drawn to the door leading outside, he stared through the windowpanes, studying the huge greenhouses behind the house. They were encased entirely in glass from what he could tell. His inner self barked, and before he realized it, his hand was on the doorknob, ready to open it and head toward the large enclosures. Movement by the one closest to the house caused Kai to jerk away and hide behind the jamb for a moment. He knew his actions were childish and chastised himself, but he couldn't help it. Peering around the edge, he saw Cole standing by a woman and talking to her. She smiled up at Cole, and Kai's other half growled in irritation. He didn't understand the emotion knotting his stomach or the sudden urge to shred her perfect face, and it only grew when Cole hugged the petite woman.

Cole stepped away from the woman and entered the greenhouse while she headed to a silver truck parked nearby. Kai watched her the entire time, studying her face as she drove by the main house. A trill of annoyance echoed in his head. "Why?" Kai demanded.

The trill came again, only this time louder, and Kai winced. He curled his fingers around the doorjamb, ignoring the desperation behind the sound. "Stop it," he snarled, angry at himself for wanting nothing more than to be by Cole's side.

The snap of the jamb beginning to splinter returned Kai to his senses, and he yanked his hands from the frame, staring at the deep holes in the white wood. He looked down at his hands to find his nails elongated and dark red fur beginning to sprout along his arms. He stumbled into the wall behind him, shaking his head furiously. It had been years since he'd lost control of the change. "No," he murmured. "Not now."

But his inner self ignored him, and the change took hold. Kai cried out a split second before his human self disappeared in a blinding flash of light and his animal side stood there instead. He tried to return to his human form, only to find he couldn't. Shit. What the hell was going on? He'd been fourteen the last time he'd shifted without knowing exactly when it would happen. A loud bark rang out through the house, horrifying Kai. Could anyone hear him?

Kai managed to gain command of his limbs and darted toward his room, the door still cracked from earlier. He managed to squeeze through and kicked it shut with his hind legs. He couldn't lock it, though. If Cole or anyone else came into the house right then, he'd be screwed. What if they found out he wasn't human? What if they wanted to use him the same way his uncle had? Panic oozed along his nerves, and Kai begged his animal half to let him shift.

The slight fear turned into full-blown terror when the back door slammed shut. Shit, shit, shit. Kai's horror grew when he heard Cole call his name. "Kai? Are you awake?"

Kai couldn't respond, and he could barely stop a stray answering bark from coming out. He sensed his tail wagging in eagerness, and Kai snapped at himself.

"Kai" came the muffled voice from behind the door. "Are you all right?"

A whimper stuck in his throat. Kai looked around wildly, desperate to find a hiding place. The closet door was closed, and he couldn't open it in his current form. His gaze zeroed in on the bed, and he scurried toward it just as he heard the snick of the doorknob turning. He darted under it and pressed as close to the wall as he could, trying to make himself as small as possible. "Kai?" Cole's voice came softly.

He saw black work boots as Cole moved farther into the room and stopped near the bed. Kai's heart beat hard at his ribs, threatening to break out of his chest. His muscles trembled and his nose quivered as his animal self caught Cole's scent. Wolves hunted his kind, didn't they? Kai worked to remember the things he'd learned from the books he'd stolen from the houses his uncle sent him into.

Movement shook him from his thoughts, and he saw Cole lowering himself to his knees. Horror spread through him, and he curled into himself tighter, pulling his bushy tail over his head. He peered through the thick white fur and waited for Cole to see him. Cole's deep green eyes met his and widened in surprise, but they held no menace, no sudden feral hunger, or at least that's what Kai hoped.

"Kai?" Cole whispered.

Kai cowered even deeper into the darkness beneath the bed, his small body shaking, but Cole's next words stilled the furious trembling. "So beautiful."

Surprise caused Kai to lift his tail away from his face a bit to peer at Cole. Unable to stop, he issued a small chirp. He fought his fox's initial urge to revel in the praise.

"I knew there was something about you, something different," Cole murmured reverently. "I could smell it all over your skin, but this... this is something I never expected."

Kai stared at Cole, still holding himself tense as he tried to anticipate the man's next move. His whiskers flickered and his animal self urged him to move closer to Cole, a longing that Kai denied. He couldn't put himself within Cole's reach. He couldn't allow himself to be vulnerable. Who knew what Cole would do to him now he knew the truth. Would he want to use him as his uncle had, or would Cole kick him out, disgusted at his ability to shift into a fox? The idea of not being around Cole, a thought which should have made him happy, sucker punched him hard with dismay. It panicked him even further. He glanced past Cole at the open door. He could probably get by Cole, but the probability of getting out of the house wasn't the highest.

"Don't run, Kai," Cole implored. "Please."

Indecision kept Kai rooted. The note of fear in Cole's voice stilled him. He tipped his head to the side, uncertain of what to make of the emotion coming from the big werewolf. He remained out of Cole's reach and waited to see what Cole would do.

CHAPTER FIVE

THE MOMENT Cole stepped into the house, the strange scent that clung to Kai's skin engulfed him. Cole stopped for a moment, lifting his head to sniff at the air. His wolf lurched to attention, and Cole's body responded powerfully—his cock hardened and his skin tingled with the desire to shift. His wolf wanted out to claim his mate and bind Kai to him forever. But he needed to approach what happened next with calculated caution.

He closed the door to prevent any possibility of Kai getting out of the house and walked toward Kai's room, the scent getting stronger, along with the smell of fear. Cole swallowed hard. This could make or break whatever progress he hoped to make with Kai. "Kai?"

His call did not receive an answer, although he didn't really expect one under the circumstances. He tried again, and when silence met his question once more, he carefully opened the door. The room appeared empty, but he could hear the sound of Kai's heart beating fierce and fast against the young man's rib cage. Cole swallowed and walked farther into the room. The sound came from beneath the bed, and he lowered himself to the floor, not certain what he expected to find. What he found stole his breath.

Copper-red and golden-blond fur, thick enough to make any wolf envious, shimmered in the dim light beneath the bed. A tail white as snow covered Kai's slender, feline-like face, while black paws were pulled close to the slight form. His mate was a fox! Cole's heart expanded, and he curled his fingers into his palm. Kai took his breath away. Cole had imagined many things since realizing Kai wasn't entirely human. Of course, he'd thought some form of wolf, not a fox! Cole had never heard of any shifters except wolves before. Did his father, or anyone in his pack for that matter, even know there were fox shifters? It also made him frown mentally at Kai's reaction to Cole shifting. If Kai could change into a fox, why had he acted so shocked and surprised on the plane?

Cole realized Kai had his gaze trained on the bedroom door and knew if he didn't try to stop him, Kai would attempt to flee. "Don't run, Kai. Please."

When Kai stilled and his attention returned to Cole, Cole hid a sigh of relief. He eased his body closer to the ground, until his belly rested on the carpeted floor. He wouldn't push for anything Kai didn't seem ready to give, but he couldn't imagine walking away anytime soon. Smiling, Cole laid his chin on his forearm. "I always thought wolf shifters were it, you know? That we were the only ones out there who could change into another form. I can't believe we never knew about others. How long have you been able to shift? Since puberty, I'm guessing. When I turned thirteen, my whole world changed, but in a good way."

Kai sort of snorted in answer, and Cole paused. "You didn't see it as a good thing, did you?"

Of course, waiting for Kai to answer seemed pointless. "Are you able to shift at will?"

Kai tipped his head in a slight nod.

"Will you change back and talk with me, Kai?" Cole asked. "Please? I'd like to know more about your kind."

Kai hesitated, and Cole figured moving away would give his mate some level of comfort. He slowly rose to a sitting position and then scooted in reverse until he hit the wall near the door. When Kai didn't come out immediately, Cole wondered if he would at all, but then he saw a flash of hazel eyes as Kai crawled from beneath the bed. Cole sucked in a breath at being able to see his mate in his entirety, out of amazement, but also out of sheer rage. He could clearly see each and every ridge on Kai's body, the way his fur clung to his rib cage and hips and how malnourished he was. It broke his heart, and he barely managed to stifle a howl of anguish. The scars around Kai's throat as a human carried over to his fox but were more evident, awful slashes of white, patchy hair circled the vulnerable flesh. Cole knew it took years and years of continuous damage or major trauma for a shifter to retain any scars. He was pretty certain fox shifters must have the same capabilities as wolves.

He balled his hands into fists, nails digging into his palms. He'd seen the damage on Kai's human body, of course, but to see it in his second form only cemented how badly he would hurt the person who'd done this to his precious mate. It also brought home the hopelessness of gaining Kai's trust. He couldn't blame Kai if the man never trusted another person in his life.

He squared his jaw, hiding his pain and anger, and tried to smile at Kai again. Did Kai change the same way his kind did? He got his answer shortly. A flash of light and then Kai crouched there in human form, shaking his head. Cole swore he would force feed Kai every second of every day if he had to. Tomorrow, he'd ask Julie to watch over the greenhouses for a bit longer. He needed to take care of some things, including spending more time with Kai while he could and making sure his mate took care of himself.

Kai finally looked up at him and sat, leaning against the side of the bed. He seemed to be nearly holding his breath for something.

"When did you first change?" Cole asked.

At the innocuous question, Kai seemed to relax a fraction. "Thirteen."

"Are there others like you?"

"None I've ever met."

Cole grunted. "What about your parents? Where are they?"

"Dead."

"I see," Cole murmured. "How long?"

Kai tensed again and dropped his gaze to the floor. "Ten years."

Cole sensed they were close to a topic Kai didn't want to discuss and dropped it. He hungered, craved, to know more about Kai's past and to know who had put those scars on Kai. "I remember my first shift. I found it disconcerting, and I couldn't have been more uncoordinated."

Hazel eyes met his again. "Yeah?"

Cole nodded. "Definitely. I expected it, though, having grown up in a pack and having my parents by my side. I felt this power trickling along my skin. Kind of tickled, actually."

A small smile flickered across Kai's lips, and Cole kept talking. He'd give anything to see a full-blown grin on his mate's face. "The hardest thing to get used to was going from knowing how to walk on two feet to suddenly having to control four, I think. Even expecting the change didn't make it any easier."

For the next fifteen minutes, Cole recounted his first shift and the way he'd felt. He studied Kai while he talked, enjoying the emotions chasing one another over Kai's features. Obvious moments of Kai's memories of his own first change were evident in the dawning light of recognition and the occasional darkening of Kai's expression.

"I love to run, to feel the earth beneath my paws," Cole said. "There's nothing as freeing or exhilarating."

Kai picked at a loose string on his jeans. "I... I have never been able to do that."

"No? Well one day, once you're healed, we'll run together, okay, kit?" Cole offered, the pet name rolling off his tongue without thought. He held his breath a bit to see how Kai would respond to his offer and the name.

When Kai nodded without comment, a tiny flicker of hope twitched inside Cole's chest. Maybe it wasn't entirely impossible for Kai to learn to trust him. "Did you eat?" Cole asked.

"Yes."

Cole glanced at his watch to find most of the day had gone. "I want to take you to meet my father. See if he has any idea about your people."

Kai instantly balked. "No!"

"Why?" Cole frowned. "He may know something about where you come from."

"I don't want anyone else to know," Kai muttered.

Cole crossed his legs and leaned forward a bit. "I know you're afraid, Kai, but you don't have to be. No one here is going to hurt you."

Kai glared at Cole. "You can't possibly know what others will do."

Cole restrained his frustration. "I do know."

"How can you? You don't read minds, do you?" Horror entered Kai's gaze, and Cole considered for a split second teasing Kai but figured it would be better to be honest.

"I don't have to read their minds, Kai. My father is the Alpha of our pack. I'm next in line to lead them, and you are my mate, which means no one will harm you."

"Stop saying that," Kai grunted, glare deepening.

"I can't stop saying it. You *are* my mate," Cole said. "No one here would dare lay a finger on you, kit. I promise you the only thing my father wants to do is to help."

Kai shook his head again. "No."

Sighing, Cole ran one hand over his face. The hopeless feeling settled in his chest again, snuffing out the small flame of hope. What would it take for Kai to trust him? "All right. I won't bring him here."

The tension in Kai's shoulders relaxed a fraction.

"I still have to tell him about you, though, Kai."

With those words, the tension ignited all over again. "Why?"

"Because you're in pack territory, and while you remain in the house, no one will pick up your scent, but once you're outside these walls, you'll encounter at least a dozen members. Quite a bit of the population here is wolf."

Kai made a small sound of terror, brought his knees up to his chest, and wrapped his arms around them. "What?"

Cole remained silent for several moments and then asked, "What do you know about wolves?"

"Not much," Kai whispered.

Cole had already gathered Kai wasn't well-schooled. Oh, Kai spoke pretty well, but there didn't seem to be much knowledge about some things in particular. "Wolves are very territorial. We live in packs with an Alpha and a hierarchy system. Beneath the Alpha are his Betas."

"Betas?" Kai interrupted.

"Betas are much like soldiers, bodyguards in a way. They'd give their lives to protect the Alpha and the pack. They're the ones called upon when something or someone needs to be taken care of."

"I see," Kai replied.

"The idea bothers you, doesn't it?" Cole asked.

Kai hesitated, and Cole gestured for him to speak his mind. "It... it seems stupid to put yourself in harm's way to keep someone else safe. What makes someone so important they would give their own life to protect them?"

"What about the President of the United States?" Cole challenged gently. "There are men and women who put themselves at risk every day to guard him. Without a leader, the nation would fall to pieces. A pack is much the same way. The Alpha is there to guide and protect his pack. Without an Alpha, there'd be no order, only chaos. Eventually there would either be a new Alpha, or the pack would scatter to the winds, hoping to join another."

"Has anyone asked them if they want one?" Kai asked curiously.

Cole smiled. "Each member is free to make a choice of whether to stay or go. The only thing asked of them is to keep our secret and to obey the Alpha when necessary. Usually during times there is danger to us or them. My father is not a dictator and neither will I be when I take over."

"Are there Al-alphas who are?"

"Yes. There are Alphas out there who do not care for their own. They are selfish and put their people in jeopardy every day. But they're usually the kind who did not grow up into the position. They are ones who challenged the previous Alpha and won. They're power hungry, willing to do anything to be in charge, even kill."

Cole gave Kai a bit of time to process the information before continuing. "Anyway, as I said before, wolves are very territorial, and if they find someone unknown on their lands, they will react. We have very keen senses even in our human forms. It wouldn't take long for them to know you are not entirely human, Kai. It's very dangerous for you to be in our area unannounced. If you leave here without my protection and without the others knowing of your presence in the area, you could get hurt. If you are insistent on my not telling anyone what you are, you must promise me you won't leave this house without me. Understand?"

Cole saw the almost imperceptible twitch Kai gave. "Talk to me, kit. Please. What's going on in your head?"

At first, he didn't think Kai would respond, but then Kai replied, "I'm a prisoner, then."

Heart clenching at the desolate tone in Kai's voice, Cole protested, "No! It's not like that at all."

"Isn't it?" Kai asked. "I'm to be held in this… this cage until you are ready to let me go."

Cole clenched his jaw as his heart broke. "Do you really see it that way? I've done nothing except take care of you from the moment I found you. There are no bars on the windows, no locked doors, nothing to keep you here. Do you truly believe you're in a prison?"

When silence met his question, Cole had his answer. Even after all he'd done to show Kai he wanted nothing except to help him, Kai still thought of him as merely a roadblock to his freedom. If he hadn't already been seated, Cole would have dropped to his knees. His lungs constricted and robbed him of air. He felt strangled. Cole swallowed several times to stem his emotions, at least long enough to excuse himself from the room and Kai's presence. His wolf had gone quiet, retreating further into Cole's subconscious.

"I will abide by your wishes," Cole managed to get out. "No one will know of your true nature."

Cole managed to drag himself to his feet and turn toward the door. He opened it and stepped through, his hand still on the knob when he stopped.

"I hope in time you'll come to understand I want nothing except to make sure you are safe and happy."

He didn't give Kai a chance to scoff at his words before closing the door behind him. Gods, if this crushing feeling crowding his chest was anything similar to what Nick had endured for six months, he commended his friend and Beta for his strength. Cole scarcely had entered his bedroom before he hit his knees. From the moment he learned about true mates, he'd always imagined what kind of person his would be. It never mattered to him about gender or looks. He'd figured they would be someone smaller since Alpha pairings tended to end up with one larger than the other. He'd never in any of his musings about his other half thought they'd be as damaged as Kai. Most people wouldn't think of such a thing, he supposed.

To have found his mate only to have to let him go again seemed beyond unbearable. Cole had suffered a broken bone or two in his life, scrapes and bruises, and been in plenty of scuffles with pack members on the night of the full moon. But the pain in his heart and soul compared to nothing he'd ever experienced. He knew he'd have no choice except to figure out how to move on, to live, once Kai left, if he could. His family and his pack were relying on him to take over from his father when Elijah stepped down. He didn't have the luxury of falling apart. However, he needed at least a little while to lick his wounds in private and build up to putting on a courageous front.

Cole couldn't say how long he knelt there, head down and hands hanging at his side. All he knew was when he finally managed to look up, the sun had begun to dip below the horizon, and his room had grown dim. The clock on his nightstand showed the time was a little after eight. Hoisting himself from the floor, Cole left his room and walked down the hallway to the kitchen. He noted the light from beneath Kai's door as he passed, ignoring the twinge of relief he felt at seeing Kai hadn't run from the house. Except it wouldn't make sense for Kai to leave. After all, he'd be getting what he wanted in a matter of a month. Why run?

Even though the walls were mostly windows, Cole felt stifled, penned in. He needed to get away. Now. He didn't even stop to consider letting Kai know. He had to get out. The front door didn't even have time to close behind him before he shifted and took off at a run, paws digging into the grass and dirt. His wolf let forth a long, mournful howl, and Cole allowed his mind to shut down, to become nothing except the animal. No more thinking, wondering, stressing. None of it mattered. He raced into the forest surrounding his property, desperate to find a release of some kind.

The skies darkened, and the almost-full moon rose higher into the night. Cole's wolf hunted and stalked a small rabbit, capturing its prey easily. The taste of blood stirred its primal urges into a greater frenzy. It wanted its mate and knew just where to find it. Cole stirred when he sensed his wolf's desire to turn back to the house, to go to Kai and end the torment in both their souls. He battled with his inner beast, struggling to keep control and stop it from doing something they would both regret. Kai would never forgive them if they took him without his consent. Cole hated the idea of being bound to a Kai who hated him more than a Kai who merely distrusted him.

Cole forced himself to shift to human form. "No!" he snarled at his wolf. "He doesn't want us."

Cole's wolf howled its grief within him, and Cole lifted his face to the moon above, his hands fisting in the soft grass and fallen leaves beneath his legs. He prayed to have the strength to get through the next four weeks without falling apart. He begged for the courage to set Kai free as he'd promised, to watch his true mate walk away from both of them.

"Cole."

Jerking slightly, Cole forgot strong emotions could stir the mental connection to the pack Alpha, his father. *"Cole, come to me."*

He shook his head. He'd promised Kai not to tell anyone what Kai was. *"Come to me now."*

The sharp bark of his Alpha sent Cole surging to his feet. A wolf could not ignore the swell of power buried in the command. Cole shifted and ran in the direction of his parents' home. They lived about fifteen miles from his own place, but a wolf could cover the distance in a short amount of time. Cole reached the pack manor in minutes, panting from the exertion. His tongue lolled out to the side as his father exited the front door to stand at the top of the porch steps. "Come inside, Cole. Your mother and I want to talk to you."

He could have refused to shift, remained in his wolf form, but his mother would kill him if he tracked mud into her foyer. Shifting, he stood before his father, head hung low in a defeated posture. His father came down the steps and put a warm arm around Cole's shoulders, urging him up those same planks of wood and into the home he'd grown up in. His father squeezed him when they entered the living room, and his mother came to him and wrapped her arms around him in a tight hug. "We've missed you, my love," she said.

"I've missed you too, Mom."

Sara released him. "Nick told us you found him."

Cole nodded, finally raising his head to meet their gazes. "I did."

Elijah gestured for him to sit and sat down in his usual chair near the fireplace. "Sit. Tell us what has happened to upset you."

Cole didn't want to rehash everything right then. His emotions were still too raw, abraded, but he knew his parents wouldn't allow him to remain silent. He began, detailing what condition Kai was in when he found him, the scars and fear his mate carried, but he let his voice fade away when he came to what he'd discovered about Kai tonight.

"What, Cole?" Sara prodded. "Please tell us."

"Dad?"

Elijah gave a small nod.

"Have you ever seen... other shifters?" Cole started tentatively. He knew he'd be breaking his promise to Kai, but he couldn't handle this on his own. Not yet.

Frowning, Elijah tilted his head in a curious gesture. "You know we have, Cole."

"I don't mean wolves, Dad. I mean other shifters who aren't wolves."

Sara and Elijah both gave him a look of surprise. "I suppose I've always wondered if we wolves were the only ones, but I've never seen others aside from wolves," Elijah answered slowly. "Why do you ask?"

Cole swallowed and looked down at his feet. He shoved the guilt he felt aside and whispered, "Kai is a shifter."

"But that's wonderful news!" Sara exclaimed. "Isn't it? Then he understands how the mating bond works."

"He's not a wolf shifter," Cole answered.

He sensed his father leaning forward before a large tanned hand came to rest on his knee. Cole took comfort in the affectionate gesture and placed his on top of his father's. He looked at his parents. "He's a fox."

Sara gasped in reaction while his father remained solemn and quiet. "I found out today. He doesn't want me to tell anyone, but I don't know what to do." Cole growled as he lunged to his feet and began pacing. "Everything is completely messed up right now. He hates me. He doesn't trust me, and he doesn't understand what a mate is."

"But—"

Cole interrupted his mother. "He wasn't raised by his parents, at least I'm assuming not. He won't tell me anything. I shouldn't even be telling you this. I promised him I wouldn't. I just don't think I can handle this on my own, Dad. I mean, I've always imagined what it would be like when I met my true mate for the first time. None of this ever occurred to me. I've never seen someone so… so broken before."

Sara stood and approached him, grabbing his arm to stop his restless pacing. She reached up and cupped his cheek, rubbing her thumb over his skin. "Oh, my love, no one is ever truly broken. Damaged maybe, hurt definitely. You have to earn his trust, to make him see how much you already care for him. I know you. I know your heart. You're a good man, Cole, and it won't take long for him to realize how good."

Cole's eyes burned with unshed tears. The last time he'd cried to his mother he'd still been in elementary school, but all he wanted now was to bury his head in her lap as he had then and weep his pain away. Blinking heavily, he gave her the best smile he could manage. "I don't know if I have enough time for him to realize it, Mom."

She frowned at him. "Why not?"

He told her of his deal with Kai, and she smacked him on the shoulder. He winced and rubbed at the spot. "Mom!"

She scowled. "Didn't Nick's situation show you how stupid that is?"

Nick had found his mate in a small town where a wolf pack believed only Native Americans could be true wolves. His mate, Thayne Whitedove, believed him to be a created wolf, a wolf who had nothing but animal instinct, dangerous to everyone around them. Despite Thayne discovering Nick had been born a wolf, he hadn't wanted anything to do with Nick and rejected Nick's claim as his mate. Nick had spent six months in a living hell. He'd run himself into the ground, a hard feat for a wolf to do. Cole and Ryan Driscoll, Nick's business partner, had been unable to help Nick through that painful time.

Then during a business trip, Nick had been unexpectedly called to Wyoming, where Thayne needed his help to cut the ties between Thayne and the created wolf he'd accidentally made. The only way to sever the connection was for Thayne to submit to what he didn't want, the mating.

Nick had agreed to help his mate and suffered even more when Thayne continued to reject him despite the bond. It took time, but Thayne accepted Nick in the end, and while their relationship couldn't be defined as perfect, they were gradually building on top of the rubble and strengthening their union every day.

"I thought I would have enough time," Cole murmured. "I didn't realize just how damaged he is."

Sara sighed and hugged him once more. "Give him the chance to see who you are, Cole. Maybe he'll surprise you."

Cole gave a shuddery breath and wrapped his mother in a hard embrace. "Maybe."

Elijah had been silent during their exchange, and it surprised Cole that he was still in the room when he spoke. "I need to understand more about him, Cole. Please sit and tell me everything you know."

Cole released his mother and looked over at his father, nodding. "I don't have much to tell you, though."

After Cole relayed the precious little information he had about Kai and his animal spirit, Elijah rubbed at his chin. "I have a few contacts I can reach out to in the other packs. Perhaps one of them has encountered others of Kai's lineage."

"Don't tell them anything, Dad," Cole said, afraid if too many people knew of Kai it might endanger him.

Elijah smiled at him. "Don't fret, son. I may be old, but I am not senile."

Cole scoffed. "You aren't old."

His father didn't look anywhere near close to his age. A few wrinkles at the corners of his eyes and a smattering of graying hair at his temples were the only things indicative of his father's years.

"Rest easy, Cole. Why don't you go on home and spend time with your mate? I will call you if I find out anything."

Cole tensed at the mention of returning home but stood anyway, giving his mother a hug and a kiss on the cheek. Once he cleared the front steps, he shifted and loped toward home, taking his time out of sheer reluctance to face the rejection waiting for him.

CHAPTER SIX

KAI HUDDLED in the same spot Cole had left him in. He leaned his head on the side of the bed to stare at the ceiling, attempting to analyze why he felt guilty. The look on Cole's face when he left made Kai uncomfortable in the pit of his stomach. When he'd heard the door open and shut, indicating Cole had gone, Kai had to grab hold of his fox to keep from running after him. Cole wouldn't leave him for good… would he? Kai had instantly dampened those thoughts. This was Cole's home, why would he leave? He'd kick Kai out first. Another thought that left him squirming in discomfort.

He'd never wanted to reveal his animal half to Cole. It made him feel vulnerable, but he now knew Cole would never use it or him to his advantage as his uncle had. Cole's awe and wonder upon seeing him in his animal form wasn't something he'd anticipated, and Cole calling him beautiful sent a warm feeling through his stomach. Kai's fox had almost preened at the compliment, and he'd been unable to stop the small sound of pleasure his fox let out. He'd noticed the immediate nickname Cole had given him. Kit. He'd managed to do a little bit of research over the years when his uncle hadn't been watching, and he knew young foxes were called kits. Somehow, it didn't offend him that Cole called him by the name. He didn't want to examine too closely how it did make him feel, though.

When he'd shifted for the first time at the age of thirteen, his uncle Jerrod's initial reaction was disgust and fear. He'd threatened to kill Kai, locked him away in his room, and called Kai a freak. It took a month, in which Jerrod almost starved him to death, before Jerrod came up with the idea of using Kai to infiltrate people's homes and rob them blind. Kai tried to resist at first, but his uncle beat him into unconsciousness. His ability to heal faster than humans saved his life each and every time Jerrod took out his frustrations on Kai. Sometimes the houses he targeted weren't as fruitful as he expected.

Kai remembered waking up the morning after his first shift to find himself shackled to a bed in the basement. He'd been terrified, yanking at the chains and cuffs in desperation to get free. Until then Jerrod had merely ignored him, giving him the bare minimum he had to. Thinking back on it, Kai didn't understand why Jerrod never abandoned him to the foster care system during the year and a half after his parents' death. In fact, it might have been better if he had.

Jerrod kept him chained to the bed in the basement every minute except when he sent Kai on a job, threatening to kill him if he tried to run away. Too afraid to do anything at first, Kai believed Jerrod and did everything his uncle asked. As he got older, he started to mouth off and tried to refuse to steal from unsuspecting people, only to end up beaten severely anytime he attempted to deny Jerrod's demands. It wasn't until he turned twenty-one that he started to plan to get away. He squirreled away money he'd stolen whenever he could, a quarter here, a dollar there. For the two years it took him to save up enough money and a small amount of food to take with him, he lived in terror his uncle would find the stash and finally carry out his promise.

Somehow Kai managed to keep Jerrod from discovering it, and he made his escape one night while Jerrod slept off his latest alcohol binge. He'd stolen the key when his uncle came downstairs to the basement to intimidate him and kick at him. Too drunk to feel it and too angry at life to see it, Jerrod didn't notice when Kai fell against him and slid the keys free from his pants pocket. After Jerrod had tired of bullying him, he'd stumbled upstairs and passed out on the couch. Kai freed himself, gathered the things he'd hidden all over the basement, stuffed them in the backpack his uncle placed on him when he sent Kai into a house, and left. He didn't stop to rest for well over twenty-four hours, putting as much distance between himself and Jerrod as possible.

He'd been moving ever since, stopping only long enough to sleep for a few hours and then running again. The last two days were the first time he'd slept for more than two or three hours at a time. Since being with Cole. Kai frowned and lifted his head up from the side of the bed. He was still in a cage, though. He couldn't leave and he couldn't do whatever he wanted to do. Cole's face when Kai had called it one flashed through his mind. Kai sensed he'd hurt Cole, and his stomach turned at the idea. Everything Kai'd expected to happen hadn't. He hadn't been tied up or locked in his room. Cole didn't actually seem to want anything from him.

Except this mate thing, he taunted himself. He didn't even know exactly what being Cole's mate meant. What did it mean Cole wanted from him? Kai rested his forehead against his knees as Cole's words echoed in his mind. *"I want nothing but to make sure you are safe and happy."* The idea of someone caring enough about him to want him to be happy seemed foreign to him. His parents had wanted him to be safe, loved, and happy, but they were his mom and dad. Cole was a stranger, someone he'd bumped into once and only known a couple of days. He couldn't accept the idea of someone who didn't even know him wanting to take care of him.

Kai knew his fox seemed inclined to believe it. The struggles he'd had with his fox made it more than clear how he felt. He'd never distrusted the instincts of his fox, but their ideas of what Cole wanted didn't align at all. Cole might also be a shifter, too, but a wolf, a completely different species. Yet Kai knew his companion would accept Cole without reservation if Kai gave it half a chance.

Kai realized the room had grown dark, and his stomach gave a painful growl. He dragged himself to his feet and clicked on the light, blinking against the sudden brightness. The digital clock on the stand beside the bed read 9:00 p.m. No wonder he was hungry. He hadn't eaten since early that morning.

He left his room and headed to the kitchen. He hoped to get something to eat before Cole returned. Where did Cole go this time of night? Maybe he'd gone to the greenhouses, or maybe he'd met up with the pretty woman from earlier. The idea of Cole meeting the dark-haired woman twisted Kai's guts, and he jerked open the refrigerator door angrily. It frustrated him to not understand the feelings raging through him whenever he thought of Cole with someone else. He'd never experienced any of these emotions before. Anger because of his uncle, yes. Fear and pain, for sure. The emotion seemed to be a combination of both, and yet another unknown element mixed with them, causing his blood to burn beneath his skin. Overwhelming agitation made his hands shake and his jaw clench.

Kai grabbed packages of cheese, sandwich meat, and mustard from the door. He'd make a sandwich and take it to his room to eat. He also snagged two cans of soda—one to drink with his sandwich and the other to put away. Once he'd finished building his sandwich and replaced everything in the fridge, he turned off the lights and trotted back to his room, shutting the door behind him. He heard Cole enter the house as he put his sandwich and the can of soda on the nightstand. He didn't want to analyze the relief that poured over him too closely. Cole hadn't been out but an hour or two, which couldn't have been long enough to have met anyone. Right?

Kai listened to Cole's footsteps trail through the house, past his room, and into the other at the end of the hall. He really needed to get out of there. The idea of running again scared the hell out of him with what had happened in Phoenix, but he couldn't stay. The longer he remained at Cole's, the more in danger he was of believing Cole's words about wanting to help him. He planned for the next day while stashing the extra soda in the same place he'd put the few packs of crackers and small bags of chips he'd already taken.

He managed to eat the sandwich he'd made, although each bite scraped harshly along his esophagus whenever he swallowed. His fox prowled and paced in his mind. Kai knew his fox wasn't happy with his intention of leaving the following evening after Cole went to bed, but he had to go. He had no other option. His ribs were almost entirely healed, and by tomorrow they'd be nothing but a bad memory and another scar on his subconscious.

He finished the last bite of the sandwich and set the plate on the nightstand before gulping down the remainder of the soda. He flipped off the light and slid between the covers, curling into a small ball. "We can't stay here," he whispered into the darkness, trying to persuade his companion but also to convince himself.

At some point he fell asleep because when he next opened his eyes, sunlight shone into the room. Kai sat up, gingerly testing his ribs, and smiled when he found he could move without pain or even tenderness. He remained in bed for a moment, listening for any movements in the house. No sounds met his ears, and he got off the bed, exited the room, and went into the bathroom to relieve himself. He decided to scope out the house to make sure he was really alone. After a thorough inspection, Kai knew Cole had gone. He returned to his room and grabbed his backpack. Guilt stabbed him briefly on his way to the kitchen, but he shoved it aside and entered the pantry to stuff as much food as he could in the bag. More crackers, a jar of peanut butter, a few ready-to-open cans of vegetables, a box of pretzels, and a tin of cookies joined the few possessions he owned. He stashed the bag in the closet for later. Tonight, once Cole had gone to sleep, he'd make his escape.

Kai had already explored the house and didn't want to leave the safety of his bedroom. He'd seen a TV in the living room, but he didn't want Cole to find him on the couch watching it. He left his room and wandered down the hallway. The house reeked of money, and Kai knew Cole had a lot. His uncle would love to hit Cole's home, to steal anything possible. The idea rankled more than usual, and Kai frowned.

The wood flooring throughout the house gleamed in the light, and Kai knew Cole took pride in his home. Thinking of his uncle defiling it made him angry. Why should someone who hadn't worked hard to get it take something from someone who had? He'd hated doing what his uncle wanted. There were a few times he'd walked away empty-handed on purpose. Pictures of a smiling family sent remorse crashing over him, and he'd lied to his uncle and told Jerrod the family had nothing. It had earned him a beating more than once, but he didn't regret his choice.

Colored photographs in frames drew him to the counter between the kitchen and the living area. He'd noticed them yesterday during his exploration but hadn't stopped to look at them. Cole had a lot of family from what Kai could tell. There were pictures of picnics, smiling groups of people, Cole as a kid with two adults—Kai figured they were Cole's parents because of the resemblance—and Cole with Nick. Kai touched the edge of one frame, studying the wide grin on Cole's face. If he'd been normal, Kai would definitely admit how gorgeous he found Cole.

Sighing, Kai moved to the small bookcase close to the couch and read over the few titles he saw on the shelf. He figured maybe he could try reading a book. He'd never progressed past a fifth-grade reading level, but he'd always been a little ahead of his classmates in most areas. There were about twenty books overall. Kai only recognized a couple of the authors: Stephen King and J.R.R. Tolkien. The rest he'd never heard of. George R.R. Martin stood out, and he pulled the book off the shelf. *A Game of Thrones* sounded interesting from the outline on the back of the book.

He grabbed an apple from the kitchen and returned to his room. It didn't take long for him to become engrossed in the story. The various characters were not easy to keep track of, but he did his best. The idea of dragons made him wonder if there'd ever been dragon shifters. After all, there were apparently foxes and wolves. Why not dragons? Kai would love to be a dragon shifter. He could have eaten Jerrod. Maybe gotten indigestion from him too. Snorting, Kai focused on the book. He became so engrossed in the story, most of the day passed by before he pulled himself away. The sun hung low in the sky, and the room had grown dark. He had started to strain to read the words in the dimming light, and he gave up, setting the book down, marking his page in the process, and sat up on the bed. Maybe he'd take the book with him in order to finish it.

The scent of body odor reached his nostrils, and Kai sniffed at his armpit, wrinkling his nose as he realized how bad he smelled. He decided he'd gone long enough without bathing and got off the bed to pick up the borrowed jeans and T-shirt he'd dressed in on the plane. He only had one other shirt and another pair of pants besides the ones he wore at the moment, also from Cole's friend, and he wanted to keep them for wherever he ended up. He needed to at least look halfway presentable to get a job. Although he wasn't sure what he could qualify for. He didn't have any official skills, and he'd never finished school because of his uncle. Despair loomed over him, but he refused to let it get to him. Someone would give him a job. They didn't need to know the truth about his past. Maybe he could be a simple dishwasher in a diner somewhere or something.

The shower felt amazing. He hadn't bathed in hot water for years. Once his uncle had locked him in the basement, he'd been forced to rinse as best he could in the sink downstairs on the nights when Jerrod was too drunk and passed out to notice the noise of the running water. The hot tap hadn't worked, and he'd only been able to use the cold side to wash off with. Kai wondered more than once how he hadn't ended up with pneumonia during the years down there. The hard, cold cement and lack of central heating during the winter months had been brutal, yet somehow he'd managed to survive it all.

He scrubbed at his skin with a bar of soap he found on a small ledge jutting from the wall, cleansing away some of the memories of the men in Phoenix and their hands on his body. Bottles of shampoo and conditioner sat on another larger shelf built into the tiled shower, and Kai used some to wash his hair, closing his eyes in pleasure. The differing clean scents almost made him dizzy. He sighed and dipped his head under the spray, rinsing off the suds. The sound of Cole entering the house made him tense, and he tried frantically to remember if he'd locked the bathroom door.

Kai needn't have worried because Cole's footsteps didn't even hesitate near the bathroom. They kept going, and Kai relaxed, but the knowledge Cole didn't seem to want to check on him as he had every other time disappointed Kai. Maybe Cole had finally given up on him. He should be happy, yet the truth caused him a small bout of depression. He really needed to get the hell out of there.

Finishing his shower, Kai turned off the water and grabbed a towel from the rack beside the tub. He dried off and dressed in a matter of minutes. When he exited the bathroom, he couldn't help but glance toward Cole's room. No light showed from beneath the door. Had Cole already gone to sleep? Kai scurried to his own bedroom and glanced at the clock. He'd taken longer than he'd thought. The red letters showed almost eight. He sat down on the bed and yanked on his shoes before retrieving his bag and putting everything in it. The backpack weighed quite a bit, but Kai had carried heavier in his fox form. His uncle never let him leave a house without taking anything of value he could fit in his bag or mouth. If he did, he'd regret it later when Jerrod beat the shit out of him for missing something. Of course, Jerrod used whatever excuse he could to hit Kai, a valuable object left behind or not.

Kai sat on the bed, waiting. His pulse sounded loud in his ears as he listened for Cole's heartbeat to even out, signaling the man had fallen asleep. It wasn't until almost one in the morning when he heard Cole finally slip into unconsciousness. Kai ignored the cry his fox gave as he stood and hefted his bag onto his shoulder. He just needed to get outside, and then he could shift and run. An acrid taste built in his throat as he crept out of the room and into the hallway. Time moved slowly, and by the time his hand was on the handle of the front door, Kai thought for sure his heart would explode out of his chest. He swallowed hard as he carefully unlocked the door and turned the knob. When it clicked, he froze, listening to the sound of Cole's heart. The sound never wavered, never increased, and Kai knew Cole still slept.

Despite the darkness outside, Kai could see as if it were daylight still, his eyes easily shifting to canine form. He didn't latch the door, just closed it to where the door rested against the jamb. An owl hooted close by, and Kai shivered a bit. The sound seemed ominous in the empty night. Kai waited to shift until he'd reached the trees. He set his bag down, closed his eyes, and gathered the energy around him. When he opened his eyes again, the ground appeared about a foot away from his face, and the slight breeze tickled each individual strand of hair covering his body. His ears twitched at the new sounds he could pick up: the same owl ruffling its feathers, the scurry of some small creature in the underbrush of leaves beneath the trees, and the howl of a lone wolf far off in the distance.

He hesitated for a moment, remembering Cole's words, but he shook his head. What sane person would be roaming the woods at one in the morning, he mused as he wriggled his legs into the arm holes of the pack and hefted it onto his back. Years of experience made it easier than one would think for a fox to accomplish. Kai trotted toward the trees and followed along the edge in the direction Nick had driven from a matter of days ago.

The night air felt cool. Drops of dew built along Kai's whiskers as he traveled, and he shook his head once in a while to dislodge the water. A sense of despair and anxiety edged in on him the farther away he got from Cole's place. He fought it and kept moving, continuing to follow the same tree line. Once in a while, he'd glimpse a light shining from a car driving by or from a nearby house. He remained hidden in the shadows, never allowing the glow to reveal his presence.

Kai couldn't be sure how long he'd been moving or how far he'd gotten when another howl came, this time closer than the one he'd heard when he first started out. The sound sent a tremble of fear along his spine, and he picked up his pace. His paws dug into the soft soil, and dead leaves crunched loudly beneath his feet. Kai heard the rustle of bushes a few yards away, behind him and to his right. His heart jolted, pounding at his rib cage. He started running faster, but the bag hindered him, slowing his stride a fraction. Oh God, was he going to die out here? After everything else he'd endured, would this finally be his end? Killed by another animal? Maybe it was his time. He'd cheated death for ten years while under his uncle's eye; it would only be right for it to be over now.

Midstride, something hit Kai in the side, and he tumbled down, the backpack dislodged and sent flying into a nearby tree with a loud crack. His attacker wrapped around him, they rolled in a ball of fur for several feet before coming to a complete stop. A heavy weight on top of Kai pinned him to the ground. Kai issued a sharp, high-pitched scream. The sound echoed eerily through the forest. He scrabbled for release, punching his hind legs at the soft underside of whatever animal had tackled him. Another cry, an alarming bark, rattled in his throat. He didn't want to die, not here, not as some wild animal's dinner. He screeched again only for the sound to die halfway when the warm length atop him shifted in a bright flash of light and Cole's human form appeared, holding him down.

Elation rushed through Kai, followed by relief and then fear. Would he beat Kai for running? When Kai met Cole's gaze, the disappointment and despair there punched him in the gut worse than a fist.

"Why?" Cole asked, his voice a broken sound in the silent night.

Kai couldn't answer, not just because of being in his animal form, but because he didn't know how to answer Cole. He didn't understand the feelings eating away at him the longer he remained in Cole's presence, or the way he wanted to bury his furry face in the hard chest above him and beg for forgiveness. Kai closed his eyes and returned to his human form, keeping his head turned to the side to avoid the piercing stare. "I don't know."

"You promised to give me a month. I didn't ask for anything else. Just one month."

"I know," Kai whispered. He couldn't even begin to sort out why Cole's hard body pressing his into the ground didn't terrify him. Rather, to his utter horror, he felt himself getting hard and twisted his body to the side, trying to hide it. Cole must have taken it as a sign of struggling to get free because he abruptly rolled off of Kai into a crouch a few feet away.

Kai curled into himself to hide the bulge in his jeans. He knew about sex. He'd experienced wet dreams and masturbated a few times over the years, even heard Jerrod with his women sometimes. He'd never once been turned on by anyone. Maybe the fear of what they would do to him if they knew the truth kept his libido in check, but his body's reaction to Cole embarrassed and shamed him.

"Is being around me so unbearable to you you'd rather live scared and alone? Rather be on the streets and hurt by strangers than let me help you?" Cole asked quietly.

Shaking his head, Kai closed his eyes again, fighting the burning sensation of tears.

"Then why? I have asked nothing of you since bringing you here. Nothing except to remain with me, get to know me, if only for a little while. Why did you agree if you can't stand to be near me?"

Kai heard a hitch in Cole's voice, and he shuddered at the intense desire to throw himself at Cole, plead for the other man to absolve him of the agonizing guilt liquefying in his veins. He'd never hurt anyone in his life on purpose, but in some way he'd deeply wounded Cole, the one man who seemed to want nothing except to help him. Kai swallowed several times past the lump in his throat. "I-I can't...."

"Can't what, Kai?" Leaves rattled, and Kai opened his eyes to find Cole kneeling now, studying him intently. Kai couldn't answer. The words stuck in his throat. "Kai?"

"Please stop," Kai pleaded. "I can't!"

"Tell me. You can't what?"

"I can't care about anyone!" Kai exploded. He sat up in agitation and gripped at the sides of his head. "I just can't!"

Warmth surrounded Kai's wrists, and Cole pried Kai's hands away, lowering them to Kai's lap. "Look at me, Kai. Please."

Kai shook his head.

"Look at me," Cole demanded gently. Several tears escaped as Kai raised his gaze to meet Cole's. "There are many things in this world not worth doing, but caring about someone is not one of them. Are you saying you care about me?"

"I-I don't know," Kai stuttered.

"Why did you run, then?"

Kai closed his eyes again, unable to meet Cole's probing stare and the hope in the depths of his eyes. "I ca—"

"Don't start with that again," Cole rumbled.

Kai sensed the lack of menace behind the growl but felt Cole's power. He shuddered and replied in a whisper, "I could."

"Could what, kit?" Cole didn't let him hide, wouldn't let him go without explaining his obscure response.

"Care. I could care, and I don't want to."

Cole released one of Kai's wrists, and Kai flinched at the touch of Cole's fingers on his cheek. A sigh tickled the hair along Kai's forehead, tousled in their struggle moments ago. Kai opened his eyes again to find Cole extremely close. A small sound, one he knew didn't come from fear, slipped free. Kai found himself frozen at Cole's nearness. When Cole began to stroke his cheek in a light caress, Kai's pulse sped up a fraction, and his heart tripped a beat. Heat trickled along his veins, spiraling toward his lower half, causing his body to respond once more. Kai prayed Cole wouldn't notice, but he knew if his own senses could pick up the scent and see through the darkness, Cole's had to be keener, sharper. The predator residing within Cole must be stronger than his own if he'd found Kai so easily.

"Why don't you want to care?" Cole whispered, never freeing Kai's gaze from his.

Kai wasn't sure how he had the strength to answer. His limbs grew heavy with the warmth spreading through him, and it seemed as if cotton suddenly filled his head. "Because it hurts," he managed.

"What does?" Cole prodded, seeming to get even closer, his nose almost touching Kai's.

"When you leave."

Cole gave a soft growl. "Never going to leave you, kit."

Kai trembled as Cole's mouth settled on his. He whimpered at the brief touch and squeezed his eyes shut tight. Cole broke the kiss, only to return again when Kai didn't object, this time deeper and firmer. Kai instinctively opened his mouth when Cole probed along his bottom lip. The slick sensation of Cole's tongue across his lips brought out another whine, louder and needier. If his body had responded before, the new feelings rushing through him now made him even harder. Cole didn't ask for more despite Kai realizing if the bigger shifter had, he wouldn't have stopped him. He'd never experienced any of the sharp bolts of desire stabbing him all over his body. When he moved, his cock rubbed at the front of his briefs, a profound dampness making him wonder if he'd come in his pants from the kiss alone.

Cole freed Kai's mouth, breathing heavily through his nose. Kai knew Cole couldn't miss the tangy scent of his arousal, and he flushed even more. He opened his eyes but refused to meet Cole's again. Embarrassment at how he'd responded forced him to fix his gaze on one broad shoulder and not look up. When Cole didn't say or do anything else, Kai wondered if they would sit in silence the rest of the night. It had to be edging on to dawn soon. Of course, he had no clue how long they'd been sitting there.

"Kai?"

He continued his study of the corded muscle along Cole's throat disappearing beneath the edge of the soft green shirt Cole wore. A single callused finger slid under Kai's chin and tilted his head up, forcing him to either close his eyes or look at Cole. Kai almost opted for the first choice, but he couldn't bring himself to deny Cole what he asked.

"Come home with me, kit. Please. Give me the agreed-upon month," Cole murmured while searching Kai's face for whatever answer he needed.

If Kai remained with Cole and Cole continued to be kind to him, his heart and his fox would never let him leave at the end of the month. Twenty-eight more days. Could he give Cole those days and still retain every piece of himself by the time they passed? His fox chirped, urging Kai to remain with the bigger shifter and accept what Cole offered. Kai found he couldn't argue with either Cole or his fox. He wanted to stay.

"Yes."

Cole seemed to sag at the single word. "Thank you."

Kai looked around in discomfort and spotted his bag. He moved away from Cole and stood, then walked over to pick it up. He hefted it onto his shoulders in a deft shrug and looked at Cole, who had also gotten up from the forest floor. No words were exchanged as they began the walk home, their shoulders occasionally brushing. When they finally entered the clearing behind the house, the sun was just peeking over the horizon, gold and red fingers of dawn spreading across the inky darkness. Kai wondered if maybe it were a sign things were going to be different for him from then on.

CHAPTER SEVEN

When Cole had awakened to a silent house, Kai's heartbeat no longer present, he'd almost lost his mind. He'd rushed through every room, searching for Kai but coming up empty. When he'd managed to stem his panic enough to think, returned to Kai's bedroom, and found the beloved pack missing, he knew Kai had run. The animal instinct in him kicked into overdrive, and moments later he was on his wayward mate's tail, praying he'd reach him before he could disappear again.

He'd never imagined the night would end the way it did. The taste of Kai's lips still crackled along his tongue, making him want more. Gods, the fire he'd experienced the moment their mouths touched had been unlike anything he'd ever known. Electricity had sparked a flame through every inch of his body. It had taken his entire being not to pin Kai to the forest floor and take him right there, everything else be damned. The knowledge Kai still didn't trust him stopped him. He couldn't risk damaging the tentative foundation their relationship perched on. Not if he wanted to keep Kai forever.

Kai's admission had made his inner beast howl for joy, but it had also been extremely telling. The battle Cole fought included not only Kai's fear of being hurt physically, but emotionally as well. The small step taken uphill gave Cole hope again, made his usual positive mental attitude return, and Cole swore he would take every chance he got to show Kai he wanted nothing more from him than to remain by his side. With every stride toward the house, his resolve grew stronger. He wouldn't give up. Not now. Not after this. He'd allowed his fear of losing Kai to make him weak, and it shamed him. He'd never given up easily and even less so when it came to something that mattered.

When they reached the house, Cole opened the door and waited for Kai to enter first. "Why don't you go get some sleep?" Cole suggested, noting the dark circles underneath Kai's eyes.

"You should t-too," Kai protested, his words broken by a yawn.

Cole smiled and reached out to pat Kai on the head. "I'm fine. Just need to check on the greenhouses first."

He couldn't sleep even if he wanted to. The progress with Kai left him too wired to relax enough to go to bed. "Go," he said, nudging Kai toward his room.

Kai yawned again and nodded, trudging down the hallway. Cole chuckled a bit and reached for the phone on the bar. He dialed Nick's number and waited. "You better have a damn good reason for calling at such an ungodly hour" came a gruff, annoyed greeting.

"Sorry, Thayne," Cole replied, "I need to speak with Nick."

Thayne, Nick's mate, grumbled, and Cole could hear the rustling of sheets before Nick came on the line. "Cole? What's wrong?"

"Sorry to wake you and your mate, but I need to see you. As soon as possible."

"Are you okay?" Nick sounded more alert, and he could hear further rustling of the bedding as Nick sat up.

"I'm fine, Nick. Something happened tonight—something fantastic."

"You've bonded?" Nick asked excited.

"Not yet."

"Oh." Disappointment sounded in Nick's voice. "Am I to guess, or are you going to tell me?" Nick mused.

Cole sat on one of the stools and grinned. "I could tell you, but I'd rather you come here. Besides, I think Thayne is about to reach through the phone and strangle me for calling..." he trailed off as Thayne finished his sentence on the other end, "...at an ungodly hour."

Nick laughed. "I'll be over as soon as I can."

Cole heard Thayne give a throaty growl just before the phone disconnected. He smirked, knowing Nick wouldn't be as quick as he indicated. "Someday," Cole murmured to himself and stood up to make some coffee.

He was already on his second cup when Nick arrived. Nick entered the house without knocking. They'd been friends for years, aside from Nick being his intended Beta when Cole took over as Alpha. Cole picked up on the just-ravished flush on Nick's cheeks, and he noticed several red marks over Nick's throat. He couldn't be happier for Nick. When Nick had returned all those months ago from Wyoming, Cole had wondered if Nick would survive. He'd watched as Nick lost weight and became a shell of his former animated self. Not even Elijah had been able to help. When Cole had received the call about Nick ending up in the hospital, having collapsed while at the airport, Cole had been certain Nick would go the route most wolves did when they lost their mates. Nick pulled through despite everyone's doubts.

Nick gave a sheepish smile and rubbed at the side of his neck. He didn't offer any excuses, merely grabbed a mug and filled it with coffee before sitting across from Cole at the small breakfast table. "You want to tell me what's going on?"

Cole spoke in a hushed voice, not wanting Kai to overhear him as he recounted what happened, including Kai's true nature.

"A fox?" Nick asked incredulously.

"Keep your voice down," Cole warned, glancing toward the hallway. "He doesn't want anyone to know."

"Sorry," Nick grunted. "How is it possible no one knew? I mean, I guess it is possible, though. Thayne's pack in Senaka thought only Native Americans could be wolves because of their ancestors. Even now they don't exactly believe anything else. Why couldn't there be others out there? What about his parents? Family? Does he know of any others?"

Cole shook his head. "No. His parents died when he was just a kid. He hasn't told me anything else."

Nick winced when Cole got to the point in the story where Kai had left, his own experience with his mate abandoning him most likely playing through his mind. When Cole finished, Nick had a wide grin on his face, and he reached out to tap Cole's shoulder. "I knew things would work out," Nick said.

"It's not as if we've bonded," Cole replied. "Things aren't settled yet."

"Maybe, but you've made progress, which is a good sign!"

Cole ran the fingers of one hand through his hair. "Is it? What if one tiny step forward means three giant ones back? I'm trying my damnedest to keep my hopes up he'll be able to trust me someday and will want to remain with me, but I promised him I'd let him go at the end of the month. How the hell am I going to keep my promise, Nick? It'll be like tearing my own heart out."

Nick reached out and gripped Cole's forearm. "You won't have to keep your promise, Cole. His fox must recognize the connection. No matter how much he may want to, he can't deny you're his mate."

"Thayne did." Cole spoke before he thought and then covered his face with his hands. "Fuck! I'm sorry, Nick. That was a shitty thing for me to say."

"It's okay. You aren't wrong. He tried to reject the connection, but couldn't. It ate him up inside every day, as I am certain Kai is slowly working his way through. He won't leave, Cole. Give him the chance to accept everything. He's gone from living a life where he's obviously been abused and believed he had no one in his corner to being thrust into one with mates and shifter packs. Try not to push him or yourself so hard."

Cole dropped his hands and looked at Nick. "How did you survive this never-ending feeling as if your chest were going to cave in at any moment?"

Nick gave a mirthless smile. "I'm not sure I did during those months apart from Thayne. Even less when we bonded at first. I took it one day at a time and tried to muffle the pain however I could."

"Was the pain worth it?" Cole asked.

"Oh yes," Nick breathed, his green eyes softening as he thought of his mate. "More than you can imagine."

Jealousy ate at Cole's insides. He wanted to experience what Nick felt right then and to know Kai waited for him in their bed, anxious to accept him instead of fearful of him. Cole's throat tightened, and his hands balled into fists. One day, he promised himself, one day soon he'd have the same kind of relationship.

"What are you going to do about the summit, Cole?" Nick asked, breaking Cole free of his thoughts.

Cole grunted. He prayed he could gain Kai's trust by then. "I have no choice. If things are not settled between Kai and me by then, I will have to tell my father I can't go."

Nick grimaced. "Are you sure that's wise?"

"What else can I do? I can't leave him here, and I won't force him to come with me to the summit."

"Perhaps things will change by the day we leave," Nick suggested hopefully.

"Perhaps." Cole held no delusions about how difficult a road lay before him. The few inches he'd gained last night could easily be lost if he didn't tread lightly. He changed the subject, needing to relax his mind for a while. "How're things with Ryan?"

Ryan, Nick's business partner and friend for eight years, had confessed his feelings for Nick during the time Nick completed his bond with Thayne. While the union of true mates was considered a sacred one, Nick and Thayne's connection hadn't been a real one. Oh, they'd bonded as a pair in the usual claiming, but the lack of acceptance in Thayne's heart kept it from being complete, a fact Ryan had hoped would send Nick running into his arms. Only Nick had rejected Ryan's feelings, and it created a rift between them. Cole didn't know if the two of them could ever repair their friendship. When love became involved, things weren't so black-and-white.

Nick sighed and rubbed at his stubbled chin. "It's only been a few weeks, but I think him seeing how Thayne and I have become over the last month has helped a bit. He sees the mating bond has strengthened. I just don't know if he'll ever truly understand, to be honest."

Cole nodded. "Maybe once he's located his own mate, he'll finally realize how hard it is to let them go, no matter how they treat you."

Nick shrugged. "It's possible. Maybe then he'll forget his feelings toward me and we can be friends again. I miss him." An exasperated expression came over Nick's face, and Cole gave him a questioning look. "Thayne doesn't like it when I think about Ryan," Nick explained.

Cole laughed even though the reminder of the depth of a mate's bond left a hollow feeling in his chest. The stronger their connection became, the more they were able to communicate, even telepathically. Thayne apparently had picked up on Nick's thoughts about Ryan. "If you need to leave to reassure him, I don't mind."

Nick shook his head. "No. Thayne has to work at the diner today. Jo has promoted him to one of the cooks."

"Jo must like him." Cole chuckled. "Not many get on her good side so quickly."

"Thayne has a silver tongue when he wants one. I figured it wouldn't take him long to graduate from dishwasher to cook."

"I need to check on my greenhouses this morning, and then we can have some breakfast if you want to stick around," Cole suggested.

Nick looked at his watch. "I actually have a conference call with a new client in an hour and still need to get to the office, but rain check?"

"Always."

Nick smiled and stood, clasping Cole's hand and yanking him out of the chair into a brief hug. He slapped Cole on the back before stepping away. "Have faith, Cole. Things will work out."

Cole wondered if Nick was right as he watched Nick leave.

LATER, AFTER taking a walk through each greenhouse and giving instructions on what to plant next, Cole pulled Julie aside.

She gave him an exasperated look. "How long?" she asked.

Cole shook his head. She knew him too well. "A week, maybe two."

Julie sighed. "Things aren't going well with your mate, I take it."

"I need to spend time with him, Jules. If I'm here in the greenhouses every day, it's not enough. You know I'd never ask you this soon after returning if it weren't important."

She rolled her eyes at him. "I know, Cole. It's fine. You owe me, though."

"A nice long vacation!" he promised.

"Paid for," she growled without menace. "To Hawaii or someplace with beaches and sun."

"Done!"

"Fine, fine. Go. Everything will be taken care of. But don't forget the meeting tomorrow with the Bryson's Market rep. Nine at their headquarters in Redwood."

Cole grinned and hugged her tight. "Thanks, Jules. You're the best."

"I know. I know. Now get out of here. Go claim your mate."

With Julie, everything was in good hands, and she grumbled just to grumble. She'd never really tell him no or mean it when she did. The only reason she even seemed disgruntled was because he'd asked so soon after the last time.

When he returned to the house, the clock read a little past ten, and he could hear Kai's steady heartbeat, indicating the younger man still slept. Cole had no idea how he would explain the summit to Kai, or if he even had a prayer of convincing Kai to come with him. Kai didn't want to meet anyone, and Cole felt pretty certain Kai would completely balk at the idea with how many wolf shifters would be there.

He made breakfast for himself and ate in silence while lost in thought. His father wanted him to take over the pack soon, but he didn't feel ready at all. How could he lead when he couldn't even convince his mate to trust him? Would he be able to do it at all if or when Kai left him? The fears and worries swirled around inside his mind, eating away at the little bit of confidence he'd gained from the kiss they'd shared. It agitated him even further because he'd never been a timid or self-conscious person before. He'd always known he'd be a great Alpha when the time came. Not because it was part of his DNA, but because of his father. Since he could remember, he'd shadowed his father during pack meetings, listened to the powerful speeches his father gave, and seen the way the pack followed him with all their hearts. Now, he faced the greatest challenge of his life, and he wasn't sure he could take it head-on without faltering and still hold on to the belief he would be as great an Alpha as his father.

A sound brought Cole out of his musings. He had no idea how long he'd been sitting there, but the remainder of his breakfast sat cold and untouched. Looking to his right, he saw Kai standing in the doorway, hesitation written on his expression. Cole dredged up a smile for him. "Good morning," he greeted. "Are you hungry?"

Kai edged farther into the room with a slight nod. Cole got up and dumped the contents of his plate into the trash before setting the dish in the sink to wash later. His appetite had fled, and he didn't relish the idea of eating cold eggs. "Anything you want in particular? I can make eggs or pancakes or anything else you want to eat."

"You don't have to go to any trouble," Kai murmured. "Cereal is fine."

Cole turned toward Kai, who'd taken a seat at the table. "I don't mind. Really. Do you like pancakes? I used to eat them a lot when I was a kid. Now it's more of a food I have to be in the mood for."

"O-okay."

"Pancakes it is."

Whatever had caused Kai's reluctance to come into the room moments ago faded away. Kai relaxed his shoulders and a slight smile crossed his lips.

"How'd you sleep?" Cole asked while grabbing the box of Bisquick from the pantry and the milk from the fridge.

"Good."

One-word answers, Cole thought to himself with a sigh. "Is the room comfortable? When I had the house built, I kind of just let my mom run with the decor."

"It's fine."

Two words! They were getting somewhere at least. Cole started mixing the ingredients in a bowl. "I took some time off from the greenhouses. My assistant manager, Julic, is going to be taking care of them for a couple of weeks."

"Why?"

Cole looked over at Kai, who stared at him, confusion on his face. "So we can spend time together and get to know each other, Kai."

Fear chased away the confusion, and Cole's heart dropped into his stomach. The kiss hadn't changed anything. His hand tightened on the wooden spoon until he heard a snap, and he worked at loosening his grip. Cole swallowed hard and pretended he didn't notice Kai's horror as he tossed away the broken utensil and grabbed another, mixing the pancake batter a little more vigorously. "It's the only way you'll learn you can trust me, and I thought maybe we could go for a run in the forest later too."

Satisfied the lumps of powder were gone, Cole took down a frying pan and set it on the stove. He stopped and stared at the wall behind the stove. "I thought what happened last night meant you were starting to realize I don't want to hurt you," he said softly.

Cole had no idea if Kai would have responded because there came a sudden knock on the front door. Kai made a small sound of terror and stood, his chair legs scraping along the floor. Cole swung around to find Kai staring wild-eyed at the door. Frowning, he moved to Kai's side and laid his hand on Kai's shoulder. "It's okay. No one here will harm you."

The panic didn't leave Kai's face, and Cole pulled Kai against his chest, wrapping his arms around him. Maybe the animal instincts within Kai caused him to accept the comfort. Kai buried his face into Cole's chest, shudders wracking his thin form.

"Who is it?" Cole called out, giving the person a chance to identify themselves before opening the door. Not normally something he would have done, but he wanted to reassure Kai it wasn't whatever demon the younger man thought it would be.

"It's your mother" came a dry response, curiosity buried in his mother's voice.

Kai gripped him tighter when he made to move toward the door. Cole would have chuckled if the situation weren't so amazingly tragic. Kai had never had a true childhood and a chance to experience the things in life that led to being an adult. It hurt Cole's heart how deep Kai's true nature had been buried inside him, stifled as he'd grown up. Cole could sense the spitfire his mate was meant to be and prayed he could someday bring out the real Kai. "The door's open," he shouted.

The snick of the handle turning sent Kai into a frenzy, and he attempted to push away from Cole—no doubt to run and hide.

Cole held on tight. "Shh," he whispered, "she isn't going to hurt you."

Kai continued to struggle but eventually grew tired, still weak from malnourishment. Cole looked up at his mother, who stood there with sympathy on her face. "Hey, Mom."

"Hi, honey. I came by to see if you needed help with any... ah... thing." Her gaze flicked to Kai for a split second before returning to him.

Cole could practically hear the thoughts chasing one another in his mother's head. She wouldn't ask, at least not with Kai right there. "We were just about to have some breakfast. Would you like some?"

His mother glanced at the stove and saw the pan and bowl. "Why don't I do that while you introduce me to your young friend?"

Cole nodded. "Sure, Mom, sounds great."

Sara moved to the fridge to get some butter for the pan and then turned on the stove. Cole looked down to find Kai's eyes pinned to his mother's slender form. "Hey," he whispered to get Kai's attention.

Kai didn't even flinch. "Kai," Cole tried again. Finally, he raised his gaze to Cole, who didn't look away while introducing them. "I want you to meet my mother. Her name is Sara. Mom, this is Kai."

His mother smiled at Kai, but remained by the stove. "Hello, Kai. It's wonderful to meet you."

Kai returned to staring at Sara. Cole attempted to help Kai to his seat, but Kai dug his fingers even farther into the shirt at Cole's lower back, clinging to the one person he knew in the sea of the unfamiliar. Cole didn't move. He remained by the table, holding Kai, and started talking to his mother, hoping the normality of the situation would help Kai calm down. "Where's Dad?"

"Your father had some pack business to handle with the upcoming summit. He wanted to check the accommodations were all in order."

Sara expertly flipped the pancake in the pan and allowed the other side to cook before sliding it onto the stack already started. "Nick tells me things are going great with Thayne. I'm glad to see things on track with those two."

"Yeah, he was over here this morning for a while."

As they talked, Cole could feel Kai beginning to relax bit by bit with the two of them not focused on him. Kai still wouldn't look away from Sara, but Cole picked up on the fear in Kai beginning to change to something else. When Sara came toward them to set a plate on the table, Kai didn't tense or shy away. Instead Kai seemed fascinated by his mother. "What do you two boys have planned today?" Sara asked as she began to clean up.

Cole managed to lower Kai into a chair without him and nudged him to pick up the fork, tipping his head to indicate Kai should eat. "I wanted to show Kai around the greenhouses if he's willing, and then I thought we'd go for a run later on."

"Sounds fun. How's Julie doing?"

"She's great, really helped me out the last few weeks. You know how I've been trying to land the account for Bryson's Market?"

"Of course. It's all you've talked about for two years!"

Sara filled two mugs with coffee and came to the table, setting one cup at the third seat and sinking into the chair across from Kai. Kai stopped moving immediately, fork halfway to his mouth, and stared at her, but when she didn't do anything except take a sip and continue talking to Cole, he resumed eating, slowly.

"What about Bryson's Market?" she asked.

Cole pulled out the other chair and sat, picking up the mug his mother had brought him. He preferred his coffee black and strong. He never understood how people could load the drink down with sugar, creamer, and everything else and still call it coffee. "George's brother Thomas happens to know the owners, and when the wife used my bath salts, she insisted her husband give me a meeting. I have a conference with a representative from their company tomorrow."

"Such wonderful news, honey!" Sara exclaimed. "I'm proud of you. You've done so well with this place."

"Thanks, Mom." Cole smiled and took a sip of the dark liquid.

His mother glanced at Kai, who still had not taken his eyes off of her, and then she looked toward Cole. "Your father wants you to be at the summit," she said without censure.

Cole knew she already suspected what he'd say. He shrugged. "We'll see how it goes. I can't guarantee I will be right now."

Surprisingly, Kai asked, "What's a summit?"

Cole raised his eyebrows but didn't make a big deal of Kai speaking up in front of his mother. "Remember how I told you there are other packs out there?"

Kai nodded.

"There's a pack in Wyoming who believed only Native Americans could be true wolves. Because of the ties we now hold with them, and in order to give the wolves of each group a higher chance for finding their mates, we've planned a summit at a lodge in neutral territory where we'll meet and spend a few days together."

"And you have to go?" Kai asked.

Cole picked up on the edge in Kai's voice. "Depends."

"On what?" Trepidation shone on Kai's face.

"Whether or not you go with me. I can't leave you here on your own."

"I can take care of myself," Kai snapped, a bit of his fire showing through. Then Kai seemed to realize how he'd responded, and fear of retribution flitted across his pale features.

Cole ignored it and calmly explained, "I know, but I can't leave you because I need you. My wolf won't allow me to be separated from you."

Kai gaped at him, surprised. Before he could recover or ask further questions, Sara chuckled and reached out to pat Kai's hand gently. "He's always had a way with words, baby."

Cole noticed Kai jump at his mother's touch, but he didn't pull away from her. Jealousy warred with satisfaction. Kai was already getting comfortable around his mother, but it also frustrated Cole at how easy he'd come to trust her and not him. He gave a humorless grin and hid his emotions behind his coffee mug by taking a sip. "Do you think you can soften the blow with Dad?"

Sara gave him a resigned look. "I'll try. You know your father wanted you to be there for more than just the reason for the summit."

"I know, Mom, but you can't tell me he would handle this any differently if he were in my place."

Kai had grown quiet again, but Cole could sense it wasn't out of fear. He picked up on a strand of agitation and frowned, studying Kai, who'd returned to eating, gaze locked on the plate.

"I understand, honey. You don't have to explain or defend yourself to me. I'm happy for you and will do what I can to help."

Cole sighed and set his mug down. "I know Dad thinks I'm ready to take over the pack, but I don't think I am."

Sara set her hand on his forearm. "Trust your father's judgment, Cole. He would never jeopardize you or the pack. He's seen the progress you've made with your business. The dedication you give it is inspiring. He knows you'll make a great Alpha. Besides, your mother wants some time alone with her husband for a change."

She grinned at him. Cole laughed and leaned over to kiss her cheek. "You're the best, Mom."

"I know," she replied cheekily.

They continued to chat about the pack and news about other members, eventually bleeding into the topic of Cole's current crops. Kai didn't speak up again, and it wasn't until he stood that he drew Cole's attention away from his mother. "I need to use the bathroom," Kai muttered and, to Cole's surprise, practically stomped out of the room.

Cole sighed. What had he done now?

Sara gave a soft laugh and reached up to pat his cheek. "He's going to be a handful, Cole, but give him time. The abuse he's endured is much worse than I expected from what you told your father and me the other night. I can see it in his eyes. Don't push him too fast or too far before he's ready. There's still a fire in him his abuser hasn't managed to eliminate."

"I don't know how to handle this, Mom. I've seen a lot of things shadowing Dad all these years: the banishment of pack members, the Created Ones, and even the deaths of other wolves. But this... this is something I don't have a clue what to do about. I don't want to push him, and I'm fighting my wolf's instincts to ignore Kai's fears and take what I want, but how do I get past the wall?"

Sara glanced toward the hallway Kai had disappeared down and lowered her voice. "He needs to speak with a therapist, Cole."

Cole shook his head. "I doubt he'd agree to. Not yet anyway. Maybe later on."

"Then I suggest you spend some time reading, honey. If you can't get him to see someone, the only answer is to try to learn what you can to help you help him."

He couldn't believe he hadn't already thought of looking things up online. Giving a wry smile, he replied, "Thanks, Mom."

She shrugged. "That's what moms are for, sweetie. I think I'm going to head out, though. I need to check in on Paulette. She's been feeling ill the last couple of weeks. I think she's pregnant again."

Paulette was a human mate to one of his father's Betas. She'd already had three pups and swore she'd never have another one. "George must have super seed or something," Cole joked.

Sara batted him on the shoulder and rolled her eyes. "Men," she scoffed. Standing, she leaned in and hugged Cole. "I'll see you later, honey. Remember what I said. Give him time."

Cole walked his mom out and watched her get into her car. He closed the front door when she'd driven onto the main road and turned around to find Kai standing in the hallway entry, arms wrapped around his waist in a protective manner. The expression on Kai's face did not give him hope time would make a difference.

CHAPTER EIGHT

WHEN COLE told Kai the reason he wouldn't be attending the summit, Kai hadn't known what to say, and the longer he listened to Cole talking to his mother, the more agitated he became. Kai didn't quite understand his own emotions toward the situation, which further frustrated him. He didn't need anyone to take care of him. He wasn't a child! Then he overheard Cole's mother suggest Kai see a doctor, and he grew even angrier.

Now he stood in the hallway staring at Cole. His skin felt tight, and his teeth were clenched hard enough it seemed as though they might crack. He knew anger, but this feeling rushing through him seemed magnified, more intense and almost painful. His head throbbed as he balled his fists together.

"Kai?" Cole questioned hesitantly.

Kai opened his mouth, but nothing came out except a rush of air. His breathing had grown shallow and black spots danced before his eyes. His chest heaved, and his heart pounded against his ribs.

"Kai?" Cole tried again, approaching him and placing his hand on Kai's shoulder.

Something snapped, and Kai raised his hands and started hitting at Cole, anywhere and at whatever he could. He slammed his fists into Cole's chest, arms, and shoulders again and again. Somewhere deep inside he knew his actions were wrong, but he couldn't seem to stop himself. His arms grew weaker with each resounding slap, and eventually it sank into his subconscious that Cole didn't try to stop him. Cole just stood there and accepted the blows. Somehow, in the midst of Kai's rage, Cole had managed to slide his arms around Kai's shoulders in a partial embrace. Tears rained down Kai's cheeks, and he went to move away, horrified at his actions, but Cole wouldn't set him free.

Burying his face in his palms as Cole pulled him closer, Kai sobbed even harder. Nothing made sense to him. He didn't know why he'd gotten angry or why he'd begun lashing out at Cole. The rage had died, leaving behind a feeling of emptiness, hopelessness. Emotions he knew only too well. He'd experienced those many nights locked in his uncle's basement. "I'm sorry," he began to babble. "I'm sorry. I'm sorry. I'm sorry."

"Shh," Cole murmured, breath stirring the hair atop Kai's head. "It's okay, Kai. Shh."

"I'm sorry. I didn't mean to."

Cole held him tighter, rubbing a palm in circles along Kai's back. "I know. It doesn't matter."

Kai hiccupped but didn't repeat his apology. He didn't understand why Cole wasn't angry at him. He'd tried to hurt Cole. The thought seemed ridiculous, considering Cole's size compared to his own. Yet Cole didn't get upset with him. He didn't attempt to stop him or hit him. All these thoughts whirled around inside his mind until his head began to throb harder.

Suddenly, Kai's world spun, and he found himself airborne and being carried to the nearby couch. He made a small sound of protest, which Cole ignored. Cole sank down onto the sofa and settled Kai in his lap. Kai tried to slide off, but he didn't put up much of a fight when Cole refused to let him go.

Cole cupped Kai's cheek and slowly tilted Kai's face up toward him. He brushed a strand of Kai's hair away from his face, causing Kai's breath to catch at the tender gesture. In a way it reminded Kai of his memories of his mother, but it was different in a whole other way. The roughened skin sliding over his cheek sent flickers of heat rushing down into his lower belly, something his mother's caress had never done.

"Want to tell me why you were mad?" Cole asked softly.

"I don't know," Kai replied, voice hoarse from his fit.

"Maybe talking about it will help."

Kai frowned, gaze locked on the tanned skin of Cole's throat. How could he talk about it when he didn't know?

"You seemed upset when you left the table earlier. Maybe start with why?"

"I don't know," Kai repeated.

"Was it something we said?" Cole probed again.

Kai fidgeted as some of the emotions returned. "No."

Cole didn't seem to want to let up, though. "Did we scare you?"

"No! I just don't want to be your excuse!" Kai exploded, surprised at his own words.

"My excuse?" Cole asked, clearly confused. "What do you mean my excuse?"

"For not going to the summit. I'm not a little kid who needs to be taken care of!" Kai squirmed to get off of Cole's lap. He managed to twist himself to the left and onto the couch, pulling his knees up to his chest and wrapping his arms around them. "I don't want you to stay here because of me."

Cole didn't respond at first, and Kai thought he might have made Cole mad for sure this time. He peeked out of the corner of his eye to find Cole staring at him, but the expression on Cole's face wasn't anger. He recognized it. The only woman his uncle dated who hadn't wanted to beat him or use him had worn it more than once. Pity. The thought of Cole feeling sorry for him made his chest hurt. Kai dropped his forehead down to his knees and dug his fingertips into the fabric of his jeans, wrapping it around the digits until they grew numb.

"You aren't an excuse for me to not attend the summit, Kai," Cole eventually responded. "I'm doing my best to not overwhelm you or make you afraid of me more than you already are, but you have to understand what I told you before is the truth. You are my mate. Nothing else matters to me. Not the summit or being Alpha of my pack. All of it could be gone tomorrow, and it wouldn't mean a thing to me. But you...." When Cole paused, Kai tensed and squeezed his eyes shut. "You are everything."

The way Cole said it sounded simple, and yet it sent tendrils of pure terror to Kai's gut while sharp needles of emotion struck his heart. His fox chirped and yipped happily, excited at Cole's words. Cole's insistence on being mates, his own animal half wanting to be near the big shifter, and the fading of his desire to run away made him begin to doubt his human side. Every day he spent here, the more his fear continued to dissipate. Kai didn't know whether to trust his fox's instincts or his own. "I don't understand," Kai murmured halfheartedly. "Why?"

"I can't explain the way the mating bond feels, Kai. It goes beyond human comprehension. It's soul deep and only the connection, once made, can truly make you understand what I feel in my heart."

Would he have understood if his parents hadn't died? Why hadn't they told him the truth about who he was? Instead they'd let him live in ignorance. For the first time in his life, Kai actually felt angry at his parents. If they'd told him what to expect, about the change at thirteen, about everything, he could have hidden the truth from his uncle. They would have saved him from years of abuse and being used to hurt others.

The sound of Cole standing forced Kai from his thoughts, and he looked up to see Cole towering over him. He couldn't help the unconscious flinch and the immediate guilt at the hurt on Cole's face.

"I want to get to know you, Kai, and for you to get to know me. Us sitting here beating a dead horse isn't going to change the facts of the situation we find ourselves in. For at least a little while, let's table this. Will you please come with me and let me show you who I am?" Cole held out his hand, waiting for Kai to reject or accept it.

Kai gave a small nod and hesitantly placed his own hand in Cole's. Cole pulled him to his feet. Instead of releasing him, Cole led the way down the hallway and out the door at the end of the hallway. Kai felt exposed the moment they stepped into the sunlight. He hadn't realized just how much he'd begun to think of Cole's home as a safe haven until then. Swallowing hard, he continued to allow Cole to lead him toward the greenhouses. "Cole?" he murmured in fear as he saw a man hefting pallets of plants onto the bed of a truck.

"It's okay, Kai. No one here will hurt you. I promise. That's John. He's one of my employees." Cole waved at the man who smiled and returned the greeting.

Kai's stomach cramped as they entered the first greenhouse and he saw three others inside. His palms started to sweat, and Cole tightened his grip. "Relax," Cole chided gently. "Would you feel better if I asked them to leave?"

"I... I don't know," Kai whispered, eyeing the others. He recognized the woman he'd seen Cole hug the other day. Jealousy nipped in, and he moved closer to Cole.

The woman looked up and saw them, smiling. "Hey, Cole," she called and walked toward them.

Kai tensed and pressed even tighter against Cole's side. He heard Cole chuckle, but continued to stare at the dark-haired woman. She stopped in front of both of them. "Hi," she directed at Kai. "I'm Julie."

He didn't respond but watched her closely.

"Julie, I'd like you to meet Kai, my mate."

Julie offered her hand to him to shake, but Kai ignored it, wrapping his free hand around Cole's bicep. She lowered it and nodded, playing off his slight. "What brings you down here, Cole? I thought you were going to take a few days off."

"I wanted to show Kai around. Would you mind asking the others to take a break for a little while?"

"No problem, Cole. I'm sure they'd appreciate it."

Kai noticed the look Julie gave Cole but couldn't quite read it. His fox growled, wanting to snarl at her, but Kai kept his mouth shut. He didn't think Cole would approve of him treating someone who worked for him in such a manner. Kai watched her walk over to the two other people and speak to them for a moment. They gave curious glances in Cole's and his direction, but they nodded and took off the gloves they wore, slapping them against their thighs to knock off excess dirt. Julie sent another wave as the three of them exited the building.

Cole reached up and covered the hand Kai had wrapped over his bicep. "You don't have to be afraid of any of my people, Kai. They would never hurt you."

Kai bit his lip and let go of Cole's arm. He tried to pull free of Cole's grip on his hand, but Cole resisted and began to talk about his business.

"We grow different kinds of vegetables and herbs throughout the three greenhouses. This greenhouse has several types of herbs, including my favorite, peppermint leaves. Each building is kept at a different temperature, based on what is planted in them."

Cole started walking along one of the rows. He pointed out the different herbs, indicating the varying types of leaves and how to tell them apart. When they reached the peppermint, Cole released Kai's hand and squatted down. He pulled one of the leaves off and stood up. He held the leaf beneath Kai's nose. "I use the oil from the plant to make bath salts."

Kai breathed in the scent of the leaf and wrinkled his nose at how potent it was. Cole laughed. "Peppermint is one of the more aromatic herbs, but our sense of smell makes it ten times deeper."

"It's very strong," Kai murmured in agreement.

"Similar to the scent, the plant tends to overrun others if you let it, which is why this section is separated from the other end." Cole walked to a cart nearby and picked up a clay pot with an herb in it. He brought it over to Kai. "Do you want to try planting one?"

Kai shook his head. "I don't want to ruin it," he protested.

"You can't ruin it. Come on, kneel down." Cole lowered himself near an empty spot. He picked up some kind of small shovel. "Come on, kit. It won't bite," he teased.

Swallowing hard, Kai got down on his knees, albeit a little less elegantly than Cole. He accepted the shovel. "Now, dig a hole right there," Cole said, pointing.

The damp smell of earth hit his nostrils the minute the tool hit the dirt. Kai closed his eyes and breathed it in deep, his lungs relishing the scent. His fox chirped in pleasure, and Kai could feel him almost bouncing in eagerness. He opened his eyes and continued to dig until he'd removed enough soil to put the plant in.

"Good," Cole praised and handed the pot to Kai. "Now place your hand around the base of the plant and tip it over, loosening it from the pot. Once you've removed the peppermint, place it into the hole."

Kai followed Cole's instructions to the letter and sighed when he'd placed the plant safely in the ground.

"Now we cover the roots up and add a little water to get it started."

Kai used the shovel and his free hand to replace the soil around the roots. Cole stood and returned to the cart nearby to pick up a watering can. He brought it over to Kai, handed it to him, and said, "You want to pour enough to dampen it, but don't drown it."

Tilting the can, Kai watched the water come out of the tiny holes, wetting the soil beneath the herb. "Great! See? You're a natural at this! I may just have to put you to work in the greenhouses," Cole commended, winking at Kai.

Warmth at Cole's praise trickled through Kai, and he smiled a bit. He passed the can to Cole and went to stand. Cole placed a hand beneath Kai's elbow and helped him up. "Let's get your hand washed off, and then we can continue the tour, hmm?"

Kai nodded and followed Cole to a spigot nearby. Cole turned it on, grabbed Kai's wrist, and pulled his hand under the water. "I can do it," Kai protested.

"I know," Cole replied simply, but continued to help rinse the soil off. He shut off the water once all traces of dirt were gone. He yanked a paper towel from the dispenser on the pillar near it and dabbed the liquid from Kai's skin. Cole's fingers brushed over the deep scars on his wrist, reminding Kai of his life before.

Kai flushed as Cole tenderly traced the gnarled flesh, and he tried to tug his hand away. Cole refused to let him go and surprised Kai by pressing a gentle kiss to his wrist. "Cole," Kai squeaked, and this time Cole released him.

Cole kept his face averted as he disposed of the paper towel, and Kai wondered what Cole thought of his scars. Did they disgust Cole? When Cole looked at Kai again, Kai saw nothing in Cole's expression except a slight smile. Cole led him through the other rows, indicating the different types of plants and explaining why he chose to grow them. It fascinated Kai to watch the peacefulness on Cole's face as the man talked. Kai envied Cole on more than one level, yet at the same time he didn't wish they could trade places. He would never inflict his awful past on anyone, especially someone as kind as Cole.

"The other greenhouses contain mostly vegetables and assorted fruits. We supply several markets in the surrounding areas, and a lot of the pack members come here to buy directly. Cheaper for them really."

"How long have you been doing this?" Kai asked curiously.

"I started the business about eight years ago, but the greenhouses took a while to build. Originally I had a small one I built myself."

"This is amazing," Kai said, bending down to look at a plant near where they stood.

Cole smiled. "Thanks. I enjoy working with my hands. There's nothing quite as satisfying as seeing others enjoy the fruits of my labor."

Kai straightened and walked a little farther down the row, still studying the different types of greenery.

"Is there anything you like to do?" Cole asked from behind him.

Kai shrugged. "Not really. Drawing sometimes, I guess."

"Anything else? What about playing any instruments?"

Shaking his head, Kai looked over his shoulder and responded, "Never got the chance to try."

Cole's expression darkened for a split second, but then he smiled. "Well let's rectify that now, hmm?"

Excitement gripped Kai for the first time in a long time. He followed Cole from the greenhouses, listening to Cole indicate which one held which types of crops. When they reached the house, Cole stopped inside the door. "Why don't you go take a seat in the living room? I need to get something from my room."

"Sure," Kai responded.

He walked down the hallway and took a seat on the couch, crossing his legs underneath him. Cole appeared seconds later with a guitar in one hand and sat next to him, leaving only a few inches between them. Kai could feel the heat from Cole's thigh.

"I haven't played in a couple of years," Cole said, strumming the strings and messing with the metal knobs at the top of the guitar.

Kai observed quietly and not without interest. When Cole started playing, his heart tripped a beat, and he sat up straight, placing his feet on the floor. Kai didn't know whether the emotions running through him were from the music or watching Cole. Somehow he suspected the answer was more about Cole than the instrument. He stared at Cole's strong fingers plucking at the taut strings and shivered at the unbidden thought of Cole's fingers on his skin. The idea frightened him and stirred something deep inside his chest at the same time.

The sounds died off, and Cole looked at him. "Do you want to try?"

"I don't know if I can," Kai muttered uncertainly. "It looks complicated."

"Not at all. Here," Cole replied and handed him the guitar. "Place the neck in your left hand and brace the bottom on your knee."

Kai took the instrument, a bit hesitantly, and did as Cole said.

"Is it okay if I get closer to show you?" Cole asked.

Kai bit his lip but nodded. Cole slid over until they were thigh to thigh. When Cole placed his arm around Kai's shoulders, Kai jerked in surprise.

"It's okay," Cole said softly.

It took every ounce of Kai's willpower not to jump off the couch as Cole began placing the fingers of Kai's left hand on the different strings. "There are six notes on most guitars. You use your other hand to strum the strings to make the sounds while controlling the notes with your left hand. Good so far?" Cole asked.

"Yes," Kai murmured.

Cole placed his fingers over Kai's at the top of the guitar and picked up Kai's right hand, placing a small triangular-shaped plastic chip in between his index finger and thumb. Kai tensed. "Relax, kit," Cole whispered near his ear.

Kai swallowed and tried to do as Cole instructed.

"Since you're just beginning, we'll start with the two basic chord types, first position chords and barre chords. First position is primarily played with open strings and pressed strings. You see the spaces marked off down the neck of the guitar?"

Kai grunted in response.

"Those are called frets. Common major chords are C, A, G, E, and D. Place your fingers here." Cole moved Kai's fingers accordingly. "This is A major."

Cole used the plastic chip in Kai's fingers to strum across almost all the strings, producing a light sound. Kai felt the vibrations of the chords against his fingers and grinned. Cole continued to move the placement of his fingers, going through each of the notes and their differing sounds. Eventually Cole showed him a few to practice at playing together. When Cole allowed him to try it on his own, Kai's fox gave a forlorn chirp at the loss of Cole's body heat and touch. Kai ignored the emotion and followed the instructions, satisfaction surging through him when he managed to do it seamlessly. "I did it!" he exclaimed.

"You're a natural at this, kit," Cole praised. "Why don't you continue to practice while I make us some lunch?"

"Okay."

Kai repeated everything Cole had shown him until he could perform the actions without a hitch. He looked toward the kitchen where Cole stood at the counter. Studying Cole's strong back, Kai's thoughts strayed to Cole's declaration of Kai being his everything earlier, and his stomach flip-flopped. He'd never thought of another man sexually before. He knew what being gay meant and wondered if his reactions to Cole meant he was gay. Would it have made a difference if he'd grown up with his parents instead of his uncle? Would he still be interested in Cole? Or did his animal side dictate who he would be with? The idea of not being in control of even who he would love or be with left a feeling of helplessness. Kai didn't know if he would ever be free to choose for himself.

"After we eat, I'll show you another chord since you've gotten those down lightning fast," Cole interrupted his thoughts, and Kai started.

Cole set a plate on each side of the small table and beckoned Kai to come sit. Kai stood, set the guitar down beside the couch, and walked over to find Cole had made sandwiches. Potato chips filled a medium bowl for them both to take what they wanted. He sat in the chair across from Cole and scooped a handful of chips onto his plate.

"You think playing music is for you, kit?" Cole asked and took a bite of his sandwich.

Kai picked up his own, cradling it in his hands. "I don't know."

"You're really good," Cole commented.

Kai shrugged.

"If it isn't something you enjoy, we can always try something else."

Instead of replying, Kai bit into his sandwich and chewed, slow and calculating. He didn't want to answer Cole because the same resentment from earlier was rising in his chest. He had no idea what words would come out, and he didn't want to hurt Cole. The thought of worrying about Cole surprised him. His fox chirped in agreement, and Kai ignored it. He'd only been around Cole for a few days, but he could sense something inside him changing. Did he react to Cole because of the mate thing? Kai almost gnashed his teeth together. Fear had been a constant thing in his life. He knew fear. These new feelings constantly bombarding his senses since he'd met Cole he didn't understand. They made him uncomfortable and distressed.

Cole set down his sandwich. "Is everything okay, Kai?"

"I'm fine," Kai snapped.

Cole raised his eyebrows. "You don't seem fine."

"What would you know?" Kai snarled, dropping his sandwich on the plate.

Sighing, Cole said, "I thought we were finally getting somewhere, Kai. What happened?"

The bottom of the chair legs scraped the floor as Kai stood and started restlessly roaming between the living area and the kitchen. Cole didn't ask again but waited for Kai to answer. Kai hadn't a clue what to tell Cole. He didn't understand it himself. Tension spread across his shoulders the longer the quiet continued. He ran a hand through his hair, fingers brushing the collar on his throat. It reminded him of the scars beneath it and Kai stopped near the couch. "Why?" he whispered.

"Why what, kit?" Cole prodded.

Wrapping his fingers around the top of the cushion nearest him, Kai shook his head. He didn't know.

Cole stood and walked to Kai's side. He placed a hand on Kai's shoulder. "Talk to me, please."

Kai heard the imploring in Cole's voice. "I don't understand."

"Understand what?"

Wrapping his arms around his waist, Kai stared at one of the pictures on the wall. "Anything. These things I'm feeling. I've never felt this way before."

Cole reached up and touched Kai's cheek, work-roughened fingers sending tendrils of heat through Kai's veins. Kai shivered.

"What are you feeling?" Cole asked, voice raspy.

"So many things," Kai murmured. "Warm inside, as if I drank something hot. Uncomfortable. Angry. Scared. I don't know. Some things I've never felt before." He sat on the arm of the couch, not releasing his death grip on the cushion.

Cole crouched in front of him, looking up at his face. "Take a deep breath." Kai complied. "Good. Now stop thinking, Kai."

Kai gave him a skeptical look.

Chuckling, Cole patted his knee. "Sometimes it's hard to shut off your brain. Try. The more you think, the more you go in circles. Believe me, I know. Enjoy being here in the moment. The past is over and the future is unknown. Today is the only thing you can control, Kai."

Kai stared at him, his words very close to the thoughts he'd experienced mere moments ago. "Do I?"

"Do you what?" Cole frowned.

"Have control?"

"Of course you do," Cole replied, confused. "Is there a reason you think you don't?"

Shrugging, Kai cast his gaze to the side. Silence met his gesture, and when Kai glanced at Cole he saw what appeared to be pain. Kai's breath caught, and guilt flooded him. The pain vanished when Cole realized Kai was studying him. Cole stood and moved to stand near the window. "You feel I want to control you."

It wasn't a question. Kai didn't know how to answer without hurting Cole again, but his silence seemed to be what Cole expected. Cole remained turned away from Kai for several minutes, quiet and brooding. Kai wondered if Cole would speak to him again. His fox trilled at him, actually furious with him over his treatment of Cole. Shame bit deep. How could his fox expect him to be okay with everything when he'd only known Cole for a matter of a few days?

"I need to go for a run," Cole said in a flat tone. "I hope you'll join me, but I won't make the decision for you. It's your choice."

Kai flinched at Cole's words. They hit him in the chest—hard, tiny arrows stabbing his heart in painful bursts. He tried to swallow around the sudden lump in his throat. Cole didn't even glance his way as he strode around the couch and into the hallway. Kai hesitated for a few breaths and followed behind. The door at the end was just closing as Kai reached it.

Cole had already shifted when Kai stepped outside. He didn't wait for Kai, loping off toward the woods. The moment Kai released his human half and became his fox, a sad cry echoed off the buildings and into the trees. Kai worked to keep himself in check as he followed Cole.

CHAPTER NINE

GODS, IT felt as if his chest would cave in any minute. The sheer mountain he needed to scale in order to reach Kai's heart loomed over him taller than the trees high above him. Cole struggled with his wolf, especially when he heard the scream of Kai's fox. The desire to return to Kai's side deepened his pain, but he couldn't give in. At every turn Kai stabbed him, not literally, but sometimes Cole felt the urge to check for a deep gouge where his heart beat against his rib cage.

Leaves crackled behind him, and Cole knew Kai had followed. It gave him a momentary sense of pleasure, one which he shoved away, refusing to give in to the hope he'd been foolish enough to let blind him. What had he expected? Kai didn't even know him. He'd met Cole less than a week ago. Yet somehow he'd thought the mating bond would make a difference. How could he have been so naïve? Cole shook his head and caught the scent of a rabbit. Feral instincts kicked in, and he spun on his hind legs, darting after the furry creature. Thoughts of Kai faded behind the glory of the chase. He raced through bushes and around tree trunks, twigs snapping, branches scratching over his body. The smell of fear from the hare only further incensed his wolf. His teeth snapped shut, and the sound of bone crunching echoed through his skull. The delicious taste of blood slid over his tongue, and he lay down where he was, heaving yet victorious.

Cole remained conscious in his wolf form, but allowed his wolf control for the time being. When Kai appeared from between two trees, his wolf scented the air, and Cole could sense his wolf's immediate desire, his own buried in there with it. Cole struggled to regain power, ignoring the intense urge to say to hell with it and let go, allow the mating to happen no matter what Kai wanted, but he knew he couldn't take away Kai's choice. It would make him no better than whoever had abused and tormented his mate before. Instead, Cole severed the rabbit in half and picked up part of it. He crept toward Kai, placed the hare on the ground in front of him, and returned to his own meal.

He watched Kai sniff the offering and then sit down on his hind quarters, tilting his head to the side in a quizzical manner. Cole realized Kai had no idea what to do with the rabbit. Even his fox's instincts were stunted. Grunting, Cole bit into the meatiest portion, holding the animal in place with his paws, and tore away a piece to eat. Kai's eyes widened and Cole saw disgust overtake Kai's features. He took another bite and another until the only things remaining were bones and some fur. His wolf gave a huffing laugh when Kai pushed the other half toward him with one delicate black paw.

Ignoring the kill, Cole stood and approached Kai. Cole bumped against him, rubbing his neck along Kai's. Joy struck him as Kai returned the affection, an almost purring sound issuing from the fox's throat. Cole nipped playfully at Kai's ear, licking the nonexistent wound when Kai growled. The smell of Kai's fur, the feel of it on his, made him long even more for the day he could call Kai his own. He wanted nothing more than to have his mate by his side, loving him. The unwanted thought of what his life would be like if Kai left at the end of the month crowded into his mind. Everything would become dull, gray, ugly. Could he stand to let Kai go? He couldn't keep Kai locked away, not after what happened to him before. The scars on Kai's neck stood out in all their garish ugliness, and Cole knew he could never imprison his mate. If it came time to let him go, he would. He could do nothing else.

He shoved away any thoughts of Kai leaving and lapped at Kai's muzzle before he turned and trotted a few feet from Kai. Stopping, he glanced over his shoulder, tossing his head as though to say follow me. When Kai stood, Cole danced several more feet from him, and each time Kai advanced closer, he would dart away again. As soon as he saw the light of understanding on Kai's face, Cole spun and dashed through the trees, satisfaction creeping in when he heard Kai pursuing him. Every thousand yards, Cole would stop, allowing Kai the chance to catch him, only to flee at the last second. He led Kai on a merry chase for several miles. Pure happiness sang through his blood. When he'd found Kai in Phoenix, Cole had believed he might never get this time with Kai. The damage to Kai's psyche and body made him skeptical of even getting close enough to fight off the demons haunting Kai.

Finally, not far from the pack manor, Cole allowed Kai to catch him, panting in pleasure as Kai tumbled him to the soft leafy floor of the forest.

He lay pinned beneath Kai, letting Kai remain in power. Surprise shafted through him when Kai leaned down and lapped at the fur along his throat. Cole couldn't stop the low sound his wolf issued or the reaction of his body. Kai rocked against him and Cole squeezed his eyes shut, close to losing control of his wolf. When Kai repeated the action, Cole rolled them, forcing Kai to hold still. It took every ounce of his willpower to control himself and his wolf. He shifted, knowing he couldn't hold on much longer in animal form, his instincts too strong. Once human again, Cole threw himself off to the side of Kai, chest heaving from lust and exertion.

A flash of light behind his lids alerted him to Kai shifting. "Cole?" Kai queried softly.

Cole kept his eyes closed and threw his arm over his face, hiding the sheer desire raging through him. His cock made a hard spike within his jeans. There could be no mistaking the bulge pressing at the fly and no way Kai couldn't smell the tangy scent of salty liquid dampening his briefs. A groan broke free when Kai laid a hand on his chest; the heat of his palm burned Cole through his shirt. "Don't," he rasped between clenched teeth.

Kai removed his hand. "What's wrong?"

Good gods. Cole wanted nothing more than to beat the everliving shit out of whoever had kept Kai locked away from the world. For Kai to not understand what was happening to Cole was pure torture. "I need a minute."

"Are you hurt?" Kai asked, concern evident in his voice.

Cole gave a mirthless laugh. If only it were something that simple. "No."

A frustrated sound came from Kai. "Then why can't I touch you?"

The thin thread holding his sanity in place snapped. Cole dropped the arm covering his face, opened his eyes, and grabbed hold of Kai's hand, dragging it over the harder than steel prick beneath his jeans. "That's why," he growled.

Kai started in shock, eyes widening. Cole sneered and released his hold on Kai, expecting him to withdraw from him as if on fire, only to jerk as Kai flexed his fingers along his cock. Cole sucked in a deep breath. "You have to stop."

"You're hard," Kai murmured, contracting his hand once more.

"Fuck," Cole snarled and thrust his hips upward, grinding against Kai's hand. "I need you to stop, Kai."

"Is… is this because of me?" Kai whispered.

Cole couldn't take it anymore. He rolled to his feet and faced away from Kai. "It's always you," he replied.

"Always?"

Kai either couldn't understand what his words meant, or he wanted to kill Cole. "I think we should return to the house. It's going to get dark soon."

Cole heard the sound of leaves being crushed beneath paws before two wolves, one dark as night and the other golden blond, crashed through the underbrush to come to a shuddering halt in front of him. Kai let out a terrified noise and scuttled away, stopping only when he hit the trunk of a tree. The blond shifted right away, and Nick stood in its place. "Cole, hey. Didn't know you were out here."

Raising an eyebrow, Cole replied, "What are you doing in this neck of the woods, Nick?"

Another flash of light bounced off the trees. "We were just out for a run after visiting your father," Thayne drawled, throwing an arm around Nick's shoulders, very obvious in his intent of showing his possessiveness over Nick. Cole would have smirked if he could have drawn up the ability to.

Nick smiled at Kai. "Hey, Kai. It's good to see you out. You're looking a lot better."

Cole glanced over and saw Kai staring in fear at Thayne. He supposed if he didn't know the stupid jackass and he'd had the same kind of past as Kai, he probably would be just as afraid. "Kai?" he prodded. "I'd like you to meet Nick's mate, Thayne."

Thayne frowned. "What's wrong with hi—*ooof*!"

Nick's elbow cut him off. Thayne rubbed the offended spot and glared at his mate. "What'd ya do that for?" he demanded.

Cole approached Kai and held out his hand. "Come on. He won't bite. I promise."

Kai took Cole's outstretched hand. Cole helped him to his feet and led him closer to the other two, engulfed by sadness when Kai crowded further into his side, one slender arm snaking around Cole's waist. Any other time, Cole would have rejoiced in Kai's embrace, but he knew the only reason Kai wanted to touch him now was out of fear. It left an acrid taste in Cole's mouth, and he gave Nick a strained look, answering the sympathy in his friend's gaze. "Thayne, this is Kai, my mate."

Nick must have explained the situation through their bond because Thayne gave a softened smile at Kai. "Hello, Kai."

Kai nodded, but didn't say anything, studying Thayne closely, wariness in his eyes.

"What brought you to the manor?" Cole asked.

"Your father wanted to talk to me," Nick said.

"About what?"

Nick hesitated.

"Nick? What's going on?"

Nick sighed. "He wanted to talk to me about what's going to happen if you aren't able to go to the summit."

Kai stiffened at Cole's side. "What do you mean?"

"I'd rather you talk to your father, Cole," Nick replied. "Please."

Scowling, Cole demanded, "Why can't you tell me?"

"Because he asked me not to."

"What the fuck, Nick?"

Thayne snarled and stepped forward a bit. Nick placed a hand on Thayne's chest. Thayne quieted down, but he kept a tight hold on Nick's shoulders. "You know I cannot go against your father's command, not until you are Alpha, Cole. All I can tell you is he understands your position and doesn't want to force you to go."

Cole wanted more than anything to smash his fist into the nearest tree but restrained himself, knowing it would only terrify Kai. "I see."

Nick gave a wry twist of his lips. "Maybe you should talk to him tomorrow, Cole."

"It'll have to wait until after my meeting with the representative from Bryson's Market."

"You still need me for tomorrow?" Nick asked, indicating Kai with a minor flick of his head.

"As long as it isn't going to interfere with your work," Cole said.

"Ryan can hold down the fort for a couple of hours."

Cole saw the distaste on Thayne's face at Ryan's name and hid a smirk. Even though Thayne had no reason to be jealous, he couldn't seem to stop from wanting to smash Ryan into pieces. "Thanks, Nick. I'll see you at eight."

"Sure thing, Cole. We need to get going, though. Have a good evening. It was great to see you again, Kai." Nick smiled at Kai once more.

Cole sensed Kai's small nod, and they both watched as Nick and Thayne shifted once more. The two wolves dashed into the trees and disappeared. Cole couldn't help but notice Kai didn't let go of him even after they were gone. "What is Nick helping you with?" Kai finally broke the silence.

Knowing Kai would be angry if he thought Cole didn't trust him, Cole gave him a half-truth instead. "I asked Nick to keep you safe while I'm gone."

Kai jerked away from Cole, mouth tight around the edges. "You asked him to babysit me?"

"No!" Cole exclaimed. "I just want him there to watch over things, to make sure nothing happens."

Kai scowled. "Afraid I'll run away again?"

Cole sighed and ran a tired hand over his face, a headache throbbing behind his eyes. "No."

"I don't need him there."

Cole wanted to snap at Kai, but he held his tongue. "I know you don't."

"Then why is he going to be there?"

"Are you afraid of Nick? He's my best friend, and I would trust him with your life. He already knows you're a fox shifter, and—" Cole stopped abruptly, realizing what he'd said. He'd promised he wouldn't tell anyone about Kai. But when Kai didn't react, probably because he was too wound up about the babysitting issue, Cole went on. "If you don't want Nick here then would you be more comfortable if my mother came to stay with you?" Cole asked.

Kai huffed and crossed his arms. "I don't want anyone to stay with me!"

Cole took another deep breath. "I am not leaving you alone, Kai."

"Why not?"

Unable to handle Kai's stubbornness any further, Cole shouted, "Because when my mother knocked on the door this morning, you almost jumped out of your skin! I am not leaving you on your own!"

Kai took several steps back, face paling. Cole swore and breathed in, letting it out on a sigh. "I'm sorry. I didn't mean to yell. You won't tell me about your past. You can't stand to let me or anyone else within two feet of you. The minute Nick and Thayne showed up here, you freaked and turned white as a sheet. I'm not... I can't leave you on your own, Kai. I'm sorry. There's no argument you can use to change my mind. Let's go. It's getting dark, and I have some stuff to prepare for tomorrow."

When Kai seemed inclined to argue again, Cole gave him an icy stare. "Enough, Kai."

Something in his face must have stilled whatever else Kai had been about to say because his mouth snapped shut and he remained quiet. A fact Cole couldn't have been more grateful for as he teetered on the edge of losing control. Cole shifted and waited for Kai, loping off into the woods the moment Kai followed suit, knowing they had a lot of ground to cover. His heart was heavy, and his spirit weighed more than a stack of the fifty-pound sacks of organic fertilizer they used in the greenhouse. Nothing in his life had ever prepared him for his mate's rejection. Cole knew deep down, even if he hadn't already accepted it, that at the end of the month, he'd be saying goodbye to Kai. His mate would never remain by his side. Kai would choose to leave him, believing he was better off alone and away from Cole, away from the sanctity of their bond. Cole wondered if he would be strong enough to take over as Alpha when it happened. His father had talked about handing over leadership after the summit, but Cole knew he wouldn't be ready, not now. Maybe not ever if Kai chose to leave him.

He couldn't stop the forlorn howl his wolf let loose. Its lonely depths echoed through the empty forest. Cole shuddered inside when several answering cries came from a long way off, offering support, love, but they weren't the ones he wanted to hear. They couldn't soothe the soul-deep ache he felt. He could hear the soft chuffing sound of Kai's paws through the dirt on the forest floor behind him, the noise reminding him of what he'd found and would lose in the coming days, time being his worst enemy, an enemy he couldn't defeat no matter how strong his muscles or how sharp his claws. Cole had never felt so helpless in his entire life. He'd never faced an enemy he couldn't overcome. Nothing had prepared him for this. How could he fight something that had no tangible form?

By the time they made it to the house, it had gotten dark, and Cole couldn't find the strength to pretend things were normal. He made a quick dinner of steaks and salads. They ate in painful silence, and when they'd finished, Kai went to his room while Cole cleaned up and retreated to his own, leaving his door open a crack just in case. Despite knowing Kai would leave him at the end of the thirty days, he still didn't want Kai to run again, didn't want his mate where he couldn't find him, alone and starving. At least Cole could still take care of him, make sure he was fed and clothed. Cole put together the business plan for his meeting with the representative from

Bryson's Market by rote, unseeing and uncaring. His heart wasn't in it. A week ago, he'd have put his all into the charts and graphs, ecstatic for the chance to impress. Now... it didn't matter.

A noise behind him alerted him to Kai's door opening, and Cole stiffened, but Kai entered the bathroom and shut himself in. Cole rubbed at his eyes with one hand, tears burning behind them. He'd never been a weepy guy, never teared up at sappy movies or funerals, but lately he'd been on the verge of crying more than he cared to admit. He'd kick the shit out of anyone for daring to even think him weak, but the title fit right then. Oh, he didn't believe crying made him weak, not at all. Tears were a cleansing wash of the body, something people needed to heal their souls from pain, even men sometimes. No matter what society believed. He was a pathetic asshole for thinking of giving up on Kai, for allowing the idea of letting his mate go at the end of the month to even form, but he had no idea how to fight gravity, inevitability, the blatant truth staring him dead to rights in the face.

Cole had been arrogant and ignorant to believe thirty days would be enough to get past the defenses Kai had built from a lifetime of abuse, neglect, and fear, to believe the mating bond would be enough to convince Kai they were meant to be together. Snorting in disdain at himself, Cole buried his face in his hands and blinked away tears, refusing to give them purchase. How could he have been naïve enough to believe someone who'd been raised outside of shifter culture would ever understand? Maybe he should give Kai what he wanted now and let him go, save them both the heartache the next three weeks would no doubt bring: the fighting, the constant paranoia from Kai, the continuous placating and pleading from Cole.

"Cole?"

Kai's voice behind him caused Cole to sit upright and drop his hands in his lap. He didn't turn around. "You should go to sleep," Cole rasped.

"Are you okay?"

He managed to stifle a sharp bark of laughter, instead straightening his spine even further. "I'm fine," he grunted. "Please... go to bed."

Cole didn't hear Kai leave and balled his hands into fists. He struggled not to put one through the monitor of his laptop, his claws extending and digging into the flesh of his palms.

"I—"

"Get out," Cole choked, interrupting him. A sharp intake of breath caused a dull pain in Cole's chest, and Cole closed his eyes, letting his head fall forward. "Please."

Kai's footsteps were soft as he left Cole's room, and Cole wanted to chase after him, wanted to soothe the hurt he knew he'd caused, but he couldn't, knowing it wouldn't matter. Cole heard the snick of Kai's door closing, almost unable to breathe through the torment crushing his soul.

UNABLE TO sleep, Cole had spent the night researching what he could about abuse victims, the recovery time, therapy. Seeing how long it could take, the last intact piece of Cole's heart shattered. Any possibility of Kai being able to accept him before the thirty days were up faded away with every story he stumbled upon. Cole read through forum after forum of shared traumas and horrors, his heart clenching with each one and his mind unable to believe anyone could be so cruel. Fury unlike he'd ever known built beneath the surface. Someone had subjected his mate to these things. Gods, he didn't even know if they'd sexually abused Kai. He realized he had no idea exactly what cruelties had been reaped upon Kai and what it would take for his mate to overcome them. If he'd felt helpless before, now it increased a hundredfold. Cole had no idea where to even begin to help Kai, to begin working through what he'd suffered.

Needless to say, some of his furniture and a lamp needed to be replaced by the end of the night, and Cole looked a lot worse for wear by the time he took a shower and dressed in a pair of dark slacks, a white dress shirt, dark suit jacket, and a green tie to match his eyes. He had no desire to attend the meeting with the Bryson's Market's representative. If he hadn't promised Julie he'd be there, he'd cancel. His head swam with everything he'd learned, and he had no idea how to even process any of it. At the end of his research, he'd dug up the names of a few therapists in Redwood City. He hoped he could see someone today, talk to someone to see if he could get some advice on how to proceed, because he hadn't a clue how to approach the situation.

Cole dropped the folder he'd made up containing his report for his meeting by the front door and made eggs, bacon, and toast, setting the table for Kai and Nick. There wasn't a chance in hell he could get down a single bite of food himself. He also set out orange juice and made coffee. Nick knocked on the door moments before Cole went to wake Kai.

"Hey," Cole said wearily as he answered the door.

Nick gave him a concerned look. "You look awful, Cole."

"Thanks," Cole said without heat or humor. "Have a seat. I'm just going to get Kai."

"Cole, wait." Cole stopped. "Is everything okay? I thought maybe...." Nick trailed off, no doubt thinking what he'd seen in the clearing yesterday made everything better.

Cole shook his head. "Don't. It's fine. I'm fine. I need to accept it, Nick. I never thought...." His voice choked off.

"Fuck, Cole, I'm sorry." Nick stepped close and wrapped his arms around Cole, rubbing his back.

Cole wanted desperately to bury his face in Nick's shoulder and accept the comfort his best friend offered, but knew he couldn't, not yet. Maybe after Kai had moved on. He breathed in Nick and Thayne's scent, jealousy biting deep, and then berated himself for being envious of the happiness his friend had found. "I'll be fine. I.... Nick, I think it's best if I leave before he comes out, okay? I can't see him right now. Would you make sure he eats?"

"Cole, you have to eat," Nick replied, worry evident in his face and voice.

"I'll get something later," Cole lied. "Just make sure he eats, okay? He's still too skinny, and he's still healing."

"I got it, Cole."

"And I... I may be a little longer than a couple hours, okay? I have a few other things to take care of." Cole picked up the folder he'd placed by the door earlier.

"Sure," Nick replied, giving his friend a sympathetic look, which caused Cole to wince, knowing he must appear a coward to Nick. "You know, if you need to talk, I'm here, Cole."

"I know, Nick, I know." Cole knew his own situation wasn't far off from Nick's from months before. Thayne's demons were also intangible, but to Cole, less daunting, less insurmountable. "I'll be home around one."

"I'll watch over him for you, bro."

"I know you will," Cole said and walked out, heading to his truck.

With the hands-free Bluetooth in his truck, Cole placed several calls until he found one of the therapists willing to see him on such short notice, a Dr. Virginia Rice. She seemed intrigued by his insistence, or maybe it was his desperation. Cole didn't know for sure. "I don't normally appreciate the haranguing of my receptionist, Mr. Ferris, but I admit I am curious. Do not be late."

"No, ma'am. I'll be there."

"Oh, and, Mr. Ferris?"

"Yes, ma'am?"

"Please apologize to Terry when you get here. I think she'd appreciate a nonfat latte."

For the first time since those stolen moments in the clearing with Kai, Cole gave a rusty chuckle. "Got it, Dr. Rice. Thank you."

Cole pulled into the parking lot of Bryson's Market headquarters and took a deep breath. He picked up the folder and slid out of his truck, closing the door behind him. Even if he didn't land this account for himself, he needed to land it for his mate, to give Kai the future he deserved and to set up the business for the next ten years, even if Cole might not be around to see it. With resolve in his step, he entered the building and approached the receptionist, determined to give Kai everything he could.

When he exited a little under two hours later, he had a five-year contract for his peppermint bath salts, a trial offer for six months delivery of several of his crops, and a resolute look in his eye as he headed for his lawyer's office. His lawyer didn't understand his insistence on creating a trust in the name of Kai Ferris or assigning Nick Cartwright as the trustee in the event something should happen to him, and he tried to dissuade Cole from moving forward with the paperwork. Cole ignored his lawyer's advice and insisted on drawing up the forms, signing them without hesitation the moment his lawyer slid them in front of him.

"I hope you know what you're doing," Lance Castle sighed as he authenticated the signature.

Cole grunted. "You've known me for over eight years, Lance. When have I ever made a decision I wasn't entirely certain of?"

Lance studied Cole for several long moments. "Who is this Kai Ferris? You've never mentioned him before."

Cole gave Lance a twisted smile. "My mate."

Lance's eyes widened a fraction. "Truly?"

"Yeah."

"That's awesome, Cole. Congratulations! But... why the trust?"

Cole shook his head. "I can't really get into it. Let's just say I made a deal with the devil, and I think the devil might win."

"I'll have Maggie make you a copy of these for your records, and we'll get everything filed immediately. Are you going to make the summit in a couple weeks?"

"Not this time." Cole left the rest of his words unspoken as he stood, holding out his hand to Lance. "Thanks for doing this at such short notice, Lance. I appreciate it."

"No problem. Congratulations on the Bryson's Market deal too, by the way. I know you've been working to get them on board for a long time."

Cole smiled but knew it didn't reach his eyes. "Thanks."

Lance showed him out of his office, and Cole took the offered folder from Maggie before leaving the building. He made a quick stop at the nearest Starbucks, ordered the expected nonfat latte, and headed for Dr. Rice's, his stomach in knots as he didn't know what the woman would be able to tell him about Kai. There were things he couldn't exactly tell her—he didn't know everything, and of course he couldn't talk about Kai and himself being shifters. He prayed whatever her words were, they could ease some of this soul-sucking hopelessness he felt. It kicked him in the balls how much stronger Nick seemed to be at handling this with Thayne. Cole tipped his hat to his Beta because if Nick had lived through this for six months, the man had more strength than fifty Alphas combined.

Pulling up in front of the building where Dr. Rice's office was located, Cole took a deep breath, picked up the coffee cup, and stepped out.

CHAPTER TEN

KAI BLINKED awake, smelling eggs, bacon, and coffee. He'd fallen asleep somewhere around two in the morning after listening to Cole through the walls, breaking what sounded like furniture. At first, he'd been terrified, but he knew in his heart of hearts Cole would never hurt him. Something had set Cole off. When he'd seen Cole sitting at his desk last night with his head in his hands, he'd been unable to resist going in to check on him. In the short time he'd known Cole, he'd always thought the man stronger than anyone he'd ever met, but the set of Cole's shoulders convinced Kai something weighed heavily on Cole. He'd been drawn in to try to help him, but when Cole had thrown him out of his room last night, Kai hadn't expected to feel as though someone had punched him in the stomach. His uncle had done it often enough that he knew the sensation.

The soft murmur of voices in the living room caused Kai to tense, and he knew Nick had arrived to babysit him. Kai scowled and sat up. He tugged on the pair of jeans he'd discarded the night before and stomped out to the living room only to stop in surprise. He didn't see Cole anywhere. Nick stood at the stove, and the table only had two sets of dishes on it. "Where's Cole?" Kai demanded.

Nick swung around and gave Kai a raised eyebrow. "And good morning to you too."

Kai didn't care how it had sounded. He couldn't believe Cole had left without a word. "He just left?"

"He needed to go take care of some things."

"He couldn't even be bothered to say goodbye?"

Nick gave him a hard look, impatience in the set of his mouth. "I'm surprised you even care."

Kai stared at Nick, shocked. "What?"

"Cole is the kindest person I've ever met in my life, and he's done nothing except try to help you. Do you have any idea what you're doing to him? No, of course you don't, because you can't see past the end of your snout. Yeah, you've had a shit lot handed to you in life, kid, but it doesn't give you the right to be so fucking selfish."

Kai gaped at Nick. The man had seemed nothing except easygoing in the interactions he'd had with him, but this side of Nick shocked Kai, and he couldn't do anything except stare at the other shifter. A plate slamming down on the counter sounded loud as Nick growled.

"I promised myself I'd stay out of it, because Cole can handle himself, but coming out here practically accusing him of abandoning you when all you've done is use him and treat him as if he's only here as a means to an end instead of giving him a real chance pisses me off, kid. He's my best friend, and I refuse to sit by while you treat him like fuck all. Now, sit down, eat, and think really hard about what you say next. Got it?"

The first instinct Kai had was to run. Nick hadn't raised his voice, though. He'd been angry at Kai, but hadn't yelled nor had he raised his hands to hit Kai. Hesitating, Kai debated on what to do next, eyeing the table and the door.

Nick sighed. "Sit. If you don't eat, Cole will have my hide as a wolfskin rug for next winter."

Kai didn't understand why the idea of Cole still wanting to take care of him despite being angry with him made him want to smile. He edged toward the table and gingerly took the seat he'd begun to think of as his. "Is Cole coming back?"

"Of course. It's his house."

Oh. Of course. Kai snorted to himself. Why wouldn't Cole return?

Nick sat down across from him, sipping at his coffee, but didn't eat, instead watching as Kai picked at his food. "Has Cole tried to tell you about what we are?"

Kai nodded.

"Then you know what mates are?"

"Yes."

"Did he tell you what happens when one rejects the other?"

Kai tensed, waiting for the expected guilt trip. "No."

"A year ago, I found my mate, Thayne—you met him the other day. I knew before I even saw him we were mates."

"How?" Kai interrupted.

"It's a scent thing. Wolves can smell it the moment they meet their true mate. I don't know if it's the same way for your kind. Of course until you, we had no idea there were potentially other shifters out there. Anyway, I'd wanted a mate since I can remember. We all grow up believing, hoping, we'll find them one day. We never know whether they will be male or female, but usually the ancestors of our people, or fate, whichever you choose to believe in, pair us with the other half of our soul with our intended proclivity. While it may sound romantic as a fairy tale, believe me, it isn't. You don't fall in love with your mate at first sight. You feel the pull, the instant lust and desire to be with them, to have them sexually, but emotionally, you could end up hating each other." Nick paused, and his lips twisted into a bittersweet smile.

"Thayne… he had witnessed something rather difficult to bear as a child, and it left him detesting the idea of having a true mate. He rejected me the moment he found out we were mates. It wasn't an easy pill to swallow. In fact, it was one of the most painful fucking experiences of my life." Nick gave a sour laugh, eyes shadowed with something Kai couldn't identify.

"But you're mated now," Kai pointed out.

"Not without a long road to get here. Thayne—" Nick's voice caught in his throat. "—Thayne made a mistake, something only I could help him break. It forced him to accept my claim, accept the mating bond, but not me. For six months, I worked myself into the ground, rarely sleeping or eating, and for a shifter, that's a scary thing. We need both and a lot of it. I ended up in the hospital with massive weight loss, malnourishment, and dehydration. You yourself know what both of those can lead to. We rarely need human medicine to survive, and most of the time it never works."

Kai shivered. "I-I remember."

"It took a lot for me to not go full wolf and disappear into the forest to die when he rejected me, Kai. If I hadn't had Cole, Ryan, my business partner, and Seth, my best friend, I would have. I've witnessed many of our pack waste away to nothing when they've lost their true mates."

"Why are you telling me this?" Kai whispered, appetite fled, not even half the breakfast gone, fork on the table beside the plate, forgotten.

"Because you need to understand what being a true mate means and because I'm a selfish prick who can't stand seeing Cole the way I did this morning. He is my friend and the soon-to-be Alpha of my pack. Right now, though… he's just my friend, and I know what he's going through. You've given him a time limit, and all he can hear is the clock ticking the more time goes by."

Kai tried to picture Cole, such a large, vibrant man, shrunken in on himself, and his heart pitched. His hands shook as he lowered them to his thighs, and his fox made a pitiful chirp inside him. Kai couldn't imagine Cole being anything less than the strong, beautiful wolf he'd met, the one taking care of Kai as though he meant the world to him. "I don't know what to do."

"Stop pushing him away. If I know Cole, he isn't asking for anything from you except to be by you, with you. He would never ask for more than you are ready to give."

Kai bit his lip. He knew Nick was right. Cole had never asked him for anything really. Nothing except to be with him, spend time with him, and get to know him. He hadn't even touched Kai without asking for permission first. Kai closed his eyes as he realized how often he'd rejected Cole over the last several days. Cole had never once gotten angry at him for it, never tried to push him or threaten him to accept Cole. He'd only gotten angry around Kai once, when Kai had been upset about Nick babysitting him. "When is Cole coming home?"

"He said he had more than his meeting to take care of and figured around one. Until then, you're stuck with me. I hoped we could spend the time together talking and maybe even watch a movie or perhaps play a video game on the PS4 he has. Unless you have something else in mind for how you want to spend the morning?"

The need to see Cole rode Kai hard, but he knew he had to wait. Cole would return, and Kai could apologize. He needed to tell Cole… what? He didn't even know what he'd say. He'd been a selfish jerk. Kai thought over every single day since he'd first laid eyes on Cole in the alley in Phoenix. Cole had saved his life, protected him, taken care of him, wanted nothing more than to help him, given him everything he could, and Kai had never once thanked him or given him a chance. He'd given Cole nothing in return. Cole hadn't expected anything from him except for Kai to get to know him.

"Let me get breakfast cleaned up and then we can decide what to do, okay? Don't let Cole know how little you ate, huh? He'll kick my ass for sure." Nick grimaced and stood. He picked up his plate and Kai's.

Kai took a deep breath and got up as well, reaching for the silverware and glasses. "Can I help?"

Nick gave him a surprised glance, one that made Kai twitch in embarrassment. Had he even forgone such a small thing as helping to clean up after himself? "Sure. How are your ribs doing?"

"They feel better," Kai said as he carried the glasses to the sink.

"Let's make sure we don't do anything too taxing. Cole showed you his greenhouses yet?"

"Yeah. Yesterday. They're beautiful."

"It's been his passion for years. I can still remember him talking about his plans to build them when he started up the business." Nick chuckled, green eyes twinkling. "The day they started construction on them was probably a step below the day he found you."

Jealousy zinged through Kai, surprising him. "You've known each other for a long time?"

"All our lives actually. Born and raised together. Oh, the things I could tell you."

"Like what?" Kai asked curiously, leaning against the counter as Nick started washing the plates.

"Oh no, I don't think I should. Cole would kill me."

"Come on, I can keep a secret. I won't tell him. I want to know more about him. Please?"

Nick eyed him for a moment and then said, "All right, but if you tell him I told you...."

"I won't! I promise!"

Laughing, Nick replied, "Let's get these dishes done first, and while we play a video game, I'll tell you some of the stories, okay?"

Kai nodded eagerly and helped dry off the dishes as Nick washed, putting away the ones he knew where they went, asking about the others when he didn't. For the first time since Kai had been at Cole's home, Kai forgot about everything else: his past, his uncle, and the pressure of being Cole's mate. After they finished, Nick set another pot of coffee to brew and beckoned Kai to follow him. "What game do you want to play?"

Shrugging, Kai perched on the edge of the couch and watched as Nick turned on the television on the wall. He knew what video games were, but he hadn't played one since before his parents' death. He'd even stolen a few video game systems for his uncle over the years, so he wasn't entirely ignorant of how they worked.

Nick poked through a shelf of neatly organized slim plastic cases. "Hmm. Let's see. What about *Call of Duty?*"

"What is it?" Kai asked.

Nick turned his head to look at Kai, an eyebrow raised, but didn't comment on his lack of knowledge. "A first-person shooting game. You're a soldier. We can either go online as a team or go against each other offline."

Kai shook his head, wrinkling his nose.

"Okay, I guess you don't like war games. What else? Hmm." Nick continued to browse through the selection while Kai settled farther onto the sofa and drew one knee up to his chest, wrapping his arms around it while watching in fascination. "What about *Need for Speed?*"

"What's that?"

"Car racing? You design your own race car and race other drivers?"

"Okay, sure. I'll probably be terrible at it, though."

"Nah, I'll teach you."

Kai watched Nick pull out a hidden drawer built into the top of the cabinet next to the fireplace, where an electronic machine was hidden, and smiled, shaking his head. Somehow it didn't surprise him Cole would find a way to make his space neat and compact. In the short amount of time he'd known Cole, the man seemed compulsive about things being in place and put together. Nick placed the disc in the machine, hit the button, and grabbed up a flat controller to turn on the television before picking up the game controllers. He handed one to Kai and sat down next to him. "We'll work on your car first and get you familiar with the game before we get into playing against each other, okay?"

"Okay."

Setting up Kai's car took longer than Kai would have thought. A lot of the color designs didn't appeal to him. They were still on Kai understanding how to drive without running into things, what buttons to press to make the car move, and how to take the curves properly when Cole opened the front door. It surprised Kai how quickly the time had passed, but it wasn't the surprise of Cole's appearance that caused him to drop the remote into his lap or the zing of happiness at seeing Cole walk through the door that made him feel guilty. It was the dark circles under Cole's eyes, the way Cole hesitated in the doorway at the sight of them sitting on the couch together, and the pain in the dark green eyes that made Kai's breath catch in his throat. "Cole."

Nick stood. "Hey, Cole."

Cole turned on his heel and slammed the door behind him, the sound as loud as a gunshot over the noise of the music from the video game. Kai flinched, and Nick swore, then sighed. "Give me a minute, buddy. I need to talk to him."

Kai nodded and swallowed as Nick hurried outside after Cole. He didn't know how to turn off the video game, and the music started to grate on his nerves. He got up and located the remote, turned the volume down on the television instead, and moved to look out the window, wanting, needing, to see Cole. The two of them were standing near Cole's truck with Cole's back to the house, but Kai could see the angry set of Cole's shoulders and the way Cole had his hands fisted at his sides. Would Cole hit Nick? Nick didn't seem afraid of Cole, though. Cole's shoulders suddenly slumped, and he brought his hands up to cover his face, a move that brought a sound forth from Kai, a desperate and wounded one that shocked him. Kai slapped a hand over his mouth, stifling it. Cole's defeated air made Kai's heart ache in a way he didn't understand. Nick laid a hand on Cole's bicep, and a fierce high-pitched growl rattled in Kai's throat, startling Kai even further. What the hell was wrong with him?

He watched as Cole lowered his hands at something Nick said, and he ducked behind the wall when he saw Cole start to turn toward the house. Kai's foot slipped on something, and he looked down to spot a manila folder on the floor. Frowning, he bent and picked it up, noticing the name of a company etched into the area where the label usually went, a law firm of some kind. He set it on the coffee table, though he couldn't help his curiosity, wondering why Cole had been to see a lawyer. Was this where Cole had gone for his meeting? He recalled the conversation Cole had with his mother about the meeting and knew it wasn't about a lawyer. It had been something to do with a market, a Ryson or Bryan or something. Kai frowned.

The sound of the front door opening caused Kai to jump, and he turned to find Nick standing there, but no Cole. "Where's Cole?" Kai asked.

"He needed to go for a run. Said to have some lunch, and he'll join us a little later." Nick headed toward the kitchen.

Kai scowled, not really understanding everything. He didn't follow Nick. Instead he rushed down the hallway to the back door in time to see Cole disappear in human form into the trees. Without giving it another thought, he thrust open the door and ran after Cole. He heard Nick call his name, but he ignored it. His fox urged him faster, pushing him to catch Cole before Cole could leave him behind. The moment Kai entered the tree line, he shifted, his animal half picking up Cole's scent right away. Giving a small yip, he barreled through the lower brush, tracking Cole until he reached a ravine where Cole did an abrupt turn and followed its jagged line through the forest. Kai threw his snout in the air, let out an eerie howl, and waited, hoping Cole would answer.

The returning howl came, several miles to the north of him, and Kai gave an answering happy cry, racing fleet-footed toward it, his tiny black paws eating up the ground at a fast clip. Leaves flew up in the air as he came to a shuddering halt when Cole appeared before him a few yards away, still in his powerful wolf form. Kai trembled, uncertain as to why he'd sought out the other shifter but knowing he needed to be with him, to comfort him. He cautiously approached Cole, sniffing at the air only to whimper when he caught the scent of hesitation and pain. He'd done that. The realization slammed into Kai as surely as his uncle's fist during one of the many beatings he'd suffered. He'd been completely blind.

Cole lowered himself to the ground, laying his large head on his paws, eyes dull but watchful. Kai gave a low trill in his throat, a lulling call of apology meant to soothe and calm. Cole didn't move. Kai stepped closer, until he stood mere inches from Cole, and pressed his nose to Cole's muzzle, nuzzling gently. Cole whined and closed his eyes, leaning into Kai. The scent of pain grew deeper, and Kai would have gasped if he'd been in human form. Despite what Nick had tried to explain to him before about mates and their connection, how it hurt when one rejected the other, Kai hadn't truly understood until then. It terrified him to know how much another person needed him. Him... a damaged soul who didn't have enough left to offer to another person. Yet Kai knew after everything he'd witnessed these last few days that Cole didn't care about any of it. Cole hadn't asked for anything. He just wanted... Kai. All of him, parts of him, anything he could get. Cole wanted whatever Kai would give him. It horrified Kai as it reminded him of a starving dog waiting for table scraps, and he'd never thought he'd be capable of treating anyone the same way he'd been treated almost his entire life.

Kai shifted. "Cole...." His voice wavered, and he choked, stroking the fur along Cole's back with trembling fingers. "I'm sorry."

Another whine left Cole's throat, and Cole shoved closer, laying his head in Kai's lap and closing his eyes. Kai leaned down and pressed a kiss to the top of Cole's ears. "I'm so, so sorry," he wept. "I didn't understand."

Tears dampened Cole's fur as Kai cried, for the pain he'd endured for many years and for the pain he'd inflicted since being relieved of his own. Cole only chose to shift when those tears finally became dry tracks on Kai's cheeks. He wrapped Kai in a tight embrace, holding him close to the warm muscles of his chest and stroking one large hand down the ridges of his spine. "It's all right, Kai."

Kai gripped Cole's shirt, fingers digging in and holding on tight. "I di-didn't know," he hiccuped. "I n-never wo-would have—"

Cole covered his lips with two fingers, shaking his head. "It's all right."

Burying his face in the crook of Cole's neck, Kai sighed, still upset. Once he could manage to talk normally, he asked, "How are you able to be nice after I've been nothing but cruel since we met?"

Cole's chest rose and fell on a breath. "Because no matter how much you hurt me, Kai, you are still my mate, and because you weren't raised in the way of shifters. You couldn't possibly understand the bond of true mates. Not yet."

"I… I'm still not sure I'm ready to be mates," Kai began. Cole stiffened, and his broad shoulders drooped. Guilt bit deep into Kai once more. "But I won't leave," he rushed on to say. "I won't leave after the month is over."

The tension left Cole. "Thank you," Cole murmured, pressing a kiss to Kai's temple.

The sheer relief in Cole's voice caused even more guilt to crash down on Kai. "I'm sorry," he murmured.

"Don't be. I'm sorry I'm an impatient ass, kit."

Kai glared at Cole. "You aren't."

Cole raised one auburn brow. "I think there are few who wouldn't agree with me."

"Well, I don't think you are, and that's all that matters," Kai replied haughtily.

Cole chuckled. "Very true, mate, so very true."

Kai stilled, uncertain how he felt about Cole using the term as an endearment but decided to let it go. He smiled at hearing Cole laugh for the first time since they'd argued the day before. He became aware of their position then as well. He was straddling Cole's lap! A flush worked its way over Kai's cheeks, darkening them to a rosy color. Cole frowned. "Are you all right?"

"I… ah…." Kai licked his lips. "We should go. I kind of left without telling Nick."

Cole grunted. "He's supposed to be watching over you. Great bodyguard he is."

"Hey, I didn't exactly give him a choice. I kind of just ran out." Kai dropped his gaze to the base of Cole's throat in embarrassment. He saw several fascinating strands of dark auburn hair peeking through the top of Cole's T-shirt and wondered if he was hairy all over, and if it was all the same color. Eyes widening and breath catching, Kai bit his lip at his wayward thoughts. He started in surprise when Cole slid two fingers beneath his chin and tipped his head upward a bit. He hadn't even been aware Cole had moved. Dark green eyes caught his gaze, and Kai watched as they got closer, giving him more than enough time to move away. But all Kai could do was part his lips, waiting for the kiss Cole obviously intended to take. A sigh slipped free the moment Cole's mouth settled over his.

Cole broke away, much to Kai's disgruntlement, but only angled his head to deepen the kiss. One of Cole's strong arms slid around Kai's waist to support him while the other came up to allow Cole to cup the back of Kai's head. Kai tentatively rested both of his hands on Cole's chest and gave an unsure swipe of his tongue along Cole's bottom lip. Cole's answering groan vibrated beneath Kai's palms, and he flexed his fingers as he repeated the movement, slick and wet against the smoothness of Cole's mouth. Kai made a small noise in his throat at just how good it felt. This time Cole wrenched his mouth away and dropped his forehead to Kai's shoulder, shuddering. "Gods," Cole gasped. "We should go."

Kai shifted a bit in Cole's lap, knowing he needed something, needed release, but Cole grabbed his hips, stopping him. He became aware of the hard bulge beneath his bottom and the muscles quivering beneath his hands. Cole wanted him. Kai rolled his body slightly and felt Cole's fingers dig into him. "Kai, don't."

He knew he wasn't being fair, knew he should listen to Cole, but his fox wanted the other shifter more than anything he'd ever wanted in his life. "Why?" Kai whispered, nuzzling at Cole's throat.

"Because I wouldn't be able to stop myself from claiming you," Cole rasped.

Kai still didn't understand how claiming another worked. He nipped at the skin on Cole's neck. "It takes more than sex to claim me?"

Cole growled, hands tightening on Kai almost painfully. "Yes. I would have to bite you as I come inside you. Fuck! Kai, stop!" Cole snarled as Kai laved at the spot he'd bitten.

Something about the way he had such power over Cole's reactions made Kai feel heady, in charge, and he didn't want to stop. He bit down again, harder but not enough to break the flesh. Before he could comprehend the movement, Kai found himself pinned beneath Cole, a very angry, very turned-on werewolf panting in his face. Hard green eyes glittered down at him as Cole held his hands over his head. "Enough!" Cole demanded. "Before you find my cock buried so deep inside your ass you won't know where you end and I begin, kit."

Kai's breath caught, but to his astonishment, not from fear. Pure lust slammed into his belly. He licked his lips. "I...."

Cole must have mistaken his reaction for disgust because Cole's weight was suddenly gone, and Kai lay there, breathing heavily and hot with desire. His fox cried out, begging for his mate to take him. Kai didn't understand the rapid change in his body or why he didn't want to head for the hills as he would have in the past. Had what Nick explained about mates changed everything? Did he want Cole to claim him? He was no longer afraid of Cole. He trusted Cole. The realization rushed through Kai, almost slapping him in the face as he saw Cole standing several feet away, facing away from him.

He managed to stand and approach Cole, setting one hand on Cole's broad back. "I'm sorry," Kai murmured.

Muscles quivered beneath his fingers. Cole spun around and crushed Kai to him. "Never believe I could hurt you, kit. Ever."

"I know," Kai whispered. "I know you'd never hurt me, Cole. I trust you."

A tremble wound its way through Cole's body, and Kai closed his eyes, unable to comprehend having such an effect on a man—wolf—as powerful as Cole. He burrowed closer to Cole and hung on tight, his fox almost purring within him. The world dropped away, becoming nothing except the two of them. Kai couldn't ever remember a time when he'd felt as safe and warm as he did right then. Maybe not even when his parents were alive. Wind rustled the trees overhead, sending several leaves to the forest floor around them. Cole's lips whispered over Kai's temple once more before Cole released him. "Let's go home," Cole murmured.

Kai nodded and reluctantly let go. He waited until Cole had shifted to allow his own change to take place, his fox accepting control again eagerly. Cole brushed against him, stroking his throat over the top of Kai's head with a guttural growl. Kai chirped and licked at Cole's muzzle, panting with happiness. With a gentle nip at Kai, Cole darted into the trees toward home, and Kai gave chase.

When they reached the house, Nick was pacing near the door, a scowl on his face. Relief immediately flooded his tense features, and his shoulders slumped when he spotted the two of them trotting from between the trees. "Dammit, Kai! What the hell?" he shouted when he spotted Kai.

Kai shifted and had the grace to look sheepish. "I'm sorry, Nick."

Cole snorted and rolled his eyes, shifting in a flash of light. "Great looking out, Nick," he drawled.

"I'm sorry, Cole! I—" Nick cut himself off, his eyes darting between the two of them. "Did you two...?" His voice trailed away as he scented the air.

Kai wrinkled his brow, tilting his head as he tried to understand what Nick asked.

"No!" Cole exclaimed, shaking his head. "No, we didn't. Let's go inside. I have something I need to talk to you about, Nick, and Kai needs to eat."

"I'm fine," Kai protested, frowning.

"You need to eat," Cole insisted, tone stern. "You're still as skinny as a reed. Until I can't see your ribs anymore, you'll eat every chance I can stuff food down you."

Kai flushed. "I'm not hungry."

Cole grunted and placed a hand on Kai's lower back, guiding him into the house. Kai could feel the heat of Cole's touch almost burning him through his thin T-shirt and bit the inside of his lower lip. He didn't understand what Nick had asked, but he had a feeling it had something to do with him. The three of them headed to the kitchen, Cole never once removing his hand, using it to direct him into the chair that had somehow become his. "Don't move," Cole directed.

Kai glared at him, but he didn't put any heat behind it, knowing Cole only wanted to take care of him. He watched as Cole handed the folder from the lawyer's office to Nick. "This isn't up for discussion," Cole instructed Nick before relinquishing it.

Nick nodded once while Kai gazed on curiously. He saw Nick's eyes flash over the contents of the folder and widen in shock, flicking up to Cole several times before returning to the document. A noise rattled in Nick's throat. "Cole," Nick choked, "no."

Kai frowned. "What?"

Cole shook his head. "Just sign it, Nick."

"I can't. You know I can't."

Cole gave Nick a sad smile. "You're the only one who can."

Kai didn't know what the two of them were discussing, but whatever the paper said upset Nick a lot. He started to stand, but Cole held him in place with a hard stare. Kai held his breath as Nick took the pen Cole offered, his long, slender fingers tightening on it until Kai felt certain it would snap. "You're asking too much, Cole," Nick rasped.

"Am I?" Cole murmured. "You're my best friend, Nick. If not you, then who? You're the only one I trust with this, Nick."

"But why?"

"You've been there, Nick. You know why."

"But you're an Alpha, for fuck's sake!"

Cole flinched, but didn't waver. "You think I'm not aware of what I am, Nick? You think it didn't cross my fucking mind? You think I don't know this makes me weaker than my own fucking Beta? Shit, Nick, I know it better than you ever could. I've done nothing except think of every single thing running through your mind, but I feel it here." Cole touched his chest, "I won't be able to handle it the way you did."

It hit Kai then that Cole and Nick were talking about him. His breath caught in his throat. Something in the document pertained to him.

"Don't ask me to do this, Cole."

"I'm already asking you, Nick. Please, for me."

"But... I thought things had changed."

Cole laughed, but it held no humor or happiness. Kai had known more than his fair share of bitterness, so he recognized it coming from Cole. He winced, knowing he'd affected Cole's life negatively.

"Nothing has changed, Nick. Nothing has changed at all. Just sign the damn paper, Nick."

Nick set the folder on the island counter, placed the tip of the pen over the paper, hesitated, but signed. He closed the folder and set the pen on top afterward. "I've known you my whole life, Cole, and this... this is a mistake."

Nervousness set in, and Kai couldn't take it anymore. "What's going on?" he demanded, standing.

The two of them looked at him in surprise, almost as if they had forgotten he was there. "Nothing," Cole said. "What do you want to eat for lunch?"

"Tell him, Cole," Nick growled.

"Tell me what?"

"Nick!" Cole snarled.

"He has a right to know," Nick snapped.

"Know what?" Kai persisted.

"It's nothing."

"Goddammit, Cole! You don't have the right to make such an important decision without telling him."

"I have every fucking right. It's my business, my life. Either shut up or get out!" Cole shouted.

Nick jerked as if struck. Kai stared at Cole, mouth hanging open, never having seen him in a rage, not even when he'd insisted Nick come stay with Kai today. Silence enveloped the house for several breaths, and then Nick stormed out of the house, slamming the door behind him.

"Fuck!" Cole swore, pinching the bridge of his nose between two fingers. "Stay here," he grunted and tore after Nick.

Kai closed his mouth and listened to the sound of Nick's car starting, but no sound of tires crunching on the gravel followed the growl of the engine, and eventually the rumble cut off. He breathed a sigh of relief, knowing Cole had felt awful immediately after speaking to Nick in anger. Turning his gaze to the folder, Kai wondered what had set Nick off. He frowned and edged closer, ignoring the warning bells at the back of his mind against prying. He opened the folder and peered at the paper. Most of the language didn't make sense to him, but he did recognize his name being printed as Kai Ferris, which gave him a jolt, as well as him being named Cole's beneficiary. Kai's lips parted on a sharp intake of breath. He didn't understand what a trust was or how it all came together, though. Nick had seemed agitated by the entire document.

The front door opening brought his head up, and Cole entered the house. Cole stopped short when he saw Kai looking at the papers. Kai scrambled away until he hit the stove.

"You weren't meant to see that," Cole said as he came forward and closed the folder.

"What does it mean?" Kai asked.

"It doesn't matter."

"It does matter," Kai insisted. "Why did it upset Nick? I know it's about me. He said I have the right to know!"

Cole sighed and rubbed at the top of his head, mussing up his hair. "Come sit down. Please." The please had been added as an afterthought, as if he'd realized how demanding he'd sounded.

Kai went around to Cole's side of the counter and perched on the edge of the couch cushion, waiting for Cole to explain. He watched as Cole started pacing between the fireplace and the windows. Cole seemed hesitant to begin talking. "Cole?"

Cole stopped at one of the wide windows and stared out of it. "The papers are a trust, a fund, naming you as beneficiary and Nick as the trustee, the one who controls the assets and helps with the business side of things. If something happens to me, Ferris Organics, the greenhouses, my home, and all of my assets become yours."

Flabbergasted, Kai stared at Cole's broad back, his eyes wide and his hands trembling. "But... why? What do you mean if something happens to you?"

Kai could see Cole's mouth twist in his reflection in the window. "I know you've agreed to stay here, to no longer leave after the month is over, and I couldn't be more grateful. My wolf couldn't be happier either, but I am not naïve enough to believe you will ever accept being my mate. Over the course of my life, I've always known what was expected of me, thought I knew how my life would go, but I never...." He trailed off, his hands tightening into fists at his side.

Heart pounding and sweat beading on his upper lip, Kai tried to understand Cole. He wanted to tell Cole he could accept Cole eventually, but fear curled in his belly at the idea. He didn't want to be in a position to be controlled by anyone ever again, and somehow, it felt as if being mated would give Cole power over him. Yet Kai also sensed his desire to remain free hurt Cole a lot.

"The trust ensures no matter what you will always be taken care of. You are my mate, kit. My everything. I need you to understand how important it is to me you know that."

"I do," Kai whispered.

Cole glanced over his shoulder at Kai, a pained smile on his lips. "I'm sorry for yelling earlier, for scaring you."

Kai shook his head. "You didn't scare me."

Turning, Cole gave him a skeptical look.

"You didn't," Kai insisted, standing and walking over to Cole's side, gazing the few inches up into Cole's eyes. "It surprised me, but it didn't scare me. I've never heard you really yell before." Kai laid his hand on Cole's bicep. "Is everything with Nick all right?"

Cole covered Kai's hand with his own, bringing Kai's to his lips and pressing a kiss to the back of Kai's fingers. "Everything is fine. I apologized for being an ass. He wasn't wrong, but at the same time, he knew he'd overstepped his boundaries."

Kai shivered at the heat on his fingers. "You're his best friend. He cares about you."

"We've known each other a long time," Cole replied, pulling Kai closer and wrapping his arms around him. "Before Nick's parents were killed, his father was one of my father's Betas. I think I will be very lucky if Thayne doesn't come over here and try to kick my ass later, if he's not already on his way here."

Kai frowned and looked at Cole. "Why would he want to hurt you?"

Cole chuckled. "When mates bond, they develop a telepathic link, kit. They can feel what the other feels, talk to each other without words. I have no doubt Thayne could sense Nick's emotions earlier."

Kai wrinkled his nose. "Really? Seems a little invasive."

"Not really. It can bring you closer together actually," Cole said, longing buried in his tone.

The sound hit Kai hard. He knew Cole wanted them to have the same type of connection. Kai leaned his forehead against Cole's shoulder and frowned.

"Let's get something to eat, okay?" Cole said, chest rumbling beneath Kai's forehead.

"'Kay."

Kai eased away from Cole, ignoring the way his fox chirped at him to not let go. "Can I make it for you this time?" he asked.

Surprise flashed across Cole's face. "You don't have to."

"I know. I want to."

"If you're sure," Cole said.

"I am," Kai said, smiling.

Cole reached out and brushed the backs of his fingers over Kai's cheek, returning the smile. "Any idea what you want to make?"

"What do you want to eat?"

"Anything is fine," Cole husked, voice raspy and thick.

Kai tilted his head in confusion. Why had Cole's voice changed? But he didn't ask. Instead, he chose to turn toward the kitchen and head into the pantry to see what he could make. They'd had pasta a few days before, and he didn't want to resort to sandwiches again. He spotted a box of instant biscuit mix and wondered if Cole had chicken in the house. A poor man's version of potpie sounded good. "Cole?" he called.

Cole appeared in the doorway suddenly. "What's wrong?"

"Oh, nothing," Kai replied. "I wanted to ask if there was any chicken by chance."

The tension in Cole's shoulders eased. "I can check. I don't know if Nick took anything out earlier."

Kai caught a whiff of cinnamon and sandalwood as Cole turned and frowned. He breathed in deep, filling his lungs with the scent, and his knees weakened. He didn't understand why he'd never associated the smells with Cole before, but his fox let out a yip inside him, almost wagging its tail in eagerness, urging him to follow Cole. Kai shivered and tried to regain control of his limbs, picking up the box of biscuit mix and leaving the pantry.

Cole stood at the fridge, door open, and Kai saw him reach inside for something. When he pulled his hand out of the fridge, he held a package of chicken. "I guess he did," Cole said with a small smile, showing it to Kai.

"I can make what my mom used to call poor man's chicken potpie," Kai said, showing him the mix.

"Sounds good. Do you need my help with anything?" Cole asked, setting the chicken on the counter near the sink and leaning against it.

Kai shook his head. "I want to do this for you. You've done a lot for me already."

Cole gave him a look. "I wanted to."

"Please?" Kai said.

Cole studied Kai for several minutes and then smiled. "All right. I need to check on some things in the greenhouses anyway. I'll only be a half hour, okay, kit?"

"Sure," Kai said.

Pushing away from the counter, Cole brushed past Kai, squeezing his shoulder on the way. Kai stopped him with a touch of his hand on his forearm. Cole gave him a questioning look. Before Kai could have second thoughts, he leaned up and pressed a light kiss to Cole's cheek. Cole made a startled noise, a small sound of air escaping his lips. "Thank you, Cole," Kai murmured before turning away to start making them a late lunch.

There were no other sounds except those of Cole's footsteps as he left the kitchen. Kai smiled and began humming as he busied himself at the stove, cutting up the chicken and seeking out the carrots and peas he needed. His heart beat fast against his ribs, but he ignored it, deciding to take it one day at a time.

CHAPTER ELEVEN

THERE WERE a lot of things Cole had expected in his life, things he'd known were certain to happen. He'd known he'd become Alpha of the Emerald Lake Hills wolf pack one day. Nick would be one of his Betas, along with Ryan, and Howard and Wilson, his father's Betas, would retain their positions until they chose to step down or reached the end of their life cycle. There were also things he'd spent time dreaming and hoping for. Cole had hoped to one day find his mate, to claim them and spend his life with them. He'd hoped to have his own business, to grow organic fruits and vegetables, and to help provide for his pack.

He'd learned a lot from his father and mother over the years about leading, about knowing when to show empathy but also when to be the Alpha his father expected him to be. The last week had tested the faith he had in himself to be Alpha, to have the strength everyone around him expected him to have. The moment he'd snapped at Nick, he'd felt terrible, but when it came to Kai, the rational side of himself went out the window. The switch went off, and his common sense shut down. He'd hurt Nick because of his own insecurities, a fact that left an acrid taste in his mouth. Never had his emotions gotten the better of him before. He wasn't sure if it was because he didn't have as much control as he thought or if he was closer to becoming feral than he thought.

Cole strode toward the first greenhouse, his expression grim. As much as it would disappoint his mother and father, his taking over the pack now would be wrong. He could barely keep it together himself; trying to lead a pack of over three hundred didn't seem manageable. The odds of the pack still being together in six months were slim to none if his reactions of late were any indication. He would go see his parents before the summit, to tell them his choice and to let them know he wouldn't be attending the gathering either.

When he entered the greenhouse, Julie stood off to the side talking to a pack member named Walter Harrison and his son, Gregory. She smiled when she saw him, but her smile dimmed. She said something to Walter and made her way to Cole. "Cole, is everything okay?"

Cole gave her a strained smile. "It's fine. I wanted to let you know how things went with the Bryson's Market rep. We got the deal."

"That's fantastic!" she exclaimed, throwing her arms around him and hugging him tight.

"Thanks," he murmured.

She raised her brow at him. "Why aren't you more excited? You've wanted their account for years!"

"I know. Thanks for setting it up."

"Things aren't going well with your mate I take it."

Cole flinched, mouth tightening around the edges. "I don't want to discuss it, Jules."

She gave him a sympathetic look. "I'm sorry, Cole. If there's anything I can do, let me know."

"What's Walter doing here?"

"Picking up a couple crates of tomatoes. Jo asked him to grab hers as well. The diner ran out this morning." Jo owned the local diner where Thayne worked as one of the cooks. "You sure there isn't anything I can do, Cole?"

Cole shook his head. "No, but thanks, Jules." He reached out and gave her shoulder a squeeze before moving away to check on his peppermint plants.

After looking over the soil beneath the leaves of his latest batch of peppermint and ensuring it wasn't too dry, Cole rinsed his hands. He could sense Julie watching him but ignored her. He didn't want her pity, and he sure as hell couldn't handle talking about his situation with Kai right now. He knew Julie wouldn't spread the gossip among the other pack members, but he couldn't hash it out again. Gods, the pack would think him weak and unable to lead if they heard he couldn't even claim his own damn mate. Cole scowled and kicked at a rock, sending it skittering across the greenhouse floor.

Figuring he needed to stop hiding, Cole left the greenhouse. The scent of spiced chicken and gravy hit his nostrils as soon as he stepped inside, and his stomach growled as his mouth watered. It seemed Kai could cook! Cole strode down the hallway to the kitchen to find Kai just pulling the pan of food out of the oven, a pleased look on his features. The flaky crust on top of the mixture in the dish was a nice golden brown and smelled amazing. Kai set the dish on the stove and prodded the crust with a fork, humming when the topping passed his test.

"Smells great," Cole praised, leaning his shoulder on the open doorway.

Kai looked up, eyes sparkling with pleasure. "Thank you. It's one of the few things I remember from when my mom used to cook. She showed me how to make it one night."

"I can't wait to dig in. I see you set the table already," Cole said, glancing over.

"Figured it made sense to while the food baked. Do you want soda or tea?" Kai asked.

"I'll get the drinks." Cole motioned for Kai to have a seat. "I think we should have your injuries checked again before you get too adventurous."

Kai scowled. "I'm fine. Besides, I ran around and played in the woods earlier and you didn't seem to mind."

Cole sighed and stepped closer to Kai. He brought his hands up to rest them on Kai's shoulders. "And I forgot how badly you were injured just a few days ago."

"The shifting helped. My ribs are fine," Kai protested. "I promise."

"Please take it easy for a couple more days. For me?" Cole asked.

Kai sighed. "All right. For a little longer."

"Thank you." Cole smiled and nudged Kai toward the table. "Go. I'll bring the food to the table. Anything in particular you want to drink?"

"Soda is fine."

Cole placed the steaming pan of potpie on the table between the two plates, then grabbed a bottle of Coke from the fridge. He filled both their glasses before having a seat. Kai scooped a huge spoonful of the piping hot food onto Cole's plate and waited for Cole to try it, almost holding his breath in anticipation. Cole picked up his fork, stabbed a huge bite, blew on it, and placed it in his mouth. The flaky crust almost melted in his mouth, and the flavor exploded over his tongue. He moaned at the taste, closing his eyes as he savored the chicken, vegetables, and gravy. Once he'd chewed and swallowed, he opened his eyes. "This is great!"

Kai grinned in pleasure at the compliment and proceeded to serve himself. Cole ended up eating more than his fair share of the pan. His stomach felt strained by the time he finished, and he sat back with a sigh, patting his belly. "Wow, it's been a long time since I've enjoyed a meal so much."

The pure delight on Kai's face satisfied Cole's wolf, and Cole knew he would do anything to make Kai smile. "I'm almost tempted to lick the plate," Cole teased, winking at Kai. A small laugh escaped Kai, the sound going straight to Cole's heart. Cole fought the sadness following on the heels of the burst of happiness. There would be time to grieve later on when he was alone again. For now, he wanted to enjoy being with Kai. "Since you cooked, I'll do the cleanup, hmm?"

"I don't mind," Kai replied.

Cole waved Kai's response away. "It's the least I can do. Afterward we can play a game or two of *Need for Speed*, or if you'd rather, we can do something else."

"Okay."

Cole stood and began clearing the dishes. Kai went to help, but Cole stopped him with a look. Kai wandered into the living area and sat down on the couch. It didn't take Cole long to wash, dry, and put away the few plates they'd used as well as store the leftovers. Once finished, he joined Kai and turned on everything before handing one of the controllers to Kai. "Did you and Nick have a good time today?"

Kai nodded. "Nick seems like a nice person."

"We've been friends for a long time. Gotten each other into and out of a few scrapes over the years." Cole navigated the menus with ease, setting it for two players, and put them on one of the easier tracks. He didn't play often, but knew the game fairly well. The race began, and Cole tempered his speed, letting Kai stay ahead of him, almost nudging him several times to stay on course. "Everything went well?"

Kai made a small noise, and when Cole glanced over, he couldn't help but grin. The sheer concentration on Kai's face was adorable. A tiny pink tongue peeked out of one corner of his mouth, and his eyes were trained on the screen in determination. Cole figured video games were something Kai would come to enjoy. He planned to order more after Kai went to sleep. There were hundreds out there. With the greenhouses, Cole didn't have a whole lot of time on his hands to play, so he only kept a few around for whenever Nick came over to hang out, which had been less and less since Thayne had come into the picture. Now with Kai, Cole figured the time would cut down even further, at least until Cole managed to figure out what their future would truly become.

Kai made a triumphant sound, and Cole looked at the screen to find Kai had crossed the finish line while Cole's car kept running into a wall. He'd been watching Kai's enjoyment of the game instead of paying attention himself. Kai turned toward him, frowning. "You let me win," he accused.

"Actually, I didn't," Cole confessed sheepishly.

"Then what were you doing?" Kai demanded.

"Watching you," Cole admitted.

Kai's cheeks reddened at Cole's words, and Kai's eyes widened in surprise, but Cole saw the irises darken. A curious response. Cole tilted his head a fraction. "Does that please you?" Cole asked, his voice husky.

Kai's Adam's apple bobbed as he swallowed, hard. "I-I don't know."

Cole wanted to press the issue but decided against it. Instead he returned his attention to the game. "Something to think about," he said.

The next couple of games Cole managed to concentrate. He won the second one, but threw the third, letting Kai win by a fraction without making it obvious. It made him happy to hear Kai's whoop of excitement as he crossed the finish line first, and Cole swore he would lose a thousand times over in order to hear Kai so pleased. When it seemed Kai grew bored with the racing game, Cole suggested another one, a shooting game that made Kai screw his nose up in distaste. Instead, he showed Kai how to play a single-player RPG game and left Kai to it, grabbing a book from the shelf near the fireplace and settled down to read while Kai ventured through the different levels of *Final Fantasy XIV*.

Cole didn't concentrate on the book but rather on the situation he found himself in with his true mate. He supposed it could be worse. At least they could be friends. His wolf didn't like the idea of not being able to touch Kai, and Cole admitted to himself he hated the idea too, but he'd never push Kai for more than Kai could give. From what the doctor had told him, Kai might never be ready to submit to a physical relationship. Dr. Rice had asked Cole to bring Kai to her office, but Cole knew Kai would never agree to see her. He'd told her as much too. Even the idea would have Kai running. She'd given him some literature to read and told him about some support groups for him to join as the loved one of a victim of abuse, but until Kai was ready to face the horrors of what he'd been through, he would never be able to move past them and have a future. Cole knew she meant Kai would never be able to have a future with him. Her words had effectively shattered Cole's heart.

After the visit, he'd sat in his truck for a half hour, numb, staring out of the windshield at nothing. How could he fight demons that weren't tangible? He couldn't hit them or break them. They weren't in physical form for him to tear to pieces with his claws or teeth, and Kai wouldn't talk to Cole. He wouldn't tell Cole who hurt him in order for Cole to remove the threat from Kai's life. Cole didn't have any idea how to banish the darkness surrounding his mate, and he felt helpless. He couldn't fight what he couldn't see.

When he'd arrived home to find Nick and Kai together, smiling and having fun, it had hit him in the chest as though a knife had been shoved into his heart. Nick accomplished something in a matter of hours Cole had been trying to for days. He'd gotten Kai to smile and forget the past, even if only for a little while. Jealousy had chomped down on Cole's soul immediately, and he'd almost lost it. If he hadn't gotten out of the house when he did, he might well have shifted and torn into his best friend. Then for Nick to challenge him on the only thing he could do for Kai had scraped over his already raw nerves. Guilt rushed in right after he yelled at Nick, but Cole couldn't have contained his outburst to save his life. He hoped Nick would forgive him and their friendship hadn't suffered too much damage to be repaired.

Cole's wolf prowled restlessly beneath his skin. The animal didn't understand why they hadn't already claimed their mate. It couldn't comprehend Kai's fear or the horrors of Kai's past. The only things his wolf knew were that Kai belonged to them and they needed to put their mark and their scent on him before someone else dared to try. Why weren't they doing it right now? A whine stuck in Cole's throat, and he swallowed the sound, fingers tightening on the edges of the book he held. He wanted to shift and run, to shed the human emotions beating at his consciousness for good, but he couldn't. Not until he'd found a way around Kai's defenses long enough to uncover the cause of Kai's fear and his haunted past.

He could hardly admit it to himself, let alone Nick, but he held on to his human self by a thread. The shame at how easily he could give in made it even harder to control and even more attractive to want to let go, release his wolf spirit and never walk as a man again. He'd faced many Created Ones, killed more than a few, and yet the slight, one hundred pound shifter beside him bested him with nothing more than a few words and a glance.

While many would consider him weak, Cole didn't care. He would never do anything to harm Kai, even if it meant losing himself to his beast.

A grunt of frustration yanked Cole from his thoughts, and he shook his head and blinked, clearing his mind. Kai appeared to be having difficulties on one of the quests, and an irritated frown marred the perfection of Kai's forehead. Cole chuckled and leaned forward, poking at the lines. "You'll get wrinkles if you keep scowling so much."

Kai scowled and huffed. "I can't make the stupid jump. He keeps falling."

Laughing, Cole took the controller from Kai. "You're the one moving him. Here. You have to make him run toward the edge but wait until he's right there to jump. There ya go!"

The character on screen landed successfully on the other side. Kai gave Cole an incredulous glance. "Where were you ten minutes ago?"

Cole held up his book, ignoring the way his intestines twisted at lying to Kai. He looked at the clock. He hadn't realized how long he'd been lost in his musings or how long they'd been sitting there. Orange rays of sun dusted the horizon, and the sky above had begun to purple. "It's almost time for dinner. Think we should order pizza?"

Kai shrugged, once more involved in the game. Cole couldn't help but laugh again, and he stood, stretching muscles burning from being in the same position for a long period of time. He closed his eyes and raised his arms over his head, bending his back slightly to elongate his spine. A warm groan rumbled in his chest at the pleasant sensation of muscles releasing tension. When he opened his eyes, he found Kai's gaze locked on the tanned skin of his belly where his T-shirt had ridden up, exposing the light trail of red hairs leading into the top of Cole's jeans. Kai licked his lips, and Cole's blood heated at the sight of his mate's clear interest, but he knew Kai wouldn't go beyond the hungry stare, and Cole brought his arms down, ignoring the sudden tightening of his jeans. He couldn't help the tiny quirk of his lips when disappointment flashed across Kai's face and Kai's gaze dropped to the obvious bulge at Cole's crotch. It felt good to know Kai wanted him even a little.

"What do you want on your pizza, kit?" Cole asked, feigning ignorance of Kai's perusal.

"Huh?" Kai returned, blinking several times before shaking his head. "Oh, uh… I'm good with anything. Except broccoli."

Cole wrinkled his nose. "Broccoli on pizza? Who the hell eats that?"

Kai giggled. The sound sent electric pulses straight to Cole's cock, and a growl almost spilled out. He wanted to pin Kai to the couch and cover his slender body with his own, to ravage those full lips until neither of them could breathe and swallow the needy noises Kai would surely make. Clearing his throat, Cole turned away from Kai and adjusted his aching prick as he used the excuse of calling the pizza place to give himself a moment to calm down. He ordered three large meat-lovers with garlic rolls and a side order of chicken wings.

When he turned back to the couch, Kai had shut off the game and disappeared. "Kai?" Cole called.

The shuffle of footsteps coming down the hallway alerted him to Kai's return. Kai entered the kitchen holding the small black notebook Cole had shamelessly looked through when he'd first found Kai, the one that contained sketches of foxes and other animals. "What ya got there?" Cole asked, pretending ignorance of the contents.

He saw Kai biting at his lower lip in nervousness as he approached the island counter and set the book on it. A faint dusting of red highlighted Kai's cheeks. "Wi-will you let me draw you?"

Cole froze in surprise. "You want to draw me?" he finally managed to ask.

Kai wouldn't meet Cole's gaze, but he gave a short nod. "If you don't want me to, I-I understand."

Cole approached Kai, caution in each step, afraid he'd frighten Kai into hiding in his room. Setting his hand on top of Kai's where it rested on the counter, Cole squeezed gently. "I would be proud to have you draw me, kit."

Hazel eyes flicked up to his, suspicion in their depths, but whatever Kai sought in Cole's expression seemed to be missing, and a small smile lifted the corners of Kai's mouth. "Thank you," Kai murmured.

Cole grasped Kai's fingers in his and raised them to his lips to press a light kiss to the tips of them. "Anything for you, kit."

Kai stilled, eyes widening at the unexpected gesture. Cole could hear Kai's heartbeat increase by half a beat, and he could smell the scent of arousal spiking off of Kai's skin. He ignored it with difficulty and released Kai instead. "Where do you want to do this?"

"Huh?" Kai asked, rather dazed.

Cole stifled a grin. "The drawing. Where do you want me to sit or stand?"

"Oh! Uh… the couch is fine," Kai mumbled, the flush on his cheeks deepening.

Cole moved over to the sofa and sat, relaxing into the corner with one arm draped over the arm and the other over the back of the couch. "Any particular pose you want me in?"

Kai shook his head and perched on the nearby recliner. He opened his book to a blank page and began to sketch. Cole didn't speak, enjoying being able to watch Kai's intensity as he glanced between Cole and the page. The only sounds in the room were their combined breathing and the gentle hisses of the pencil on the paper. Kai brought a knee up enough to rest the book on at one point, but his concentration never wavered. Cole studied the lean line of Kai's neck, hating the black collar that broke up the paleness of the soft arch, knowing what lay beneath it. He slid his perusal farther down to Kai's shoulders and slender chest, noting how ragged the shirt appeared, making him want to take Kai shopping immediately. Tonight, when he ordered more of the games for Kai, he'd also purchase clothing, things that suited his mate. His wolf wagged its tail in eagerness at the idea of providing for their vulnerable other half even in such a small manner.

The whole drawing couldn't have taken more than fifteen or twenty minutes, but Cole would have remained where he was for much longer if it meant spending time with Kai, being studied by his expressive hazel eyes. When Kai lifted the pencil away from the paper for the final time, Cole couldn't quite keep disappointment from zinging through him, but he buried it behind a smile. "Done?"

Kai nodded and shyly turned the book around. Cole sucked in a breath at the image of himself staring back at him. "Kai," he murmured, leaning forward and reaching out to take the black sketchbook from him. His fingers trailed over the strong lines of his face in wonder. "You have so much talent, kit."

A blush worked its way up Kai's neck and into his cheeks. Cole would have given anything to have had the right to kiss Kai right then, but he controlled himself, his wolf whining at the restraint.

"You really like it?" Kai asked.

"I do. It's beautiful." Cole picked up the page and, even though he'd already looked through it before, asked, "May I?"

Kai gave a small tip of his head in assent. Cole began to flip through the pages, noting the new sketches Kai had added since his arrival. Kai had even drawn Cole's wolf, and Cole stopped to stare at it, realizing Kai had captured every detail of his beast, including the scar above Cole's right eye. The scar had come from a particularly nasty fight with a Created One a few years ago, one that ended in the death of a pack member as well as the Created One. Cole had nearly lost his eye in the fight.

"You should take a class at the local college, kit. I bet you'd enjoy it." Cole closed the book and handed it to Kai. "I could pull up the site on the computer for you."

"Oh no, I couldn't." Kai shook his head. "I—"

"Yes, you could. You have such a gift, kit."

Cole could see the longing in Kai's face and how much Kai wanted to take Cole up on what he offered. "Come on," Cole said, standing and holding out his hand.

Kai bit at his bottom lip in indecision but then hesitantly set his hand in Cole's. Cole pulled Kai up from his seat and led him down the hallway to his room. He opened the door and urged Kai into the seat at the desk. Kai sat rigid in the chair, staring at the laptop screen as if the thing would bite him, and Cole bent forward over him, placing his hand on the mouse. He clicked on the internet and then googled the local college. It only took a moment to bring up the site for the school, but the heat from Kai's body against his chest invaded every pore on Cole's flesh. He breathed in the earthy scent of Kai, wanting to nuzzle his mate's crown, but knew it wouldn't be welcome. "They—" He paused to clear his voice, which was husky with need for Kai. "—have several art classes, including drawing. See?"

Cole clicked on the link for the information for the art course, and Kai drew a breath at the images on the screen. Heart clenching with the need to please Kai, Cole continued to encourage Kai's desire to learn and opened more of the pages for other courses: art history, graphic drawing, architecture, and even photography. The small trill Kai released at the photos on the screen and the way Kai leaned closer to see them better sent warmth rushing through Cole. To make Kai happy in any way made Cole feel a thousand feet tall.

"You interested in photography, kit?" Cole rasped, his cock hard and aching in his jeans, fingers tightening on the mouse to stop him from grabbing Kai and yanking him out of the chair and into his arms.

Kai nodded, still staring at the pictures. Cole's fangs itched at the sight of the pale skin at the nape of Kai's neck through the reddish locks of Kai's hair. His wolf begged to sink its teeth into the tender flesh, to mark Kai as his own. Licking his lips, Cole dipped his head, breathing ragged. The second before his mouth could make contact with Kai's neck, the doorbell rang. He jerked away, horrified at what he'd almost done. "Pizza," he managed to gasp and darted out of the room, hurrying to the front door.

When he flung it open, one of his pack mates stood there holding the food. "Hey, Cole," Devin Murphy greeted, smiling. "Got three large meat-lover's, chicken wings, and an order of garlic rolls."

"Devin," Cole replied, voice harsher than he intended.

Devin frowned. "You okay, Cole?"

Clearing his throat, Cole said, "I'm fine. Just a little tired. How're your parents?"

"Good, good. The auto shop has been doing well. Dad even said after the summit next week I can quit Vinnie's and start working at the garage again."

Cole knew the Murphy's had struggled for a while, and Devin had found another job to help his parents out in the interim. Once the others in the pack had found out, they'd pulled together and started bringing their vehicles to Murphy's Garage instead of one of the more mainstream places. "That's good to hear, Devin. I'm glad everything is working out."

He pulled out his wallet and took out the cash for the food along with a slightly larger tip than usual. "Tell your dad I'll be by sometime next week with the truck. Need an oil change and some new tires, okay?"

Devin passed him the food and accepted the money. "Sure thing, Cole. Can't wait to attend the summit. You're going, right?"

Cole shook his head. "Not this time, Dev. Maybe next time."

Frowning, Devin tipped his head. "But why? Don't you want to find your mate?"

I already have, Cole thought but kept it to himself. "I'm not worried about it. Besides, I doubt my mate is there."

"Why do you think your mate won't be there? Do you think it's not a good idea to attend the summit?" Devin fidgeted. "Mom is worried the other pack may not be open to us being wolves. Are you worried about the same thing?"

"No!" Cole denied. "Not at all, Devin. I have a lot of stuff going on right now and can't take the time away. I promise you it is definitely worth it to go."

Devin still had the shine of skepticism on his face. Cole set the food on the small table near the door and stepped closer to Devin. He reached out a hand and cupped the nape of Devin's neck. "It'll be okay, Devin. You know I would never lie to you or put you in any danger. As future Alpha, it is my duty to protect you just as it is my father's."

Devin nodded, the doubt fading from his expression. "Everyone will miss you, Cole."

"I—"

A strange noise hit Cole's ears, and Cole frowned. Devin's eyes widened as he stared at something next to Cole's shoulder. Cole turned to see Kai standing in the door of the hallway, darkness on his features. The noise issued again from Kai. The sound had a dangerous element. "Kai?"

Devin stumbled away from Cole. "Uh… I'll see you later, Cole."

Devin scurried to his car, and Cole could hear the tires scrambling for purchase on the gravel as Devin tore out of the driveway. Cole shut the front door, never taking his gaze from Kai. "What's wrong, kit?"

"Who was that?" Kai snarled, eyes flashing between human and fox. Sharp fangs glistened in the overhead light, Kai's animal very close to the surface.

"A pack member. He delivered the food, and we were talking about the summit." Cole moved closer to Kai, unafraid of his slender mate, more fascinated by what he saw before him. If he didn't know any better he'd swear Kai was jealous. "Did he frighten you?"

Cole stopped a foot from Kai and waited, carefully watching Kai's expression.

CHAPTER TWELVE

WHEN THE sound of Cole talking to someone had first penetrated Kai's stupor over the beautiful images on the computer screen, he'd been too scared to leave Cole's room, but the longer the voices vibrated against his eardrums, the more curious he grew. He'd gathered his courage and left the safety of Cole's room. The sight of Cole standing in the doorway with his hand on some stranger, the look almost intimate, had caused a sharp pain in Kai's chest. But the pain had dissolved into rage. How dare Cole touch someone else? Cole had sworn they were mates, hadn't he? Wasn't being mates supposed to mean something? His fox chattered furiously in his head, demanding Kai set him free to rip off the pretty blond boy's balls with his sharp teeth.

He hadn't even realized he'd made any noise until Cole turned to look at him. Satisfaction and the urge to give chase shot through him when the boy turned and ran to his car, obviously intimidated by Kai. When Cole asked him if the other man had scared him, Kai glared at him, offended at the same time as furious. "Why were you touching him?"

Cole stepped closer. "Does it matter?"

"Yes, it matters!" Kai snapped.

"Why?"

Kai froze, chest heaving from his rage. Why did he care so much? His fox made a high-pitched, aggressive sound inside his head as he thought about Cole being close to someone else. He cared because… because Cole belonged to them. The idea caused Kai's heart to pound against his rib cage harder than it had the first time he'd ever stolen into someone's home to rob them of their valuables for his uncle. "I-I…."

Cole moved until they were mere inches from each other. Kai almost gasped when Cole cupped his chin and tilted his head up. "Were you jealous, kit?" Cole murmured, rubbing his thumb along the line of Kai's jaw.

"No," Kai croaked.

"Liar," Cole accused softly before covering Kai's mouth with his.

Kai did gasp this time, his lips parting on a swift intake of breath, allowing Cole access in the process. Cole's tongue surged inside, filling Kai, only to dart away before Kai could taste Cole in return. A whimper broke free, and Kai grabbed the front of Cole's shirt, fearful Cole would leave him wanting… wanting *what*, he didn't understand, but he tangled his fingers in the soft material of the T-shirt and held on tight. "Cole," Kai begged.

Cole slid one strong arm around Kai's waist while cupping Kai's cheek in the other hand. "I've got you, kit," Cole rumbled before diving in for another kiss.

A heavy warmth settled between Kai's thighs, causing his cock to harden and his balls to throb with the need for release. He eagerly opened his mouth, accepting the erotic thrust of Cole's tongue, this time meeting it with a tentative swipe of his own. Cole's low groan vibrated all the way into Kai's chest, and Kai loosened his death grip on the shirt to wrap his arms around Cole. Kai whimpered when Cole nipped at his bottom lip, mind fuzzy and pulse pounding in his ears, blocking out everything except the scent of Cole in his nostrils and the taste of him on his tongue.

He couldn't have said how long Cole ravaged his mouth. All he knew when Cole stopped was that he didn't want him to. He chased after Cole's lips, but Cole prevented him from his goal by cuddling Kai close to his shoulder. Cole struggled for breath, every ragged indrawn gasp shuddering through Cole's large frame. Did he really affect Cole to such an extent? The idea caused butterflies in Kai's stomach, and he unconsciously nuzzled close to Cole's throat.

Cole moaned and tightened his arms around Kai. "Kai," he rasped.

Kai brushed an openmouthed kiss over the pulse point at the base of Cole's neck. He drew in deep drafts of Cole's delicious fragrance, the rich, earthy smell calling to his fox on a profound level. Flicking his tongue out, he tasted the salty, smooth skin.

"Fuck!" Cole howled, and Kai found himself pressed against the wall beside the bar separating the kitchen from the living room, blanketed by Cole's larger, harder body.

Cole shoved his thigh between Kai's legs while running his hands down the sides of Kai's body and around to cup Kai's ass. Kai squeaked in surprise, but he didn't get a chance to voice any possible objection because Cole's mouth captured his again, demanding and urgent. Kai opened under the onslaught, a moan slipping free as he ground against Cole's thigh. He grasped at Cole in the rising storm, anxious for an anchor before he could be swept under, unable to find the surface again. Cole's kiss grew more passionate, eager, and hungry the longer it went on, and surprise crashed through Kai when Cole lifted him up to fit himself between Kai's legs. Apprehension began to set in, and Kai gripped Cole's shoulders, pushing at him a little, trying to break the kiss to protest. Only Cole didn't notice. Kai's nervousness deepened, and he grew more frantic, shoving harder and struggling to turn his head.

When Kai began to cry, his tears seemed to bring Cole to his senses. Cole pulled away, dazed at first, and then horror dawned over his handsome features. "Kai," Cole managed to gasp as he lowered Kai to his feet. "I-I'm sorry. I...."

Cole stepped away from Kai, running a trembling hand through his hair. Disgust and bitterness twisted his lips. Kai didn't know how he remained standing, his legs weak and shaky, but he wasn't afraid of Cole despite his reaction to the hot make-out session mere moments ago. He reached out a hand toward Cole, but Cole moved even farther away from him.

"Don't," Cole said angrily. "I'm sorry, kit. I didn't... I...."

He broke off whatever he'd been about to say, spun on his heel, and slammed down the hallway and out of the house. A piercing, mournful howl seconds later broke Kai's heart, and he raced toward the door, knowing he was too late to catch Cole but needing to try anyway. An empty moonlit yard met Kai when he reached the open door, and Kai closed his eyes, sagging against the wall to sink down to the floor. He hadn't meant to hurt Cole, but everything had been moving too fast. He'd never even kissed someone until Cole. The idea of anything more had terrified him, but at the same time Kai knew he wanted Cole. He needed to explain to Cole, to make Cole understand what he felt, but Kai wasn't even sure he understood it himself.

Kai remained by the door for hours, never moving, watching the trees for Cole. The moon moved across the sky, constant in her bathing light, but Cole didn't appear. At some point, Kai began to nod off. His eyelids grew heavy, and he sensed he was falling asleep. He tried to stay awake but lost the battle sometime after midnight. What time it was when Cole returned, Kai didn't know, but he roused when he felt strong arms sliding beneath him, lifting him from the floor. He struggled to wake up, to tell Cole what he wanted to say, but he could do nothing more than grunt.

"Go back to sleep, kit," Cole's voice rumbled in his ear.

Kai mumbled something unintelligible, but he couldn't pull himself out of slumber enough to be cognizant of anything except Cole's broad chest beneath his cheek and the arms cradling him close as Cole carried him. Then the softness of his mattress welcomed him, and Kai knew no more until he awakened the next morning.

LIGHT STREAMED in the window, and Kai sat up, rubbing at his eyes. He glanced at the clock and saw it was already morning. Memories of the night before set in, and Kai shoved the blanket aside to scramble out of bed. He needed to find Cole, to make him understand.

He made a pit stop in the bathroom first and then continued on his hunt for Cole. Kai followed the smell of freshly brewed coffee and fried eggs toward the kitchen. He noticed the pizza boxes were gone from the table by the front door and wondered if they had been wasted. His stomach gave a loud growl as he remembered he hadn't eaten since lunch the previous day. He found Cole seated in the breakfast nook, sipping a mug of coffee, and he couldn't help noticing the dark circles under Cole's eyes and the way Cole wouldn't meet his gaze when Kai entered the kitchen. Cole stood and began preparing a plate of food for Kai. Ignoring everything else, Kai approached Cole, and when Cole turned toward him to offer the food, Kai stepped forward and wrapped his arms around Cole's waist. With a swift intake of breath, Cole tensed.

"What are you doing, kit?" Cole asked.

Kai laid his head on Cole's shoulder. "I'm sorry."

The tension in Cole's body eased, and Kai closed his eyes when Cole set the plate of food on the counter to return Kai's embrace. "For what?" Cole murmured.

"I wasn't afraid," Kai whispered.

Cole grunted. "Don't lie to me, kit. I should be whipped for what I did last night."

Kai made a horrified sound and stared at Cole. "No!" he protested. "I wasn't afraid, I swear. I...." He looked down at the dark green shirt Cole wore, noting how much it reminded him of Cole's eyes. "I've never...."

Cole took Kai's chin between thumb and forefinger and gently urged Kai's gaze to meet his. "I overwhelmed you."

"A little," Kai admitted. "I-I'm not scared of you, Cole," he added.

"I made you cry," Cole replied, his tone pained, eyes haunted.

Kai reached out to smooth away the lines of stress at the edge of Cole's brow. His fingers shook as he waited for rejection, but Cole leaned into his touch, eyelids lowering to half-mast with what Kai could only identify as pleasure. It fascinated Kai to be able to influence someone as powerful as Cole. He'd never take advantage of it, ever, but he couldn't understand how someone as beautiful, strong, and amazing as Cole could ever be hurt by him. He was insignificant, a nobody, a freak.

"I've never done any of those things before," Kai explained, "and everything moved faster than I knew how to handle. It's not your fault."

Cole tightened his arms around Kai. "I should have noticed you were upset. You never should have gotten to where you had to cry. I'm a selfish bastard."

"You are not! You're the kindest, most generous person I've ever met," Kai admonished. "Since my parents died, no one has cared whether I've eaten or even if I lived or died. I pushed you last night. You tried to stop, and I didn't want to. If anyone is at fault, it's me."

Leaning his forehead against Kai's, Cole sighed, the rush of breath fanning over Kai's cheeks, sending warmth through Kai's veins. "I never want to be a reason you cry, kit. Ever."

Kai's heart swelled, and a piece of the wall he'd erected over the years broke off and fell away. Swallowing hard, Kai managed a trembling smile and kissed Cole's cheek, breathing in the sandalwood and cinnamon smell he'd become familiar with around Cole. He opened his mouth to reply to Cole, but his stomach chose to growl at that moment, loudly. Kai flushed in embarrassment.

Cole chuckled and nuzzled Kai's temple. "Let's eat, okay? Then I challenge you to a rematch at *Need for Speed*."

Kai frowned. "But I kicked your butt yesterday."

"Big words when I couldn't concentrate because of a certain distraction."

Kai's breath hitched at the implication, and he hid a pleased smile as he stepped away to pick up his plate from the counter. "Sounds to me as if someone doesn't want to admit he lost fair and square."

Cole laughed out loud as he followed Kai to the table. "You keep telling yourself that, kit. We'll see how bad you kick my butt today, hmm?"

"You're on," Kai replied.

The conversation caused a shift in their relationship, and everything seemed to get easier. Kai found himself shying away from Cole less and less with every passing second. He caught himself studying Cole whenever Cole wasn't paying attention: his movements, the way his eyes crinkled at the corners when he laughed, the curve of his mouth when he smiled, the way the red in his hair shone in the right light, how his laughter rumbled in his chest, reminding Kai of the deep thrum of bass in a stereo, and the way he would catch Cole staring at him from the corner of his eye when Kai wasn't looking his direction. All of it caused his belly to tighten with warmth and his fox to chirp in satisfaction. Kai made the conscious decision not to worry about any of it and to accept the emotions and see what would happen. His fox wanted to be there, and his animal spirit had never steered him wrong before.

By lunch, they'd played several rounds of *Need for Speed*, and Cole had given Kai another guitar lesson. "You're picking it up fast," Cole praised when Kai finished.

Kai beamed. "Thanks."

"Are you hungry yet?"

He considered his belly for a moment and then shook his head. "Not yet."

Before Cole could say anything else, a knock sounded on the door, and Kai tensed, his momentary lapse into happiness forgotten. Cole placed a hand on his shoulder. "Relax, kit. It's just my mother."

Kai frowned. "How can you tell?"

Cole tapped his nose. "Scent."

"Oh." Kai still hadn't grown accustomed to using his sense of smell to identify others.

Cole squeezed his shoulder and released him before walking to the door to let his mother in. Kai didn't cower this time, merely watched with caution as the pretty redhead entered the house and greeted Cole with a huge hug. She turned to Kai and smiled. "Hello, Kai."

He nodded to return her greeting, never taking his eyes off of her as she moved farther into the living room.

"Did you tell Dad already?" Cole asked her.

Sara Ferris frowned. "I did. He wasn't thrilled, but he understands."

"Who knows? Maybe in six months at the next summit, things might be different."

Kai tried to interpret Cole's meaning, but he couldn't come up with anything. Guilt bit deep again. Cole wasn't going to the summit because of him. Before he thought twice about it, Kai blurted out, "I'll go with you."

Cole, who'd turned his back to Kai to speak with his mother, visibly tensed. He spun to look at Kai. "No, kit."

Regret had already begun to edge its way in, but Kai stiffened his spine. Setting his mouth in a determined line, Kai said, "I want to go."

Cole approached him and set his large hands on Kai's shoulders. "Are you sure, Kai? You know there are going to be dozens of people there. Other shifters."

He hesitated for a second. "Will you be staying in hotel rooms?"

"Lodges. To keep the possibility of any infighting, our pack will be staying in several on one side of the campus, and the other pack is staying in the other. We would have a private lodge, though. Just you and me."

Kai bit his lip, gathered his courage, and replied, "Then I can stay in the lodge for the duration of the summit."

Sara smiled. "See? It's all going to work out. Your father is going to be thrilled."

Cole still didn't appear convinced. He peered into Kai's eyes. "Tell me the truth, Kai. Why?"

"For you," Kai replied. "You've already made it clear you won't go without me. If I need to go in order for you to, then I will."

Cole huffed, but Kai could see a slight flush on Cole's cheeks. "You don't have to do it for me. I can always go to the next one."

Kai took Cole's hand between both of his. "I really want to."

Cole swept him up in a tight embrace, and he could sense Cole's emotions—sheer elation and something much deeper. Pride. Kai didn't understand how he could pick up on Cole's feelings or what Cole was proud of, but nothing mattered to Kai at that moment save making Cole happy. He had done so much for Kai already that to be able to do something for Cole in return seemed small in comparison.

"Thank you," Cole murmured near his ear.

Flushing, Kai kept his face burrowed against Cole's chest when Cole released him to continue the conversation with his mother. "I guess we're going to the summit."

"Magnificent! I'll let your father know. We've chartered a private jet for the trip, which means no worries about arrangements." Sara moved closer to them, and Kai tensed a bit. "Kai?"

He lifted his head to look at her. She held out her arms with a warm look on her face. "May I hug you?"

Kai started, but after a contemplative minute of silence, nodded. "Okay," he whispered, stepping away from Cole.

Sara slipped her arms around his body, and Kai forced himself to stand still as she tightened her hold briefly before letting him go. She reached up to touch his cheek. "You are going to be a wonderful mate for my son."

"Mom!" Cole admonished.

Kai widened his eyes at her as she moved away. He swallowed hard at the sudden weight on his shoulders of being considered Cole's mate. But hadn't he told himself he would give it a chance? For Cole? He hadn't thought much past the time they'd spent in Cole's home, to the future and what it might mean for him, for them. Cole would be Alpha one day. Kai couldn't imagine standing by Cole's side, not when his scars and the things he'd done made him hideous. He would never be good enough to be Cole's mate.

"What, sweetie? He is your mate. I'm not saying anything new or shocking." Sara pouted at Cole.

Cole gave her a look Kai couldn't interpret. "Just leave Kai be, Mom. Don't push anything on him, okay?"

"Me?" she asked in feigned surprise. "I would never!"

Skepticism shone clearly on Cole's features. "Uh-huh," he replied, tone derisive.

She rolled her eyes and shrugged her elegant shoulders. "Can't blame a mother for wanting the best for her son."

Kai winced. If she knew everything about his past, she wouldn't be saying he would make a great mate for Cole but rather chase him out of Cole's home and their pack territory.

"Ignore her, kit."

With a wan smile, he turned his gaze away from the both of them. The patterns in the flooring became interesting, and he stared at them while Cole and his mother continued to talk.

"We're leaving next Friday morning. Your father wants to get there before everyone else and make sure there are no issues with the reservations.

You know how things can be sometimes. We want to make sure we have the entire compound rented."

"I'll make sure we're ready on time. Are Kasey and Seth going this time?"

"I am pretty certain they are. Kasey wants to see his brother."

Cole grunted. "It's hard to believe they have such an outdated law. Thayne didn't do it on purpose."

Kai looked up at Cole, curious about Nick's mate and what he'd done. Cole must have seen the question on his face because Cole started explaining. "A few months ago, Thayne was exiled from his pack."

Kai frowned. What had Thayne done to cause them to throw him out?

"Thayne made a Created One."

"What's a Created One?" Kai asked, tilting his head a bit.

"It's when a born wolf completes a certain ritual and turns a human into a wolf."

Kai raised his eyebrows. He didn't know they could do such a thing. "What's wrong with making a human a wolf?"

"Created Ones are… unnatural, and they rely on their animal instincts more and more the longer they're wolf, to the point where they become dangerous," Sara interjected. "Not only could they expose us, but they also begin to crave flesh. Any flesh."

Shock and awe caused Kai to gape at Sara. He'd never considered eating a human, even in his fox form.

"In Thayne's pack to make a Created One is punishable by death or exile," Cole finished. "But in Thayne's case it wasn't intentional. He didn't know he'd turned a lover of his until later. It doesn't excuse the tragedy of the lives lost because of his mistake, but he did help destroy the Created One."

"Destroy?" Kai asked in horror. "You mean killed them?"

"Yes. There is no choice because eventually it will become too dangerous to remain alive and could even expose our kind."

"But—"

"We cannot risk humans finding out about us, kit," Cole interrupted him. "Or allow it to hurt innocent people. Our pack does not have such unbending rules as Thayne's old pack regarding mistakes made. We do not exile or put someone to death for making a mistake, but if someone does it intentionally, then they are punished and removed from the pack."

"Oh stop, Cole. You're scaring him," Sara admonished.

Kai shook his head. "No."

"There's no need to hide how you feel, Kai."

"I'm not scared. Just shocked."

Sara gave Kai a sympathetic glance. "I know it's a lot to take in, sweetie, but we aren't as ruthless as it sounds. You'll find we are mostly a peaceful lot unless provoked."

Kai remained silent, lost in thought about what he'd just learned. What if they found out about his past activities? Would they banish him as well? The idea of not being able to be with Cole sent a sharp pang to his chest. His fox chirruped at him in melancholy.

"My job is done here, then," Sara said. "Betas attending the summit will be meeting with your father this evening to discuss rules and what to expect from the other pack. I really think you should be there. Hopefully both of you, but I understand if being around so many people might be overwhelming, Kai."

A shudder wound its way through Kai at the idea. "I think I'll stay here."

Sara embraced him again before he could protest, and then she was on her way out of the house. Kai stared after her as the front door closed behind her. She reminded him of a whirlwind, fierce and wild.

"Don't worry. You'll get used to my mother's ways," Cole said as if reading his mind.

"I've never met anyone like her," Kai replied honestly.

Cole smiled. "She's definitely one of a kind. I wouldn't change a thing about her."

Butterflies tickled Kai's innards with warmth at Cole's affectionate grin. He turned his head to hide the flush warming his cheeks.

"Let's get something to eat, kit." Cole ruffled Kai's hair and turned toward the kitchen.

Kai trailed behind him, not all that hungry as he thought over the enormity of what he'd promised. At least he could remain in the lodge while there. What the hell had he gotten himself into?

CHAPTER THIRTEEN

COLE COULDN'T stop his worry for Kai from dominating his mind as he prepped a simple meal of soup and sandwiches for lunch. He could scarcely believe Kai even volunteered to go, but the idea of exposing Kai to a situation Cole knew would frighten Kai dimmed his joy at being able to attend the inaugural summit with his pack. The others would definitely be able to pick up Kai's distinct fragrance. Even remaining in the lodge wouldn't prevent them from scenting Kai's presence. He would need Nick and Thayne's help protecting Kai. They were the only ones who knew about Kai's true nature aside from his parents.

Neither of them spoke much during lunch. Cole wondered if Kai regretted his decision to go, but he didn't ask the question, letting it hang in the air between them. The afternoon went by fast afterward. Cole gave Kai his next guitar lesson before putting in a movie for the two of them to watch. After it ended, Cole made Kai a quick dinner and then put on his shoes and grabbed his keys and wallet. "Will you be all right on your own for a little while?"

"I'll be fine," Kai promised. "If it's okay, can I use your computer again?"

"You don't need to ask. This is your home too, kit."

"It's still your room."

Cole waved away his concerns. "Feel free to use the computer whenever you want, as much as you want."

"Thank you," Kai murmured.

"No worries, kit. I'll be home as soon as I can."

More than anything he wanted to have the right to kiss and hug Kai, but he restrained himself and patted Kai on the shoulder before leaving. The sun dipped below the horizon as Cole climbed into his truck, started the engine, and backed out of the driveway. He was uneasy leaving Kai alone, but he prayed to whatever ancestors he might have to watch over his mate while he tended to business.

There were already several other vehicles at the pack house when Cole arrived. He recognized Howard's red Ford F-150 and Wilson's black

Dodge Charger. They were his father's trusted Betas. Cole had known them since he'd been born, and both men were like family to him.

"Hello, Cole" came from his left, and Cole turned to see Nick standing there, hand entwined with Thayne's. They hadn't exactly parted on the best of terms the other day, despite Cole's apology for being such an ass.

"Nick, it's good to see you." Cole meant it. "Hey, Thayne."

Thayne offered his hand to Cole in greeting. "Cole."

"I'm surprised to see you here," Nick said.

"I'll be attending the summit," Cole replied, watching Nick to gauge his friend's reaction. Surprise registered on Nick's face. "Kai agreed to go."

"Really?"

"Yeah. Mom came by earlier today, and Kai volunteered to go. Except he'll be staying in the lodge for the duration."

"I'm happy for you, Cole," Nick replied.

Cole sighed. "I worry for him and his safety while we are there."

Nick frowned. "Why? You'll be there to protect him."

"Yes, I'll be there, but there will most likely be times I can't be with him. There's no chance someone will not pick up his scent, especially since we aren't mated."

"Are you sure it's wise to go, then?" Thayne asked. "Someone may challenge you for the right to mate with him or even challenge your right to lead this pack someday. They'll think you're weak for not being able to claim your mate."

Cole let out a fierce growl. "Let them challenge me. I'll take down anyone who dares to think they can."

Nick reached up and slapped Thayne on the shoulder. "Why the hell did you have to say that?"

"Because it's a reality!" Thayne protested. "The pack will see it as a failing on his part if he can't claim his mate."

Cole's vision shifted, and he blinked heavily, took a deep breath, and struggled to keep his wolf under control. "My pack mates would never believe such a thing. You must be speaking of your *former* pack and what they will assume of me. Do not underestimate my desire to claim Kai. They live under old laws, outdated ideas. Not giving in to my wolf and marking Kai as mine is the hardest thing I've ever done and takes more strength than anything I've ever withstood. Created Ones included."

Thayne flinched at the stress Cole placed on the word *former*. He clenched his hands at his sides. "I did not mean to insult you. I merely meant to give you warning of what may happen if they were to find out your situation."

Snarling, Cole tossed his head, sending several strands of auburn hair across his forehead. "They can try, but know this, anyone who dares to challenge me for Kai or the right to lead this pack will die."

Thayne blanched at the sheer power rolling off of Cole. He struggled to remain on his feet.

"Cole!" Nick grunted, also having trouble staying upright.

Cole closed his eyes and took several deep breaths to calm himself. The idea of anyone trying to take Kai away from him caused his entire being to vibrate with rage. After several moments, he regained control and reined in his instinctual need to tear someone's throat out. "Sorry," he muttered.

Nick wiped at the sweat on his forehead, his hand shaking a bit. "We just want to help, Cole. Thayne didn't mean anything by it."

Thayne swallowed visibly. "I'm sorry, Cole."

Heaving a sigh, Cole hung his head in shame. "No, I'm sorry. The whole situation has me and my wolf on edge. It's not an excuse for what I did, though."

Nick moved closer and set his hand on Cole's shoulder. "Believe me, I understand."

Cole reached up and set his hand on Nick's, squeezing in thanks before letting go. He straightened up and lifted his head higher. "I know I don't have the right after being an ass yesterday, but I wanted to ask you both to help me watch over him while we're at the summit."

"Of course!" Nick exclaimed. "No matter what, I'm still your friend and will stand by you."

Relief washed over Cole. "Thank you."

Thayne gave Cole a brief nod. "We'll be there for you."

"I'm more grateful than you can know." Cole looked up at the house. "Let's get in there, I guess."

The three of them entered the pack house and headed to the back deck. At least half of the pack stood outside, looking at Cole's father, waiting to hear what was expected of them at the summit. Cole joined his mother off to the side while Nick and Thayne trotted down the deck stairs to be with the others.

"Everyone knows why we're here," Elijah began. "Next week we will travel to Bear River Lodge in Kamas, Utah. We have reserved most of the available property, but some of you will have to bunk together in order to accommodate everyone attending the summit. Sara has put together an assignment list for each of you to make it easier. You will be able to shift and run as you wish, but still, remain alert to the possibility of humans in the area."

He paused for a breath. "The Senaka pack will be extremely skittish at first. Until Thayne's brother met our previous pack mate Seth Davies, they believed they were the only true-born wolves. We are meeting on neutral territory to try to reduce the aggression they might feel. I expect every single one of you to do your best to set their minds at ease. There will be no tolerance for fighting, posturing, or signs of aggression from anyone attending. Is there anything unclear about those rules?"

Everyone nodded almost in unison.

"If someone should happen to find their mate this time around, approach the situation with care. Your true mate may not be as receptive right away as you are."

Sara stepped forward to take Elijah's hand. "We must remember the purpose of this summit is about opening more doors to finding our other halves as well as building the foundation of peace and trust between us and the Senaka pack."

There were a number of murmurs among the members, but Cole sensed they were all good things. Until one person asked, "Are the rumors true? Has Cole found his mate?"

Cole started in surprise. The only ones who'd known about Kai were his parents, Nick, Thayne, and Julie. How had anyone found out? His father turned toward him with a question in his eyes. Cole took a deep breath and moved to his father's side. "Yes, it's true."

"Where are they? Why haven't we met them?" another pack member shouted from the crowd.

"My mate has been through a lot in a short number of years. He is still recovering from a traumatic experience. One day I will present him to you." Cole hoped he told the truth about introducing Kai to everyone.

"Why can't we meet him now?"

"What's wrong with him?"

"Are you still attending the summit?"

Questions came from several directions. Cole held up a hand. "I know you're all curious, but I ask you, please respect my request for privacy for now. When the time is right, I will bring him in front of the pack. Yes, I will be at the summit."

Cole could see a number of the others were skeptical, while some radiated disappointment. He knew the pack didn't understand. All he could do was pray to the ancestors he would be able to give them what they wanted sooner rather than later.

His father spoke up once more. "Please see Sara before you leave in order to get your airline ticket. If anyone has to change their flight time or cannot go, make sure you let Sara or myself know."

The crowd dispersed, some heading immediately inside to meet Sara and others milling around the yard talking among themselves. Cole glanced at his watch anxiously. He'd been away from Kai for over an hour, and it felt wrong. "I need to go," he told his father.

"Go. Take care of your mate. The pack can wait to meet him until he's ready."

Cole hugged his father tightly. "I love you, Dad."

"Love you too, son. Now go on. Meet us here Friday morning at ten."

"We'll be here," he replied before hurrying into and through the house and out the front door to his vehicle, wishing he could be sure once and for all that Kai wouldn't run.

The trip home seemed interminable, and he couldn't stop the sigh he let out when he turned his truck into the driveway. He caught sight of Kai peeking out of the front window as he shut off the engine. A smile edged its way over Cole's lips at seeing his mate waiting for him. Cole jumped out of the truck, shut the door, and rushed into the house. Kai had sat down on the couch by then, but Cole couldn't resist the urge to scoop Kai up and into his arms. "I missed you," he murmured into Kai's dark locks.

His heart tripped a beat when Kai returned the embrace. "Did everything go okay?" Kai asked once Cole released him.

"Everything went fine. We will meet my parents at their home Friday morning and fly out shortly after."

Cole sensed Kai's instant fear, and he frowned. "Are you sure you're ready for this, kit?"

Kai nodded. "I can do it."

"Okay. I won't ask again, but promise me the second you're uncomfortable, you'll let me know."

"I promise."

"Good. Now, let's get some dinner going, okay?"

THE DAYS leading up to the summit were spent wholly with Kai. Cole made it a point to start telling Kai about the pack members and showing him pictures to ease his transition into meeting everyone. He also told Kai more about himself, dying to ask questions about Kai as well, but he knew he needed to be patient and wait for Kai to trust him enough to tell him about his past. Someday Kai would tell him everything.

Kai's new clothing arrived two days after it was ordered, and Cole couldn't help but smile when Kai tried to hide his excitement. He knew Kai still felt bad Cole had spent money on him, and he guessed Kai didn't want to appear too eager because of it. The clothing was a little loose on Kai, but Cole had ordered a size bigger to accommodate Kai gaining weight. Pride at being able to provide for Kai made him more hopeful things would work out over time.

They continued the guitar lessons, but Cole had the notion Kai would prefer art supplies and bought several things from Amazon: colored pencils, charcoal, a sketchpad, paints, brushes, and a couple of small canvases. He couldn't wait to give them to Kai. They would arrive while they were gone to the summit, unfortunately, but Cole could surprise Kai with them when they got home.

Kai's wariness of him seemed to be dying away, and he no longer jumped out of his skin whenever Cole touched him or entered the room. Kai's expression would light up whenever he saw Cole, and Cole hoped it meant their bond was growing stronger with each moment they spent together. Every day found Cole more and more reluctant to let Kai disappear into his room each night alone. He wanted to wake up with Kai in his arms, see Kai's face on the pillow next to his, and know without a doubt Kai would never leave him.

Cole found it difficult to sleep the night before they were due to leave for the summit. He eventually gave up around four in the morning and got out of bed. He listened for Kai's heartbeat and found the steady rhythm he knew better than his own by now. After stuffing his feet into a pair of beat-up sneakers, Cole slid on a T-shirt and left his room.

The rest of the house remained silent as he let himself out the back door. He made the short walk to his first greenhouse by the last sliver of the waning moon. Maybe the soil would calm his nerves about the summit and Kai being there. He flicked on the lights as he entered before breathing in deep. The fresh, overturned soil around newly planted vegetables tickled his nostrils, and Cole smiled. Even after all this time, he still enjoyed the scent. It humbled him and reminded him of what he did for his pack and the local businesses.

Organic veggies and fruit grown without chemicals were becoming more popular. Still, many foods were treated, injected, or made with some sort of substance that made people sick, fat, or unhealthy overall. Cole tried his best not to ingest anything he didn't grow himself.

Grabbing a small trowel, Cole made his way over to one of the half-planted soil beds and, after checking what Julie had already started planting there, began to dig several evenly spaced holes, in which he planted seeds. Light had started to fill the sky when Cole unwrapped the hose from the wall and turned on the faucet. He sprayed a light mist over the area until the soil darkened and grew damp. He didn't want to overwater them as that would ruin the freshly sown seeds.

The sound of the greenhouse door creaking open surprised Cole. He turned and found Kai standing inside. "Hey, kit. It's a little early to be out of bed."

Kai shrugged. "I couldn't sleep anymore."

Cole smiled. "Neither could I. Nervous about the summit?"

Kai looked away from Cole. "A little."

Cole turned off the hose and wrapped it around its rack. "Just remember I'll be there, kit. I'll never let anything happen to you."

He saw Kai nibbling at his bottom lip and approached him. "Do you trust me, Kai?"

Without hesitation Kai nodded.

"Then trust I will protect you, and my parents will too. No one there will hurt you."

Kai fingered the leaf of a still-growing tomato plant. "Okay," he murmured.

"Let's go get dressed and eat something. We have to be at my parents' place by ten."

Cole turned off the lights on their way out. They wouldn't be needed during the day, and Julie and the others would be there soon to start their shift.

When the two of them entered the house, Cole went to his room while Kai headed to his. They met in the kitchen about forty minutes later, fresh from showers and ready to head out after eating. It was just after nine thirty when they placed the bags they'd packed the night before into the bed of Cole's truck and climbed into the front seat. Kai sat huddled as close to the door as possible, looking terrified out of his mind. Cole didn't know if his mate could handle this as well as he'd said he could. "One last chance to back out, kit," Cole said quietly.

The only noises in the cab were those of the wheels on the asphalt and their combined breathing. Cole heard the audible sound of Kai swallowing, hard. "No."

Tightening his hands on the wheel, Cole wished with all his heart he could take away whatever in his past made Kai afraid of everything. He still didn't know the truth of Kai's history, but he had a feeling when Kai did finally open up to him, he would want to find the person or persons who had done Kai wrong and rip them into bloody pieces.

He reached out and grabbed Kai's hand, pressing it to his right thigh and holding on tight. "Whatever you need, tell me. Okay? I'll make it happen, no matter what."

Kai gave his hand a slight squeeze in response.

They arrived at the pack house a little before ten. Cole's mother stood on the front porch, waiting for them. She smiled the instant Cole pulled into the driveway, but she remained standing at the top of the steps as if she knew Kai would need space and didn't want to crowd him. Cole released Kai's hand and opened his door. "Ready?"

Kai took a visible breath and reached for his own door handle. They met in front of the truck, and Kai immediately took Cole's hand again, much to Cole's surprise. As they approached the porch, he saw his mother's gaze flick downward and then away, a small smile teasing her lips.

"Hello, Kai. How are you?"

"Okay, I guess," Kai said.

She reached out to touch his cheek. "Everything will be all right."

"Where's Dad?" Cole asked.

"He's on the phone with Howard, going over some last-minute instructions."

"They aren't flying with us?" Cole frowned.

"No. Your father figured it would be best if we traveled with just the four of us. They'll join us tomorrow with everyone else."

Before Cole could respond, his father came out of the screen door. He came forward and stopped next to Sara. "Hello, Kai," he greeted gently.

Kai moved closer to Cole and managed a nod in return. "Kai, this is my father, Elijah Ferris. Dad, this is Kai, my true mate."

"I've heard quite a bit about you. Cole tells me you can draw."

Kai shrugged. "A little."

"*Pfft*," Cole scoffed. "More than a little, kit. You're beyond talented."

Flushing, Kai looked at the ground.

"Oh stop, you're embarrassing him," Sara chided. "Let's get your bags into the car and we'll head to the airport. Gives us time to get a coffee and talk."

"Sure thing, Mom." Cole tried to step away from Kai, but Kai refused to let go and remained glued to his arm while he grabbed the bags from the bed of the truck. He brought them over to his father's SUV and tossed them into the cargo area. He helped Kai into the back seat and slid in beside him.

Kai stared around in awe at the inside of the vehicle. "It's my dad's pride and joy," Cole said. "He got it less than a year ago and is still demanding people take off their shoes to ride in her."

With a squeak, Kai bent to remove his shoes, and Cole chuckled out loud and stopped Kai. "I was teasing, kit."

"Don't let him fool you, Kai," Sara interjected from the front seat. "My husband is most assuredly protective of his girl, but you don't have to remove your sneakers."

Kai gave Cole an exasperated look. "You're mean."

Laughing again, Cole replied, "I'm sorry. I didn't think you'd take it so seriously."

It warmed Cole's heart to see Kai open up at least a little with his parents around. Kai rolled his eyes and folded his arms over his chest in an adorable pout. "How would I know you were kidding?"

"Because he didn't take off his before he got in the car," Elijah answered.

154

Cole slid closer to Kai and put his arm over the back of the seat behind Kai. "You mad at me, kit?"

Kai looked at Cole for a moment from the corner of his eye and then dropped his pout. "No."

Cole chatted with his parents the remainder of the trip to the airport while Kai stayed quiet. The closer to the airport they got, the more edgy Kai became, leaving him twisting his hands together in his lap. Setting his hands on top of Kai's, Cole leaned in and whispered, "Relax, kit. I'll be by your side the entire time."

Kai gave a wan smile and turned his hand upward to link fingers with Cole. "I don't mean to be such a pain."

"You aren't. Someday you'll feel comfortable enough to tell me what happened to you, but until then we'll take it one step at a time." Cole squeezed Kai's hand in comfort.

Ten minutes later they arrived at the airport in Redwood City, and after his father located a spot in the parking lot for private charters, they headed inside. It was a lot calmer than the commercial airport, and only a few others were waiting for their own flights. Cole led Kai to a seat and urged him down into it.

"Can I get you anything? Chips or a drink?" Cole asked.

Kai shook his head. "I'm not hungry."

Cole didn't press the issue even though Kai still needed to add on several pounds to be at a healthy weight. He figured nerves kept Kai from being interested in food. "We'll get you something when we get to Utah," Cole said.

Elijah checked in with the desk and then guided Sara to seats near Cole and Kai. Cole casually chatted with his parents while keeping an arm around Kai. A couple of people looked at them with distaste, which Cole ignored, not caring what strangers thought of him or his holding on to Kai. When a man finally came to advise them they were ready to board, Kai tensed again, and Cole squeezed Kai's shoulders in a reassuring manner and stood, holding his hand out to Kai who took it right away.

A few moments later, they were buckled into their seats. Cole had urged Kai to the window seat, so he could be on the outside to offer a shield of sorts to his mate. The flight to Utah passed without incident, though Kai did remain on edge throughout the entire time. They landed in Salt Lake City where they rented a car to drive the remaining 120 miles to Bear Lake

Lodges. Kai fell asleep on the hour and a half drive, slumping into Cole's side at one point, resting his head on Cole's shoulder.

When Bear Lake came into view, Cole took note of the awe-inspiring view, his keen senses picking up the multiple scents of prey in the area, the clean smell of fresh water, and the tall grasses nearby. "Wow, great choice here, Dad."

"Thanks, son. I came here once a couple decades ago and thought it might be a great place for this. Neutral territory and lots of space between the rentals. I figured it best to do this in the off-season and to rent out as many of the lodges as possible. There might be a stray human or two, which means we will still need to be careful, but I think we'll be fine overall."

After a quick stop for his father to check in at the gatehouse and grab the keys, they continued toward the lodges. They pulled up in front of a sprawling two-story cabin, the façade fashioned from logs with tree bark for the trim. Trees surrounded the property, but there was plenty of open space for the younger pups to play in.

"Where are Kai and I staying?" Cole asked.

"There's a small place up the hill behind the lodge. This is where our pack will be staying, and about half a mile to the west, there's another large cabin the Senaka pack will reside in."

His father put the rental in Park in front of the house while Cole gently shook Kai's shoulder. "Time to wake up, kit." Kai muttered and burrowed his face harder against Cole's arm. Cole chuckled and tried again, cupping Kai's cheek with his other hand. "Come on, baby. Open your eyes. You can rest in our cabin, okay?"

Kai snuffled and then opened his eyes, peering at Cole for a second in confusion. Cole wished the innocent expression would remain on Kai's features, but it faded away and remembrance set in, along with trepidation. "Sorry," Kai murmured and sat up, rubbing at his eyes to clear the sleep out of them.

"No worries," Cole replied. "Let's get our stuff together and we'll head up to our place and get settled in. Tonight we'll have dinner with my parents and tomorrow we'll be on our own."

"Okay."

They got out of the rental and grabbed their bags from the back. Cole took the key from his father and headed in the direction of the smaller cabin. Kai followed behind at a slower pace. Their cabin had three rooms:

a bedroom with a decent-sized bathroom, a kitchenette, and a small living area. A huge king-size bed dominated the bedroom. "There's only one bed," Kai whispered.

"I'll sleep on the couch," Cole said while placing Kai's suitcase on the bed. "It'll be fine."

Skeptically, Kai peered into the living room at the barely love-seat-sized couch. "You're too tall and won't fit."

"I will in my wolf form," Cole replied easily. "Do you want to take a shower while I unpack?"

"I can put my stuff away."

"I'll do it. Try to relax for a bit. We'll head over to the other lodge in a couple hours for dinner."

Kai shook his head. "I'd rather be doing something than just sitting."

Cole wanted to insist but held his tongue. He didn't want to crowd Kai's need for independence. He could sense Kai's nervousness, and he figured if something as simple as putting his own clothing away gave Kai even a small slice of peace, Cole didn't want to argue. "Sure, kit."

They worked in tandem in silence. Cole took the top two drawers in the dresser for his underwear, socks, and tanks. The jeans went into the second drawer, and he hung his shirts in the closet. Kai took longer, but Cole didn't rush him. He sat on the bed and leaned against the headboard, watching Kai slowly fold a few items for the dresser. "When we get home, we'll have to see about getting you some more clothes. The new stuff is great, but I think you could use some more jeans and maybe some shorts for the hotter weather."

"What? No. I'm fine. I don't need anything else."

Cole snorted. "You scarcely have enough to get through a few days without needing to do laundry."

"I-I don't want you to keep buying me things."

"You still don't understand, do you?" Cole replied and stood from the bed to approach Kai. He set his hands on Kai's shoulders. "You're my mate."

"But—"

"You're my mate. It means I take care of you. No matter what you need, I will get it for you."

"I feel as though I have nothing to give you in return."

Cole smiled and brushed a light kiss over Kai's head. "You have no idea how much you've given me already."

"What have I given you?" Kai asked. "I've hurt you more than once. You almost disappointed your parents because of me. I don't see how I could possibly have given you anything."

"It's okay. You don't have to see. Just know when I tell you something, I mean it."

Kai still appeared skeptical, but he gave a small nod. "Okay."

"Good. Now, let's take a look around the rest of this place and then head over to dinner with my parents."

They took their time checking out the cabin before following the same path back to where the rest of the pack would be staying. His father already had the grill fired up and had steaks ready to go on for a minor searing. Cole grabbed a soda for Kai and a beer for himself. Sara led Kai away from the two of them to help her set the table. While keeping an eye on Kai, Cole asked his father, "I would assume the Alpha of the Senaka pack is attending as well?"

"Jeremiah, yes. He'll be here with his mate, his son Kasey, whom you've met, and of course, Seth."

Seth, their former pack Rho, had mated the Alpha-to-be, Kasey Whitedove. They'd had a tumultuous mating as well. Kasey had been extremely prejudiced against white men and didn't believe Seth could be his mate. Kasey almost lost Seth when a crazed wolf from Seth's past had kidnapped him, determined to never let him go. Thankfully, Kasey rescued Seth at the last moment and came to his senses about their mating.

Cole had met Kasey and trusted his instincts that Kasey was a good man. Even though Cole hadn't grown up with Seth because of Seth's parents moving around all over the country, he still felt responsible for him as another member of his pack. Kasey had proven to be a great mate since their brush with tragedy, and Cole was thankful Seth had found an honorable man like Kasey.

"You think his father regrets exiling Thayne?" Cole asked.

Elijah sighed. "What man wouldn't regret having to hurt his son in such a way? As a father I can't fathom doing something so gut-wrenching, but as an Alpha, I can understand why he did it. To show weakness in any form leaves his position open to challengers who intend great harm to the pack. If he lost, the pack would suffer exponentially."

Staring at the horizon where the sun hung low over the trees, Cole took a sip of his beer. "I don't know if I would have the strength to do something so painful to my own son. To choose the pack over blood... seems harsh and heartless."

Elijah flipped a couple of the steaks. "As Alpha you have to make the hard decisions, to do what's right for the many, not the few. Even if it means hurting someone you love."

"Would you have chosen the pack over me or even Mom?"

"I know I love you and your mother with all my heart. The idea of choosing the pack over her or you seems unfathomable. Sara is my true mate. You are my only son. I wouldn't want to give up either of you for the world. I would most likely choose to step down and allow you to take over."

"You'd give up being Alpha?" Cole asked, shocked.

"If it's the best path I could take for the good of the pack and my family."

"Do you judge Jeremiah harshly for doing what he did?"

"No. He did what he felt best for his people. Thayne broke their laws, and if he hadn't upheld the law, they would have lost faith in him as their Alpha, which leads to unrest and possibly further problems among the pack."

"I see," Cole murmured.

"See what?" Sara asked, walking up to slide her arm through Cole's.

"Just discussing some pack stuff," Elijah answered.

She seemed to take the hint in Elijah's words and didn't press for more details. "The table is all set."

Cole glanced around for Kai and frowned when he didn't see him. "Where's Kai?"

"He went to use the restroom, baby. Try not to worry. Nothing is going to happen to him here."

The idea of possibly dozens of unmated shifters around his mate set his teeth on edge already. Not having Kai in sight at all times only increased his agitation. "I think I'll go check on him."

"Really, he's fine," Sara chided, but Cole ignored her and headed inside anyway.

CHAPTER FOURTEEN

KAI ZIPPED up his jeans and moved over to the sink to wash his hands. The bathroom in the big lodge was quite nice. A huge shower stall lined one wall, with multiple showerheads, and the same rustic decorations were set about in a random yet cohesive pattern. His hands shook as he dried them, and he curled his fingers into his palms. He wouldn't be meeting the people arriving tomorrow. He'd be safely ensconced in the cabin up the hill, but that still didn't settle the gut-twisting butterflies wreaking havoc on his insides.

Looking in the mirror, he could see his fox gleaming through in anxiety. To wolves, his kind were prey, something to be hunted. The idea of being around strangers who were also wolf shifters made every nerve ending tingle with fear and incited the desperate desire to run and hide before they got there. Despite his instincts screaming at him to leave immediately, Kai trusted Cole to protect him. Cole would never let anything happen to him.

The thought of Cole calmed his nerves dramatically, and Kai smiled—a small lift of his lips, but he reached up and touched the curves of his mouth. It had been so long since he'd truly had anything to be happy about, and the expression felt almost foreign to him. He dropped his hand to the counter and leaned in closer to the mirror, studying his features. Did Cole truly want him? The skinny little nobody with pale skin and enough baggage to weigh down a thousand men? What would Cole do if he knew Kai wasn't a good person? If he knew how Kai had stolen from people for his uncle?

Huffing, he shoved away from the mirror and yanked open the bathroom door. Kai stopped in surprise when he saw Cole standing there, ready to knock. "Cole," he breathed.

Cole let his arm return to his side. "Everything okay?"

Kai nodded. "I'm fine."

"Dinner is almost ready. You ready to eat?"

"Sure."

Cole grabbed Kai's hand and entwined their fingers together. He hesitated and looked at Kai again. "My wolf is already on edge about this

160

weekend, Kai. Knowing there will be unmated wolves and our own bond is incomplete, I need you to stay in the cabin unless I'm with you, okay?"

"Okay."

Smiling, Cole lifted Kai's hand to his lips and pressed a kiss to the back. "Thank you."

Kai had no intention of leaving the cabin during the time they were there. He'd have enough trouble controlling his fox's instinctive need to hide once the other wolves arrived. Cole led him out to the house, where Elijah and Sara were already sitting at the table, waiting on them to start eating. It hit Kai hard. They looked like a family, one that wanted Kai to be a part of it. Blinking heavily, Kai slid onto the bench next to Cole.

"You okay, Kai?" Sara asked, a frown on her face.

"I'm fine," he managed to say, his voice husky with emotion.

He could tell Sara wanted to question him further, but she accepted his word and moved on. The conversation flowed around him for a little while as he ate, distracted by his earlier realization. Eventually he heard his name.

"Kai?"

Looking up, he saw all three of them watching him. He flushed. "Sorry."

Cole placed his hand on Kai's knee. "You seem as though you're not here. Are you worried about tomorrow?"

"Oh no. I'm fine!"

"Are you sure, honey?" Sara questioned.

"Yes, I'm sure. I think I'm just tired," Kai fibbed.

"Do you want to go and lie down?" Cole asked.

Shaking his head, Kai said, "Not yet."

"I hoped you could tell me more about what you know about your parents and your shifter history," Elijah said.

Kai tensed. "Not much at all. My parents didn't tell me anything except only my mother could shift. I didn't understand what that meant until I shifted, and even then, I didn't know much."

"They never told you where your family came from? If there were other fox shifters?" Sara asked.

"No. Mom had no other family."

"Your father was human?"

Kai nodded.

"What about any of his family? Did they know about your mother?"

He clenched his fingers around his fork, hoping his distress didn't show. "No, no family either," he mumbled. No way would he tell them about Jerrod.

Elijah hummed in disappointment. "I admit you are the first of your kind we have encountered. I wasn't naïve or vain enough to believe wolves were the only shifters, of course, but we've never come across another before now. I did inquire among some other Alphas I have connections with, but their answers were pretty much the same as ours."

Kai shrugged. He didn't have anything else to tell them.

"I assume you were adopted after your parents died?" Sara asked.

Sara's question was unexpected, and Kai stiffened, sweat breaking out over his brow. He tried to swallow, but his throat felt so tight the saliva didn't want to go down. A loud buzzing noise reverberated in his ears, and he could barely catch his breath. The sound of Cole's voice filtered through the static, and Kai leaned closer to Cole, who wrapped an arm around Kai's shoulders.

"Mom, enough. He doesn't want to talk about his past."

"I'm sorry, sweetie. I didn't mean to upset him. I didn't mean to pry, Kai."

Kai turned his face toward Cole's chest and breathed in deep, the scent of earth flooding his senses. The warmth of Cole's body and the smell of his familiar musk sent waves of calm through Kai. "It's okay, kit. I've got you," Cole said, rubbing a hand over Kai's bicep.

"I'm sorry," Kai whispered.

"There's nothing to be sorry for."

Without lifting his head from Cole's chest, Kai looked at Sara, apologetic. She smiled at him and reached out a hand to touch the one still gripping his fork on the table. "You never have to talk about anything you don't want to, honey. We're your family now, and whatever it is, we'll understand."

Tears stung Kai's eyes as he stared at Sara. He'd been without anyone in his court for years, and the idea of having a family again overwhelmed him. "Thank you."

Sara squeezed his hand and then let go. "Let's finish dinner. I brought one of Jo's famous cheesecakes."

Cole nuzzled his chin against the crown of Kai's head. "Finish up, kit. Jo's cheesecake is to die for."

Kai swiped at his cheek, cleared his throat, and sat up straight. "I've never had cheesecake. What is it?"

Sara gasped and stared at Kai in shock. "Never had cheesecake? Oh my! You're in for a treat, then. It's the most sinful, amazing dessert on the planet."

"Is it made with cheese?" Kai asked.

Cole chuckled. "In a sense. It's made with cream cheese, sugar, and a few other ingredients."

"I look forward to trying it."

The conversation flowed around Kai again while they finished their meal. When Sara brought out the cake, Kai gazed at it in wonder. Several inches thick with fresh strawberries on top, the dessert smelled heavenly. His fox chirped its eagerness to taste the confection. Sara cut him a large slice, placed it on a plate, and passed it to him. He eagerly dug in, taking a huge forkful and stuffing it in his mouth. Creamy rich flavor exploded over his tongue, and he moaned, eyes closing in lust. Kai had never tasted anything as sinful or amazing.

He opened his eyes to see Sara and Cole watching him, bemusement on their features. Kai flushed, but took another bite, though a smaller one this time.

"You like it?" Cole asked.

"It's amazing," Kai answered when he'd managed to swallow.

Cole smiled. "I'll make sure we get more. There are other flavors we can try as well."

"There's more?" Kai asked in surprise.

"Lots more. Chocolate, cookies and cream, caramel, banana cream, too many to name."

Kai dropped his fork to his plate in astonishment. "Caramel? Really?"

"Is caramel your favorite?" Cole asked.

Kai nodded in excitement. "I didn't get to have it often, but I love caramel."

"Well we'll try that one first, then," Cole said, running his fingers over Kai's cheek before standing. "I'll help clear the dishes, Mom."

"Thanks, baby. Your father brought some of his favorite whiskey if you want to grab the bottle out of the bag by the front door."

Cole started stacking plates. Kai jumped up to help, but Cole waved his hand at him. "Don't worry, kit. I've got this."

"But I should help!" Kai protested.

"How can I impress you with my muscles if I let you help?" Cole said with a wink and a grin. He placed all their dinner plates onto the platter that had held their steaks and picked up the plate with the leftover cheesecake on it in the other hand. "Honestly, don't worry about it, kit. You just sit there and relax."

Kai sighed and sat down again as Cole went into the cabin with Sara. He stared at the scratches in the wood of the table, uncomfortable being left alone with Elijah.

"I don't want you to think you can't trust us, Kai," Elijah said. "Our pack would never let anything happen to you or judge you for your past. No matter what it is."

Biting the inside of his lip, Kai remained silent and kept his gaze on the table.

Elijah didn't press any further. Kai heard the rustle of fabric and glanced up under his eyelashes to see Elijah pull a cigar and a packet of matches out of his front shirt pocket. The door behind Kai opened, and Cole appeared at his side. This time he held two glasses and a bottle with brown liquid inside. The smell of alcohol hit his nostrils the second Cole opened the bottle. Flashbacks caused by the scent of it flashed through Kai's mind: his uncle's hot, disgusting breath in his face as he yelled at Kai for screwing up again, the feel of his uncle's fists slamming into his face and body, and Jerrod tossing liquor on him and threatening to set him on fire because he hadn't found anything worth a damn from a house he'd stolen from.

A whimper lodged itself in his throat as cigar smoke wafted over his face. Kai almost fell as he struggled to get off the bench. Cole asking him what was wrong brought Kai's attention to Cole, but Kai flinched away when Cole reached for him. The sound of a dish shattering on the floor and a loud curse from inside the house released the small cry Kai had stifled at first. Kai whirled on his feet and raced off toward the cabin he was sharing with Cole. "Kai!"

He didn't stop, running swift and terrified. The dark had no impact on his ability to see as he rushed up the hill to the front door. He shoved it open, went inside, and slammed it behind him. Kai darted into the bedroom, shifted, and hid under the bed. His body heaved with each shuddering breath, and tiny yips of fear rattled in his throat.

The sound of the front door sent Kai curling into an even tighter ball. He brought his tail over his face and tried to remain still. "Kai!"

Cole's voice sent a shiver through Kai. "Kai, are you in here?"

Kai wanted to give in to his animal self and go to Cole, but he couldn't bring himself to leave the safety of his spot. The bedroom light flicked on, slivers penetrating the fur of his tail. A soft intake of air alerted him that Cole had spotted him. Cole's next actions shocked Kai. Instead of attempting to coax Kai out, a flash of light briefly lit his hiding space, and then a warm body joined him beneath the bed, curling around him as much as Cole could in the tight confines.

He pressed closer to Cole's wolf, absorbing the comfort and protection Cole offered. There were no sounds aside from those of their hearts beating and the soft in and out of their breathing. The terror that had encompassed Kai ebbed away with each moment. Faster than ever before when he'd been alone. His blood no longer roared in his ears, and the uncontrollable tremors receded a little at a time.

Kai couldn't tell how long they remained under the bed together, but eventually he fell into a light sleep. When the warmth of Cole's body left him, Kai protested with a small chirp, but Cole shifted and shushed him, pulling him out from under the bed. Cole placed him in the center of the bed and lay down with him, once more wrapping his larger frame around Kai. "Will you shift for me, kit?" Cole whispered.

At first, Kai debated denying him, but in the end he returned to his human form, his legs entwined with Cole's. "I'm sorry," Kai mumbled into Cole's chest.

"For what? There's nothing to be sorry for."

"I was rude to your parents by leaving the way I did."

Cole sighed, his breath feathering the hair on top of Kai's head. "My parents didn't see it as rude. They were worried about you. You weren't rude. Something obviously terrified you."

Kai picked up on the question in Cole's tone. He warred with himself, but finally he said, "The smell of the alcohol."

"I don't understand. Why did it scare you?"

Kai picked at a piece of lint on Cole's shirt and swallowed hard. He had to force the words past the lump stuck in his throat. "My un-uncle. When he drinks, he hits me."

A sharp intake of air and Cole tightened his arms around Kai. "He's the one you thought I was taking you to, isn't he?"

"Yes," Kai murmured.

"How long?"

"What?"

"How long did he abuse you?"

"Ten years."

"Jesus!" Cole growled.

"After my parents died, I didn't have any other family except him. He didn't start hitting me until a few months after they were gone. I broke a dish while trying to get something to eat for myself, and he had been drinking."

"You were eleven years old, for fuck's sake!"

"I was a burden he didn't want," Kai said. "If I hadn't proved useful, he probably would have abandoned me years ago."

"Is he the one who caused the scars on your throat and wrists?" Cole asked.

Nodding against Cole's chest, Kai replied, "When I shifted for the first time, it terrified him. He demanded to know what I was, and he locked me in the cellar. Eventually, after I'd gotten out a couple of times, he put a collar and a chain on me, shackling it to one of the support beams in the basement."

"Fucking hell. No one noticed you weren't going to school? What about Child Protective Services?"

"No one noticed because he never let me go to school. Once they'd handed me over to my uncle, they were finished with me and didn't care enough to check in again. My uncle's neighbors were almost as bad as him and couldn't care less what happened to me."

"How did you get away?"

Kai didn't want to tell Cole about his uncle forcing him to steal. He didn't want Cole to hate him. "I stole food and a little bit of money, change mostly, over a couple of years. I hid it as best I could to keep him from finding it. Took some time, but one day, my uncle blacked out in the basement, and I managed to steal the key to the chain from him. I escaped and have been running ever since. Twice, he almost caught me, but I shifted and disappeared."

Cole hugged him harder, pressing his lips to Kai's temple. "He'll never hurt you again, kit. I swear it on my life."

Kai slid an arm around Cole's waist and clung to him. "He will find me. He always does."

"If he shows up, he'll wish he hadn't. You have me and the entire pack by your side, Kai. He won't live to see another day if he even comes near you."

Shuddering at the cold tone in Cole's voice, Kai didn't say anything further. Would the same coldness be directed at him if Cole found out about him stealing from innocent people?

They both eventually fell asleep, and Kai only woke once the sun shone through the curtains, casting a ray of light across his face. Cole had already left the bed and Kai could hear the shower running in the bathroom. The idea of a naked Cole just a few feet away sent a surprising heat through his entire body. He'd never really considered being sexually attracted to anyone, considering what he'd seen with his uncle and the multitude of women he'd gone through over the years. But with Cole it somehow seemed different.

Kai heard the shower turn off and sat up. He ran his hands through his hair and tried to straighten the mess it had become overnight. Cole exited the bathroom at the same moment Kai went to stand from the bed, causing Kai to yank the blanket over his lap in a hurry to cover the reaction between his legs. The sheer expanse of tanned skin on Cole's chest shone with dampness. A simple terry-cloth towel hung low on his hips, and Kai almost fainted when the towel slipped a little.

"Good morning, kit," Cole greeted, smiling. "I thought we'd have breakfast with my parents before the others start arriving."

"Okay," Kai squeaked.

"I'll get dressed while you shower. Don't take too long, though. It's already after nine, and the other pack members and Senaka pack arrive at eleven, so we only have a short window."

Nodding, Kai scooted into the bathroom and closed the door. He leaned against it and sighed. Holy crap! His fox half chirped in his head, and Kai agreed. "Tell me about it, buddy," Kai whispered.

He moved fast, showering and washing his hair in less than ten minutes. He turned off the water and grabbed one of the towels on a rack nearby. He dried his body and then rubbed at his hair, ruffling it and squeezing out as much of the water as he could. Tying the towel around his waist in a similar fashion as Cole, Kai grabbed up his comb from the sink and made short work of the shoulder-length, ragged locks. He'd cut his hair himself over the years but never managed to make it even. Most of the strands in the back tended to be longer than those on the sides. He had no bangs.

The mirror began to defog and reveal the deep scars around his throat and Kai winced. He snatched up the collar he'd removed prior to his shower and wrapped it around his neck again. It didn't take long to brush his teeth and use a splash of Cole's mouthwash. When he exited the bathroom, Cole had already gotten dressed and sat perched on the edge of the bed. Kai halted in the doorway, uncertain and shy.

He tried to cover his chest with his arms. His ribs were less obvious after Cole had kept feeding him every chance he got over the last two weeks, but he was still ashamed of his body. Nothing could have prepared him for the hunger he saw crowd onto Cole's features. Hunger was one emotion he knew. It looked the same no matter what the person wanted—food or sex. Somehow he knew Cole wanted him. "I-I should have brought my clothes into the bathroom with me," Kai mumbled, making a beeline for the dresser to take out a pair of jeans and underwear.

"Kai," Cole growled a split second before Kai found himself pressed up against the dresser and a very hard body covering his. Cole cupped the side of Kai's face and leaned in, capturing Kai's lips. Kai gasped in surprise, which quickly faded, and he brought his arms up to wrap around Cole's neck, holding on for dear life in the tidal wave of lust emanating from Cole.

A deep groan rattled in Cole's chest, and then the weight of Cole against him disappeared, leaving Kai panting and struggling to remain standing by gripping the dresser. "Cole?" Kai asked, bewildered.

Cole left the bedroom without a word. Surprise kept Kai immobile for a moment, and then a frown worked its way across his face. What had he done to make Cole stop? Kai dressed quickly in jeans and a black T-shirt, then shoved his feet into his sneakers. He entered the main room of the cabin to find Cole standing at the window facing the huge cabin the main pack members would be staying in. "Cole?"

Turning, Cole gave him a smile. "Ready?"

"Did I... did I do something wrong?" Kai asked.

"What?" Cole's smile faded, and his brows furrowed. "What are you talking about?"

"The kiss," Kai mumbled. "You just... left."

Cole walked toward Kai and stopped in front of him. He gripped Kai's upper arms and leaned in close. "If I hadn't left, it would have gone a lot further than you were ready for. I don't want to rush you into anything, and the more I touch you the harder it gets to remember you aren't ready."

Eyes widening, Kai stared at Cole. "Oh."

Grinning, Cole repeated, "Oh."

Kai's face heated, and he knew he had to be blushing furiously. Cole chuckled and pulled Kai into a brief embrace. "Let's get some breakfast."

They left the cabin and headed to the main house. Sara was already in the process of making eggs, bacon, sausage, toast, and fresh-squeezed orange juice. "You're amazing, Mom," Cole said, dropping a kiss on the top of her head. "What can we help with?"

"If you could butter the toast, Cole, and Kai, if you could set the table that would be a big help."

"Sure," Kai said. He grabbed the plates already sitting on the counter, along with silverware, and walked outside to the same table they'd used last night. The temperature outdoors was perfect, warm enough to be pleasant with a slight breeze, and Kai breathed in deep. The smell of grass, trees, and flowers bombarded his senses. While he'd been on the run, he hadn't had the chance to slow down and absorb being out in the fresh air again or seeing the grass and sunlight. In fact, he couldn't remember the last time he had enjoyed the sights and scents.

The sound of an engine reached Kai's ears before he saw the vehicle. Tension tightened the muscles in his shoulders and fear engulfed him. He couldn't bring himself to move until he felt Cole's hands on his shoulders, and Cole crowded him into the lodge. "It's okay, kit."

Kai couldn't catch his breath.

"Mom!" Cole called out.

Sara rushed into the main room of the cabin. "What's the matter?"

"Someone arrived early. I thought we had until eleven."

The sound of car doors opening and slamming shut caused Kai to whimper. He tried to struggle free from Cole's embrace to run back to his safe space in their cabin. "Kai, stop," Cole murmured.

"Let me go," Kai begged.

"Kai!" Sara said sharply.

Kai stilled and looked at her.

"No one is going to hurt you here, Kai. This is our family, our pack, and once they know you're Cole's mate, they will protect you as they would Cole. You can't live your life afraid."

Kai stared at Sara for a few heartbeats, then gave a minute nod. Sara broke into a smile and said, "Cole, can you and Kai grab a few more place settings? I'll go see who is here already."

Cole drew Kai into the kitchen to get a few more plates and sets of silverware. He put them on the counter and then turned to Kai. "If you really can't handle meeting some of our pack members, we can go to our cabin together."

The offer appealed more than anything else, but he knew Sara was right. "No. I have to stop being scared. Not everyone will treat me like my uncle did. You and your parents have shown me nothing but kindness since I've been here."

Cole placed his hands on Kai's shoulders. "You are amazing, kit."

Kai shook his head. "I'm nothing special."

"But you are," Cole insisted. He leaned toward Kai and gave him a gentle kiss, no more than a simple brush of his lips over Kai's but enough to warm Kai from the inside out. "I've never known anyone as strong as you are. Anyone else who had gone through the horrors you have wouldn't have been able to withstand half as much as you without going crazy."

Biting his lip, Kai flushed and dropped his gaze to the hollow at Cole's throat. He didn't know what to say. Cole squeezed his shoulders and let go. "We should get out there, okay?"

Kai nodded and without a word picked up the plates while Cole grabbed the silverware. Terror made Kai tremble, and his breathing grew shallow as they exited the lodge. Since Sara had referred to them as pack, Kai could only assume the four people standing there talking to her were shifters. A blond woman wearing blue jeans and a white tank top stood next to a dark-haired young man who looked to be in his late teens or early twenties. Two other men were next to her, smiling and chatting. One of the men had black hair while the other had platinum blond. Their attention immediately centered on Cole and Kai, and Kai retreated slightly, edging a little behind Cole.

"Cole!" the blond exclaimed, coming toward him.

"Hey, Maggie," Cole greeted, wrapping her in a tight hug.

A low growl rattled in Kai's ears, and he realized when everyone stared at him in surprise that the sound came from him. Cole released the woman named Maggie and took his place next to Kai, sliding an arm around Kai's waist. "Everyone, this is Kai, my mate." He said it proudly, and Kai couldn't help but feel bad for being jealous.

"I'm so happy to meet you!" Maggie cried. She started to move toward Kai, but Cole shook his head.

"He's a little shy about being touched," Cole said without further explanation.

Maggie stopped. "Oh, I'm sorry! Hello, Kai. My name's Maggie. I'm Cole's cousin-in-law."

"Hi," Kai murmured.

"This young man who is badly in need of a haircut is my son, Travis."

"Sup?" Travis grunted.

"He's not the most eloquent," Maggie said, rolling her eyes. "The big lug standing next to him is my mate and Cole's cousin, Daryl."

"Congratulations, you two," Daryl said with a grin. "Nothing better than being mated."

Maggie linked her arm with Travis's. "And this"—she gestured at the platinum blond—"is my brother Maddox."

Kai nodded in greeting, leaning into Cole's side a little farther. "Hello."

Maddox smiled. "It's great to meet you, Kai. Congratulations, Cole."

"Why don't we sit down to eat?" Sara said. "I made eggs, bacon, and toast, and there's plenty for everyone."

"Oh, we don't want to intrude! We should just go get settled in."

"Nonsense, Maggie. Put your bags inside the door and come sit down."

"Thank you, Sara," Maggie replied. "We are a little hungry after the trip."

Kai scrunched in closer to Cole's side as the three of them moved past to set their stuff down. Cole made sure Kai was between him and Elijah when they sat down. Kai sensed eyes on him several times during breakfast. They all seemed curious about him. Did they find him lacking as a mate for Cole? Were they staring because he didn't measure up?

"How did you two find each other, Cole?" Maggie asked.

"We just kind of bumped into each other in town," Cole replied.

"Isn't that the best? Finding the one person meant for you by being in the right place at the right time?" Maggie said with a dreamy expression on her face. "Was it love at first sight?"

"Not exactly," Cole chuckled. "Still working on winning him over."

Maggie furrowed her brow. "He's a shifter, right? The pull between shifter mates is undeniable."

Kai tensed and dropped his fork to the table, staring at the plate in front of him as if he could burn a hole in it with his gaze. Cole wrapped a strong arm around Kai's shoulders.

"Maggie, why don't you tell us about the new remodel to your kitchen?" Sara interrupted.

The tension eased out of Kai as Maggie launched into the details of what they'd done to their home. Cole nuzzled at his temple. "You okay, kit?"

CHAPTER FIFTEEN

"I'M FINE," Kai murmured to Cole. The unease radiating from Kai set Cole's wolf on high alert. He kept his arm around Kai while eating with his other hand and only half paying attention to the conversation.

While Cole knew the other two would never do anything to his mate, he still felt edgy around Maddox and Travis since they were unmated and he hadn't claimed Kai yet. Throw in Kai's nervousness, and he couldn't help but feel as though his wolf could take control at any moment, if only to protect Kai.

He couldn't be prouder of Kai for what he knew had been a huge step for his mate. In fact, Kai had taken more than one step outside of his comfort zone. Telling Cole about his uncle and his past couldn't have been easy for Kai. When they returned home, he'd find out what had happened to the prick. Though he didn't know how he would since he had very little information to go on, but he'd figure it out.

When they'd finished eating, Cole stood and drew Kai from the bench with him. "I think we should return to our cabin now. Kai needs to rest."

"I'm fine," Kai protested.

Cole ignored him. "Thank you for breakfast, Mom. I'll see you all later."

"Of course, sweetie. Try to get some sleep, Kai."

"I'm so happy to have met you, Kai," Maggie said. "I look forward to chatting with you again soon."

"Nice to meet you too," Kai murmured.

Cole led Kai away from the big cabin and up the hill to theirs. He didn't speak until they were inside. "I'm sorry, kit. Having you around two unmated males is a bit more than my wolf can handle. If we'd remained and they'd made any moves toward you, innocuous or not, I am not sure I could have stopped from shifting and trying to hurt them."

Kai stared at him, eyes wide.

"I really wish you understood, kit." Cole ran a hand through his hair in frustration. He wanted to claim Kai more than anything, and he wondered if he'd be able to retain his hold on his wolf when running with the pack.

"Can you explain it to me?" Kai asked.

Cole didn't know how to make Kai understand the difficulty in accepting that Kai didn't want him or how much it hurt whenever Kai pushed him away. "I don't think there is a way to explain it, Kai. It's just… instinct."

Kai frowned and looked ready to protest, but Cole gave him a lopsided, sad smile. "It's okay. We'll talk about it again later. I want to take a short nap as I don't think there will be much sleeping until late tonight."

"Tonight?" Kai queried.

"I will be required to run with the pack each night I am here."

"Oh."

"I will only be gone a couple hours at most." Kai dropped his gaze to the floor. Cole pulled Kai into his arms. "I don't want to leave you, but I don't want the others asking questions before you're ready to meet everyone."

"I see."

Cole cupped Kai's chin in one hand and tilted his face up toward his. "You trust me, right?"

It pleased Cole when Kai didn't hesitate to answer. "Of course."

"Then trust I won't let anyone harm you. It's best you stay in the cabin because you are unmated and because you aren't a wolf. They will be able to scent it."

"All right," Kai whispered.

Cole brought them both to the couch and sat, pulling Kai down onto his lap. He urged Kai to rest his head on his chest and began running his fingers through Kai's hair. "Will you tell me about your parents?"

At first, Cole didn't think Kai would answer, but after several moments of silence, Kai started talking. "It's getting harder to remember what they looked like. I only have the one photo of us taken a few months before they died. My uncle threw out almost everything else he couldn't sell for drugs and alcohol. They were good people. My mom always smelled of sunshine and daisies. She never got angry and always sat with me after school to have a snack and help me with my homework.

"My dad, he was a big man. I can still hear his deep laugh and remember how it felt like flying whenever he would pick me up and put me on his shoulders." Kai's voice hitched a little. "They left me with a babysitter the night they died. It'd been raining, and the only thing I can remember is the police telling the woman watching me how they must have hit a puddle and skidded across the road into a ravine. The car exploded on impact, and they died."

Wet heat soaked through Cole's shirt, and Cole sucked in a breath, pain shafting straight to his heart. "I'm so sorry, kit," Cole murmured, rubbing his hand over Kai's bicep.

"They took me away the same night. The babysitter, a friend of my mom's, helped me pack some clothes, and then the police took me to their station. A lady cop sat with me until another came to get me. She took me to a strange home for the night, and a couple days later someone else came to take me to my uncle's." Kai sobbed harder. "H-he never wanted m-me. I thought for sure he'd leave me, and I wish he had before I shifted."

"Shh," Cole crooned, hugging Kai tighter. "I wish I could take your pain away, kit, but that part of your life is over."

Kai shuddered and took a deep watery breath. A few moments passed as Kai began to calm down, and then he said, "I'm sorry."

"There you go again, apologizing for something you don't need to," Cole teased.

Kai huffed a slight laugh. "I got your shirt wet."

Cole shrugged. "Doesn't matter. I have more. Besides, it's good for you to get it out. I'm glad you told me."

A sigh rattled Kai's slender frame, and he burrowed farther into Cole's chest. Cole dropped a kiss on the crown of Kai's head. "Rest, kit."

"But I'm not tired," Kai muttered. Only his words were disputed by a large yawn he let forth.

Cole chuckled. "Uh-huh."

"Maybe a little," Kai said.

Cole waited until Kai relaxed against him, indicating Kai had almost fallen asleep. "Kit?"

Kai snuffled. "Hmm?"

"What was your uncle's name?" Cole held his breath, hoping his question wouldn't stress Kai out again.

"Jerrod, his name is Jerrod," Kai whispered and then a slight snore came from him.

Cole closed his eyes and released the breath in a hard rush of air. At least he had a name now. Kai had never told him his last name. A situation he'd have to rectify as soon as he could. Now he knew Kai trusted him, he didn't think Kai would hesitate to tell him. He figured since Kai's last name most likely belonged to the uncle, it would make it easier to find the son of a bitch. "I've got you, baby, and I'm never letting you go," Cole murmured against Kai's temple.

Kai mumbled in his sleep and snuggled harder against Cole. Cole picked up Kai and carried him into the bedroom, where he took off Kai's shoes and covered him with the comforter. He left the room, closing the door behind him, and pulled his cell from his pocket to call Nick. Nick answered the phone after letting it ring several times.

"Hey, Cole, how are things with Kai being there? Any problems?"

"No. Actually he did well today. He met cousin Maggie and her family."

"Are you doing okay?"

Cole moved to stare out the window at the big lodge. A pickup truck, two SUVs, and two luxury sedans were already parked there. "Knowing he's around so many other unmated wolves makes it hard to keep my wolf in check. He's restless."

The wolf hadn't settled down since his cousins had arrived. Cole could feel him pacing in his head, waiting for his chance to take control.

"No one will touch him, Cole. Our pack respects and trusts you. They would never betray you."

"Our pack, perhaps, but they aren't going to be the only ones here."

"Thayne's father would never allow any harm to come to him," Nick swore. "I know it will be expected for you to be present during the pack run. If you're really worried, Thayne and I will stay behind and watch over him. Make sure no one comes near your cabin."

"That would help more than you know, my friend," Cole said. The knowledge his Beta and best friend would be there to protect Kai settled his nerves, and his wolf began to lose some of its agitation.

"We are just now leaving the airport and should be there in about an hour."

"Thanks, Nick."

"No worries, bro. You know I'll always be there for you."

Cole heard a growl in the background and grinned. "Don't think Thayne liked your declaration too much."

Nick huffed, and then an unmistakable grunt came from Thayne. Laughing out loud, Cole ignored the twinge his heart gave as he doubted he and Kai would ever have such a relationship.

"You didn't have to hit me!" Thayne shouted.

"Stop being boneheaded and then maybe I won't have to."

"You wouldn't get jealous if I declared my undying devotion to someone else?" Thayne challenged.

"I'll let you go, Nick. Tell Thayne I said thank you," Cole interjected.

Nick sighed. "We'll be there soon. Hold down the fort till we do."

"See ya soon." Cole hung up and shoved the cell in his pocket again.

He spent the hour before their arrival pacing and thinking, worrying more than anything. The sound of Kai's steady heartbeat assured Cole his mate still slept. Every once in a while, he'd glance out the window to look for Nick and Thayne. They'd flown commercially and had to rent a car, so he wouldn't know what kind they would arrive in. When a dark blue truck pulled up outside the main lodge and Cole spotted Nick in the passenger seat, Cole heaved a relieved sigh. He went to the door, opened it, and stepped out onto the porch. Nick glanced up toward the smaller cabin, and Cole waved.

Nick smiled and waved in return. He said something to Thayne and began to walk in Cole's direction. Thayne hefted a bag onto each shoulder from the bed of the truck and went into the lodge. Cole hugged Nick the second he walked up the two small steps. "Where's Kai?" Nick asked.

"Sleeping. He still needs rest."

Cole ushered Nick into the cabin and shut the door. He gestured to the sofa. "He told me about some of his past."

Nick raised a brow at Cole. "And?"

He shared a short version of the events Kai had revealed. Nick stared at him in horror as Cole spoke. "Jesus."

"Yeah, tell me about it."

"He's strong," Nick said with admiration. "To have suffered through so much and survived? He's truly amazing."

"I need to find the bastard. My wolf is going crazy at how Kai has been hurt. He told me the fucker's name is Jerrod. I just don't know how to find him."

"Hire a private investigator. It's what they do for a living."

Cole grunted. He'd thought about it, but he didn't want anyone else knowing Kai's business without Kai's agreement.

"Well, whatever you decide, you know I'll help however I can," Nick said.

"I know. Thank you, Nick."

They chatted for a while longer before Thayne showed up. Cole thanked Thayne in person for offering to help. He knew this would be the only time Thayne had to spend with his family for at least six months due to his father's banishment. "I won't stay out long. Just enough to show my support of the summit and introduce myself to your pack."

"They aren't my pack anymore," Thayne growled.

Cole winced. "I know. I'm sorry."

"My father did what he felt was necessary for the good of the pack and his position as Alpha. He had no choice. After all, I'm the one who fucked up."

Nick leaned against Thayne's side. "I'm sure your parents will be happy to see you."

"Maybe."

The two of them left a few minutes later, leaving Cole to his thoughts and brooding. Kai woke as the sun went down, and Cole phoned Nick to ask him to bring food to the cabin when they came. "Nick and Thayne are going to watch over you while I'm out."

Kai frowned. "I don't need someone to babysit me."

"It's not babysitting, Kai. They're going to make sure no one bothers you. It's the only way my wolf will allow me to leave you. I need you to be okay with this."

He didn't think Kai would accept it, but after a few breaths, Kai nodded. "Okay."

"Thank you, kit. They're bringing some food for you to eat as well."

Once the other two had arrived, Cole joined his family in front of the main lodge. Cole couldn't quite hide his shock at the number of shifters there already, and he saw several of his own pack had already paired off with others he didn't know. His father and mother stood with a couple he assumed was the Alpha of the Senaka pack and his wife. The man resembled Thayne, and Cole figured he had to be Alpha Jeremiah. Kasey and Seth were also with them. Seth smiled when he saw Cole and waved, beckoning Cole to join them.

"We weren't sure you'd make it down," Seth said, giving Cole a hug. "Nick told us you'd found your mate. I'm happy for you, Cole!"

"Thanks," Cole grunted. He wondered if Nick had told them the whole story.

"Where is he? Did he come with you?" Seth asked, curious.

Cole stifled a wince, but he had his answer. Nick had kept his secret. "He's a little people shy."

"Oh, okay. Well, I'd love to meet him before the summit is over," Seth said.

"I'll talk to him and see. How's the practice?"

Seth, a veterinarian, had actually met Kasey because he'd moved to Senaka to take over the practice from another vet. "Doing well. Of course, now I'm mated to Kasey, the business doesn't stop."

Kasey grinned and held out his hand to Cole. "Good to see you again, Cole."

"You too, Kasey. Seth keeping you busy?"

Seth huffed and rolled his eyes. "You Alphas are all the same. As if I'm the troublemaker."

"I actually keep him busy. I'm a bit of a slob," Kasey replied sheepishly. "It's more a lack of time to do anything, though."

"*Pfft.* You can toss your dirty clothing in the hamper. You just choose to throw them on the floor!"

Cole chuckled, ignoring the pang of longing in his chest. Would he ever have such a relationship with Kai? "I'm glad to see you're both happy. I also noticed several of the Emerald Lake Hills pack have already paired off with some of yours, Kasey."

"It seems we've been successful in uniting a few mates," Kasey replied.

Elijah interrupted their conversation. "Cole, come meet Jeremiah and Emily."

Cole excused himself and joined his father. "Hello. It's good to meet you both."

Jeremiah, an Alpha with much wisdom in his eyes, stood tall and muscular next to Cole's father. He had shoulder-length black hair streaked with gray, and Cole could feel the power in the other man. It set his wolf on high alert.

"Hello, Cole. Your mother has told me a lot about you," Emily greeted.

"I hope we have the chance to talk privately this weekend," Jeremiah said. "Your father told me a bit about your mate, and I admit to being very curious about him. There have been a handful of rumors over the year, but we've never met another species of shifter."

"I don't know much at all, sir. Kai wasn't raised with others of his kind, and his parents died before he made his first shift."

"None of that sir business. Call me Jeremiah. I'm sorry to hear about his family."

"What were the rumors you've heard before?" Cole asked, curious.

"Not a lot, I'm afraid. Just how there were other types of shifters. Stories about fox and bear shifters being sighted, but unfounded due to no evidence. I am certain much as we have the rule of not revealing our existence, they do as well."

"There isn't a whole lot to go on. Is there anyone else we'd be able to talk to? Someone who may know where Kai and his family came from?"

"I'm afraid I only know of one other pack farther east of our own, and they had no more information than us."

Of course, up until recently the Senaka pack had believed only Native Americans could be shifters, so it made sense they wouldn't have many contacts outside of their pack. "Thanks," Cole said.

"I wish I had more to tell you," Jeremiah said with regret.

A big bonfire had been built in the nearby fire pit, and many of the others had already shifted and were lounging near the open flames, waiting for Elijah to give the go-ahead for the run. Cole noticed Devin sitting with his parents and gave him a smile. Nick's cousin Carter sat close by, but Carter looked miserable. Cole felt bad for him. He knew Carter wanted to find his mate more than anything, and with how sad he appeared to be, he hadn't been one of the lucky ones this time around.

"When does the run start?" Cole asked.

"We were waiting for you to arrive before we spoke to the packs," Elijah replied.

Elijah and Jeremiah moved together to stand atop the highest step. "Good evening," Elijah started, catching everyone's attention, even those already shifted. They all stood to attention and waited for him to continue. "Welcome to the first summit between the Senaka and the Emerald Lake Hills pack. The whole point of these next couple of days is to allow for us to work together to create unity between our packs and for our peoples to hopefully find their mates. I'm very pleased to see several of you have already found your true mates."

"There are only a few rules we must follow while we are here." Jeremiah took over. "No fighting or squabbling. Treat each other as you would any pack member. There is still the chance of encountering humans while in these woods, so please be careful where and when you shift. I ask my own pack to remember we are all born shifters, no matter our race."

"Thank you, Alpha Jeremiah." Elijah grew serious. "I have one announcement to make. I will be retiring by year's end, and my son will be taking over as Alpha."

Surprised whispers and gasps came from the attending pack members. Cole detected a few glances his way. Did they not believe he could rule as well as his father? He hadn't thought his father would go through with retiring right now since his mating with Kai wasn't going the way he'd hoped it would. Pressure weighed down on his shoulders, and Cole wanted to refuse to take over at the end of the year.

"All right, everyone, let's run!"

Cole chose to back-burner any thoughts regarding becoming Alpha and shifted into his wolf form. He stretched with a whining yawn and dug his paws into the grass. The lingering scent of Kai trickled over his senses, and Cole closed his eyes. He wanted desperately to claim Kai and make him his forever, but he wouldn't force Kai into something he didn't want. Opening his eyes, Cole darted after his father, pushing himself away from the area.

The moon shone overhead, almost full, and spotted the ground beneath with shafts of light. Cole ran alongside his father, keeping pace quite well. A few feet from the edge of a ravine, Elijah turned and traced the edge, Cole easily keeping up. The scent of a rabbit caught Cole's attention, and he began hunting it, breaking away from his parents and the others. A split second before he could capture the rabbit in his teeth, another slim wolf snatched the critter away and ran off into the woods.

He didn't move for several breaths, shocked, and then tore after the other wolf. There weren't many wolves with the tawny black-tipped coloring, and he couldn't remember any of his pack being the same color. Cole felt pretty certain the wolf had to be from the Senaka pack. He reached a clearing to find the slender wolf had stopped and lay beneath a tree, enjoying its catch. Cole snarled and stalked forward, slow and calculating. The wolf merely gave him a bored look and tore off another piece of the rabbit.

Where the hell did this wolf get the nerve to steal his kill? When Cole stood within a couple of feet, the tawny wolf tossed the remaining carcass at Cole's paws. Cole snorted and growled, but it had no effect on the smaller one. He stood and stretched and padded forward, rubbing against Cole. Shock held him immobile for several breaths before he spun and grabbed hold of the slim wolf by the throat with his jaw. He pinned the other beneath him only to feel the hard cock pressing against his fur. Before Kai, he would have taken what the stranger offered, but now he felt dirty. Cole shifted to his human half. "Shift," he snapped.

The tawny wolf lolled his tongue to the side in a funny smile before a bright flash of light found Cole atop a gorgeous, slim male. Black hair cut short on the sides with a thicker bundle on top and bright violet eyes made an enticing package. "Did you not hear my father earlier?" Cole demanded.

The younger man smirked. "About your mate? You haven't claimed him yet."

How the hell could the other wolf know anything about his mating? "I have found my mate. Claimed or not, it makes no difference."

Violet sparkled with lust. "I can provide some relief since your mate is clearly leaving you wanting."

Cole jerked when he felt a hand cup his cock through his jeans. He snatched the shifter's wrist and yanked his hand away from him. "This is unacceptable behavior. If this is how you intend to act during a summit until you find your mate, you will no longer be welcome."

A pout forced the wolf's bottom lip outward. "You're so damn sexy. I only wanted to fuck."

The tawny wolf shifter strained upward, rubbing himself against Cole again. Cole gave a rumbling growl. "Stop. If I catch you coming on to another mated wolf again, I will be forced to speak with your Alpha."

Cole's threat seemed to give the younger wolf pause. "You wouldn't."

"Don't test me, pup. Now get the hell out of here."

Sighing, the wolf shifted and slid free from beneath Cole, giving him one last look at the edge of the trees and then turning and darting off into the darkness. Cole felt unclean, and the other wolf's scent permeated his skin and clothing. Kai would smell him for sure. He headed back toward the lodges while telepathically letting his father know the evening was over for him. He needed to hold his mate in his arms.

CHAPTER SIXTEEN

KAI STARED, unseeing, at the television set. Cole had only been gone a little over two hours, but already his skin felt tight. He couldn't stop the anxiety trickling along his nerve endings. His fox paced within his headspace, chirping to be set free, to be with Cole. His entire world for the last two weeks had revolved around Cole.

Howling in the distance sent a shiver down Kai's spine. To be surrounded by predators with no way to escape spiked the restlessness to even higher levels. Kai got up and walked to the window. He saw Nick and Thayne lying together in the grass out front of the cabin. Thayne had his head on Nick's back, eyes closed. He must have realized Kai was watching them, for one eye popped open. Kai leaned his forehead against the window and sighed, his breath fogging the glass for a split second.

Thayne nudged Nick, and they both stood, stretching, and then shifted. They headed up to the door and knocked. Kai hesitated but then went to let them in. Nick smiled at Kai as Thayne shut the door. "Missing Cole?"

Kai widened his eyes at Nick, surprised by how he'd easily picked up on Kai's emotions.

"It's okay. It's natural to miss your mate." Nick gestured to the couch. Kai shook his head. "Don't want to sit down."

"He should be here soon," Nick said. "It's merely a formality to show his support of the summit and the partnership with the Senaka pack. Especially since he's already found his mate. There's no need for him to spend a lot of time with the other unmated wolves." Nick winked at him.

The idea of Cole being around wolves who didn't have their partner caused Kai to frown. "Is it possible for a wolf to have two mates in their life?"

Thayne leaned against the wall near the front door. "No. There is only one. Though it is possible to have a relationship with another if they haven't found their mate or their true mate dies."

"What if they find their mate and they don't claim them?"

Nick winced. "It's hard on both if either one doesn't accept the other. It's almost impossible not to claim them. But if it happens, they are capable of moving on, if they're strong enough."

"What do you mean?"

"There are some wolves who find the loss or rejection of their mate too hard to bear and will take their own life."

Kai stared in horror at Nick. Would Cole actually do that? He remembered the papers he'd seen on Cole's counter and what Nick and Cole had fought over. Did Cole intend on taking his own life because Kai wouldn't become his mate? "Nick—"

"Quiet," Nick said sharply, turning his head to listen to something.

"But—" Kai shut up when Nick gave him a harsh look.

Nick and Thayne stood and crept toward the door. Nick visibly relaxed when he peered out the window. "It's Cole."

Relief and excitement flooded Kai. Nick opened the door and Cole, in his wolf form, padded into the cabin. Another scent mingling with Cole's slapped Kai in his face, and he frowned, sniffing at the air, trying to identify the new smell. The new odor had a sharp edge to it, a harsh red pepper or something. Kai moved closer to Cole and breathed in deeper. Cole shifted to human and Kai saw a guilty expression on Cole's face. Jealousy sank its teeth into Kai. Anger followed behind it. Cole had found someone else. He reeked of whoever had been all over him.

Kai retreated, furious yet not even sure he had the right to be.

"Kai," Cole said, holding out a hand.

Nick glanced at Thayne, and they both slipped out of the cabin. Kai glared at Cole, but didn't say anything. "Nothing happened, Kai."

"You stink," Kai snapped.

Cole winced. "He stole the prey from my wolf. My wolf chased him down, and he wanted to, but I would never betray you, kit."

Kai didn't understand why he felt betrayed. He wanted to believe Cole, but his fox even stayed quiet. "You promised," Kai whispered.

Anguish darkened Cole's features. "I didn't do anything with him, Kai. He wasn't you. The only one I want is you. Haven't I shown you nothing else since Phoenix?"

Biting his lip, Kai wrapped his arms around himself. "I-I don't know."

The light in Cole's eyes seemed to go out then, and Kai knew he'd hurt Cole beyond anything he ever had before. His own heart wrenched, and Kai darted forward to wrap his arms around Cole's waist. "I'm sorry. I'm sorry."

Tears swept down Kai's cheeks when Cole didn't immediately embrace him. "I can't keep doing this, kit," Cole murmured. "I can't keep having my heart torn out."

"What? What are you saying?" Kai asked, lifting his head to peer into Cole's eyes.

"When the summit is over, we'll return to Emerald Lake Hills, and I'll leave. Julie can handle the greenhouses, and Nick will protect you." Cole sounded flat, lifeless, and Kai could see emptiness in Cole's eyes. Something he had put there.

"No!" Kai protested. "I-I don't want you to leave."

"I can't stay."

Cole attempted to extract himself from Kai's arms, but Kai held on tighter. He hadn't been educated as most people were, and he might not understand everything about being a shifter or being a mate, but he knew he didn't want to lose Cole. No one had made him feel safe since his parents died except Cole. He also sensed his fox would never forgive him if he chose to ignore the way his heart insisted he let Cole in. "Claim me," he whispered.

Cole jerked. "What did you say?"

"Claim me," Kai said again, stronger this time.

A choked sound came from Cole, and then he thrust Kai away. "Don't," Cole said through gritted teeth. "Don't do that."

"Do what?" Kai asked.

"Don't ask me to do what you clearly don't want."

"How do you know I don't want it?" Kai challenged.

Cole snorted. "It doesn't take a whole lot of smarts to see you're still afraid of me."

"No! I'm not afraid of you! I just… I just don't want anyone to have control over me ever again!"

Cole froze, horror dawning over his features. "You think being mated to me will be about my controlling you?"

Kai remained silent. Nothing in the time he'd known Cole had made him believe Cole would attempt to control him, but he couldn't stop the human side of him arguing Cole would change after they were bound together. Cole must have taken his silence as affirmation.

"Being mated is about being one, about taking care of each other and loving each other. It's about finding the other half of who we are." Cole's shoulders slumped. "A mate can never hurt a mate."

Approaching Cole once more, Kai reached up to touch his cheek. "Then claim me."

"I—" Kai cut off whatever Cole intended to say by placing his hand over Cole's mouth.

"Please, Cole."

A shudder visibly ran through Cole's large frame, and then Kai found himself swept up in a hard embrace and his mouth plundered by Cole's tongue. Kai returned the kiss eagerly, inexpertly, but Cole only groaned and then cupped Kai's bottom, lifting him up and carrying him into the bedroom. Kai gasped when the cold sheets met his warm skin. Cole followed him to the mattress and continued to kiss him, dragging his tongue over Kai's lower lip while his hand snaked underneath Kai's T-shirt.

Heat seared through Kai's flesh when Cole's palm pressed against his belly. Cole slid his hand higher still, smoothing over his ribs to his pec and then down again. "Kai," Cole groaned. "Touch me."

Kai tentatively brought his hands up and rested them on Cole's lower back. Cole's shirt had bunched around Cole's chest during their movements, and warm, muscled skin met his fingers. He pushed Cole's shirt higher, tracing his fingertips along the same path. He tensed when Cole unsnapped the collar he wore and removed it, but then Cole slid his mouth down the line of Kai's jaw to his throat. A sharp intake of breath and then a moan escaped Kai when Cole scraped his teeth over the sensitive skin on the side of his neck.

Cole did it again, and Kai gripped at the rippling muscles on Cole's back, eyes wide in shock at how good everything felt. He'd always imagined sex to be quick, hard, and uncaring of the other person because of how Jerrod treated his women. The pure pleasure of Cole's hands and mouth on his skin seemed almost unbearable, but Kai wanted more. When Cole's mouth latched on to his throat and suckled the flesh, Kai couldn't stop the small cry he let forth or his hips thrusting up, grinding his hard cock against Cole's thigh.

"You taste amazing," Cole murmured, swiping his tongue over the bit of skin. He grabbed the hem of Kai's shirt and pulled it over Kai's head. Kai moved to cover himself, embarrassed of how emaciated he still appeared.

"Don't," Cole rasped. "Don't ever hide from me. You're beautiful."

A flush worked its way over Kai's face. "I'm not."

Cole cupped Kai's cheek. "You are. You're the most beautiful shifter I've ever seen. It's a privilege having you for my mate. Everything you've survived shows me how strong you are. Weight can be gained, and scars only show your strength outside. You have a pure heart and a pure soul. Nothing else matters to me."

Kai tried to protest again, but Cole silenced him with a deep kiss. A sigh of delight slipped out when Kai opened beneath Cole's lips. Kai jerked when he felt Cole caress his chest, and then Cole began kissing his way down Kai's body. Each nibble, lick, and suckle caused Kai's cock to throb. By the time Cole reached his navel, a fine sheen of sweat covered Kai's skin, and he thought for sure he would come in his jeans. Cole snaked his tongue into the shallow indent, and Kai gasped, arching his back and digging his fingers into the sheets.

Cole slipped the button free from its slot and began tugging down the zipper. Kai trembled, afraid, but yet he wanted nothing more in his life than to be touched by Cole. Cole tugged the jeans down a bit, exposing Kai's hip bones and abdomen. The tip of Kai's cock peeked from the top of his briefs and Kai couldn't help the keening cry torn from him when Cole slid his tongue around the mushroom-shaped knob. "Oh my God," Kai moaned.

Shudders wracked Kai's body with each swirl of Cole's tongue. He was too far gone to notice when Cole slid the briefs down and tucked them underneath his balls, freeing the entire length of his dick. The second Cole swallowed him whole, Kai curled his toes inside his socks and couldn't stop himself from falling over the edge and coming down Cole's throat. He cried out and thrashed his head from side to side, nails shredding the sheets beneath him.

When he could think again and process what had happened, Cole had every piece of their clothing removed and Kai tucked tight to his chest. "You okay, kit?" Cole murmured.

"I had no idea anything could feel so good," Kai rasped.

Cole nuzzled the area behind Kai's ear. "It only gets better."

Oh God, if it got any better Kai might not survive. Cole flicked his tongue over Kai's skin and then wrapped his hand around Kai's half-hard cock. He began to stroke Kai until Kai stood at full mast once more. Kai couldn't help the tiny groans and whimpers he choked out over and over. The calluses on Cole's hands felt almost sinful and beyond wonderful. He didn't think he could handle Cole doing anything more to him, but Cole once again made his way down Kai's body, and Kai gasped when Cole lifted his thighs over his shoulders. But the sensation of Cole separating his bottom and the swift swipe of his tongue caused Kai to almost buck them both off the bed. "Cole!"

"Relax," Cole whispered, and then he repeated the action. Kai couldn't imagine how Cole could be doing something in such a place or how it could possibly feel as good as it did. A shocked moan escaped Kai when Cole pressed his tongue inside him, breaching the tight muscle of his entrance.

If Kai hadn't already come, he would have right then. Kai grabbed hold of the already torn sheets again, unsure how he'd endure all the new sensations Cole inflicted upon him without flying apart. Cole thrust his tongue in and out of his hole, simulating the action of fucking. Kai couldn't prevent the sounds he made as Cole ravished him, flicking his tongue again and again, probing inside of him. The noises embarrassed Kai, but everything Cole did unleashed a whole uncharted world of awareness of his body.

When Cole stopped, Kai released a small choke of disappointment, but the choke turned to a loud gasp when Cole slid a finger inside of him. Cole slipped the digit deeper inside of Kai. The whole thing felt strange, and Kai fidgeted a bit, causing Cole to continue to lap at his entrance again. It took several moments before Kai could relax and it no longer seemed as if he had to go to the bathroom. Until Cole added a second finger and Kai felt a twinge of pain, but it disappeared almost immediately.

Then Cole touched something inside of him, and Kai cried out, lightning rippling through his entire being. What the hell was that? Kai couldn't think or speak, and he realized his hips were pushing down on Cole's fingers. He hadn't even known he'd been doing it. Cole placed several kisses along Kai's inner thigh, suckling as he went. "Don't move," Cole commanded as he pulled his fingers free of Kai and climbed off the bed.

Kai wondered if he'd done something wrong. Those thoughts lasted for about half a second, and then Cole joined him on the bed again. The snap of a cap roused Kai enough to register Cole held a small white tube in his hand. He looked on curiously as Cole squeezed some kind of clear gel onto his fingers, but he lost interest the moment Cole slid one and then the other finger back into him. The coldness made him shiver. Kai didn't know how the stuff didn't sizzle when it came into contact with his heated skin. Then, as Cole moved the digits inside of him, Kai realized the purpose of the gel, and he flushed, biting his lip. It smoothed the way for Cole to fuck him.

The knowledge caused his gaze to drop down to Cole's crotch, and his eyes widened when he saw the size of Cole's cock. The head had to be almost as big as his fist, and the thickness as wide as his arm. How the hell would it fit inside of him? Cole must have sensed his perusal, and he picked up Kai's hand and brought it down to his cock, wrapping Kai's fingers around the shaft. A gasp caught in Kai's throat at how hot the hard length felt in his palm, the skin smooth and silky. He tentatively stroked as he would himself, and Cole hissed. Kai darted his gaze up to Cole's face, but he only saw pleasure on Cole's features.

"Kai," Cole groaned and then kissed him, hard. Kai tightened his grip and tugged faster, beginning to enjoy the way Cole throbbed in his hand. But Cole stopped him, grabbing his wrist. "I'll come if you keep touching me, and I need to be inside you."

Kai's doubts resurfaced again. "Will it fit?"

Cole nuzzled Kai's throat. "It will. It may hurt a little at first, but then it starts to feel good."

He still didn't believe Cole's cock would be able to go inside him, but he nodded. Cole picked up the little tube once more and drizzled a lot more gel into his palm, which he proceeded to slather over his dick. Kai couldn't stop himself from tensing as Cole rose up over him. "You need to relax, kit," Cole murmured, pressing a kiss to the corner of Kai's mouth.

Cole slotted the head of his cock at Kai's entrance, but Kai couldn't force himself to calm down, and he winced as Cole attempted to push a little. After a second failure to enter him, Cole started kissing him, drawing Kai into a mini make-out session, and then suddenly Kai found himself on top of Cole. Surprise caused Kai to sit up a bit, and he stared down at Cole. "What?"

"It's easier if you control how fast you take me, kit," Cole explained, lips swollen from their kisses and eyes half-lidded from lust. "Do whatever you're comfortable with. I don't want this to be something you remember with hatred or disgust."

Kai sucked a breath and then let it out slowly. He knew he wanted Cole to claim him, and he knew from what Cole had told him before Cole had to come inside of him and bite him. He rolled his shoulders and sat up farther. The head of Cole's cock bumped along his crack and came to rest above the crease. He experimented with the motion, rocking up and down a bit.

Cole gripped Kai's hips. "Don't tease," he growled.

A smile flitted over Kai's lips. He liked having power over someone else. It made him feel more in control than he ever had before. Leaning forward, he reached behind him, guided Cole's shaft to his hole and, taking a deep breath, bore down a bit. His eyes flew open wider when the tip began to ease into him, and a popping sensation tore through him as the crown breached him entirely. "Slowly, kit," Cole encouraged. "Take it slow and easy. Fuck, you feel good."

Sweat burst out over Kai's forehead and upper lip, and his thighs began to burn from the effort. He braced himself on Cole's chest and eased a bit more of Cole inside. Cole slid his palms over Kai's thighs, along his abdomen and belly, and higher to his pecs. "God, you're beautiful."

A flush suffused Kai's entire body. Cole thought he was beautiful? Even with his body all scarred and skinny? Kai managed to take a couple more inches before he had to stop and allow himself to accept the invasion of Cole's flesh.

He had no idea how long it took before his ass met Cole's balls, but his entire body shimmered with sweat and his thighs were on fire. Kai remained still for several breaths, and then he shifted to find a more comfortable position, only to gasp when Cole's cock touched the same place his fingers had. He rocked his hips experimentally, tilting his head back and closing his eyes at the ecstasy engulfing him. Cole made some sort of noise, but Kai couldn't comprehend anything beyond what he felt.

Cole gripped his hips and stilled his motions. "Kai, stop."

Kai opened his eyes and stared down at Cole. Had he done something wrong?

Cole reached up to caress Kai's cheek. "I need a second. You're so fucking tight I'm not going to last long if you keep moving."

Tilting his head a bit, unable to understand why Cole wouldn't want to come, Kai asked, "Don't you have to come inside me to claim me?" Kai asked.

Smiling a bit, Cole replied, "I want it to be about more than just claiming you, kit. I want to make love to you."

Kai frowned. He'd never heard the term before. "Make love? Is that the same thing as fucking?"

Cole winced. "Making love is what two people do who care about each other. It's about ensuring we both feel good and showing our affection for each other. Fucking, though I do want to fuck you, isn't the same. It's hard and fast and not at all about anything except pleasure."

Still seated on Cole's cock, Kai tried to understand the difference, he'd only ever seen or heard mention of fucking. The other seemed nicer, though. Something he could enjoy. "I see."

Cole wrapped his arms around Kai, pulling him down to his chest and then rolling them until their positions were reversed. He remained embedded deep inside Kai. "Do you, kit? Do you know how much I want you?" Cole rolled his hips. Kai grabbed at Cole's forearms, letting out a moan. "You need to understand before this is over, once I claim you, you and I are tied forever. There's no running away, and there's no way to undo the bond. Do you agree to be my mate, Kai? To stay by my side until the day I die?"

Kai stared at Cole, the man who had taken him in such a short time ago, the one who'd given him everything and never asked for anything in return, the one man who he couldn't imagine his life without. "Yes."

A growl rumbled in Cole's throat and he began to move, thrusting deep and slow. Kai moaned and gripped Cole's arms tighter. Everything outside the bed they were in no longer existed. Kai had no idea how he'd ever lived before Cole. He brought his legs up higher around Cole, gasping when it allowed Cole to reach even farther inside him. Cole's movements caused a sweet friction on his own cock and he knew it wouldn't be long before he came. He pulled Cole tighter against him, welcoming the peak just seconds from consuming him. A loud cry echoed through the cabin as Kai came, hot, wet splashes of semen coating his and Cole's abdomens.

The friction became a sweet, slick glide, and then Cole grunted. If it were at all possible, Cole swelled even larger as warmth spread through Kai's insides, and then a piercing, sharp pain in his shoulder ripped another howl and another orgasm from Kai. He arched from the mattress, clawing at Cole, shuddering and sobbing at the overwhelming crash of emotions pouring over and through him. "Cole, oh God!" Kai wailed.

Cole withdrew his teeth from Kai's shoulder and lapped at the wound. Kai shuddered and collapsed to the bed, boneless. A hiss came from Kai when Cole slid free from his body and then Kai found himself pulled to Cole's chest. "Sleep now, kit. I've got you."

Kai struggled to stay awake, but the stress of the trip and the hours spent without Cole along with the massive overload on his senses yanked Kai deep under. He couldn't be sure how long he slept, but he knew when he woke daylight shone through the edges of the curtains. He sat up and winced, his bottom protesting being sat on after the previous evening's activities. The sound of the shower told him Cole hadn't left him at the cabin on his own again, and Kai couldn't stop the relief and satisfaction at knowing he wasn't alone.

He climbed off the bed gingerly and walked toward the bathroom. He could see Cole's outline behind the translucent curtain. "Cole?"

Cole stuck his head out from behind the curtain. "Good morning, kit. Give me a sec and I'll be right out."

Kai, after a split second of hesitation, opened the curtain and stepped inside with Cole. Surprise flashed over Cole's face, and then Kai found himself pressed against the shower wall, his mouth covered by Cole's. Cole took advantage of the slight gasp he let out when the cold tiles met his back to allow his tongue to plunge in and coax Kai's tongue out to play. Kai moaned and brought his arms up around Cole's neck, his fingers tunneling through Cole's wet hair. Cole picked him up, urging Kai to wrap his legs around Cole's waist, which he did without hesitation. When Cole broke the kiss, Kai panted for breath and buried his face in the crook of Cole's neck. "Thank you, kit," Cole said.

Looking up, Kai gave Cole a questioning look.

"For trusting me. For having the courage to come in here. For bonding with me and for coming to the summit."

"Oh," Kai said.

"Are you hungry? I can go down to the main cabin and get us some breakfast."

Kai might have accepted Cole as his mate, but he still didn't think he could handle being around all the other shifters. "Okay."

Cole smiled and set Kai on his feet. "Why don't you take a shower while I get dressed and go get the food?"

"Okay."

Cole pressed a kiss to Kai's temple. "I won't be long, baby."

The nickname, different from the usual one Cole used, caused Kai to wrinkle his nose. "I'm not a baby."

Cole laughed. "You are definitely not a baby. Especially considering what we did last night. It's just a term of endearment, kit. It isn't meant in a derogatory fashion."

"I prefer kit."

Affection lit Cole's features and he leaned in to kiss Kai again. "Okay, kit. Go on. I'll have everything ready before you finish."

Kai nodded and watched Cole leave the bathroom before pulling the curtain closed the whole way. He grabbed the small bottle of shampoo and started soaping his hair. His mind drifted to the night before and what had happened. He'd actually let Cole... no, he'd actually asked Cole to claim him. His fox seemed content, more settled than Kai had ever experienced since his fox had taken over when he'd turned thirteen. But his human mind couldn't settle as easily. He prayed Cole wouldn't turn around and try to control him.

Stop thinking so hard, Cole's voice brushed through his mind, and Kai jerked, shocked and horrified. "Cole?"

A gentle laugh whispered through his head. *I'm not actually there, kit. Remember I told you being able to talk to each other this way is part of the bond.*

Kai felt as if his privacy was invaded. Could Cole could see his memories? Panic struck him, and Kai struggled to understand what he could possibly do to stop Cole from learning about the things his uncle made him do. *Calm down, Kai. Just relax. We can talk about it in a few minutes.*

Kai wrenched off the shower and almost slipped on the tiled floor as he yanked open the curtain. Oh God. Cole couldn't find out about his past. He grabbed a towel, dried off briskly, and rushed into the bedroom to grab clothing. If he'd recalled what Cole had told him before, he never would have let Cole claim him. A sharp sadness stung him, and Kai almost collapsed under the weight of it. *Is that really how you feel, kit? After everything?* Cole murmured in his mind.

"Cole, I—" Kai stopped. How did he respond?

Silence stretched on, and Kai could sense Cole had cut himself off from him. He didn't know how he knew; he just did. His fox chirped at him in annoyance. "I know, I know! But he can't find out!" Kai berated his other half. "He wouldn't want me anymore."

The front door opened and shut a few minutes after Kai had finished getting dressed and sat on the edge of the bed, head down with his hands between his knees. The smell of eggs and bacon wafted through to the bedroom, and Kai's stomach growled. He wanted to go out there, but the idea of facing a hurt Cole kept his butt firmly planted on the bed. Cole must have figured Kai wouldn't be coming out and brought the food into the room. He quietly handed Kai a plate with a fork and moved over to sit on the chair in the corner of the room. The slight snub hurt, but Kai didn't know what to say. They ate in silence.

Once their plates were clean, Cole took the plate from Kai, set it on the dresser and turned to look at him. "Why are you worried about my being able to sense your emotions and talk to you through our link?"

"I just... I feel as though I don't have any privacy anymore," Kai managed.

Cole frowned and sank down on the bed beside Kai. "I can't read your thoughts, kit. I can sense what you're feeling, and I can talk to you, share my feelings with you, but I can't see whatever you don't want me to. Eventually, as the bond grows stronger, the walls will lower, and we'll be able to hear each other no matter where we are and see what we see. But it will be only if you want me to. Although I have to admit the idea you have some sort of secret you aren't willing to share with me hurts."

Kai winced. "I don't—" He cut himself off because he didn't want to lie. "There are just things I am not ready to talk about."

Cole turned toward Kai and picked up his hand in his. "You're my mate, kit. Our link is another benefit of being bonded. I'll know if you're in trouble no matter where I am. Whatever it is, I'm willing to wait until you are ready. But don't shut me out because you're afraid. You could be a former spy and I wouldn't care."

"I'm not a spy," Kai muttered.

Chuckling, Cole entwined his fingers with Kai's. "I know, kit. I just want you to understand I don't care what you did in your past, and I will do whatever it takes to help you through whatever you went through. If you think talking to a human psychologist would help, I can arrange it."

"No!" Kai gave him a look of horror.

"Maybe talking to someone would help. Even if it isn't me."

"I can't talk to anyone about it." Cole swallowed hard, and Kai knew he'd hurt Cole. "I'm sorry," he whispered.

Cole gave him a look of sad acceptance. "What have I told you, Kai? You don't have to be sorry. You obviously went through a lot, and there are things we will have to find a way to get past. I understand you may not ever want to tell me. But you're my mate, and I want you to know you can tell me anything. I will always be there for you."

Kai nodded but didn't answer. Cole put his arm around Kai and sat in silence for a long moment. "Do you want to go for a run together? The others will be at several events my parents planned in order for the two packs to work together during the day. It'll be just us."

"Okay. Sure." Kai was eager to get out of the cabin for a little while. He was going a bit stir-crazy since being holed up in there for practically the last twenty-four hours. He followed Cole from the cabin, and as soon as they were within the coverage of the trees, they both shifted. Kai took the lead and ran, his black paws digging into the earth to push himself faster. Cole never fell behind but allowed Kai to set the pace.

CHAPTER SEVENTEEN

RESTLESSNESS POURED off Kai. Cole didn't try to guide or stop Kai from whatever direction he'd chosen, just followed him while keeping a close watch on their surroundings. He could only offer whatever reassurances his mate would allow him to. If Kai still didn't trust him yet, Cole couldn't force Kai to change his mind. He knew trust came with time.

He'd lied to Kai, sort of. While he couldn't see Kai's memories, he could still see whatever came into Kai's thoughts about his past or things he'd experienced. During Kai's moments of panic at the cabin, Cole had caught sight of an image of a man he had no doubt was Kai's uncle. The man had dark hair and similar features, yet he looked meaner than a rattlesnake and had a scar over one eyebrow. Cole burned the image into his head because he fully intended on taking out the bastard when they returned to Emerald Lake Hills. No matter what he had to do to find him.

When Kai scented a hare nearby, he took off after it, Cole still close on his tail. Kai caught it easily, and Cole stood guard while Kai gnawed on the little beast. He couldn't shake the sense they weren't alone and were being watched. He didn't pick up on any smells, their pursuer staying downwind the whole time. There were no noises aside from those of the birds and occasional rodent scurrying through the dead leaves on the forest floor. Yet he couldn't ignore the odd prickling sensation along his spine, especially since it could cost him or his mate's life if someone intended them harm.

After Kai finished the rabbit, he trotted to a creek a little farther over from where he'd caught it and bent down to take a drink. Cole stayed a Kai's side and waited. A twig snapped a few yards to their right, and Cole snarled, head whipping toward the direction of the sound. Nothing moved in the foliage. Kai bumped his head against Cole's side, a clear questioning look on his face. *Someone's out there.*

Fear rolled off Kai, and Kai crowded closer to Cole, peering at their surroundings as well. Cole couldn't stop the small bite of satisfaction at knowing Kai trusted him to protect him. Another twig snapped in the opposite direction, and Cole growled, maneuvering Kai behind him.

The same wolf who'd tackled him the evening before stepped out of the shadows, an amused look on his furry face. Cole shifted. "What are you doing here?"

The other wolf shifted and grinned at Cole. "You mated. How traditional of you. Though I have to say I've never seen a fox shifter before. Very interesting."

"You shouldn't be here."

The wolf pouted. "But we had such fun wrestling last night. I wanted to see if you were interested in playing again."

Cole heard Kai make a strange noise in his throat. He gave Kai half of his attention, never looking away from the stranger. "It's okay, kit. Remember what I told you."

"Aww, how cute. He's jealous." The wolf laughed.

Cole couldn't help but wonder if the other wolf had something wrong with him. He sniffed at the air, but there were no sharp scents of illness. "You need to leave. Now."

"But you're both fascinating."

The wolf continued to eye Kai, and Cole drew himself to his full height. "If you don't leave, I will be forced to take it as a challenge."

Excitement glinted in the tawny wolf's eyes. "I'm stronger than I look."

"Would your Alpha be okay with you attempting to violate the treaty before it's even begun?" Cole challenged.

The wolf huffed and crossed his arms over his chest. "You really are a buzzkill."

"You're challenging me in front of my new mate and acting rather aggressive. Buzzkill is hardly the word."

Sighing, the other wolf dropped to the ground gracefully to sit cross-legged. "I'm just bored. The ones who found their mates are ignoring everyone else, and the only people I know are my parents. Everyone is too busy with trying not to piss anyone off to have any real fun."

Cole raised an eyebrow. "What is 'real' fun?"

"Fucking, for starters," the wolf said with a grin.

Kai made the strange angry noise again and came to Cole's side. Cole dropped his hand on Kai's head. "No, kit." He eyed the other wolf. "What's your name?"

"Cheveyo, but my friends back home call me Che."

"None of your friends came to the summit?"

Che snorted. "No. They're not even eighteen yet. I'm the only one who is. My parents didn't want to bring me, but they figured if I stayed home, I'd get into trouble."

Cole grunted. Somehow he figured the kid gave his parents gray hairs. "There are many others close to your age here."

Che scoffed. "They're all squares. None of them have any interest in sex, or at least not with me."

"There's more to life than sex," Cole said dryly. He couldn't fault the boy for wanting to have sex, though. The drive of a man started early, and most wanted to sow their oats before settling down with someone for good.

"I just want to try it. Everyone in Wyoming knows me and won't come near me. No one here seems to be interested." Che gave a scowl. "Why is it so difficult to lose your virginity?"

Cole wanted to laugh but stifled the urge. He didn't know why Che was in such a hurry to no longer be a virgin. "Maybe it's your approach?"

Kai sat down on his haunches and stared at Che. Cole stroked the fur between Kai's ears. It seemed Kai had an interest in the boy now he knew Che wasn't a threat.

"How else are you supposed to find someone to fuck?" Che asked. "I've come right out and asked. Flirted. Been subtle. Can't seem to find someone willing to take the bait."

Cole couldn't help it this time. He chuckled and shook his head. "You have a very powerful presence, Che, and most wolves would be intimidated by you to begin with, but you also are very young, even if you are eighteen."

Che rolled his eyes. "How am I supposed to get experience if no one will give me any?"

"Ever had a boyfriend or girlfriend?"

Che shook his head.

"Why?"

"There isn't anyone interesting in Senaka."

"Are you going off to college soon?"

"No."

"Why not?"

"Parents can't afford it, and my grades aren't good enough for a scholarship."

"What are you interested in?"

"I like math."

Cole's brows went up. For someone who wanted things to be interesting, Che having a love for math seemed contradictive. "I'll bring my business card down to the main lodge later and give it to your parents. I sponsor deserving students for college scholarships whenever I see a need for it."

Che stared at Cole, shocked. "Really?"

Cole nodded. "Really. We'll see what we can do."

"Cool, thanks, bro!" Che stood and seemed about to shift and stopped. He gave a bashful look at Kai. "I'm sorry for hitting on your mate."

Kai moved toward Che, sniffing slightly. Che seemed wary of Kai. Cole suspected Che thought Kai would bite him, though Cole wouldn't blame Kai if he did. Kai surprised both of them, though, when he pressed his nose to Che's hand in a seeming accepting of Che's apology.

Che brought his hand up and set it on top of Kai's head. "Thank you."

Cole couldn't be prouder of Kai as they both watched Che shift, turn, and race off into the trees. "Ready to go, kit?"

Kai chirped at him, tongue lolling from the side of his jaw. Cole laughed. "I'll assume you said yes."

Cole shifted and followed Che's trail. They returned to their human form inside the tree line. Cole took Kai's hand and led him into the cabin. He grabbed a couple of business cards from his suitcase. "I want to get these down to Che's parents and also want to get some more information on Che. Will you be all right here by yourself for a bit?"

Kai nodded. Cole dropped a quick kiss on Kai's lips. "Keep the door locked, okay?"

"Okay."

Before Cole reached the main lodge, he could hear the raucous laughter and chatter from his pack members. The first thing he noticed when he rounded the corner were several Senaka shifters standing or sitting with some of his own. Cole smiled, happy to see his father's efforts were working out. His mother sat at the picnic under the large tree in the middle of the yard. Cole made his way to her, dropping a kiss on her cheek and taking the seat next to her. "You mated!" Sara cried with glee.

Cole grinned. "We have."

Sara clapped her hands. "I'm happy for you both!"

Cole still wasn't entirely sure Kai was. He didn't know if Kai had wanted Cole to claim him out of fear of being alone again or if something else had prompted Kai to accept the bond. Either way, if Kai left him now, they'd both suffer, and though he knew Kai would probably be able to survive with how strong his mate could be, Kai would still struggle. "Hey, Mom. There's a Senaka member I wanted to see if I could find out more information about. I told him I'd give his parents my card and ask them to call me after the summit to see about setting him up with a scholarship to college."

Sara gave him a tender look. "You always did have a huge heart, baby. What's his name? I'll find out what I can and make sure the card gets to them."

"Cheveyo. He said everyone calls him Che, though." Cole handed the cards to his mother. "I don't want to be away from Kai for long. Not after we just bonded. Do you think Dad would let me bow out of tonight's run?"

"Of course, sweetie!" Sara patted his cheek. "Your father will understand. He's proud of you and your mate for being here this weekend. Your presence the first night couldn't have been more important."

Cole gave his mother a one-armed hug and got up from the table. "I'm going to take enough food for dinner and breakfast. We'll see you tomorrow morning for the trip home."

"Tell Kai welcome to the family officially," Sara chortled.

"Will do, Mom."

Cole stopped in the main cabin, grabbed some sandwich fixings, a few apples, an orange, and some drinks, then returned to their cabin. He didn't see Kai upon entering the front door. Cole dropped the food on the counter and walked to the bedroom. He stopped in the doorway to watch Kai sleep. He could hardly believe how gorgeous, sweet, and amazing his mate had turned out to be. Once Kai shed his shell entirely, Cole felt sure Kai would become the person he truly was meant to be. When they returned to California, he'd find out more about Kai's likes and see if maybe he could hire a tutor, someone to help Kai study to get his high school diploma and whatever else Kai wanted to do in his life.

He stripped off his shirt and joined Kai on the bed, gathering him close. Contentment washed over Cole as Kai snuggled into his arms, not even waking at being touched by Cole. A short time ago, Cole had thought he would never hold Kai this way, let alone claim him. His mate's unconscious acceptance humbled him. Cole couldn't imagine not having Kai in his life.

He breathed in Kai's scent, filling his lungs with it, and closed his eyes. He never wanted to let Kai go.

AT SOME point, Cole fell asleep, still wrapped around Kai. Not until Kai tried to extract himself from Cole's arms did he rouse enough to ask, "Where are you going, kit?"

"Bathroom," Kai murmured.

"'Kay," Cole rumbled, rolling onto his back and scratching his belly.

He heard Kai close the door and then the water running a minute later. Kai reentered the bedroom, and Cole held out his hand. Kai crawled onto the bed and took his hand. Cole tugged Kai down to him, savoring the weight of Kai on top of him. "You hungry?" Cole asked.

Kai hummed and shrugged. Cole ran his fingers through Kai's hair. "I brought some stuff over from the other lodge. If you're hungry I can make us some sandwiches."

A yawn broke out from Kai before he answered, "Not overly."

"You should eat something at least. You still need to put on some weight."

Frowning, Kai asked, "You think I'm too skinny?"

"I think you're perfect, but you aren't at a healthy weight. Especially as a shifter."

Kai traced a pattern through the light sprinkling of red hairs on Cole's chest. "I've always been kind of skinny, though. Even as a child."

"Skinny is one thing, kit. Unhealthy skinny is a different story. I know you don't want to talk about it, but your uncle rarely gave you food, did he?"

Kai tensed against him and then relaxed with a deep breath. "I was lucky if I ate every other day. Either he'd remember to throw something at me or I'd steal it when I had the chance."

"Jesus, kit," Cole said.

Kai shrugged. "It was better if he ignored me."

"I wish I had found you sooner. To protect you and stop your uncle from hurting you."

"You couldn't have known," Kai said.

"Maybe not, but I still can't stop from thinking it."

A howl rose up several miles away, followed by several answering howls. Cole gave Kai's temple a kiss. "How about I make us something to eat and we can see what they have for TV channels all the way out here? I make a mean sandwich."

"Okay."

The two of them got up and exited the bedroom. Cole went to make their food while Kai surfed through the basic channels to see if he could find anything worth watching. He settled on an animated movie called *Cars*. Cole brought two plates in and handed one to Kai before sitting down next to him. "*Cars*—haven't seen this one in a few years."

"What's it about?" Kai asked.

Cole gave a rundown about a young race car named Lightning McQueen and the arrogance that led him to being stuck in a small town he soon came to love as his own. Kai laughed several times at the tow truck during the movie. Hearing Kai giggle so happily caused Cole's heart to swell. He could see Kai had already begun to heal and learn to relax a bit around him. Maybe their future together really had a chance.

After dinner, Cole cleaned the small coffee table of their leftovers and plates, and they watched another movie together. By the time Cole turned off the television, the night had grown late. Kai had already fallen asleep against his side, and Cole shifted enough on the sofa to lay Kai down on the cushions, then carefully picked him up to avoid disturbing him. The sheets were still messy from their earlier nap, and Cole set Kai on the mattress and covered him with the blankets.

Cole went into the bathroom to relieve himself and wash his hands. He removed his pants, tossed them over the nearest chair in the bedroom, and climbed into bed with Kai. He aligned their bodies, spooning with Kai, and wrapped his arm over Kai's waist. Tomorrow morning they would be leaving to go home, and Cole couldn't wait to introduce the rest of the pack to his mate. They'd love him just as much as Cole did. Cole's breath stuttered, and then he smiled, nuzzling the back of Kai's head. He loved Kai. The idea of loving someone in such a short time should have scared the hell out of him, but it didn't. It felt right.

He closed his eyes, hugged Kai tighter, and drifted off to sleep, content in the knowledge his life couldn't get any better.

THE NEXT morning progressed quickly, and after his parents and Cole said their goodbyes to everyone still remaining at the lodge, they loaded the car with their luggage and started the long drive to the airport. Cole noticed a drastic change in Kai and the way he received the world around him. He didn't seem as scared about the flight or being out in public as much. At least he didn't appear to be as concerned with his surroundings.

The return flight seemed to take longer than the one to Utah. A nagging feeling hit Cole halfway home, and he couldn't put his finger on what bothered him. They hadn't left anything behind, and the summit had seemed to go great. Yet Cole had a ball of anxiety in his chest bigger than a baseball. He didn't say anything to his parents or Kai about it. He didn't have anything concrete to share with them anyway. Maybe he'd eaten something for breakfast that hadn't agreed with him.

They arrived home without incident. Cole did a quick inspection of the house to reassure himself. "I want to go check on my greenhouses."

Kai smiled at him. "Can I come with you?"

Cole held out his hand to Kai. "Of course. You don't even have to ask."

Kai took his hand, and Cole led him to the greenhouses. He waved at one of the men working greenhouse number three as they entered the first one. Julie stood talking to someone on the phone at the rear of the greenhouse and didn't see them immediately. Only once she'd ended the call, made some notes on a form, and glanced up did she realize they were there. Her eyes widened, and she set down the notepad she held and rushed over to them. "Cole! How did the summit go?"

Cole grinned and said, "Hey, Jules. The summit went well. I think everyone found it to be a pretty big success. Several individuals found their mates."

"Amazing news!" Her gaze had never left Kai as Cole gave her the rundown. "Hi, Kai. How are you?"

Kai gave her a soft smile. "Hi," he said.

"You two mated, didn't you?" she asked. "Oh man, everyone is going to be happy to meet you, Kai."

"Not quite ready for the whole pack," Cole replied. "But soon. How've things been here?"

"You were only gone for two days," Julie said, rolling her eyes. "I promise the greenhouses are safe. We just got an order for twenty boxes of the peppermint bath salts."

"That's great!"

"I told you people would love the stuff. It's practically a miracle product."

Cole looked around and didn't see anything out of place, but the ball in his chest still didn't dissipate. "Everything's been fine? Nothing happened while I was gone?"

"Nope. Business as usual."

Grunting, Cole took Kai's hand, bid Julie goodbye, and headed over to inspect the other two greenhouses. He introduced Kai to his other employees as they came up to greet Cole. Everything appeared as Julie said. Cole rubbed at his chest. Kai noticed.

"Are you okay?" Kai asked.

"It's nothing," Cole said. "Tomorrow I need to start working in the greenhouses again. I've been AWOL for too long."

"AWOL?"

"It's a military term. It means absent without leave."

Kai frowned. "Is it because of me?"

Cole pulled Kai close, wrapping his arms around him. "If it means I have you here with me, I would have been gone longer."

"But—"

Cole cut him off. "Stop. It's fine. Julie is an excellent manager. She kept everything running smoothly the entire time I was gone."

Kai still looked uncertain. "I just don't want to be the reason you aren't giving your business the attention it needs."

"No one would begrudge me spending time with my new mate so we can get to know each other and spend time together. You are my focus, kit. Nothing else matters. I hired Julie because I knew she could handle anything in my absence. Now please, relax. I want to spend the rest of today with you without worrying about tomorrow."

Kai hesitated but then nodded. "Okay."

"Good." Cole took Kai's hand again and tugged him toward the house. "I have a surprise for you."

Tilting his head, Kai asked, "What?"

Smiling, Cole shook his head. "You'll have to see."

They entered the house, and Cole headed toward the front room. Kai trailed behind him. A large box sat inside the door, and Cole smiled in eagerness. "It came."

"What did?" Kai asked.

"I got you something. I think you're going to love it."

"Cole!" Kai protested. "You can't keep buying me things."

"Yes, I can. Now sit."

Kai didn't look convinced. "I feel bad because I know I can't pay you back."

Cole waved his excuse away. "Money doesn't matter, kit. I just want you to be happy."

He hefted the box from the floor, brought it over to the couch, and set it by Kai. Cole ripped off the tape sealing the top and gestured for Kai to start digging, sitting next to Kai on the couch. Kai hesitated, but eventually opened the box top and started taking out item after item, awe on his face. Sketchpads, colored pencils, paints, brushes, charcoal, and several other items littered the coffee table when he reached the bottom of the box. "This is too much!" Kai exclaimed, but Cole could see the longing on his face.

"Stop. I want you to pursue what you want in life, kit. You love to draw, and I know you'll be amazing at painting too."

"This must have cost a fortune," Kai murmured, picking up the box of professional colored pencils.

"Doesn't matter. I make enough money to live comfortably and still afford things to make you happy." Cole brushed a strand of Kai's hair behind his ear. "I want to do these things for you, Kai. Seeing your excitement and joy makes me happier than my hands in the soil of my greenhouses."

Kai held the pencils to his chest and looked at Cole with tears in his eyes. "Thank you."

Cole smiled, wiped away the dampness at the corner of Kai's eyes, and cupped Kai's cheeks in his hands. "You're more than welcome."

After yanking Kai across his lap, Cole kissed him, soft and gentle. He stood up, holding Kai, and took him through the hallway to the bedroom. He carried Kai over to the bed, where he followed him down to the mattress. He captured Kai's mouth again, deepening the kiss further. Shoving his hand under Kai's shirt, he smoothed his palm across Kai's stomach. Kai moaned into his mouth, and Cole moved higher until he reached the light brown buds of Kai's nipples.

He plucked one, and Kai gasped. Cole did it again and then moved to the other nipple. "Take off your shirt," Cole murmured.

Kai managed to move enough to remove the offending article of clothing. Cole lowered his head to suckle at one raised nub, flicking it with his tongue. "Cole," Kai groaned.

He captured the nipple between his teeth and rolled it lightly. His wolf gave a growl of satisfaction when Kai grabbed at his hair. He soothed the skin with his tongue again before continuing on, nuzzling, licking, and kissing along Kai's rib cage and belly, then stopped at his navel. Their claiming hadn't been as romantic as Cole would have liked. He'd been too anxious to tie Kai to him. He wanted to take the time now to explore every nook and cranny of Kai's body, learn where every freckle spattered his limbs, seek out every "hot spot" that turned Kai on, and enjoy every sound his mate let out.

No skin was left uncharted by the time Cole took Kai's cock into his mouth. He savored the taste of Kai on his tongue, lapping around the flared head and down the shaft to suck on first one testicle then the other. Kai quivered and gasped at every touch of Cole's mouth. The effect he had on Kai made Cole feel powerful and humbled all at the same time. He could sense Kai getting close and stopped, reluctantly pulling away from his cock. Kai let out a small sound of protest, which Cole cut off by circling the entrance to Kai's body with his finger. He leaned over Kai and wrenched open the nightstand to grab the tube of lube he kept there. It seemed like forever by the time he'd removed his clothing, slathered his cock, prepped Kai, and aligned their bodies.

He nudged his cockhead at Kai's hole. "I love you, kit," Cole murmured as he began to stretch Kai open.

Kai's eyes went wide, and surprise shimmered in their depths before Kai slammed them closed in pleasure. Cole stemmed his disappointment that Kai didn't return his declaration. He knew he couldn't expect Kai to love him already. He gathered Kai closer as he started to thrust, moving in and out of Kai's warm, tight body. Kai gripped at the muscles in Cole's back, nails scratching him, but Cole only hissed and drove into Kai harder, faster. The way Kai's insides tightened and caressed the length of his cock pushed Cole toward orgasm sooner than he wanted. Using every ounce of willpower, he held out, his breathing ragged with his struggle to retain his control.

Cole slipped his hand between them, wrapped his fingers around Kai's prick, and stroked in time with his thrusts. Kai moaned and tossed his head against the pillow. "Oh God," Kai cried.

"Come for me, kit," Cole urged, increasing the speed of his movements, shifting his hips around until he pegged Kai's prostate.

Kai screamed out Cole's name as hot liquid splashed across both their chests and Cole's hand. Cole growled, leaned down, and sank his teeth into Kai's shoulder, embedding himself deep as he gave in to his own release. Hard shudders wracked Cole's body in time with each pulse inside Kai. Eventually, he collapsed atop Kai, panting.

The only sounds were both of them breathing. It grew cooler in the room as the sweat dried on their skin, and a shiver ran through Kai. Cole drew the sheets over the two of them, reluctant to let Kai go, but also not sure if he was ready to face Kai's reaction to his previous disclosure. Would Kai freeze him out again?

The light dimmed as the sun sank below the horizon, and Cole finally released Kai in order to go prepare dinner. He pulled on his jeans sans briefs and left off his shirt. "Anything you're hungry for, kit?"

Kai stretched, arms over his head. "Not really."

"I'll make some pasta, then."

"Do you need any help?"

"No. Why don't you take a shower while I make dinner?"

Kai sat up, and Cole swallowed at how sexy his mate looked with his hair disheveled and the just-fucked flush on his features. "I can help. I don't mind."

Cole smiled and leaned over to kiss Kai. "I know. I like doing things for you."

"It makes me feel weird," Kai mumbled.

"It's okay. You're just not used to it. I'll win you over yet," Cole replied. "Go grab a shower. Dinner will be ready in thirty minutes."

"Okay."

Cole left Kai among the sheets and padded barefoot down the hallway to the kitchen. Maybe if he'd been paying attention instead of lost in the afterglow of sex with Kai, he'd have noticed the door was open a fraction or the smell of a stranger in the house. But he didn't and paid for it with the crack of something hard against the back of his skull. Cole didn't even see the floor rushing up to greet him.

CHAPTER EIGHTEEN

KAI SIGHED and stood from the bed. He knew he'd disappointed Cole by not saying anything in return, but he didn't know what he felt, and he certainly had no idea how to know if he loved Cole. Did he feel more than gratitude toward Cole? He cared about Cole. The idea of any harm coming to him pierced Kai straight through the heart. Was it love, though?

He entered Cole's bathroom and turned on the shower, staring at himself in the mirror as he waited for it to heat up. He saw the still-healing marks of Cole's fangs in his shoulder and touched them with the tips of his fingers. He thought of the way Cole felt inside him, and he blushed. There had been nothing in his life to compare to the way Cole brought his body alive. Every touch, every kiss, made his entire being sing with pleasure and most definitely lust.

A noise from outside the bedroom brought Kai's attention to the door. "Cole?" he called.

No answer came, and a shiver traveled down Kai's spine. He grabbed a robe off a hook on the wall, slipped it on, and peeked into the bedroom. A shadow stood in the darkened entrance to the room, and Kai sucked in a harsh breath. The shadow didn't belong to Cole. He slammed the door and locked it as a body hit the wood.

"Open this door, you little freak," Jerrod screamed, banging on it. "I knew I'd find you! Did you think I wouldn't?"

Kai sobbed and looked around him in a panic. A small window ledge above the shower stall seemed to be the only other exit, but he couldn't fit through as a human and wouldn't be able to reach it as his fox. He didn't even see anything he could brace against the door. Jerrod kept throwing himself at it, trying to break through. What happened to Cole? Had Jerrod hurt him?

The banging stopped, and Kai heard nothing for several heartbeats. Then there came a thump on the ground outside the room. "If you don't open the door, Kai, I'm going to kill this fucking piece of shit fag!"

Cole! Kai had no idea how to save Cole. He couldn't let Jerrod kill Cole, and he reached a shaking hand for the latch and unlocked the door. When his eyes adjusted to the darkness after the bright lights in the bathroom, he saw Cole lying in a heap on the floor, Jerrod's foot on his windpipe, waiting to crush it at a moment's notice. "Pl-Please don't hurt him, Jerrod," Kai begged.

An ugly sneer crossed his uncle's face at his begging. Jerrod resembled Kai's father, a lot, but for the beer paunch bulging beneath the sweat-stained T-shirt, several pockmarks on his face from poor hygiene over the years, and the repulsive yellowed, jagged teeth visible for a second when Jerrod spoke. Every day for ten years, Kai had clung to the image of his father in the picture, afraid it would be overwritten by the one before him. He didn't want his father's kind smile, laugh-lined face, and slim form to take on his uncle's visage. "Please, Uncle Jerrod," Kai tried again.

"Shut up, you sniveling bastard. Thought you'd shack up with some disgusting excuse for a man and hope I wouldn't find you, didn't you? People remember freaks. It wasn't hard to track you." A flash of silver caught Kai's attention, and he sucked in a breath. Jerrod had a gun in one hand. An evil grin cut across Jerrod's face, and he waved the gun at Kai. "I should shoot him. Make you watch your boyfriend die as punishment for leaving."

"No!" Kai cried, dropping to his knees, tears coursing down his cheeks. "Please, don't."

Jerrod increased the pressure on Cole's windpipe, and Kai didn't know what to do. "I'll come back with you, Uncle Jerrod. Just please don't hurt him."

"You're coming with me anyway!" Spittle flew out of Jerrod's mouth, and Kai winced as some of it landed on his cheek and forehead. "Get up!"

Kai struggled to stand on wobbly legs. Jerrod stepped away from Cole and grabbed a pillow, stripping the case off of it. He tossed it at Kai. "Put everything of value in there."

Jerrod wanted him to steal from Cole. He shook his head in refusal. "No."

The sound of the gun cocking sent a shudder through Kai. "Do it or I'll shoot him in the head!"

Kai cried as he started going through the nightstands, drawers, and anywhere he could think of. A Rolex and a smartwatch, some expensive-looking cufflinks, and Cole's wallet went into the pillowcase. Jerrod motioned to the bedsheets. "Tear some strips off those."

He set down the pillowcase and picked up the sheet. His hands shook as he tore at it, flinching when the fabric ripped. "Hurry up!" Jerrod shouted.

Kai struggled to get a couple of pieces of the sheet. He figured Jerrod intended to tie Cole up with it. When he held the two strips up, Jerrod grunted and gestured with the muzzle of the gun. "Tie him to the bed."

Lowering himself to the floor beside Cole, Kai surreptitiously checked him out. He saw blood on the back of Cole's head and a trickle of it across Cole's temple. Jerrod had hit him hard with whatever he'd used. Kai cried out as Jerrod kicked him in the ribs with a steel-toed boot. He whimpered at the sound of something cracking, and red-hot pain flared out from his side. "Jesus fucking Christ. You're worthless! Tie him up!"

Lifting Cole's arms above his head to the foot of the bed, he tied both strips to Cole's wrists and then knotted them around the leg of the frame. A change in Cole's breathing alerted Kai that he was returning to consciousness. A moan flittered from Cole's lips, and Jerrod jerked the gun toward him. "Get up and pick up the bag. Let's go."

Kai saw Cole's eyelids flutter a split second before they cracked open. He gave a slight shake of his head and managed to keep himself in front of Cole as Jerrod shoved him. "Please, Jerrod, just let me go."

Jerrod scowled and backhanded Kai, sending him flying into the nearby dresser. A scream of agony wrenched itself from Kai as the rib already injured broke completely and several others protested the impact. A low growl came from close by, and Kai managed to lift his head enough to see Cole wrenching at the bindings. "Touch him again, you son of a bitch, and I'll kill you!"

A chortle of harsh laughter rattled in Jerrod's throat. "What are you going to do about it? Not even sure I can call you a man considering you stick your dick in another man's ass."

Cole snarled at Jerrod, tugging harder at his bindings. "I'm more of a man than you are, you fucking piece of trash! Beating on a little kid all those years! When I get loose I'm going to rip your balls off and shove them up your ass!"

Kai used the dresser to pull himself to his feet. He pleaded with his eyes for Cole not to antagonize Jerrod. Cole ignored him, glaring at Jerrod. "Why don't you cut these loose and take me on like a real man?"

Jerrod sneered and pointed the gun at Kai. "Willing to take a bullet for a little freak, huh? Did he tell you what he is? Huh? Did he tell you what he's done all these years?"

Cole didn't even hesitate. "I don't care. Whatever he did, I'm sure he did it because you forced him."

Rage flooded Jerrod's face. He pointed the gun at Cole again. "Not even how the little freak used what he can do to steal from dozens of innocent people, huh?"

Kai's gaze remained locked on Cole's face. He needed to know what Cole thought. But instead of censure or revulsion as Cole looked at Kai, Cole's anger at Jerrod faded away to a soft, tender look. Kai's breath caught in his throat. "Not even a little bit, kit. I love you."

He'd thought for sure Cole would hate him. How could he not when he'd done such terrible things? But Cole still loved him!

Jerrod lashed out and brought his boot down toward Cole's face. But to Kai's shock, Cole grabbed hold of Jerrod's foot and wrenched it to the side, bringing the paunchy, balding prick to his knees. Tatters of the bedsheet hung from one wrist, the other having made it free entirely. Jerrod swung the hand with the firearm around, trying to point it at Cole, but Cole grabbed his wrist, banging it against the side of the bed frame. Jerrod gave a squawk of pain, but didn't let go of the gun, instead swinging his other fist into Cole's stomach. Cole grunted, but held on tight.

Frozen in time, Kai watched the two of them fight and struggle over the gun. He screamed in terror when the pistol ended up locked between them and a loud bang rang out. "Cole!"

He scurried over to where both men had fallen to the floor, ignoring the agony in his ribs. Jerrod lay on top of Cole. "Cole!" Kai sobbed, tugging frantically at Jerrod's immobile body in a desperate need to get to Cole. "Please be all right."

A groan shattered the silence, and Jerrod started moving. Kai stumbled a few paces away, terrified. "No, no, Cole!"

Instead of standing, though, Jerrod rolled to the side, and it took Kai several seconds to realize Jerrod lay there, eyes open, unseeing. Cole had blood all over his chest from where Jerrod had been shot. "Cole!" Kai cried and managed to drop down next to him and start raining kisses all over Cole's face.

Cole slid an arm around Kai's waist. "Kit," Cole breathed.

He hugged Kai hard, and Kai yelled out in pain. Cole immediately loosened his grip and sat upright, bringing Kai with him. "What is it? Are you okay?"

"I think he broke my rib," Kai panted, holding a hand to his side.

Cole swore and parted the robe Kai wore to probe at the offending area. A huge bruise had already begun to form. Kai hissed when Cole prodded his ribs. Cole helped Kai stand and move to sit on the bed. "Don't move," Cole demanded.

He grabbed up his pants from the floor where he'd dropped them earlier and pulled out his cell. He punched a number and then hit Send. "Nick? I need you. I'll explain when you get to the house. Bring Jack."

He disconnected the call and tossed the phone on the bed. "Let's get some ice on your ribs. Jack is our pack healer. He'll be able to alleviate some of the pain."

Kai clutched Cole's hand when he went to close the robe again. "Cole?"

Cole stood without looking at him. "Stay here while I go get some ice. Nick and Jack should be here soon."

"Cole," Kai said again. This time Cole's eyes settled on Kai, but somewhere about midear or thereabouts. Kai didn't recognize the emotion on Cole's face. "Does it really not matter?"

Confusion edged out the unfamiliar emotion, and Cole finally met Kai's gaze. "What?"

"That I-I stole from people."

Cole's eyes widened and he sat down by Kai. "What? No. I told you it doesn't matter to me. I know you only did what you had to in order to survive."

"Then why won't you look at me?" Kai murmured.

Sighing, Cole took Kai's hand in his. "I failed you."

"Huh?"

"I promised you your uncle would never hurt you again. I failed to protect you."

Kai stared at Cole in shock. "What? No, you didn't. He'd have taken me away again if you hadn't stopped him."

Cole reached out and gently touched Kai's side. "He still broke your rib."

"And? It'll heal. I'm just glad you're okay," Kai said. "I thought for sure you'd been shot."

A knock on the front door stopped Cole from replying. "Stay here," Cole said, and he left the room to let Nick in.

Kai stared at his uncle's body in stunned silence. He could actually go out and not worry Jerrod would find him. He didn't have to live in fear anymore. The weight he'd carried for ages lifted off his shoulders, leaving behind a sense of wonder and awe at how much choice he had now.

"Gods, Cole," Nick exhaled as he entered the bedroom. "Thayne, can you grab the sheet off the bed?"

Thayne came toward the bed. "Hey, kid. Gotta get you to stand for a sec."

Kai scowled at being called kid, but stood from the bed. He watched Thayne yank the already torn sheet from the bed and lay it over Jerrod's prone form. He didn't witness anything further because Cole and a blond-haired stranger came to him, distracting him from what Thayne and Nick were doing.

"Kai, this is Jack Foreman. Jack, this is Kai, my mate."

Jack set a small bag on the bed, smiled, and held out his hand to Kai. "It's nice to meet you, Kai."

He couldn't put his finger on it, but Kai instinctively trusted Jack. He placed his hand in Jack's. "Hello."

Jack squeezed his fingers, and warmth trickled through Kai's palm and up into his chest. He stared at Jack, surprised. Jack guided Kai to the bed. "Let me take a look at you."

Kai allowed Jack to part the robe and examine his side. Jack hummed and frowned. "Well, it's definitely a broken rib, and perhaps a couple cracked as well."

Running his palm over Kai's side, Jack closed his eyes. He didn't push on the injury, but Kai felt a sort of pressure, and he glanced at Cole in question. Cole lay his hand on Kai's shoulder. "He's our pack healer. He's an empath and is able to sort of coax the cells in your body to enhance the healing process."

Jack opened his eyes and smiled again. "You'll still be in pain for a couple of days, but it will heal much faster now."

Kai couldn't help noticing how attractive Jack was. The man had a slim yet toned body and blue-green eyes that almost seemed to swirl in a strange pattern. A small dark freckle graced his right cheek underneath his eye. Lashes most women would kill for swished against Jack's cheeks with each blink. "Thank you," Kai said.

"Don't thank me yet. I still need to wrap your chest. You're going to want to make sure to take the bandage off when you bathe."

Nodding, Kai couldn't stifle his curiosity as Jack turned to the bag he'd brought in with him. There were bandages, scissors, some sort of tape, and from what Kai could tell, needles. He'd only ever seen the latter when his uncle or one of his latest girlfriends had been shooting up with heroin. Jack took out a roll of bandage and indicated Kai should shrug off the robe.

Cole growled. "Be careful, Jack."

Kai frowned at Cole.

Jack held his hands up. "Calm down, Cole. I know he's yours."

Realization dawned. Cole was jealous. Warmth worked its way over Kai's cheeks. "Cole," Kai admonished.

Cole leaned down and murmured in Kai's ear, "I'm a very possessive wolf when it comes to you, kit. Don't want anyone stealing you away from me."

"I would never!" Kai protested.

Jack remained silent as he wrapped Kai's ribs. He finished off with several pieces of white tape. Cole immediately covered Kai's body from the others' eyes with the robe. Although, Kai noticed, Thayne and Nick were gone with Jerrod's body. He hadn't even seen them leave. "Where'd they take Jerrod?"

"They took his body to be disposed of," Cole said.

Kai didn't know how he felt about Jerrod's body being discarded as trash. His uncle had been a bastard, but he didn't know if anyone deserved such a fate. He supposed he should just be grateful Jerrod couldn't terrorize him anymore. "I see."

"I think we're good here, Cole," Jack said, returning the rest of his things to the bag. He stood and once again offered his hand to Kai. "Welcome to the pack, Kai. You're going to have your hands full with this one."

Kai shook Jack's hand lightly. "Thank you, Jack."

"No worries, Kai. Take care of those ribs. I'll be back in a week to check on you. In the meantime, if anything changes, give me a call, Cole."

Cole walked Jack out of the room and to the front door, or at least so Kai assumed. He remained in the room, staring at the blood on the carpet. When Cole returned, he stopped in the entryway. "Are you okay, kit?"

He didn't look away from the stain. "It's really over."

"Yes," Cole replied, moving to sit beside Kai. "It's over. He can't hurt you anymore."

Kai raised his gaze to Cole's. "I can hardly believe it."

Cole picked up Kai's hand in his. "Do you know what you want to do now?"

"I don't."

Disappointment flashed through Cole's eyes and Cole cleared his throat. "Do you... want to stay here?"

"What?"

Cole shrugged, looking down at their joined hands. "Since you can do whatever you want now, I just wondered if you were still going to stay here. With me."

"Of course!" Kai exclaimed. "Why would you think I wouldn't?"

Relief etched its way over Cole's face. "I didn't know if you'd only bonded with me because of your uncle."

"No! I wanted you to claim me. Don't you believe me?" Kai asked, hurt.

"Yes, of course I do. I'm sorry. Forgive me, kit?"

Kai studied Cole for a moment and then nodded. Cole still seemed uncertain of him, and he figured he couldn't blame Cole for wondering if he would leave. Their meeting and mating hadn't exactly been conventional, according to what Kai had witnessed. "I want to meet your pack," Kai said.

Cole sucked in a deep breath in surprise. "Really?"

If he had Cole introduce Kai as his mate, Cole couldn't continue to believe Kai'd only mated him out of necessity. "Yes."

Cole swept him up in a hug, and when Kai hissed he loosened his hold. "I'm sorry, kit. I got excited."

Kai laughed. "It's okay."

"Let's get some clothing on you—despite how much I don't want to cover such a delectable body—and grab something to eat."

They stood, and Cole helped Kai into a pair of Cole's sweatpants, tightening them a lot at the waist and tying the laces into a knot. Next he carefully lowered a T-shirt over Kai's head. Cole kissed Kai and then took him by the hand to lead him out of the bedroom. He followed Cole down the hallway, lost in thought.

The way Kai's life had dramatically changed over the last ten days made him feel faint and overwhelmed. Nothing could have prepared him for Cole or how things would turn out. He supposed not many people would be able to anticipate anything even close to what had happened. After all, Cole had tracked Kai to a city of thousands, in spite of his fake name, and then stumbled across him in an alley in time to save his life. Kai would be forever grateful to whatever god or unseen hand had led Cole to him. It might have only been a short time ago, but he could scarcely remember his life without Cole in it. Knowing Cole loved him made him feel complete, and he thought maybe, just maybe, everything would be all right. Only time would tell, but Kai had a feeling he'd be okay.

Six weeks later....

KAI GAZED at a box of organic pasta in the pantry and wondered if Cole would be okay with spaghetti, too tired to bother with much else. The last six weeks had gone by so fast he could hardly catch his breath. A week in, his ribs had healed completely, and after meeting the pack a few days after the incident with Jerrod and having a chance to decompress, Cole had insisted Kai enroll in an adult education class in order to get his high school diploma, which would allow him to take some college courses. Kai had spent the last month studying himself crazy. He'd taken the GED test in the morning and could only wait to hear if he'd passed or not. He prayed he had because he hated to disappoint Cole or himself.

A shadow came over the wall behind him, and suddenly he found himself swamped by the heady scent of his mate, the earthy smell of cinnamon and loose soil flooding his nostrils. "Cole," he protested as Cole spun him around and pressed him tight to the cabinet shelves.

"Kit," Cole growled before covering Kai's mouth with his own, thrusting his tongue deep between Kai's lips.

Kai moaned, opening under the onslaught, eager and hungry for it. He thrust his hands into the smooth auburn locks and tugged Cole tighter to him. Two months ago, the act would have frightened him, terrified him to his core, but now he craved it, needed it in a way he'd never thought possible. Cole cupped his bottom and lifted him high enough for Kai to wrap his legs around his waist. "Oh," Kai whimpered as Cole carried him out of the pantry into the kitchen and set him on the island counter.

Cole nipped at Kai's bottom lip as he grabbed the hem of Kai's shirt, slid it over Kai's head, and dropped it on the floor. "Need you, kit," Cole rumbled. "Need you now."

"Yes," Kai whispered. "Please, Cole."

Lips settling at the side of Kai's throat, Cole suckled heatedly at the spot he'd bitten deep to claim Kai, leaving a dark bruise for the world to see. "Mine," Cole husked, thrusting his hips forward, grinding their cocks together.

"Yours," Kai agreed with a sigh, running his shaking hands over Cole's broad shoulders and down to Cole's hips. "Off," Kai whined. "Clothes off."

Cole crossed his arms and snatched at his shirt, yanked it over his head, and tossed it aside carelessly. Nothing mattered except skin-to-skin contact. Kai gasped when Cole's bare chest touched his. He grappled Cole's shoulders and biceps, wanting to sink into his mate, to be a part of him. Cole practically tore their jeans off in eagerness. Kai groaned in pleasure at the sight of his mate's hard cock standing at attention. He reached down to wrap his fingers around the hot length, but Cole didn't give him time to savor the feel of it in his palm. He pulled Kai off the counter, spun him around, and pressed him facedown on the counter, ass hanging over the edge.

A loud moan tore from Kai when Cole spread his cheeks and dove in, shoving his tongue in deep. They'd had sex in the shower before Kai'd left to take the test, but no matter how many times they made love, neither of them seemed able to get enough. Cole had encouraged Kai to explore and taught Kai about sucking cock, eating ass, and eventually allowed Kai to fuck him. Kai still preferred Cole inside of him, although the reverse experience had been amazing.

Cole lapped at his ass while one of his hands tugged his cock and the other fondled his balls. Kai gave a mewling cry of disappointment when Cole left him for a moment, a chill racing through him when the air drifted over his saliva-dampened hole. Cole didn't leave him long. The snick of a bottle opening reached his ears, and then a pair of slick fingers pressed at his entrance. "Cole," Kai sighed, his forehead resting on the counter.

He had no idea what Cole had used for lube, but his cock spasmed as bolts of electricity shot along his spine when Cole grazed his prostate with those two digits. Cole quickly replaced his fingers with his cock, breaching Kai with little to no resistance from Kai's outer ring of muscles. A grunt vibrated against Kai's rounded cheeks when Cole bottomed out. Cole gripped Kai's hips, holding himself deep inside Kai.

"God," Cole rasped. "I can never get enough of you, kit."

"Fuck me," Kai begged. "Please."

Cole began to move, pulling out a fraction before pushing back in, eventually reaching full strokes. Their breathing grew erratic, moans and growls echoing through the entire house and sweat building on their skin. Cole changed his pace, removing his cock entirely, then plunging deep again. Kai scrabbled to keep from sliding forward with the brutality of Cole's thrusts. He was close to coming almost too soon.

"Cole," he sobbed. "I can't—"

A growl rumbled in Cole's chest, and he fucked into Kai harder.

"Oh God, Cole," Kai shouted as he tripped over the edge, semen splashing over the side of the counter.

Nails dug into his skin, and Cole let out a howl as he followed Kai into orgasm, hard pulses filling Kai's ass. Cole kept moving, increasing the pleasure of their climaxes. Kai reached behind him to grip Cole's thigh, begging, "No more, please. Oh fuck."

Cole slowed to a stop, still buried deep in Kai. He collapsed on top of Kai, panting. "Gods, kit, you're amazing."

"I think that's you," Kai huffed out with a breathless laugh.

Cole nuzzled Kai and dropped a kiss between his shoulder blades. He stood up and slid out of Kai's warm body. Kai hissed and shuddered, supersensitive. Cole helped him stand and gathered him into his arms to kiss him tenderly. "Love you, kit."

Kai swallowed hard and managed to get out the words he'd wanted to say for a while. "I love you, Cole."

A strange sensation of fullness settled in the center of his chest, and Kai gave a small gasp while rubbing the flesh over his heart. He didn't know how to identify the emotion that lanced through him. But his fox gave a thrilled chirp in his head, and Kai smiled, looping his arms around Cole's neck.

Surprise followed by affection flitted over Cole's face. "I've wanted more than anything to hear you say it."

"I'm sorry it took me so long."

Cole shook his head. "No—"

Kai covered Cole's mouth with his hand and said, "I know, I know. I don't need to be sorry."

Warmth sparkled in Cole's green gaze. He removed Kai's hand from his lips. "Let's go take a shower."

Kai smiled. "Okay."

Cole led the way, Kai watching Cole's muscular rear end flex with each step. He couldn't stop the grin spreading over his face. Things might have started out rough between them, and maybe life would never be perfect, but it could definitely come close. Kai knew he wanted to spend the rest of his life with Cole showing him just how much he loved him. Nothing else mattered.

It didn't take long for the shower to heat up, and Cole turned to Kai and held out his hand. "Ready, kit?"

"Absolutely."

J.R. LOVELESS began her adventure in writing romance at the young age of twelve. Her foray into creating her own worlds and telling her characters' life stories was triggered by her own love of reading. She currently resides in South Florida with her two dogs and two cats, volunteers for an animal rescue in her spare time, and works as a manager for a financial lending institute. Someday she hopes to begin writing as a full-time career and bringing more of her ideas to life.

Her journey into gay romance began in 2005 when she began posting her original fiction on a forum for feedback and readers' pleasure. In 2010, a good friend urged her to submit to a publishing company, and the day she received the acceptance and contract was the best day of her life. Since then, she has been noted to be one of the most purchased audio books after Fifty Shades of Grey on Audiobook.com, received best gay romantic fiction for Touch Me Gently in the 2011 TLA Gaybies, and even received an award for Chasing Seth in 2012.

J.R. adores her fans and loves hearing from them. She can be reached via her website http://www.jrloveless.com or through Facebook https://www.facebook.com/authorjrloveless/.

J.R. LOVELESS

CHASING
SETH

A True Mates Novel

Veterinarian Seth Davies comes to Senaka, Wyoming, looking for peace and anonymity, trying to escape his past. He's always been a target for trouble and pain, and Seth has had more than his share of both. Kasey Whitedove takes one look at Seth and assumes the worst. No white man could love animals the way the mostly Cheyenne population expects, and Kasey makes Seth's first days in Senaka more than unpleasant.

Then an accident puts Kasey in the uncomfortable position of eating crow—and helplessly desiring Seth—despite the danger of Kasey's life as a werewolf and Seth's stressful secrets. Chasing Seth down and keeping him safe from his past has just become Kasey's most important job.

www.dreamspinnerpress.com

J.R. LOVELESS

FORGIVING
THAYNE

A True Mates Novel

Nicholas Cartwright has done everything in his power to forget that night six months ago in Senaka, when his true mate rejected him, leaving him shattered and disillusioned. Burying himself in his work, he pushes himself to the point of exhaustion while finding the touch of another unbearable. Suddenly his mate needs his help, and he may be asking for more than Nicholas can find it in himself to give.

Thayne Whitedove has always been a wanderer, spending his days on the road and his nights wrapped in the arms of whatever random hookup he meets, until a fateful mistake sends him rushing for the comforts of home. To his utter dismay, the only way to correct his error in judgment is to accept the one thing he's never wanted… his mate. Thayne must decide whether to keep running or to stay and fight for Nick's forgiveness.

www.dreamspinnerpress.com

J.R. LOVELESS

HIS SALVATION

THE ADA CHRONICLES BOOK ONE

The ADA Chronicles: Book One

In an attempt to atone for his sins and find some solace, ADA Agent Gabriel Romero helps other Deviants in need. But with threats from both sides—Normals and the Deviants who despise them—he finds it harder and harder to outrun his ghosts, especially after a difficult mission to rescue twin brothers held at an enemy compound, where Gabriel meets Alexander Ryker. Gabriel finds his new charge unexpectedly attractive, and that's a complication he does not want—one he thinks he doesn't deserve.

Despite the frosty reception from the stubborn agent who rescued him, sheltered telepath Alex feels an instant connection through the pain he sees in Gabriel's eyes, and he does everything he can to gain his attention. The realities he must face while mastering his ability are hard, but failing to learn to defend himself is not an option. Soon he'll need his newfound strength to convince Gabriel he deserves to live and love again.

www.dreamspinnerpress.com

LOVE AND
SNOWBALL
FIGHTS
• A CHRISTMAS VALLEY STORY •
J.R. LOVELESS

Lane Freeman supposed there were worse places to be dumped than a place named Christmas Valley. After being ejected from the foster care system, he spent the past five years hitchhiking and moving around. But six months of a steady job at Tal's Bar and Grill, an apartment, and even a three-legged cat have him almost ready to risk putting down a few roots when Tal's brother comes home for the holidays.

Dallas firefighter Trey Jenkins reluctantly accepts that Lane isn't like the other drifters who've come through his brother's place. A fragile attraction begins to bloom between them in spite of the many reasons they each have to fight it. Trey wants to give Lane a family, but experience has taught Lane to depend on no one but himself. Will winter love burn hot in the town called Christmas Valley or will Lane return to his wandering ways?

www.dreamspinnerpress.com

J.R. LOVELESS

YOU BELONG WITH ME

Scott has been in love with his best friend Craig for years, but watching Craig with his manipulative boyfriend has worn Scott down, and he knows he needs a break from the pain and maybe a change of scenery and perspective. His twin sister, Karen, convinces him to spend a summer in Paris.

Karen is sick and tired of seeing Scott suffer, and she's not going to stand for it anymore. She confronts Craig and tells him what he's been missing by spurning Scott's affection in favor of a jerk who mistreats him.

When Craig unknowingly breaks Scott's heart, Craig opens his eyes—and his own heart—to the possibility of a future with Scott. He plans to use the time while Scott's abroad to orchestrate a romantic surprise that will show Scott they belong together. But when he sees Scott with another man at the airport, Craig fears he's too late.

www.dreampsinnerpress.com